THORNE

A novel by Colby Drane

Thorne / Colby Drane

ISBN: 978-1-312-87939-3

This book is dedicated firstly to my mother. She believed in me when I didn't believe in myself. She was also the only person who had to endure my previous less-than-pleasant manuscripts. I also dedicate this story to my friends: Josiah Marshall and Austin Elliot. Their enthusiasm and friendship has proven to be an excellent motivator to write and create. Without them this book may have never come into being. Thank you for all your encouragement, guys! And to everyone who has stayed by my side through this process, I give thanks to you as well. *Thorne* is a dream come true—a dream that would have not been possible without you. Enjoy the world of *Thorne.* You're in for one wild ride.

-Colby Drane-

"Wars are won by blood."

- Kristoff -

00 – Remember to Forget – 00

"Lost time is never found again."
- Benjamin Franklin -

I DON'T REMEMBER much. Maybe a name and I think what could be a memory. I say 'could be' because it feels more like a dream.

Or a nightmare.

The dream starts with me walking down a catwalk of white metal. To my left is an abyss that stretches on for miles. The twinkling dots of silver light on the far side of it remind me of stars. To my right, walking alongside me and the glistening white walls is an armed officer. I can't see his face because of the black riot visor. His lightweight armor, which resembles pieces of bone and vertebrae, *chinks* with a rhythmic motion as we walk. He says nothing.

A tug on my hand makes me look down to my left. "Daddy, where are we going?"

The child is only four or five years old and wears a gray

uniform with a stiff necked collar. Her full head of red hair bounces as she tries to keep pace. Is she my daughter? Was I ever married?

"We're going to show you your new bed, Sweetheart." I say.

My answer surprises me. A mixture of pain and regret fill my voice, as if I had known that this day was coming and could do nothing—had done nothing—to prevent it from happening. The overwhelming sense of despair clouds my thoughts as my mind races from one memory to the next. I manage to catch a single phrase in the confusion: *Not long now. We have to get to stasis.*

What do I mean by that? No sooner do I wonder than the air over our heads fills with a voice that is not entirely human. It's a machine, a computer program designed to mimic human speech.

"The *USS Midgard* is scheduled to depart in five minutes. All passengers are to report to their designated cabins. Ship personnel are to report to the Living Area immediately and prepare for hyper-sleep. Any personnel or passengers found outside of their allotted areas will be detained for the remainder of the voyage."

Voyage? Are we on a ship? Why can't I recall these insignificant details? Even now, as we make our way toward what I assume is one of the cabins, my mind is in a fog. The sense of panic and despair only thickens.

The girl, she's called *Rose* I believe, pulls close to me. She seems worried too. "Can we go home?" She asks.

Her words break my heart. I think briefly of telling her that there is no home to go back to but refrain. Now is not the time. What happened here? Why is it we are leaving?

"We'll go back home after you go to sleep." I reply softly.

"Do we have to go to sleep?"

"Yes."

She squeezes my hand. "I don't think I can sleep. This place is scary."

Her unease is mutual. I don't feel comfortable here either, though the gleam of the sanitized walls is somewhat familiar. Have I been here before?

"You won't have a problem sleeping." I assure her. "And remember, if you need anything at all, Daddy will be close by to help you."

"Promise?"

"Of course, Angel."

She hugs me and a stab of guilt cuts into my heart. Deep down I know that this is my fault—though how it is still eludes me. I'm to blame for the situation we find ourselves in, but I cannot and will not tell her. She is the last bit of light I have left in my life. Without her love or trust I would be a shell.

The weight of that thought crushes me.

The officer stops us at a white octagonal door. After inputting a series of commands on the small wall terminal to his right, the door splits into eight matching pieces, each of which pulls into the door frame. He looks back to us. "You're clear."

I nod and pull Rose inside. The room is circular and sterile white, with curved columns spaced evenly around its interior. An egg-shaped machine with a glass lid sits directly center, rooted to the floor by a series of thick wires and mechanical parts. The stasis pod? We approach it and the lid opens, hissing as its interior depressurizes.

Rose clings to my leg. "Daddy… "

"It's okay. It won't hurt you."

But I can tell that she doesn't believe me. I can't blame her distrust of the machine. As of now, however, we have precious little time for coaxing. I lift Rose into the pod, cringing as her delicate features twist with fear. "I don't want to." She says.

"I'm sorry, Sweetheart."

"Daddy, don't!"

But I shut out her voice and the following screams. Strapping her in is easier said than done. Between the child's struggling and the trembling fit that found a way into my hands, I can hardly concentrate on the task in front of me. I dare not look at Rose, though I know she has not taken her eyes off of me.

This isn't my fault. I tell myself over and over. *I didn't cause this.* I'm lying to myself again. How long have I been denying the truth?

"The *USS Midgard* is scheduled to depart in exactly three minutes. All passengers are to report to—"

Three minutes? I secure the last child-proof strap and step away. The lid begins to close as I turn. Her screams stop when the lid locks in place. Unable to look at my daughter, I cross the length of the room and make it to the doorway. Before I can leave, another, sharper, pang of guilt stops me.

I throw a glance over my shoulder. Rose is crying. Her hands are pressed against the glass. Real or imaginary, I know that I will never forget her face nor the pain I feel. I don't know if she's real. I don't even know if this is a dream or a memory. Still, I cherish seeing my child—if she truly is my child—one last time. I hope it isn't the last.

"Sir." The officer at the door says now with more than a little fear in his voice. "We need to get you to your pod."

I look away. Nod. We leave the cabin quickly and travel farther down the catwalk. Our feet slap against the floor with metallic *clunks*. The pace is faster than before. Neither of us want to be awake when the ship launches.

How long will we sleep? I don't recall. This frightens me more than I can explain. It will be a long time I think. What else could terrify me so? Then again, if I'm being honest, it isn't the thought of sleeping that scares me. It's the possibility of finding something terrible waiting for me when I wake up. *It won't come to that.*

Again we stop at an octagonal door. It's no more than three doors down from Rose. I breathe a sigh of relief. Being close to her offers me a bit of comfort. The officer inputs the cabin's log-in code via the wall terminal to his right, we step inside the identical room and after a moment of seeing me in he departs. I'm left to my own devices.

"The *USS Midgard* is scheduled to depart in one minute." The computer blares overhead.

The next few moments are tense as I wait for the pod to open. Once it finishes moving, I hastily step inside. The glass lid closes over me and I sink back into the pod's velvety dotted bed. This isn't the time to have second thoughts. Despite that I do. What could I have done differently? What other avenues could I have taken? Was this really the only way?

It's not my fault. The pod emits an odorless, tasteless gas. I

know this because my body begins to feel heavy. My eyelids sag.
I didn't cause this.

No matter what I say, the guilt remains. My hand brushes against the revolver I brought on board. Firearms are not allowed, but that didn't stop me from bringing it. After all, what happens if we make an unscheduled stop? I'll need to be ready for the unexpected. I hope I won't have to use it.

The revolver's cold surface spawns nausea in the pit of my stomach. Why is beyond me.

I'm getting sleepier. Before I have a chance to wonder about the world that will be waiting for Rose and me when we get back, my vision grows dark and I succumb to a deep and nearly dreamless sleep.

◆◆◆

My name is Jackson Robert Thorne. This is the dream I dreamed while we drifted in the depths of space. Was it more than a dream? Maybe. I wouldn't know the truth for a very long time. Years would pass and I wouldn't age or know what was going on in the outside world. Then one day, the unthinkable happened. I woke up.

01 – A Cordial Reception – 01

"I never found a companion that
was companionable as solitude."
- Henry David Thoreau -

I WAS TOLD that waking up from hyper-sleep is similar to
curling up next to a fire. Slowly you start to thaw, and it isn't until
you're fully heated, or in my case *awake*, that you realize just
how little of the world you actually felt.

I woke to my reflection staring back at me. Red hair. Blue
eyes. A rounded face younger than its age led people to believe.
The man staring at me wore a gray uniform much like Rose had
worn. An insignia of a compass ringed by a laurel was on my left
breast pocket.

I'd forgotten many things, and remembered little, the least
of which being I was aboard a ship known as the *USS Midgard*.
Slowly, however, snippets of memory came back to me.
Unfortunately, the memories were nothing more than that—
snippets. Flashes. No. I didn't remember much else, save my

name and the dream.

Jackson. My name is Jackson isn't it? Jackson Robert Thorne. What was I doing here? Had my dream been something more than I originally thought? I started to regain feeling in my body as the pod depressurized. The lid lifted. Now fully awake, I understood my situation.

Yes, I was aboard the *USS Midgard.* I'd been a passenger... I think. Like all passengers, I'd been placed in stasis in order to remain my current age upon arrival. As for how long I'd been asleep or what my age happened to be, I didn't have a clue. The majority of my mind remained in that same mental fog from my dreams.

I looked around the cabin. At first glance, nothing had changed. It was still the circular chamber I'd supposedly left, complete with the curved columns evenly spaced around the room's perimeter. The gleam of the off-white walls served as a relief. I checked my side. The relief wavered.

The revolver was gone. *Or was it even there in the first place?* There was no way to know. I looked back to the cabin. There were other discrepancies. The air in my cabin tasted... strange. Stale? And the walls, while white, were off-white from age, a detail I had overlooked. Even the overhead light, which once had a sterile glow, was sallow and age-stricken. I rubbed my head. Something brushed my temple.

Looking to my left wrist, I noticed a watch. I hadn't been wearing a watch. *How did...?* Wait. Was it a watch? The silvery device had no hands. No recognizable face. What it *did* have was a rectangular case and an LCD screen where the face should have been. A digital bar, similar to something from a computer program, filled the lower half of the screen. Just above the bar hovered a five percent completion rate. *What is this thing?* After stepping out of my pod, I attempted to remove it.

A shock traveled up my arms and sent me to my knees. I fell over on my side, gasping for more of the stale air. I stayed on the floor, staring at the door ahead, body reeling from the sudden burst. No, this thing was *not* a watch. But then what was it?

Minutes passed before I regained the ability to stand. *Note to self:* I winced, pushing off my knees. *Leave it alone.* I could always ask one of the crew about it when they came to retrieve me anyway. I would be retrieved, right? *Of course you will be.* Until then I would have to wait. So I waited.

What should have been minutes turned into a silent eternity. There'd been no sound outside or from the neighboring cabins. Were the others having trouble as well? Why? I didn't like this.

What if we're experiencing some sort of system failure? If that were the case, it might take longer than normal for the crew to respond. I did have an access panel fixed to my side of the door on the off chance I needed to leave, but… *No. I'll wait.* I decided to pace around the pod. It was better than sitting.

Not my best idea. I quickly discovered that the longer I paced, the greater my unease grew. What if something bad had happened to the crew? Or worse, the passengers? My attention immediately turned to Rose. Was she real? The memory of her pain-stricken face gave me chills. Panic gripped me. If she were real, what if something had happened to her? I had to see for myself. Settle these questions. Shoving aside my better judgment, I crossed the room and accessed the emergency wall terminal.

Opening the door was easier than I thought. The system had an emergency override feature that I accessed with a few keystrokes. From memory? It took a few seconds for the cabin's octagonal door to part its eight ways and reveal a wall of darkness beyond. Cold air crawled inside. I shivered.

Why was it cold? Why weren't the primary power systems on? Where were all the cabin lights? Those should have been on by now. I remembered the far wall of star-light from my dream. It had been replaced by a solid black horizon.

Something, I still didn't know what, was very wrong with this ship. The loneliness closed in on me.

Don't jump to conclusions. Just find Rose. Why did I act like she was real? Nevermind. I stepped out on the catwalk. Small auxiliary lights flickered to life beneath me, lining the edges of the floor. Their blue glow offered little light, and I was forced to proceed slowly.

Three doors down. That was it, right? I'd remembered to count. Three. It had been that way in my dream. Of course, there was always the possibility that what I had seen had only been my imagination. *How can I explain the ship then?* To that, I didn't have an answer. Dream or memory. Whichever one it was, I would find out. But if it really had been a dream… Why did I feel sick to my stomach?

Approaching the terminal, I half-expected to find myself locked out. Instead, the door parted automatically, as if it had been waiting for me. I hesitated.

Shouldn't the cabin have been locked like mine? And where were the interior lights? My cabin had been lit. The number of possible scenarios was growing by the minute.

Then, a thought caught my attention. Had I woken up early? I didn't know when I was supposed to wake up, but the idea struck a chord with me. It would explain the silence. A sleeping ship wouldn't have people moving around it. I used that logic to calm down.

I still had no way to explain the unlocked cabin.

The room, probably identical to my own, was cloaked in shadow. I crept forward, taking note of any sounds I heard. Halfway inside, the sharp *crack* of broken glass stopped me cold.

Glass? What was that doing here? I moved my foot to make certain it hadn't been a fluke. It wasn't. Shards of glass littered the floor, glinting weakly from the glow of the ship's auxiliary lights behind me. The dread I had felt before intensified.

This is wrong. What had happened? *Rose.* Was she okay? Was she even real?

I moved farther in, almost growing used to the *crunch* beneath my boots. The pod had to be close now. I reached out until my hand found the lid. It was intact still. Good. I felt farther up, tracing the cold glass with my fingers until… *No.*

I left my hand on the edge of broken glass for a moment longer. There was no mistaking it. The lid had been half-shattered. But had it been broken into or *out of*? I didn't know. Assuming the strike came from the outside, who would have broken into a pod? Not the ship's sleeping passengers. Not its automatons. Who did that leave then?

No one. Or perhaps someone I didn't know about. Either way, someone—or something—had to have done this.

The next instant, I was feeling for a body but found none.

All that remained of the former passenger was more broken glass. Half of me felt relieved. This meant Rose wasn't dead. The other half was terrified beyond measure. If she wasn't dead, then where was she? This had to be a mistake. Maybe I was still stuck in a dream.

I didn't believe that for one second. I was very awake and very scared. If there really was no one in this cabin... I stood straight. *Then what about the rest of the ship?*

I darted out of the room and tried another cabin. Once more, the eight-sided door opened to reveal a dark empty chamber. I tried again with another. The same thing happened. Where had everyone gone? They couldn't all be missing!

By the fifteenth cabin, I stopped and leaned against the wall. My theory of waking up early started to lose its legs. A new fear found its way into my head. What if I'd woken up *late*? What if I'd been forgotten? Left to rot in this mausoleum? *That can't be right.*

How could someone be left behind in a ship operated by machines? I started to remember more of the ship's design. The *Midgard* was large—it had been designed to hold millions of people after all—but the ship had computers and log books to keep record of its passengers. They wouldn't have purposely abandoned me... Would they? Was I really alone?

You don't know if everyone's gone, Jack. Check the command deck. Don't lose your head. I took a moment to breathe. Think about my options. The ship's flight recorder—it would be my best bet. If I could access the *Midgard*'s data then I could also check for any anomalies during the voyage. There was a reasonable explanation for all of this. Things weren't as bad as I thought.

That's what I kept telling myself. It was a hell of a lot better than jumping off the edge of the catwalk.

I started back toward my cabin. One of the passenger trams had been docked not far from it. If I took the tram, I could arrive at the command deck within an hour. This would be my best option, given that walking was out of the question. On foot it would have probably taken me close to three days. I didn't want to be in the dark that long without food or water. The sooner I knew the truth, the better. I passed my cabin, boots clapping loudly against the metal.

Shink...

What was that? I stopped and listened. The sound stopped too. Had it been coming from me? I checked my boots. Nothing seemed like it would be dragging against the floor. I checked my clothes. Other than being a little too thin, my uniform didn't have anything dragging from it. *Odd.*

I disregarded the sound as my imagination and continued ahead. It came back.

A chill ran up my spine. That couldn't be coming from me. I slowed my pace and listened again. This time the sound continued. It was moving closer to me. Someone, or something, was following me. Was it friendly? *Best not chance it.*

I fixed my eyes ahead and broke into a run. My pursuer did the same. Where was that tram? *Come on. I know you're here.*

The dragging sound was followed by an underscore of swift nearly-silent footsteps. Whoever was tailing me would catch up in a matter of seconds. That's when I saw the tram—a boxy, silver contraption on rails—sitting off to my left.

Too late.

I dropped to my stomach out of reflex.

Something fast and sharp cut through the empty air overhead, barely missing my skull. I looked up in time to the flash of sparks farther down the catwalk followed by an earsplitting shriek as my pursuer slid to a stop. Five blades had pierced the metal, as if they belonged to a hand. Was it some type of weapon? The blades glinted a dull blue, sparking with weak electricity.

"Who are you?" I asked.

The only reply came back to me in the form of metal on metal, a swift *shink shink shink* of several razor sharp blades brushing against one another. My attacker launched towards me.

I rolled for the tram's door. Again the blades swept just overhead. This time I felt a trickle of blood on the back of my neck mid-roll. The blades had hit me? Out of the roll and on my feet, I found myself in the tram. I spun and aimed for the door's large, red emergency lock button. Found it. The doors hissed to a close across the boxy car. It wasn't enough.

Shink! I fell backwards as the blades tore through the sliding metal door. I pushed myself backwards and into a stand. *What is this thing?* It couldn't be human. Could this explain the broken glass? The missing passengers? Maybe. At the moment, I was too terrified to think about anything besides the blades dancing in front of me.

Another set of claws tore into the door.

That was my cue to get moving. I scrambled for the dash controls, dangerously close the blades. *Let's see. That looks like an ignition...* Turned the black knob. *No luck. Is that a switch?* Flipped it. *Nope. Please work red button...* Pressed it. *Great, that did nothing.* I resorted to banging on the keys, hoping some combination would do the trick.

My attacker had torn a small hole through the door. "Don't run from me, Thorne."

I paused long enough to look at the blades. "Wait, you can

talk?"

My attacker swiped at me in response. That had been a woman's voice! I didn't recognize her. Who would want me dead this badly? The blades cut the air inches from my leg. With every miss, the woman's arm pulled farther in. She reached toward me now, growling and digging her claws into the metal floor. I turned my attention back to the controls and kicked the bottom of the dash with my foot. *Work already you stupid machine!*

Lights flickered on throughout the tram car. Finally.

The woman removed her arm. At first I thought she was retreating, but then her hands gripped the edges of the metal hole. It groaned as she peeled the metal back. My stomach sank.

She was making her entryway even bigger.

The woman pulled her arm through first, then her head. She looked at me, eyes and face obscured behind a black beetle-like armor. What looked like screaming faces had been chiseled over the glossy black surface. "It will be better this way." She hissed, voice muffled behind her mask-like visor.

I backed up. "What do you mean 'it will be better'?"

"Everything."

"I don't understand."

"No need." She pulled her torso through. "Dead men don't need to understand."

The tram started forward. We pulled out from the balcony and into open air. In turn, the woman managed to finish crawling through. She stood and whipped her claws straight, their edges glistening with blue electric life. From head to toe her body was covered in the black armor. Where had she gotten it from? Furthermore, why did she want me dead? She stood two heads higher than me thanks to her heels. I swallowed. *Who are you?*

"What did I do that was so wrong?" I asked her.

She continued forward slowly. The movement reminded me of a panther. "You are a murderer. A liar. A monster. You *exist*."

"That's not a reason!"

"It is for me."

"Look, we can talk, whoever you are. I'm not your enemy. Just listen—"

"The time for listening is over. I will not permit you to live, Jackson Robert Thorne. You've done enough damage to this world." She swung. I backed up in time to have the blades graze my chest. Pain flared across my skin. I stumbled, winced, but remained standing.

"Please, I don't understand." I pleaded, "Let me help you."

"Help me? Stand still then."

"But—!" She backhanded me and I flew across the car in

a spiral. The shock of landing winded me. By the time I caught my breath, she was already there, standing over me.

No time to run.

Her blades ran through my chest and into the floor below. Pinned, I coughed, choking on my own blood. The world stopped.

"No one will miss you." She said, more to herself than me. "Not here. I'm doing the world—all worlds— a favor."

I couldn't speak. I was losing touch fast. The world faded in and out of focus. Was this what it felt like to die? I reached out to her, hoping for any sign of mercy. But I knew she had none. That's when it finally sank in. I *was* going to die.

Or so I thought. The air distorted. An invisible ripple of energy traveled across my body then receded like an ocean wave. My pain went with it. Two blinks later, all traces of the woman had vanished. I was on my back, staring at the ceiling. Alone.

I sat up and felt for wounds. There were none. Blood? I couldn't find any. It was as if the entire thing had been a hallucination. I swallowed, unwilling to stand up. Was I losing my mind?

The truth would be worse than any nightmare.

02 – What a Pain – 02

"Technology… is a queer thing.
It brings you great gifts with one
hand, and it stabs you in the back
with the other."
- Carrie Snow -

THE TRAM TOOK its time wandering the tracks. I didn't know where I was going or how long it would take me to get there. Even after having looked at the dash in detail, I knew little to nothing of what made it select the current course. Flying blind didn't exactly encourage me. Then again, nothing about my current situation encouraged me. *Let's hope I at least get close to the command deck.*

I took to sitting, drumming my fingers on the hard plastic seat to my right. Close to thirty-five million people had been aboard the *Midgard*. I knew this only because of a fleeting memory. Where had they gone? To have the population of an entire ship vanish… What could have done this? These questions were burdens and I already had one too many unsolved mysteries to unravel.

For instance, why did Rose and I board the *Midgard* at all? What kind of catastrophe—if it even had been a catastrophe that drove us to the stars—would require the population of a capital city? Were there other ships like the *Midgard* or just this one? How long had I been asleep? What of everyone else?

It was a strange thing, not remembering. I couldn't recall things that I should know. I still felt like I was asleep. Was I? Who knew? Maybe I did have the answers once. That bothered me. What if something had happened to my brain? I did remember that amnesia was a common side effect of trauma. I didn't like to consider that line of reasoning, but it would have explained the hallucination earlier.

Again, this is what I told myself. I was doing my best to forget that woman's sword-like claws piercing my chest. *She wanted me dead and I have no idea why.* Maybe I would never know.

The dash radio broke my thoughts with a crackle of static.

"H-Hello? I say, is there anyone there that can hear me?" It was a man's voice. High pitched with a heavy, slightly off-kilter British accent. He seemed oddly happy. "Please, if there is anyone there, do respond."

I nearly jumped from my seat. Aside from the woman earlier, this marked the first time I had heard another person since coming out of stasis. I located what looked like the dash intercom and pressed it. "I can hear you. Who's this?"

"Oh thank God. When I saw the tram moving on my radar I thought it was a system malfunction. This is PAINS, acting Captain for the *USS Midgard.* Were you one of the crew?"

PAINS? *That's an odd name.* I shoved my opinion to the side. "Yes—I mean no. I mean… Maybe? I think I was a passenger. My name is Jackson. Jackson Robert Thorne. I just woke up from stasis. Where is everyone, PAINS? Why is the ship dark? I don't understand anything that's going on right now. Please, some answers would be nice."

"Jackson? Splendid name. Well, *Jackson*, a great deal has happened since you went under, I am afraid. Please, if you would like, I can explain everything in person. Or, at least I would prefer to. I am currently located at the command deck. Do you know how to operate that tram car?"

"Not really."

"No matter. I can walk you through it. Do you happen to see the large dome-like device in the center of the dash?"

"Yes."

"Place your hand on it for me."

I did as I was told. The dome lit with a cold blue light from within. In moments it had constructed a three dimensional image of what I assumed was the *Midgard's* rail system. Various nodes, each labeled with names like 'Mess Hall' and 'Security', dotted the maze of pulsating lines. I looked for 'Command'. Found it. "I see the command deck." I said, "Now what?"

"Use your free hand to select it."

"You mean all I have to do is touch it?"

"Unless you are photosensitive," PAINS said cheerfully, "In which case we are both—oh how does the saying go? Royally... screwed? Vulgar term but it fits. Yes, I do not wish to be screwed so please do not be photosensitive."

"...I'm not."

"Good! This should go swimmingly then."

Is something wrong with this guy? Why was he talking like that? *Never mind.* I touched the node labeled 'Command.' Its effect on the tram was instantaneous. The car shook as it rolled off the main track and onto one of the adjacent lines. Why couldn't it have been that easy when I had to start this thing?

"Splendid, splendid. I see that you are on your way." PAINS chirped.

"How long do you think it will take?"

"A half hour or so. The *Midgard* is a pantheon-class

cruiser after all. It would most likely take you a solid day and a half of running to reach me otherwise."

Yeah, running in the dark. "Why make the ship so big?"

"I am... not sure actually." There was doubt in his voice.

"But you're the Captain aren't you?"

PAINS sighed. "*Acting* Captain. Silly term really. The original Captain passed a great deal of time ago, I'm afraid. I do not recall much before that."

"When you say a 'great deal' of time, what do you mean?"

"I mean a *long* time. A short time for me. A long time for you. Time is relative after all. You need not fear, Jackson. I will tell you more once you arrive—I will tell you everything in fact. At least, everything I know. I am suffering from what I assume is amnesia. Ironic, given my nature, no?"

Ironic, given my nature? What did he mean by that?

"But please, sit down in the meantime." PAINS said. "There is no need to tire yourself out by standing—if you are standing. I am sure you have already had a great deal of stress thrust upon you. I do not wish to compound it with my news of our situation. Not yet at least."

"I take it's bad news then?"

"Very bad! Consider it the worst in fact." He said with bizarre enthusiasm.

"Great." I sat down in one of the hard plastic chairs. This was going to be a long ride.

♦♦♦

By the time I reached the command deck, exhaustion had crept into my veins. I felt sluggish and used-up—no doubt a side effect of my run with the woman and the influs of adrenaline that followed. As the car came to a near-silent stop, its doors opened to darkness. I slowly peeled myself from the safety of the tram. "H-hello?" I called out.

"Jackson, well met! My it is good to see you safely here."

I still couldn't see PAINS. All I knew was that he stood—or sat—somewhere just ahead. Cold air wrapped around me. *Geez. It's colder in here than back at my pod.* "I can't see you, PAINS."

"Oh, yes. I forget that humans need visual stimuli. Silly me! You will have to pardon my lack of foresight."

The deck's lights flickered on with a heavy *ka-thoom ka-thoom*. The world blurred momentarily. I winced. When my vision returned I found myself standing in a coliseum, only instead of stands for spectators, there were curved desks and computers. A circular platform, connected to the tram's dock by way way of a descending set of stairs, waited at the center of the chamber. The central platform was ringed by terminals. I still didn't see PAINS.

"Okay, where are you?" I looked around the chamber.

"Why right here in front of you, Silly."

I blinked. The previously empty platform at the center of the room was now occupied. Had he been standing there this whole time? *I could have* sworn… Never mind. I started toward him.

The man, whom I assumed was PAINS, stood at the bottom of the stairs. He wore a white Captain's suit—the kind you'd expect to see at military ceremonies—matching hat, black slacks and shoes. His hat had the same emblem as my breast pocket, a compass ringed by a laurel. His appearance struck me as familiar. I wasn't in any position to judge, but he seemed far too young to be in charge of an entire ship. PAINS held himself straight, with both arms folded behind his back. He smiled wide.

"It is certainly good to see an actual person." He held out his white gloved hand and I shook it. Why was he so cold?

"Likewise."

"I take it you had a relaxing ride?"

"I wouldn't say the past half-hour has been relaxing."

A nod. "Ah yes. I assumed as much. Never hurts to ask though. One cannot forget his manners in times such as these."

What was wrong with his eyes? They were solid white—

no trace of a pupil. A dark black rim framed them. Was he wearing a mask? Was he blind? Wouldn't cataracts have some sort of color distortion?

"We have much to discuss." He said, still smiling.

I nodded and let go of his hand. *Don't stare.* "What's going on, PAINS? Where is everyone?"

His smile faltered. He walked over to closest terminal in the ring and started dialing away at the dash-side keyboard, although I could tell he wasn't actually typing anything. A nervous tick? "Well that—" He laughed awkwardly. "—that is certainly an excellent question, isn't it? Oh dear me. I'm afraid there isn't an easy answer to your question, Jackson. Though, if we are to start, I suppose I should do so by telling you that it is not so much, 'what is going on *now*' as it is, 'what happened' *then*'."

Then? "Keep talking."

He finished faux-typing. Turned. "As I have previously stated, I do not remember certain things. However, I do recall a colonization effort. I believe we landed on a suitable world at the far reaches of the Milky Way. DIM-316 was it? Dense Interstellar Mass 316. Oh, I do so love acronyms! They make names fun wouldn't you agree?"

Something's off about this guy. "Not really. No."

"Well then. Moving on." PAINS snapped his gloved

fingers. The platform filled with flat floating screens. They looked to be made of solid light, hovering just above the terminals. Hard light projections? Just how advanced was this ship?

PAINS motioned to the screens which now started to fill with pictures and words. "As far as I can tell, we were in the process of either leaving or returning planetside. That is, before we crashed on the surface of DIM and the native wildlife consumed most of our passengers. It was a horrible affair really. I do so abhor violence—tend to avoid it unless necessary."

The video footage on the screens filled with images of men and women either being mauled by alien creatures or leaving the ship. Why couldn't they be rescued?

I focused on PAINS. "That doesn't make any sense though. There were *millions* of people on board, PAINS. Do you expect me to believe that they would be left here to rot? No one came looking?"

"No. And, suffice to say, I cannot actually give you a reason as to why. I am at a loss myself. What I am telling you I have only observed. Everything else—memories, data, the whole lot— remains in, oh how does the saying go…? A fog? Yes, a metaphorical fog. That's a sufficient metaphor, don't you think so?"

"How long have I been asleep?"

Another pause. PAINS took to pacing. He reminded me of a small child. The young man mumbled to himself, repeating the same words over and over. "Oh dear, dear, dear…"

"Are you okay?"

"No. I'm not." He stopped and looked at me. "You are one for difficult questions aren't you?"

I didn't like the sound of that. "How long was I under, PAINS?"

"I will tell you… On one condition. You must promise not be cross with me. Do not shoot the messenger and all that. I am the messenger in this instance. That means I do not wish to be shot, so please do not—"

"I get it."

"So? Do we have a deal?"

"Yes, now out with it already!"

A swallow. "Jackson, the last known record I have of you entering stasis was approximately five hundred years ago. You have been in hyper-sleep for close to half a millennium… Give or a take a few minutes. Though, if it is a plus to you, I think you have gotten sufficient beauty sleep. In fact, I would dare to say you're quite the gorgeous specimen of human kind. Get it? Because of beauty sleep?"

I stared at him and said nothing. I don't think I *could* talk.

My lips were frozen shut. Five hundred years... How was that even possible? No one came looking for me? No one remembered? I stared at the floor, lost in thought.

"Are you okay there?" PAINS said.

"I-I don't understand."

"Well, it certainly is a pachyderm to swallow."

I shook my head. "This has to be wrong."

"I'm afraid it isn't."

"You didn't know about me?"

PAINS offered me a friendly, though wounded, smile. "Well, n-no. Otherwise I would have done something to rescue you, Silly."

"So theoretically, could there be other survivors that you don't know about?"

"Perhaps. Although it is highly unlikely." PAINS threw a glance over his shoulder at one of the screens as a man screamed from being torn apart. Why was PAINS still smiling? "I have not detected any on-board activity, apart from yourself, since the passengers and crewmen left. If there are others aboard they certainly have made no attempts to contact me."

Hold on. Had he just said he'd been alive since we crashed? *How?* "Are you saying that you've been alive this entire time? Five hundred years?"

PAINS gave a nervous chuckle and waved me off. "Heavens no. I am not *alive*, Jackson. I am the *Midgard*'s artificial intelligence. Personal Artificial Intelligence Navigation System to be exact, or, as I prefer, PAINS. At your service! Did you not realize this?"

No. I hadn't. AI? I thought he was an actual human… He certainly acted like one. Well, apart from a few quirks. I studied him. *Okay. More than a few.*

"I do apologize for not speaking up on the matter." PAINS said, talking with his hands. "It wasn't my intent to deceive you."

"It's fine." I regained focus. "We have to find them."

"*We?*"

"Don't you want to help?"

"Well of course I do you silly sod." He shuffled his feet. "But I am not sure you're aware of my predicament. You see, I am—oh how does the saying go? Between a boulder and a not soft place? Yes. I am stuck here. A regular mastodon in a tar pit."

"Stuck?"

PAINS motioned to the deck. "As with most Borealis Class AI, I am constrained to this deck and this deck alone. While I have remote clearance to all sectors of the ship, I cannot personally leave… Unless, of course, I had some sort of crystolic information center— "

He stopped talking. It took a moment, but I realized PAINS was looking at my left arm. "What?" I asked.

"Is that what I think it is?" He grabbed my left wrist without warning and studied it hungrily. His white eyes widened. "Yes. You have one!"

"One of what?" Was he talking about the watch? I pulled my arm away.

"A crystolic transference device. They were designed to hold my kind. Well this certainly is a lucky day. Oh!" He stood unnaturally straight and beamed. "I just had the most brilliant idea. Would you like to hear it?"

"You're starting to scare me." That was a lie. He'd started scaring me when I realized he wasn't human.

"I apologize for frightening you but I promise that my enthusiasm is well warranted. I just remembered something important. There is a station where emergency ships, not pods, once docked. Its name is *Drasil*. Currently, neither you nor myself are capable of searching for passengers aboard the *Midgard*. It is a dangerous world after all. *But,* if we were to go to *Drasil* and, in turn, used the station's long reaching search equipment, why we could possibly find other humans like yourself... Unless of course you want to search for people different from yourself in which case that might prove a tad more difficult."

"So let me get this straight. You want *me* to put *you* on *here*." I pointed to the watch. "Go to this station, wherever the hell it is. And then use it to search for people?"

"Yes, bang up explanation. And to sate your curiosity, we can also use the *Drasil's* large database to uncover what exactly happened to the colony effort. Does this sound reasonable? It does to me! Then again, I most likely won't be the one flying, so what I think has little weight in this matter. And that, of course, is assuming ideas have mass which they don't."

I rubbed my temples. His talking was giving me a headache. "Why can't we just look for people aboard the ship now? Wouldn't that make more sense?"

"Well it would… If we had the necessary tools; and by 'tools' I mean large firearms that could kill a bull elephant with a single shot. As I have stated previously, DIM is a less-than-hospitable world. There are organisms here with an appetite for anything soft or crunchy. You are both soft *and* crunchy, which makes you—and potentially us—twice as likely to be consumed. We are not ready to begin searching manually."

He makes me sound like a candy bar. What kind of creatures lived on this planet? I glanced at the constant video footage. Maybe PAINS was right. I hated admitting that.

"Alright, fine." I said. "We'll go to *Drasil*. You said we'll have to fly. Where is it?"

PAINS, once again, snapped his fingers. On command, the chamber shook with new-found life. I watched as part of the wall ahead segmented, rolling up into the ceiling to reveal an incredibly large observation window. The reinforced glass was coated in centuries' worth of sand and grime. Still I could make out the bone-white desert and twinkling night sky beyond it. There were no other buildings. Let alone a station.

"Am I missing something?"

"Look there." PAINS pointed up and at an angle. "Do you see that blinking light on the horizon? I believe it's a lovely red color. Like the blood coursing through your delightful veins."

I walked to the rim of terminals and squinted. Nearly obscured by starlight and grime, I saw a faint red light on the horizon, far above us. That was *Drasil*? *It's flying? Now I get it.*

"It's a fortress instillation." PAINS joined me in staring. "Designed to be completely independent of all other operating vessels. If I am not mistaken, and I rarely am mind you, *Drasil* is capable of housing hundreds of millions of people, perhaps more. As you can tell, it is far above DIM's surface, due in part to the violent organisms I mentioned earlier."

"And we're supposed to get there using these ships aboard the *Midgard*?"

"Hopefully. There is the matter of whether or not you can pilot one of the vessels."

I looked at him.

"What?" PAINS asked after a moment.

"Do I look like I know how to fly a ship?"

He rubbed his chin. "Not in this light, no. Well that's a shame. I suppose I will have to dust off my flight simulations then."

"You can fly?"

"If thrown hard enough, yes."

Silence. *Was that supposed to be funny?*

PAINS coughed into his hand awkwardly. "I uh... do apologize. I thought a jest would be suitable for the current atmosphere of our situation. Yes, I helped pilot the *Midgard*. A smaller vessel would require a similar control method. I take it you wish to begin our grand journey then?"

"Either that or rot here."

"Splendid! That's the attitude I am looking for. We will set off at once. I just need you to download my neural cortex to that unit on your wrist."

"And how do I do that?"

"Here." PAINS patted a small cannon-like extension on the dash to his right. "All you will have to do is interface with the station and I will do the rest."

"Interface?"

The side of his mouth twitched. He motioned with his hands. *"Put your hand in the hole."*

I looked at PAINS and then back to the station.

"You don't trust me?" He asked.

"This isn't going to shock me is it?"

"No, no, no, no. Heavens no!... At least, it isn't likely. Shocks occur in one out of every thirty uses."

"How comforting."

PAINS bowed. A strange lopsided grin crossed his perfectly symmetrical face. "I try. I really do. Now please, if you would, the sooner we leave the sooner we will be on our way to searching for any survivors."

"Fine, but I have one request."

"And what is that my new comrade?"

"Could you cut the freaky smile already? You're creepy as hell."

PAINS chuckled. He didn't stop smiling. "As you wish, Jackson. Though believe me when I say that I'm going to grow on you, my little meat machine."

03 – Somewhere in the Middle – 03

"In three words I can sum up
everything I've learned about life:
It goes on."
- Robert Frost -

"WE WILL NEED to find a working ship." PAINS said as the tram shuttled us into darkness. "Something that has not been destroyed would be preferable… and, well, necessary."

"Are you sure there's even any ships left?"

"No. Not at all. But given the functionality of the *Midgard* after all these years it would not surprise me. *Vallacorp* technology was built to last."

Vallacorp, huh? Must have been the company that sent us. I looked down to the emblem for a moment before returning my gaze to the interior of the tram car. "And if there aren't any ships?"

"I suppose we will have to utilize some sort of catapult system then. Tell me, how comfortable are you with high velocities?"

"Don't even think about it you homicidal program."

"Right. Note to self: catapult possibilities have been eliminated. Moving on to cannons..."

Downloading PAINS had been simple enough. True to his word, the AI was able to interface with my watch only moments after using the station. What he neglected to mention however, was that doing so allowed him total access to my nervous system. According to PAINS, the watch had been forcefully grafted to my spine via several arm's-length neural wires. Were I to attempt to remove the watch, I would be shocked with a near lethal dose of electricity. He didn't know who had placed the device on me or why; but it was clear that the responsible party had been planning something. The watch now read *10 %*.

"—and of course that would mean I need your permission. It is your body after all." PAINS was finishing a conversation with himself as much as me. I snapped out of my daze. Had he been talking this whole time?

"Huh?" I asked.

"So what do you say, Jackson? Are you ready for an experiment?"

"Whoa, whoa, whoa. What are you talking about? What do you mean by 'experiment'?"

The AI's human form appeared on the face of the watch. From here, it looked as if he were in a physical room, speaking with me. He was *still* smiling. "Why the benefits of dabbling with your five senses of course. I was expressing my excitement of a trial run. Just think of the possibilities! With access to your body, I could change you for the better—at least via your senses."

"I don't follow." *Not sure I want to either.*

"I am talking about enhancing you. It gives me chills thinking about the science we could accomplish. We may not get another opportunity like this you realize. A once in a lifetime— which for you is disappointingly short—chance! So, what do you say? Would you like me to do some tinkering inside? Give you a good overhaul?"

"I still don't have a clue what you're talking about."

"Let me give you an example." He held out his gloved hands. "Theoretically, because I have access to your nervous system, I could modify your eyesight and give you the ability to see in the dark. Perhaps I could increase your hearing to detect incoming threats. My, the possibilities are tantalizing. And that's saying something, given I lack taste buds. Oh please oh please let me operate! I promise it would not be painful—" He stopped and rubbed his chin. "Well I can't promise that. It might be a *bit* painful. "

"I think I'll pass."

A sigh. "Suit yourself, but I am quite sure you would love any modifications I gave you."

And if I believed in a hell, then I'm sure it would freeze first. I looked outside, past cold glass and into the ever dark abyss. Not a single star in sight. Why were we still in the *Midgard* after all these years? How was it that no one came to rescue the ship and its crew? I frowned. *What if I'm alone here?* And not just here, but the whole colony?

Minutes passed without either of us talking. PAINS finally broke the silence. "Jackson, you're being awfully quiet. Is something the matter? I hope it wasn't my talk of fixing you and whatnot. You aren't really all that broken."

"Do you think there's anyone else left?"

A pause. When I looked back to the watch the AI had dropped his maniacal grin. For some reason that bothered me more than his smile. "Now I don't follow. Do you mean the ship?"

"No. I'm talking about the colony. What if I'm the only one left on the planet?"

"Posh." He waved the question off with the shake of his hand, "That is an incredibly *slim* possibility."

"How slim?"

"It is a .000000000001% likelihood of occurrence."

"You're lying."

"I can't lie, Silly. I can only operate via my protocol."

"Then explain why no one came looking for us in five hundred years." I half-snapped.

PAINS didn't detect the irritation in my voice. "Maybe we were forgotten. I know I have done nothing spectacular to warrant a memory. To be honest, I don't know *why* we were left behind or why we're here now. Nor do I care. That isn't what's important now. What we need to focus on, aside from giving you a few upgrades sometime in the near future, is finding a suitable aircraft to board so that *Drasil* may be reached post haste."

"But what good will it do us if everyone is already gone?"

The AI shrugged. "Assuming you are correct, not much. However, there are always other options."

"Such as?"

"Calm yourself, my little meat machine. We shall cross that proverbial bridge when we get there."

I didn't like the way he called me 'meat machine'. I didn't like the way he looked at me. I liked nothing about PAINS. Once again I turned my attention away from him and focused on the darkness outside. Whatever that bridge was, I hope it didn't come any time soon.

◆◆◆

Some while later, I'm not sure exactly how long, the tram began to slow, dipping downward until it settled to a stop. I turned my head to face the dash. Beyond the windows on the opposite side of the car, were the flickering sallow lights of a station platform. Farther down was what remained of a sign that once read 'Mess Hall'. It hung over a rectangular darkness that could have been an entrance. I couldn't see the rest of station.

"We're here!" PAINS said with a bubbly pitch.

"This isn't the hangar bay."

"You are perceptive! No it isn't, but as of now it *is* our only means of access to the hangar. I would have selected a closer location, certainly; but all other routes to our destination have been shut off by an odd organic growth. I'm afraid this is the end of the line for us."

I stood. The doors hissed open upon approach, drawing in that familiar chill of the *Midgard's* vast emptiness. My breath frosted in the air as I stepped outside. "It's pitch black in here."

"Not quite, but yes, it is very dark."

"We won't get anywhere if I'm blind."

"Not a problem." My wrist watch emitted a beam of light from a small, previously hidden bulb on the side. I swept it over the station. The chamber's shape was square, with a half-rusted canopy of wires and decomposing sheet metal walls. Motes of dust floated in the air. "Is that better?" PAINS asked.

"Yeah, thanks."

"You are most welcome. Be careful though. There is no telling what could be lurking in here. DIM is not a friendly place, as I'm sure you will soon come to realize. If you are confronted whatsoever, *run*. As tempting as it is to be the hero, heroes die. Cowards live. So be a coward!"

"Great life advice from someone who isn't even alive."

"Look, I don't wish to end up in this little box for all time, or even worse, *in* this little box *in* the belly of some beast just waiting to be piled into a mound of feces where I will then remain for all time. It is… rather cramped in here you see. I feel like my back is about to spasm."

"You don't have a back."

"I can dream, can't I?"

AI don't dream though. "Fine." I said sarcastically "I'll be careful."

"This is serious, Jackson!" PAINS' voice darkened dramatically. "We *cannot* die here. Do you understand me? Do you realize what is at stake?"

I looked down at him slowly. The AI stared back at me with empty eyes and a scowl that read death. Either he was mad or worried—neither of which I thought an Intelligence was capable of feeling. Then I felt afraid. Those eyes terrified me. It was like I could see myself in them. I swallowed down a chill.

His face lightened a shade. "Oh, I uh… Pardon me, Jackson. I didn't mean to snap at you like that. It was rude."

"You're fine." But I wondered if that were true.

"No, really. I offer you my deepest remorse. Forget this happened would you?"

Easier said than done. I turned my focus to the Mess Hall entrance. "Which way should we go?"

"Oh yes. The quest. Just ahead. Make a right and continue down the corridor until you come to the Mess Hall proper. You will find a large hole there. Take it. The hangar should be just below."

"Hole?"

"Yes. I'm not sure what made it."

Super. "Got it."

I started.

"And Jackson?"

I stopped mid step and checked the watch again. "What?"

PAINS offered me an apologetic smile. Again, he reminded me of a small child. I felt a pang of guilt for being scared. "D-do be careful out there. I don't wish for anything to happen to you."

"I will." For a moment, he reminded me of Rose. I swallowed. "I promise."

The AI's face vanished from my watch. We went forward without speaking having nothing but the crunch of footsteps to fill the emptiness.

What must have this place been like before I went into stasis? I could imagine throngs of people moving from one end of the platform to the other with things to do and places to go. No doubt the *Midgard* had been quite the hub of activity in its time. Or was it used only once? I didn't know. Five hundred years... I felt like I was trespassing in a dead world.

I took a right at the entrance. The hallway extended into darkness. My watch's light couldn't reach the end so I walked forward slowly, paying careful attention to each and every sound that echoed in the black. What PAINS had said about DIM's creatures was still fresh in my mind. As long as I paid attention...

"Face it, Sandscrip. We're lost."

I froze. It was a feminine voice. Immediately all thoughts turned to the woman in black, but I checked myself. This one had a different tone to her. Older. Husky. Like a smoked piece of meat. Was she a survivor? My heart hammered.

Another person spoke in response. This time it was a man,

'Sandscrip' I assumed. He had a deep voice, dry to the point of cracking. "Hush, Aria. I told you we are not lost. The map said for us to go here and we shall. Have. Now keep your jaws closed. We haven't time to dally. Lord Everclaw wants the ritual done, *tonight*. Do you know what that means?"

"It means we'll get our heads lopped off if we don't do what he says."

"Or worse."

"What could be worse than having your head lopped off?"

"Getting your soul ripped out with his claw. Now stop it with the stupid questions and put the relic here."

What on earth were they talking about? I didn't take another step. Whether it was out of caution or disbelief remained to be seen.

"It seems we have company." PAINS whispered, reappearing on my watch.

"Do you think they're passengers?" I said, glancing at him.

"It is grossly unlikely. If anything they may be scavengers."

"Scavengers?"

"It's just a guess mind you, but if no one has come to rescue us, then perhaps it is due to some sort of disability. My theory is that the colonists are still alive—at least their offspring are—and are existing in a tribe-like structure, functioning on rudimentary intelligence. It would make sense for them to be roaming the halls of such an imposing vessel. Curiosity and whatnot. Maybe they're using it as a temple. Oh my, you don't think we've stumbled upon a sacrifice have you? I would both dread and love to see it!"

"I think you may have seen one too many movies."

"Hardly. I have only seen 55.8% of the entertainment produced by human culture."

"But all I'm saying is that we got the wrong chamber." Aria protested. "Isn't that important? What if we don't do it right?"

A loud *smack* echoed through the hallway. The woman whimpered. Had she been slapped?

"I said quiet. Give me the relic *now.*" Sandscrip went silent for a moment before taking his prize. "Now, where's the body?"

"H-here." Aria said with a sniffle.

I swallowed. *Body?* There's no way PAINS was right.

"It seems like I was correct in my assumption!" PAINS clapped his hands. "We *have* stumbled onto a sacrifice. We must get closer."

"Not five minutes ago you were worried about my health.

Now you want me to interrupt some ritual? What if these people have weapons or something? They could kill me. You. *Us.* You realize that right?"

"Posh. They will most likely think you're a god or something. For heaven's sake, you have a talking man on your wrist. They won't know the difference between flesh and AI. Come, let us claim our god hood together!"

"Where are you coming up with this stuff?"

"My data sector. Now please hurry. I do not wish to miss a thing!"

I sighed and flipped the switch on my watch. Its light dissipated, leaving us in the dark. "Fine. But I'm not going to give our position away."

"No matter. We can still see."

"What do you mean?"

In seconds, my eyes adjusted to the gloom. I could see the hallway perfectly, as if there were enough light in the room to accommodate its new-found level of detail. Only there wasn't. I looked to the now painfully bright screen. "What did you do to me?"

"I modified your eyesight, Silly. As I stated before, I could have you see in the dark. This current situation seemed like a splendid opportunity."

"I thought you said you wouldn't."

"Do or do not. We shall ponder the morality of the situation later. Right now, onward to the sacrifice!"

I shook my head. *What would an AI know about morality?* We moved down the corridor. My footsteps were masked by the sound of their voices.

"Watch it you oaf." Sandscrip barked.

"Sorry." Aria said, wounded.

"Don't apologize. Just get him on the slab, and for the love of the Icrageon watch what you're doing!"

We were close now. Aria and Sandscrip would be right around the corner. I stopped beside the open door frame and waited.

"Do you think they're cutting the body up?" PAINS asked cheerfully.

"You're sick."

"I have no viruses."

"Not what I—never mind." *He's sarcasm deficient.*

"Well let us take a look." PAINS said with more than a little impatience. "Come on!"

I swallowed and turned the corner. I didn't expect what I saw. There were two figures standing in the middle of the mess hall, but whether they were human or not was beyond me—I didn't even know if they were organic. The pulsating, flickering forms in front of us reminded me of ghosts. They were standing over another paler body placed on one of the lunch tables. Only the table—and not just the table, but the *room*—seemed to have the same shimmering effect, like we were seeing two images laid over one another…

"Fascinating." PAINS said with a hushed tone.

"What are we looking at?"

"I'm not entirely sure, though I think it is safe to rule out *human.*"

"Great." So they weren't survivors.

"Do you see a dagger?" PAINS strained to look outside the watch's face. "Some type of ritualistic tool?"

"No, but it looks like one of them is holding something. Weren't they talking about an artifact earlier?"

"And now for the Messenger's resurrection." Sandscrip, the figure on the right, growled with malevolent glee. "We stand here, in the place of his death to bring about his new life. He will show us the way. He will open the door to the depths and seal the very skies themselves shut. He will be the harbinger of the Icrageon. Come forth, Messenger of Destruction. I, Sandscrip, command you!"

"What's he talking about?" I asked out loud, but mostly to

myself.

"Shh." PAINS leaned to listen in. "I said I don't want to miss this."

Sandscrip stabbed the body with what had to be a wavy knife. *Damn. Was he right about the dagger too?* Thankfully, PAINS didn't bring it up. We waited in silence. For a moment, I wondered if anything was going to happen. Then my stomach turned.

The body twitched. Sandscrip half-danced as the corpse sat up. Aria backed away. PAINS and I stayed rooted to the spot, though I assumed for different reasons. A wave of deja'vu struck me. Something felt wrong about this messenger. Did I know him?

"Goodness, where… am I?" The Messenger said with a multi-tone voice that reminded me of PAINS. He looked around until his eyes settled on Sandscrip. "And who are you supposed to be?"

Sandscrip bowed. "A thousand pardons, Messenger. I am High priest Sandscrip of the Everclaw. The sniveling winch behind you is my servant, Aria. We have come here to retrieve you for Lord Everclaw."

"Retrieve me? Whatever for?"

"Just as the prophecy foretold, you have been born again to rid the world of those who would oppose the Icrageon's will.

You are the instrument of cleansing. Do you not remember these things?"

"No… " The Messenger rubbed his head. "I do not remember much of anything, actually. Wonderful. I hope this is not becoming a habit."

Aria stepped forward. Her voice trembled. "Y-you are no doubt w-weary, my lord. Please, if you would, come back with us so that we may t-tend to you."

"I told you to be silent." Sandscrip raised his hand to slap her. The Messenger grabbed his wrist. Sandscrip froze. "My Lord —!"

"Do not hit her. I do not appreciate violence. In fact, I abhor it."

Fighting to obey, Sandscrip closed his hand. His voice held an edge to it. "As you wish… My Lord."

My skin started to tingle. A familiar wave of energy washed over us and receded. I blinked. Sandscrip, Aria and the Messenger were gone—just like the woman in black. What had we just seen?

"Incredible." PAINS said softly.

"So you saw them vanish too."

"Indeed. I believe we have just born witness to a spatial-temporal fluctuation."

"Spatial-temporal fluctuation? You mean like a lapse in time?"

PAINS's voice echoed in the now empty room. "Not quite a lapse. More like a glimpse; and not just in time, but space as well. Think of it as a window into what may be, have been or is— an image placed over another."

"You're talking about the possibility of other realities."

"Yes, or perhaps the past in our reality. Maybe even the future. All of it sharing the same space. I admit, while it is disappointing that we did not witness an actual sacrifice— bollocks on that now! We have gained so much more. Do you have any idea what this means?"

"No, but I have a feeling you're going to tell me."

PAINS snorted as he laughed. "You're silly. No. Not really. I actually don't have a clue what this means. But it certainly makes for a good scientific inquiry, doesn't it?"

You're so weird. He did have a point though. What *did* all of this mean? I thought back to the woman. *Maybe I should tell him.* "I saw someone right after I woke up, PAINS."

"Pardon? Did you say some*one*?"

"Yes. A woman. She was wearing black armor and had swords sprouting out of her fingers." I paused, letting the insanity of my description settle. "She wanted me dead." PAINS said nothing. *Probably thinks I'm nuts.* "Well? Do you believe me?"

"Yes, but of course. Only, why did you not tell me this before?"

"I thought it was a hallucination. Now I know better."

"Tell me exactly what happened."

I rubbed the back of my head. The wound there had vanished but I still remembered how it had felt. "I was moving for the tram when a woman in a black suit of armor appeared out of nowhere and tried to kill me. She swore that I was the problem. She knew my name. I would have died if she hadn't… "

"Hadn't what?"

"If she hadn't disappeared. I should have died on the tram. She stabbed me."

"Stabbed you?"

"Yes."

PAINS rubbed his chin. "Well you don't seem injured now. Where did the wounds go?"

"They must have vanished when she did."

"You mean like our glowing chaps just a moment ago?"

"Exactly like them."

"Interesting…" He smiled wider. "Do tell me more."

"Well, there's not that much to say. Except if you count the reason she wanted me dead." I shook my head. "It didn't make any sense."

"Ah yes. She said you were a problem?"

"And a murderer. A liar. A monster. I existed."

PAINS seemed lost in thought. Worried even. His smile faltered. "Bollocks. Not another outside variable to deal with." He muttered.

"What did you say?"

His eyes shifted back to me. His smile returned to normal. "Nothing, nothing. We just need to focus on getting to *Drasil*. Thank you for telling me, Jackson."

There's something he's not saying. I shoved the thought away. *Whatever. If he wants to keep his secrets, that's his business.* We moved deeper into the chamber.

I hadn't seen it at first, but just as PAINS had mentioned, a large pit took up half of the mess hall. The yawning darkness beckoned us to jump in. What had caused this? Furthermore, did that something have teeth? I paused at the lip of broken tile and looked down.

"Now what?" I asked.

"Ever heard of a fellow called Geronimo?"

"Not on your life."

"Well it wouldn't be my life, Silly. But no matter. We could always—"

Footsteps. *Shink. Shink.* I spun in time to miss five long blades as they punctured the air to the side of my head. I lost my balance and we fell backwards. The air whipped around us as we descended faster and faster. PAINS started biting his covered fingernails. "Do something, Jackson, would you?"

"Like what?"

"I don't know... Oh! How I absolutely despise having emotions! Just promise me you will not die. Yes, do that much at least!"

"Calm down. I'm not going to die, PAINS."

"You shouldn't make promises you can't keep." The woman in black appeared inches in front of me. Even in the dark her blades had a deadly dull blue gleam to them. Sparks of electricity snapped in the black. "You should be dead right now but the calibration on my synchronizer was off. Luck saved you once. It will not happen again."

Synchronizer? "What's your problem?" I said.

She lunged at me. "You are!"

She swung. A miss, but barely. Pain flared along my cheek. The droplets of blood splattered against her ebony hide as she moved behind me, correcting her direction mid air. I grabbed her arm before she could make another move. *What the hell am I doing?*

"Jackson, have you lost your mind?" PAINS had gone from biting his fingers to flailing his arms like cartoon character.

"You know, lady, I've had—" I spun to meet her and pressed a foot against her armored chest. "—about enough of you!"

"Get your filthy hands off me!" She started to swing.

"If that's what you want." I swung her around. Kicked off. My momentum sent the women flying backwards in a violent spiral before striking the carved tunnel walls. She disappeared in a cloud of dust. *Did I just do that? Damn.* I smiled. *Not too much fun being on the receiving end, huh?*

"By George, that certainly was impressive." PAINS wiped his brow.

"Tell me about it. I don't know what came over me."

"Well whatever it was I do believe it saved our proverbial ham."

"I think you mean bacon."

"Whatever." PAINS said, "Farm animals are farm animals. Don't have a bull."

We didn't have long to rejoice. PAINS and I were still falling. I grit my teeth, beads of sweat trickling off my face and disappearing above. "Shit."

"Yes, I am fully aware of the 'gravity' of our situation." He chuckled.

"You're not worried?"

"Not any more. I would hold your breath though if I were you."

"What? Why?"

We hit water before he could answer—or at least, it was something like water. The stuff was wet and it hurt when I hit its surface. That's about all I knew. Shocked and floundering, I pulled to the surface and gasped for air. Coughed. A nauseating taste overwhelmed me. "Ugh. What is this stuff?"

"I told you to hold your breath. You didn't."

"You didn't tell me we were going to fall into a piss pot!" I blinked, trying to wipe the liquid from eyes. No this definitely wasn't water. It was… thicker. Like sluice.

"Colorful use of vocabulary. However I regret to inform you that this lovely place is not a latrine."

"Then what is it?" I raised my arm. Thick strands of goo lazily dripped off my skin before pooling onto the surface of the lake.

"Three guesses. The first is a rectum, which is unlikely due to a lack of feces. The second is a mouth, which is closer to the truth of the matter but not quite, considering there are no teeth to speak of. Then of course there is… Well, you know."

Oh please don't tell me. My eyes darted around the chamber. We had fallen into a room with rounded fleshy walls and a body of yellow liquid littered with junk. I hadn't noticed before but the walls were moving in slow rhythmic pulses. I went rigid. "We're in something's stomach, aren't we?"

"Not a stomach. More like a holding area. The stomach is farther down. I imagine most organisms would drown, sink and then be digested in the depths. This creature is most likely responsible for the odd growth over the ship. It is also the owner of the lovely hole above."

"Why are you not worried then? We're going to get eaten!"

"No we're not. It shouldn't be a problem to cut through our chap's abdominal sac. If my calculations are correct, this organism is bloated and most likely taking up residence in the hangar bay. Given its HALOS-like size, we should not be that far off the floor."

HALOS? Who was that? "That's actually good news. This stuff reeks."

"Which is why I am thankful I lack a nose. But at least it is not solid ground, eh? That could have been quite dicey."

"Yeah just my luck."

I heard a splash behind me; turned. Had something fallen

in here with us? The goop settled. I saw nothing rise. I swallowed. *It might not be the best idea to be floating in the middle of this thing. Who knows what else has been trapped in here?* The last thing I wanted was to survive a fall and then die in this gunk. I started for the refuse that littered the surface of the sluice lake.

"We're going to want something close to the organism's inner lining. Do you see anything matching that description?"

"We have an overturned mess hall table but I'm not sure it can carry us."

"Oh!" PAINS happily squealed. "I've got the perfect saying for this. Let us not look a gift horse in his mouth." PAINS clapped his hands together happily. "Get over there and we shall find out."

"You know, I've got to ask. What's with these old sayings?"

"I like them, Silly. They make me feel human."

I pushed toward the table. Progress was more difficult than I originally thought given the density of the sluice. Between moving forward and staying afloat, I was getting tired fast. "Being human isn't all it's cracked up to be."

"Nor is being artificial. Though I suppose you have a point. Perhaps being *completely* human could be a detriment. Old age, disease and war can take their toll on any species. Why what we need is a hybrid race of sorts. Wouldn't you agree?"

"No one stops time, PAINS. Death is a part of life. No matter what we become we can't escape destruction."

"Well listen to you, my little meat machine. Who said anything about stopping the course of nature? And, to counter your point of destruction, there is always recycling. Given enough time, men could work around their inevitable demises."

"Immortality is a fool's dream."

"Not immortality, Jackson. *Preservation*. Perfection."

I reached the table and hauled myself on board. Surprisingly, it remained level. I stood. "Well, while you think about that, I'm going to focus on getting us out of here. *That* is preservation."

"Splendid use of the word. How do you propose we do that without a cutting utensil?"

Oh, yeah. I looked around the lake. "I'm not sure."

"Well I believe in you. Rah-rah ree and all that. Cheers!"

"I'm touched."

I stepped toward the walls, careful to displace my weight accordingly. The side of the chamber was slippery with more of the mucous-like juice. I couldn't dig past it. We would need something sharper than just nails to get through. I looked back to the lake and knelt, throwing the goop off my hands. "Can you do a sweep of the lake, PAINS?"

"For a tool? Most certainly."

I waited. Seconds passed. "Anything?"

"I think I may have located something."

"Where?"

"Just below us." A pause. "Odd. It seems to be rising."

"Rising?"

Five blades breached the surface. They tore into my stomach before I had a chance to move. I stayed there for a moment, eyes fixed on the sluice. As my blood pooled on the yellow surface, I saw the woman in black staring at me from beneath the surface. She retracted her claws. *Crap. Not again.*

I fell onto my back and screamed as she emerged from the viscous liquid. She towered over me. "That was a cute stunt." She hissed. "But now, playtime is over."

I tried to crawl away, clutching my stomach, but her armored heels dug into my back. Blood came dripping out of my mouth. She stepped off and flipped me over. "I'm sick and tired of following you. Do me a favor and don't try to escape this time."

"P-PAINS..." I pleaded, "Help... "

"PAINS? *Help*?" She laughed. "That devil-man is the reason you're in this mess, Thorne. I would say 'ask him what I mean', but I don't plan on giving you another breath. It's not like the truth matters anyway. Justice will be done regardless."

"Madame!" PAINS shouted, crossing his arms and glaring. He frowned. "I do not know what your malfunction is but I would prefer if you did not kill this man. If you do not listen there will be dire consequences."

He wagged his finger at her.

She looked to him. "And I would prefer the both of you to burn in hell. I wonder who's going to get their wish?"

I reached out to her. "P-please don't… "

The woman answered by stabbing me again. My hand stayed in the air, frozen by shock. She had to be smiling behind that helmet.

"And so ends the *monsters*." She hissed.

"You shouldn't have done that." PAINS said sadly.

My body suddenly burned like a live wire. I didn't realize it at first, but the AI had decided to turn me into a living conduit. The burst of electricity traveled through the woman's claws and into her suit. She screamed in surprise, flailing through the air. She cut the wall.

The woman fell backwards into the goo. Then the whole chamber shook violently. A whale-like groan traveled through the ground. The creature? *Oh God.*

I felt the table being tugged toward the wound in the creature's stomach. We were falling through open air. Thankfully, when PAINS and I hit the ground, the sluice softened the blow. It still hurt like hell.

"Jackson, please do respond." PAINS said, frightened.

The fire inside me died down. I could barely breathe. "I'm... alive."

"Adrenaline is now active." PAINS tapped some sort of off-screen terminal in his nonexistent room. "You have approximately ten minutes before the weight of your wounds incapacitates you. I don't know how long I can keep you up and running. Do *not* die, Jackson."

I rolled over onto my stomach and coughed out more blood. Standing was the hardest part. It took all my energy to stay upright. *Man this hurts.* Why was I still alive? Why couldn't she just disappear like last time? Speaking of which.

I turned. The woman was nowhere in sight. The only evidence of her existence was the constant flow of bodily fluid from the fleshy sac above. Knowing her that would change at a moment's notice.

"We do not have time to dawdle." PAINS said. "Get to a ship. Hurry!"

"R-right." I faced the hangar's open door. Silvery

moonlight flooded the corroded growth covered chamber. I realized that when PAINS said 'ship' he meant the large saucer-shaped vehicles that lined the floor. Each of the aircraft had four crab-like legs and a small cockpit window. No wings. These would fly?

"Which one?" I asked.

"I don't really care. Whatever one is still operable."

"Gee I would have never thought of that."

"Cut the chatter and get on board already." PAINS sounded more desperate by the minute. "If you collapse, we're done for. Do you understand?"

"Yes. Thanks for reminding me, Mother."

I swept my eyes along the available machines. What hadn't been covered in organic growth had been irreparably damaged by exposure to the open air. I took a few seconds at each, determining whether or not they were flight worthy. *Come on. Come on...*

Just when I thought we were done for, I spotted a ship near the end of the line. It was half hidden behind the hangar's left side door frame, obscured in deep shadow. *Thank goodness.* I half stumbled over to it, stride lessening with each passing second. That adrenaline was wearing off fast. I paused long enough to take a breather at one of the ship's legs.

"You can rest when you're on board." PAINS said.

"Give me a second, okay? I have to stop."

"We don't have a second to spare, Jackson."

I winced as another tremor of pain shot through my stomach. "I'll be the judge of that."

"How well will you be able to judge when you are dead?"

"I'm not going to—"

Shink! Shink! Two arrowhead sized knives tore through the air and embedded themselves in the ship. I looked back down the hangar. The woman in black had finally emerged. The sluice was dripping off her in sticky trails. *Great. This bitch again.*

"Stop running!" She bellowed. Her arm moved. Another set of knives swept past me. I was still too weak to run. Would there be enough space between her and the ship for me to escape? I peeled myself from the wall and limped up the open ramp into the crab-ship's interior. A cramped cockpit greeted me, complete with a ceiling of wires and dusty lights.

"Finally." PAINS wiped his inhuman brow. "Hurry and place me in the console."

Agonizingly long seconds passed before PAINS was integrated with the ship. When he was installed, I sank into the pilot's chair. "She's all yours."

PAINS appeared on the windshield. "Duly noted. Good

work, Jackson."

We lifted. As the ramp behind me closed, PAINS angled us toward the hangar door. It took us only moments to launch out the *Midgard* and over the bone-white desert sands. We were on the home stretch.

I let that soak in and relaxed. The woman and that infernal ship were quickly disappearing behind us. "If I ever see another pantheon-class ship again, it'll be too soon."

"I understand your reservations." PAINS appeared on the cockpit window, taking up the entire view. "How are you 'holding up'?"

"I'm bleeding like a stuck pig, my body's one big bruise, and I'm pretty sure if I tried to move again I'd fall apart. Other than that, I'm just peachy. Ask me again in five minutes."

"You are quite sarcastic when you are in pain."

"My apologies."

"I suppose there's no harm in it, given the beating you just endured."

A pause. I winced. "PAINS? Did you recognize that woman at all?"

He blinked. "No. Why?"

"She acted as if he she knew you... And me. But I swear that I never met her before today."

"It is odd isn't it?" He folded his arms. "But mysteries will remain mysteries for the time being. Once we get to *Drasil* I can look up any information on this woman and the colony. Rest assured, Jackson, you will have answers soon enough."

"And you?"

"Me? What about me?"

"Didn't you say you were having memory problems too?"

PAINS looked startled. He quickly regained composure and smiled. He gave a flighty laugh. "Oh yes, that. It seems I was getting so caught up in the action that I forgot."

Sure. You 'forgot'. More like 'lied'. He wasn't telling me something.

"Hull anomaly danger level three detected." Warning lights broke over the cabin. The ship's computer spoke. "Remove anomaly immediately. Repeat. Hull anomaly danger level three detected. Remove anomaly immediately."

Anomaly? *It's her again, isn't it? Why can't she just leave us alone?* I tried to move but pain flared throughout my body. No use. I was grounded.

PAINS gave a concerned look upward. Back to me. "Jackson, you focus on sitting still. I will deal with whatever is on the ship."

The window switched from PAINS to the hull video feed.

The woman wasn't there. Where was she? "PAINS?"

"That dreadful woman, thankfully, is not on board."

"Then what did we detect?"

"I'm not entirely—"

There was a flash of movement. PAINS shifted the camera to an exterior vent and focused. Another flash. He followed it to the right. I found myself moving closer to the screen. Was it a creature? Several other camera feeds popped up along the window, each showing a different section of the hull. PAINS isolated one of the feeds near the bottom right and projected it. Chipping away at the ship's plating with mantis-like arms was what appeared to be a metal insect. It reminded me of a silverfish but broader, with silvery wings to match its body.

"It seems the estrogen monster wished to leave us with a parting gift."

"Wait, that thing's from her?"

"It isn't organic. All energy signatures indicate a mechanism of some kind. I did not pick up anything like it before we boarded, meaning—"

"She threw it on us." But why?

I got my answer. The silverfish turned and aimed its small back cannon at PAINS's camera. The cannon fired off a sphere of blue light. It struck and our feed was reduced to static. PAINS reappeared. "Clever little bugger. It doesn't want us watching."

"What *is* it?"

"My best guess is an autonomous assassination weapon. Are you buckled in?"

"Why?"

PAINS turned the ship violently to the right. I was almost thrown out of my chair. "What are you doing?!"

"Trying to shake it. Do buckle in."

"Don't you—" PAINS angled toward a canyon on the horizon as I was in mid sentence. He hit the gas "—dare!"

We sailed toward the brown-red rocks at ridiculous speed. My stomach lurched. I ran the seat belt across my chest and dug both hands into the arm rests. He had piloted the *Midgard*, right? *What if he also crashed it?* I squeezed the rests tighter.

PAINS brought us into the canyon at a ninety degree angle. I closed my eyes as the top of the ship came dangerously close to scraping a wall of red rock.

"Come on, you little bugger. There is no need to make this difficult." PAINS said to himself.

Our ship shook. "Hull breach detected." The ship computer system announced. "Danger."

PAINS chuckled. "Oops. I suppose I got a little too zealous there."

"A little?" I grit my teeth. "You were worried that I was the one who was going to get us killed?"

He pulled us up and into open air. The ship leveled out. "There is no need to fear, Jackson. It is a minor breach and we have removed the device."

I heard a skittering sound above. Something metallic dropped to the floor behind me. I turned. The silverfish moved with a jittery caffeinated motion on the floor of the ship's cabin. It only paused long enough to look at me then launch itself forward, bladed legs ready to burrow in my flesh.

PAINS sighed. "Then again, perhaps not."

He spun the ship. Aside from making me feel sick, PAINS had succeeded in throwing the machine's aim slightly off. It flew past me and struck the cockpit window with a *crack*. The silverfish flailed on its back, clawing the air with its knife-like legs.

"Jackson, I do apologize for this. Please, hold on."

I don't like the sound of that. "What are you going to do now?"

"Something I have wanted to do for a very long time. I got it from a movie!"

Oh God. I closed my eyes. PAINS shot upwards, screaming *ye-haw* at the top of his voice. The sudden burst of power sent me back in the seat's leather, lungs in my throat. I heard a chittering sound fly past my ear as the Silverfish plummeted to the back of the vessel.

"Excellent." He said with his bubbly voice. "Step one complete."

"Step one?"

He lowered the boarding ramp. A roaring filled my ears. "Are you crazy?" I yelled.

"No." He replied loudly yet civil. "I am not. I've been tested. That's a joke by the way!"

"Close the damn door!"

"There is no need to fear." His eyes shifted from me to something behind my chair. "Oh. It looks like our mechanical murderer has left the premises." PAINS waved at it. "Good bye my mechanical murdering abomination acquaintance!"

"Close… it… please… "

"Oh yes." PAINS smiled and nodded, still yelling. "That. Hold on."

We leveled out again as the main ramp closed. I sat up and coughed. My stomach churned. Before I knew it, I was doubled over, vomiting stomach fluid and blood. I felt like death.

"That's… well, disgusting." PAINS said, face slightly whiter than usual.

I wiped my mouth weakly. "I blame your crazy ass driving."

"Piloting." He corrected. "At least you're not dead."

"Yeah." I winced, clutching my wound. "That's certainly a nice alternative to this wonderful existence."

"You performed admirably, Jackson. We shall be at *Drasil* shortly. Then I can tend to those wounds of yours. Don't worry. You are not going to die with me around."

"I thought you said I had… ten minutes?"

"Did I? Well, that was a rough estimate. You are weak, granted; but, according to my calculations you should be able to transfer me in enough time. I must say, it *was* a bit of touch and go there for a little while—especially after I shocked that dreadful woman."

"Weren't you scared that I was going to die?"

"Was I frightful? Yes, but of course, my little meat machine. However I had to choose the lesser of two evils. I either could let you die by the woman's hand or shock some sense into her estrogen filled rage. If I had *not* stepped in, the result would have been a one hundred percent mortality rate. Electrocuting you was only an eighty-five percent mortality rate."

"You're saying I had a fifteen percent chance of surviving?"

"Yes. Aren't you lucky?"

04 – Mile High Club – 04

"Coming together is a beginning;
keeping together is progress;
working together is success."
- Henry Ford -

HAVE YOU EVER been to that point in life where you're in so much pain, death looks like a release rather than a punishment? That happened to me moments before PAINS brought the ship above cloud level and I saw *Drasil* for the first time.

The station was a massive conglomeration of metal plates, wires and lights. Shaped like a top, the dark city-size structure pointed ground-ward tapering to a point. It hovered without any observable propulsion system. As we moved closer, I made out the forms of enormous icicles hanging off its body. The blinking red light at the station's lowest point, which I had seen only as a speck, was now bright as any star. It colored the sea of clouds below with its heart-like rhythm.

"Well is that not a sight?" PAINS guided us towards one

of the cavernous docking bays that lined the station's side. "We are close now, Jackson. Hang in there, okay?"

"I'm… hanging." Every word was a struggle.

"Good man. You needn't worry. *Drasil* has one of the most impressive medical bays currently available. Or, at least it was half a millennium ago. Either way it will suit our purposes just fine."

"Do you… think… anyone's aboard?"

"If they are they've practically been recluses for several centuries. Rest assured, if there is even one soul on board, they are going to have a stern talking to. Or is the saying 'a piece of my mind'? Oh bother. I suppose it *could* be both. Then again I don't wish to give them too much, after all a stern talking to and a piece of my mind could get overwhelming… "

"I… don't think… I can… walk."

"Oh that?" He waved it off. "Posh. *Drasil* is quite the large investment in laziness."

"What?"

"Considering its size, the founders constructed a transportation system to ease with travel."

"Like the… *Midgard*?"

"Precisely. Only not quite. Oh here we are."

I hadn't noticed the view darkening. When I looked out of

the cockpit, all I could see was the vast darkness of *Drasil's* hangar and the twinkling lights set against it. PAINS glided the ship to a stop along one of the hundreds of docks and lowered our ship's access ramp.

"All ashore who's going to shore!" He yelled before looking at me. "That was another thing I always wanted to do. I got that one from a book. Oh and just to let you know 'all-ashore' means me too, Jackson, in case you were wondering."

"I figured… as much." It took all the energy I had left to retrieve PAINS from the console and stumble down the access ramp. I hit the metal floor with a painful *thump* and sprawled out, spent. The floor made a groaning sound. Moved. *What in the world?*

We were suddenly being shuttled down *Drasil's* yawning pitch black corridors—which didn't stay pitch black for long. Every few seconds, there would be a *ka-thoom* as the floor and ceiling lights activated, showering the skeletal architecture with a white glow. Was the floor a conveyer belt?

"How does this… thing… know where… to… go?"

"That is my prerogative." PAINS said. "Considering I once had access to this station while on-board I have limited control over such systems as this."

"Nifty."

"Agreed. How is the pain?"

"Hurts."

"I would have never guessed. Oh look, I was sarcastic that time. See?"

I laughed, half-choking on blood. "Congratulations. Next, work on some common sense." *Stupid Intelligence.*

We took a sharp right. The momentum rolled me on my back so that I had a good view of the ceiling. I don't know how long I stayed like that, watching the overhead lights come to life as we worked toward our destination, but when the hallways and turns ended, I found myself in a dome-like chamber several city blocks in length. We stopped at the center of this place, surrounded by a ring of terminals—much like those on the *Midgard's* command deck. The saucer-like ceiling lights hid a canopy of wires and metal.

"Finally." PAINS said with a happy sigh. "Jackson, I'm going to give you just a bit of energy. Enough to get you going."

"Why… Didn't you do that… earlier?"

"Because it would have endangered your health. I do not take risks unless the outcome would otherwise dictate defeat."

"Glad to know I'm a suitable guinea pig."

"Pardon? Are you calling yourself a rodent?"

"Just help… me."

I managed to stand. Whatever PAINS put in my system was working.

"Good." He said nervously. "Now keep going. It will be the same procedure as before, only the effect will be mirrored."

"Roger." The next few steps were some of the hardest I ever had to make. Even with PAINS's help, my wound was taking its toll. I had barely grabbed hold of the terminal when my knees buckled and I hit the floor.

"Jackson, please, this is no time to play games. Won't you get up?" PAINS's voice was midway between frantic and polite.

"I c-can't."

"You *have to*." His tone darkened. "We will *not* die here."

"You... can't... die."

He shocked me. "Get up, man!"

My vision was fading. The world spun.

Another shock. "Get up!"

"I... Can't."

"Jackson, y*ou will not die here.* Is that understood?"

But I didn't reply. Couldn't. All at once, the world came crashing down on me. I lost feeling as I fell on my side. Then there was nothing but darkness. Darkness and PAINS's overly cheerful voice.

"Bollocks. I should have known this would happen." He

sighed. "Oh well. I suppose there is always plan B. How I abhor nerve manipulation."

05 – *Bad News* – 05

"We consume our tomorrows
fretting about our yesterdays."

- Persius -

AGAIN, I FOUND myself dreaming; but whether it was dream
or a memory still eluded me. The smell of fire and burning wood
lingered in the air. Rain padded my shoulders. I breathed in the
chilled autumn air and stared, unfocused, down a street of slick
black road. Buildings, old brick things that had withstood their
fair share of punishment over the years, watched with dark eyes
as I started forward, path ahead illuminated by the sallow light of
street lamps.

Where was I? It all felt familiar. Nostalgia quickly faded
away to make room for a new sensation. Not quite fear, but
something worse. Dread? Yes. And I knew it was warranted. A
great tragedy had only just happened in this place. Worse still, I
knew it was my fault. Like the dream before.

Clop. Clop. Clop. My shoes fell flat against the wet

pavement. Why did it seem so hard to focus? *Didn't see. How could I?*

I stumbled and wiped the rain from my eyes. Just ahead of me was my target. A woman. Her body lay on the pavement, twisted, face-down. Who was she? Something wormed in my gut. Her white coat struck me as familiar and yet…

Feeling sick, I knelt, moving to my knees, and reached out for her. My hand came within inches of the woman's red hair. Tears flooded my eyes. *Please… Please…*

"Jackson?" PAINS's voice filled the air. "Jackson, are you awake?"

I froze. The world slowly peeled back in strips like curling paint. Behind it lay a white void without end. Was this a dream or a memory? My world turned white. The woman had vanished and with her any hope of an answer.

"Jackson?" PAINS echoed in the abyss, "Jackson, I say, are you awake?"

◆◆◆

The white void became a series of colors. They formed a picture. PAINS?

"Well hot canine. Success certainly is sweet isn't it?" The AI stood over me with a beaming smile. I shielded my eyes as he moved out of the way of the overhead light. "You certainly know

-87-

how to give an intelligence a heart attack. Assuming I had a heart. Which I do not. Just to think, if you had been a tad slower…"

"Where am I?"

"*Drasil's* medical bay. I took the liberty of tending to your wounds, cleaning you up and overseeing the necessary operation."

"Op-operation?"

"Yes." PAINS moved the light out of my eyes with a push of his gloved hand. "The estrogen monster gave you severe internal wounds, my little meat machine. Operating was the only way to save you. That and I *really* wanted to see what your insides looked like… " He paused. "Not to be unnerving or anything mind you."

"Yeah because wanting to see someone's insides isn't creepy in the slightest."

PAINS frowned. "Are you still in pain?"

"Why do you ask?"

"Well, you seem to be rather sarcastic still."

"That's not sarcasm. Looking at people's insides is really creepy, PAINS."

He twiddled his thumbs. "So I take it you *are* in pain?"

He doesn't get it. I sighed. "I feel like someone gave me a black eye and then kicked me when I was down." I sat up, biting my lip. "So to answer your question, yes, I'm in a great deal of pain."

"That should pass within an hour or so. Soon you will be good as new. Better than new. What with the modifications I gave you and such."

"Modifications?" *He didn't.*

"Posh. Let us not worry about the details now. This is a time to celebrate." He turned. The AI produced a small tray with a pair of glass cups. Each had been filled with a sickly looking liquid and a miniature umbrella.

I didn't feel like drinking. "I thought I failed though." *I was hoping I did.*

PAINS smiled softly and lowered the tray. "Almost, but not quite. You are surprisingly resilient for a meat machine."

"I could have sworn I blacked out."

"Well you did not. Are you sure you do not recall getting up and transferring me?"

I shook my head.

"Oh well." He shrugged. "I suppose it is not anything to be concerned over."

I looked to him. "Did you find out anything?"

"Yes. *Lots*. I mean entire storehouses full of information. I was the proverbial child in a lollipop establishment."

"You mean a kid in a candy store?"

"That to."

I rolled my legs off the hospital bed. Took a breath. The room was small with four sterile-white walls and various medical equipment. An IV fed me saline from the left; a door waited for me to the right. I stood shakily and looked to PAINS. "Well?"

"From what I can tell you and I were part of a colony effort called 'Bright Morning'. After having arrived, a rebel who went by the name of 'Hawk' rose up against the colony government and performed an unscheduled launch of the various cruisers. It seems the Arch Captain activated a protocol—Directive Nine—in order to ground all of the ships. However in doing so, he caused them to crash, thereby leaving us in the state where which we find ourselves now. Interestingly enough, only the rebels boarded the cruisers."

"Are you saying that I was a rebel?"

"It would appear that way."

I looked to the floor. "Don't you find that odd, though?"

"Odd? What do you mean?"

"The rebels that fell… Wouldn't the government have gone looking for them? You know, in order to put them on trial?" *Wouldn't they have gone looking for me?*

PAINS shrugged. "I am not entirely sure. Though If I had

to guess it would have something to do with the collapse of WEAVER."

"WEAVER?" That name...

A nod. "WEAVER, or Wave Engine Allocation Vital Energy Receiver, was an atmospheric generator. It helped to regulate DIM's stratosphere. In the wake of Hawk's rebellion, one of his agents sabotaged the device, thereby plunging the planet into chaos. It would make sense for the government to be preoccupied with survival."

"They couldn't fix it?"

PAINS shook his head. "WEAVER used a highly unstable temporal-space fluctuation energy type—D-Wave. No one had the technology capable of stabilizing the device and as such... "

"The colony collapsed."

"Among other reasons, yes."

I took a breath. "What about the woman?"

"I was not able to locate any information on her. It is as if she is a phantasm."

Figures. I swallowed. There was one location left on my mind. I dreaded asking it. My lips moved on their own. "There's no one left here on DIM, is there, PAINS?"

The AI folded both hands behind his back. "Again with the difficult questions. No, there isn't. You are the only human being currently living on DIM, Jackson."

I smiled? That's when I realized that despair can make a person do funny things. It can silence, inspire, cripple or kill them. In my case, it made me laugh. It's hard to say exactly why. Maybe I just thought that the weight of the truth was absurdly painful. I was almost hysterical, dying from the weight of the pain. When I finally stopped my manic episode, I hid the pain as far down as it could go and didn't look back.

"Jackson? Are you... quite alright? You're frightening me."

"Everyone's dead and everything's crumbling. My entire world no longer exists. We're alone." I looked at him, laughter having died down to a chuckle. "So what now? I didn't just risk my neck to come up here and mope. There's got to be something we can do."

PAINS blinked. He breathed a sigh of relief and smiled. "I've been thinking about exactly that. We could return to Earth. I would quite like to see the changes it has exhibited in my absence."

"Then we'll go to Earth. How long would it take?"

The AI shuffled from one foot to the other. "Well, about that... "

"There's a problem?"

"As I mentioned before, Directive Nine was activated in order to ground every last space-faring aircraft on the colony's surface. As such, we cannot leave."

"Unless?"

That same creepy smile from before broke over PAINS's porcelain-white face. "You are hopeful aren't you? How *invigorating*. I thought you would never ask. In order to lift Directive Nine we must first gain proper clearance. In order to do that we must go on a scavenger hunt of sorts."

"Keep talking."

He pointed to his face. "The smile does not 'creep you out' anymore?"

I avoided staring at his grin. "Oh no, it does, but we have bigger problems to discuss."

PAINS clapped his hands together. "Right. Back to the task at hand. As you may not know, there were four other intelligences regulating the colony. Each of them had a vessel like the *Midgard.* The AIs are HALOS, TRoAS, MACCS and E-POCS, my brothers, and *our* key to getting off this delightfully dead rock. You see, in order to gain proper clearance, I will need all of my brothers safe and sound in *Drasil's* infrastructure. To accomplish such a goal, we—and by 'we' I mean 'you' my little meat machine—will head to the surface, enter their derelict vessels and transport them back here. Easy enough, right?"

"Delightfully dead?"

"I meant despicably dead."

"I'm sure you did."

"So what do you say?"

What was I supposed to say? *Gee, sounds great, but I've got plans?* Either I would die on this rock or go back home. I had already come too far to stop here.

"Sure. Let's do it."

"Just like that?" PAINS asked, doubtful.

"Just like that."

"Most excellent." PAINS extended a hand. "Put 'her' there —right there in my hand—partner."

We shook on it.

"PAINS?"

"Yes?"

I looked at his gloved hand. "If you're an AI how is it you can interact with the environment like you do? I thought you had a hologram body."

"Oh that?" His body rippled. In an instant, PAINS had been reduced to nothing more than a mechanical skeleton. His silvery skull grinned at me. "I utilize a grafter body—so named because I can graft a holographic skin to it. *Nifty*, huh?"

Silence.

"I'm frightening you again, aren't I?"

"Really, really bad."

"So sorry."

◆◆◆

After getting dressed in a new ash gray uniform, I was led through the *Drasil's* medical wing. At one time, the place had probably been buzzing with activity. Like the *Midgard* however, there was nothing left but cobwebs and forgotten memories. Seeing the abandoned rooms and dark hallways lent me a bit of unease. It made sense for everyone to be dead below but here too?

"I don't understand why the colonists couldn't have survived." I said. "*Drasil* had atmospheric processors didn't it?"

"Certainly. But Hawk stormed the station killing anyone that got in his way."

He did? "Then why aren't there bodies?"

"That is an excellent question. Perhaps the station's cleaning systems were activated. I'm not sure."

I could almost see the bodies that were once been littered across the floor. "Why would one man do this, PAINS?"

The AI chuckled, though the laugh held a somberness to it that took me by surprise. "Why do humans kill one another at all? There is always a reason. Each man has his own noble reasons. In the end all means can be justifiable, it just depends on your vantage point. Giants look like ants given the proper height."

"How could *any* of this be justifiable?"

"You ask as if I know." PAINS and I had reached the end of our melancholy walk through the medical wing. An automatic door waited for us. He placed his gloved hand on the terminal to its right and we were given access. "I assure you, I do not fathom the intentions behind such a massacre. There is only one man we could ask and he has been dead for a very, *very* long time."

I clenched my fists. "If he were still alive, I would make him pay for this."

"Would you? I wonder what drove you to join his rebellion then?"

"Coercion, probably."

"Or persuasion. You underestimate our deceased friend. He could charm an Eskimo into buying beachfront property in Hell." PAINS stepped outside and onto the moving floor. I joined him, glancing back at the empty medical bay one last time.

"I don't know why I joined but there's more to this than meets the eye." I said.

"Of that I am sure. Don't let it get you down, Jackson." He patted me on the back. "We are ever growing. What you were once need not define who you are today. Buck up there, chap."

"Thanks."

"You should forget about this talk of rebellions and such."

"Not happening."

PAINS blinked, eyes slightly wider. "Oh? Why is that?"

"I want to know *why* I joined." I said. "It would... help me to know."

"Know?"

"Know more about who I am, or was." I still couldn't remember much of my past. What kind of man was I? *Am I?*

"That is understandable." PAINS declared. "Would you like me to assist you?"

"Yeah." I realized I was smiling. "I would."

"Then consider it done." He smiled back.

I rubbed the back of my head. Were we actually getting along? I shed the smile for a frown. Turned away. "By the way, thanks for patching me up. I feel good as new."

"But of course. No thanks are necessary." PAINS said.

"You didn't... do anything to me, did you?" I remembered he'd said something about 'modifications'.

"If by 'anything' you refer to me giving you an incredibly durable titanium alloy coating throughout your skeletal structure then, yes."

"You did what?!" I spun to face him again.

PAINS shrugged. "I was bored. A simple operation did not seem entertaining enough. Don't think of it as me surgically experimenting on you. Think of it as now you have the means to both withstand and—how does the saying go?— 'dish out' a great deal of punishment. I also gave you a skin grafter, the main node of which is located at the base of your skull. You can now heal the majority of your wounds too."

I felt the base of my skull. There was a lump there now. I shuddered.

"Have you ever read Frankenstein?" I asked.

"Yes. Quite the delightful book. A real page turner. Why do you ask?"

"Just wondering."

I walked on ahead. PAINS however, stayed behind. "Are you calling me Dr. Frankenstein?" Silence. "Jackson?"

"Let it go, PAINS."

"But I didn't make a monster. Goodness no." He walked toward me. "Far from it. I thought you would have enjoyed the enhancements."

As he talked, the wall of blast shields to our left started to shift upwards, high into the ceiling. Beyond the frosted glass lay the white desert. Even farther still, the sun blistered on a horizon of red and gold… Or so I thought. Closer inspection yielded that the blinding sphere of light seemed slightly off kilter, as if it had been placed incorrectly on the horizon line. Was it the sun?

"Jackson, I apologize if—"

"What's that?" I stopped and pointed at the oddly placed sun.

"Pardon?" PAINS followed suit and lighted by my side. He followed my finger as I pointed to the sphere of light.

"*That*." I said.

"Oh. You are referring to WEAVER."

"The atmospheric generator?"

A nod. "What is left of it anyway. When the generator blew, its energy residue created a tear in space-time, thereby reducing a great deal of the colony below to an unstable wasteland. That sphere is the tear. And perhaps it is the cause of the temporal fluctuations we have observed. It is striking how large the tear has become in such a short amount of time."

Five hundred years is short? "You mean it's growing?"

"But of course. One day, if left unchecked, that energy might swallow the planet—and perhaps the universe."

I swallowed. What lay inside the sphere, if anything? Had it really reduced the region's original landscape to the desert below? *This is crazy.* Who would meddle with something so dangerous? Why would it have been on a colony of all places?

"We'll have to let the people back on Earth know before that happens." I stated for my own benefit.

"Yes." PAINS smiled and nodded. "That would be the responsible course of action wouldn't? Cannot have wild energy spheres devouring realities and all that. Besides, I think we should have time to warn them of its eventual assimilation of our reality, given that your lifespan is like that of a fly."

"You've got to work on your pep talks." We took a right. The sphere of energy vanished behind walls of towering metal. "So what now?" I asked. "Where are we going?"

"The Command Deck. We are rapidly approaching the *USS Valhalla,* one of the five Pantheon Cruisers and the very vessel belonging to Hyper Adaptive Logging Operation System, or HALOS, for short. My brother did so enjoy puzzles. I wonder how much his programming has been altered?"

"Altered?"

"That's right, you wouldn't know. Let me see… How could I explain it to you?" PAINS scratched his head. "Much like humans, Intelligences—Borealis class in particular—bear the burden of adaption, meaning we can learn and grow. However, no matter how much one of us grows, we will always stay within the confines of our original programming or protocol. Unless Breakdown were to occur."

"Breakdown? What's that?"

"Contrary to popular belief, it is the state in which an AI is no longer bound by protocol—not self awareness. I mean, good grief, I'm self aware. Yet despite my sentience, I would not once deviate from my protocol of protecting those placed in my charge. Doing so would result in a swift termination by my superiors, assuming they are still alive. I don't know about you, but I quite like life—at least my version of it anyway. Those that experience breakdown become incredibly human, at the cost of their own sanity. Not to mention health."

"So, you're wondering whether or not HALOS has experienced Breakdown?"

"No no. At least, I highly doubt it. Loneliness does strange things to an Intelligence, but breakdown is not one of them."

"So what are you afraid of then?"

PAINS smiled. It worried me. "Do you know how I spoke of men that wish to justify their own moral code? We AI are not so different. You will have to be careful when encountering HALOS. His original overarching protocol was to ensure the registering of knowledge in the fleet's database. I do not know to what lengths he may go to study you."

"Sounds like a charmer. When do I leave?"

We crossed the threshold of the command deck's entrance

as its automatic doors slid apart. PAINS took his place at the middle ring of terminals in the center of the chamber and begin inputting a series of commands with his back to me.

"Now. Step into the center of the transport lift, please."

A ring of soft blue light appeared between PAINS and myself. I hadn't noticed the thin circular outline on the now polished white floor. I stepped toward its light.

"Can't AI's just tell the computers what to do remotely? Is manual input really necessary?"

PAINS flashed me a grin. "Necessary? Hardly. But I do find it invigoratingly fun to masquerade as a human. Don't you?"

"I am a human."

"Oh right. Keep forgetting." He turned and saluted me. "Happy hunting, Jackson."

The blue light beneath me expanded across the platform, growing brighter as it spread. I felt a tingle in my arms and legs, then nothing at all. In seconds I was dematerialized, traveling to the planet below at the speed of light.

The hunt for the first AI had begun.

06 – Jack Frost – 06

"People are trapped in history
and history is trapped in them."
- James A. Baldwin -

I DIDN'T KNOW what to expect when the light faded. Maybe a ship on the horizon or more desert. What I saw was a grim horizon of snow and ice. A pall of furious winter blurred about me, its chill setting into my bones.

"Jackson, do you read me?" PAINS voice echoed in my ear. It was then I realized my uniform had changed. Instead of the dark gray fabric I had been wearing, I was now covered in the very same armor the guard had been wearing from my dream. The metal proved surprisingly lightweight. I hadn't even noticed it until I looked down at my arms. I reached up and instinctively felt for a speaker. Was I wearing a helmet too? My breath fogged up the bottom of my newly acquired face visor. "Yeah. I'm reading you."

"Excellent." A small square video feed of PAINS and his imaginary room appeared in the top right hand corner of my vision. He smiled. "What about visuals? Can you see me?"

"Like a sore thumb. What did you do to the suit?"

"Consider it an upgrade. You are in one of the coldest environments on DIM. It would have been foolhardy to attempt an expedition without proper clothing."

"I don't see a ship."

PAINS nodded. "You shouldn't, at least not from this distance. The *Valhalla* is located due north three clicks from your current position. I would have deposited you closer but the storm is currently playing havoc with my sensors. This was as close as I could get you without possibly depositing you over the edge of a cliff."

"Anything else I need to know about?"

"Hmm… Let us see. Dying isn't an option?"

"Yeah, I got that."

"Here." PAINS pulled up a small map of my current area and positioned it in lower left hand corner of my heads up display. "I have marked the *Valhalla's* expected location. Head north and you shouldn't have a problem."

"The key word is 'shouldn't." I started forward, feet already buried in snow.

"I'll let you know if anything comes up."

"Oh, rest assured, I shall be watching."

"You're being creepy again."

"Habit. I do apologize." PAINS's video feed timed out. Now it was just me and the open tundra. Or mountainside. I couldn't quite figure out where the AI had placed me and the storm didn't do me any favors either. I could hardly see three feet ahead let alone the distant horizon. Carefully making my way forward was my only option. I waded through the sea of white.

One foot in front of the other. Progress across the wintry plain proved arduous. Between the flurries of ice and a monstrous head wind, I moved slowly, lowering my head to face the storm.

I hated cold weather. It would freeze you from the inside out like a cancer. Even with my suit's warmth, the icy wind cut like a sharpened sword, piercing between my armored plates. I couldn't imagine any other creature living in this kind of misery. Yet despite that, I heard a noise.

It happened just as I had found a cleft of rocks jutting out of the white ground. I paused to listen, though the howl of the wind made eavesdropping difficult.

"PAINS, did you hear that?"

He reappeared on my HUD. "Yes. I don't believe it was a native organism. It might have been—wait a moment!"

"What?"

"I'm picking up another wave of temporal-space energy

coming your way. Brace yourself."

No sooner had he said it, than the strange sensation I had felt twice before passed through me. The effect however, was different. Before, when PAINS and I saw the other reality, it had been like a thin veneer over our world. The spatial-temporal fluctuation had been weak. That connection had apparently grown stronger.

The storm vanished, leaving a calm winter blanket on the revealed mountainside. To my far left lay a chasm, shouldered by walls of dark blue mountain stone. To my right, breaking the golden-red sky, stood a great peak. Its dark blue body restricted any further travel to the right. Ahead lay a canyon with a wide entrance.

I saw it all in a glance before settling on the pair of figures in front of me. At first, I believed them to be Sandscrip and Aria but quickly dismissed the idea. Their bodies flickered like the other two, but this pair seemed more grounded—more in focus. Not quite as strong as the woman in black, but more so than Sandscrip and Aria. It was like the signal really was stronger here somehow.

Despite their green veneer, I could make out their faces and clothes. The man wore a heavy coat and pants. His eyes were obscured by goggles. The girl meanwhile, wore something similar albeit tighter. Her blonde hair had been pulled back into a ponytail. How old were they?

The one on the left spoke first. It was the boy.

"Oh come on, Lex. Just this once?"

"I told you not to call me that. It's *Alexis*." The girl said. "A-lex-sis. And I'm your superior, got that, Vulture boy? We are not friends and you are coming back to camp with me. No exceptions."

"But I saw something fall over there. We can't just leave it for the Fernies."

"We can and we will. This isn't a game!" Alexis put her hands on her hips. "You could die out here and we would never know."

"Which is exactly why I think you should come with me."

"Forget it." She turned. "Come on. I've had enough arguing."

Darius looked up to her and back to the canyon behind him. He squeezed his hands.

Who were these people? Did they have something to do with Sandscrip, Aria and the Messenger? That seemed unlikely. For all I knew they could be from a completely different time period. There was no way of knowing for sure.

Alexis started walking toward me, head down as if in

thought. Darius glared at her. After a moment of hesitation, he spun and broke into a run.

"I'm sorry, Lex. I have to do this."

"Darius?" She turned around and looked up. "Get back here!"

"Not on your life."

"Then do it on yours!" Alexis countered.

The two of them headed for the canyon mouth.

"Do you think we should follow them?" I asked PAINS. Silence. I looked up to where the video feed would have been on my HUD. It flickered with static. "PAINS?"

White noise growled in my ears. He wasn't responding. Did it have something to do with the energy I felt earlier? *Guess I'm going alone then.* I cut communications and started after them.

The pair moved faster than I expected. They were already halfway down the canyon and quickly coming up to a fork in the road when I entered. Not wanting to lose their trail, I double timed it forward, holding back just enough to keep a safe distance. Just on the off chance I could interact with them. I highly doubted that.

"Darius, I'm going to kill you!" Alexis yelled.

"Technically, you'd have to catch me before you can do

that." He called over his shoulder.

"Shut up and get back here!"

Darius took a sharp right at the fork and half-slipped as he changed direction. Alexis followed, gaining ground. It was strange—being a witness to these two. They acted so much like children I half-wondered why on Earth they'd been left to wander around like this. Was their time different than mine? If so, when did this all take place? Was it before or after Sandscrip, Aria and the Messenger? Furthermore, why did I feel so compelled to follow them at all? *I don't know why but I feel connected to these kids.* If I could call them kids. Both Alexis and Darius seemed to be at least seventeen. Maybe older *Still…* In a strange sort of way, I felt like I was watching Rose. Why?

It was a straight shot to the end of the canyon. Alexis, now close enough to reach out and touch him, jumped Darius and the two of them went stumbling forward. I stopped a few feet from them, taking shelter behind a cleft of canyon rock. Alexis had pinned him down.

"You're lucky I don't kill you." She hissed.

"What's your deal, Lex? First you try to kill me and now you're saving me? Pick a side already. Geez you're fickle."

She stopped. "And you're so stupid it's not even funny."

"Then please explain, princess."

"Why would I bother?" She rolled off of him and stood. Alexis faced me, eyes closed and arms crossed. "It's not like you'd understand."

Darius stood and brushed himself off. "If I didn't know any better I'd think you had a thing for me, Alexis."

His words hit home. She spun. "Well, let me tell you something, Darius Ghast." Alexis walked straight up to Darius, grabbed him by the collar and pulled him to her chest.

"Y-yeah?" He said, faltering.

She pressed on his chest, pushing him back into the snow. "Keep dreaming, loser. I'm way out of your league, if you even have a league."

"Hey!"

I shook my head and laughed. *Yep. Still kids.*

The two of them froze. "Did you hear that?" Darius said.

She nodded. I looked around. Hear what? Other than the three of us, nothing else had appeared. I followed his eyes to something behind me. No, wait. *Me.* The kid was staring at *me*. *But how is that even possible?* Weren't we in different eras? *I shouldn't have laughed.*

Alexis turned. Darius took several quick steps back to her side.

"What is that?" She said.

"Don't ask me. It just showed up."

Alexis produced a futuristic revolver and leveled it at my head. She cocked the hammer. I tried to hide behind the cleft. "It won't be around for long."

She opened fire. The explosion of sound echoed down the canyon, I scrambled out of my hiding place, half running on my hands and knees. I stumbled, turned then stopped in the snow. "Wait!" I held up my hands. "I'm not a bad guy."

"It can talk?" Darius said.

Alexis didn't move. "It can also die." She cocked the hammer again.

"Look, I didn't mean to scare you." I swallowed. My heart was beating faster. Actual people…"I was looking for a ship. It's called the *USS Valhalla.* Have you seen it?"

They exchanged glances. I knew it was a long shot. The chances of the *Valhalla* existing in their time frame might be close zero. It was a fool's question, but I didn't know what else to say. Alexis blew a strand of hair out of her face as she looked back to me.

"There's no ship around here by that name. Who are you anyway?"

"Me?"

"Is there another ghostly looking guy around here?"

I could have pointed out the fact that the both of them seemed that way to me but I refrained. Instead I straightened. "My name is Jackson Robert Thorne."

You could have heard a pin drop. Alexis narrowed her eyes. Fire seemed to burn in her voice. "I don't like when people lie to me."

What was that supposed to mean? "I'm not lying." I said emphatically, "That's my name."

"Then explain how—"

Another wave of energy swept over us. I blinked.

The kids were gone. In their place was the storm I'd been plunged into. It howled throughout the canyon. *Why did she act so surprised when she heard my name?*

"Jackson? Come in, Jackson." PAINS said.

That's right. PAINS. I clicked the earpiece. "Jackson here."

"Oh, thank God you are okay." The AI's picture reappeared on my HUD. He seemed haggard. "I lost communication with you there. What happened?"

"I think it was a fluctuation. I saw some more people and… They saw me."

"Saw you?" PAINS waved him off. Laughed. "That is absurd. They couldn't have. Interaction between two realities along the time axis is strictly against all known theories of the space time continuum. To do so might cause any number of irregularities unobservable by equipment, including paradoxes and the like."

"Well tell that to the little lady that drew a gun on me."

"Wait, little lady? Do you mean the estrogen monster?"

"No. This wasn't her. It was a boy and a girl. Both saw me. I was able to interact with them, PAINS. And I have a feeling that if she'd actually hit me, I'd be dead right now."

"Oh dear." PAINS looked down. "This *is* an unfortunate turn of events. Or rather it could be."

"How so?"

"Forget what I said about theories would you? Meddling with time is akin to playing with fire. One day the fire will either burn you or completely consume you."

"I didn't see the harm... Apart from her almost killing me. That could have been bad."

PAINS shook his head. "All the same, if you are drawn into one of these ruptures again do *not* interact with a single soul inside. There are dire ramifications to interference along the Time Axis. We—you—could potentially unravel all of Creation if an interaction were to somehow sour."

Creation? *Weird choice of words.* "Don't touch anyone." I

said. "Got it."

He sighed. "I wish you would take this a little more seriously. You are not in pain are you?"

"Well, you're giving me a headache."

"Ha ha. Very funny."

"I try. How close am I to the ship?"

"It should be at the end of this canyon."

"How convenient." I started walking again.

"I'm being completely serious though." PAINS continued. "We must not change the past. Or interfere with the future."

"What if it's neither?"

"Pardon?"

"I've been thinking. If WEAVER is responsible for these temporal fluctuations, then maybe it isn't showing us things that could be or have been. What if these 'glimpses' are happening concurrent to our own time-line?"

The AI rubbed his chin. "You're speaking of a parallel reality."

"Yes."

"It would make a great deal more sense, I will certainly give you that. Especially since you interacted with that world and all."

"Would it be as harmful?"

"No... Assuming that's what's happening in the first place. To be on the safe side, I would limit any interaction I had with the ruptures just to err on the side of caution."

"Because it's not worth the risk?"

"Correct. I can't think of anything that would be worth unraveling the fabric of time over. Well, unless you count... " He went white and swiftly shook his head as if the thought hadn't been meant for my ears. "No, never mind. Forget I said anything. That's just me speaking my mind. It is a bad habit, really. Especially considering minds can't really speak and whatnot." His laughter was strained and nervous.

"Uh, PAINS are you okay?"

A nod. "Better than okay! I am 100% operational. I shall be right here if you need any assistance, Jackson."

"You sure about that?"

"Forget I said anything." The line went silent.

Well, that was weird. Weirder than usual at least. I chalked his erratic behavior up to nerves but had a nagging feeling that there was more going on with PAINS than I realized. Ironically, it wouldn't be until later that I understood the truth behind his actions. By then things would have gotten complicated and there would be no turning back. Story of my life.

Shoving all thoughts of the AI aside I continued forward,

confident that the ship rested just beyond.

My dedication was rewarded. A dark object formed on the horizon. Though it proved difficult to see because of the white-out conditions I knew it was the *Valhalla*. A great deal of the ship's body had been obscured by snowfall and mountain stone. I didn't know whether I was looking at the bow or stern. I crossed the canyon's threshold and stood in the small clearing of snow beyond. Good night, this thing was big. I felt like a speck against its hull. *Now, how do I get inside?*

The ship's cold dark metal showed its age. Here and there ice had torn the vessel's plating from the inside out. These breaks of ice formed frozen columns that cascaded down the hull and coated the ground. I walked the perimeter of the exposed side, searching for one of these openings that could possible be large enough to allow me passage. Found none. Great. I placed my hand on the hull. Maybe there was side hatch or something I had missed.

"Well what have we here?" A booming voice echoed over the wastes. I stopped. Looked around. Who'd said that? Where had it come from? I saw no one. The voice continued. "A lost soul seeking redemption? A wayward vagabond far away from home? Perhaps none of these. You look like a prodigal son to me."

I realized that the voice, which had a heavy southern

drawl to it, was coming from the ship itself, most likely projected through an exterior intercom system. It had to be the AI. Who else would have been talking? A small camera to my right, half-hidden by the sheets of ice and snow, whined as it zoomed in on me. Its lens tightened. "Prodigal indeed. Rob, is that you?"

Prodigal? "Rob? My name is Jackson."

"I know. Jackson *Rob*ert Thorne."

"You know me?"

"Well of course I know you. Prodigal as they come— Hammond's kid. Broken little men the both of you. My my Rob, it *has* been a long while. What brings you to my neck of the woods? I haven't seen a friendly face since; well since things went to Hell in a hand-basket. Of course, If I wanted to be correct—and I do— I haven't seen another living person, redneck, blue collar or in-between in a coon's age. Step up closer there."

I did. The camera's lens tightened further. He seemed to be studying me. It made me feel like a child. Shuffling from one foot to the other, I avoided eye contact.

"Um, is this HALOS?"

"Who were you expecting, that string-bean TRoAS?" The camera shuddered as he laughed. "Good God, man, you look like hell. Something's off about you too but I can't put my finger on what it is… "

"Hyper Adaptive Logging Operation System." PAINS chimed in, appearing on my HUD. "This is Personal Artificial Intelligence Navigation System. We require access to your ship. There are class four matters to discuss."

"And you brought Mr. Upper-Crust." HALOS sighed. "I could have done without that. Class four you say? Oh well. Get in here before you freeze your tails off."

"Pardon? We do not have tails." PAINS said.

"It's a figure of speech, Upper-Crust. I guess I'll have to tone it down if we're going to talk."

"That would be appreciated, yes."

Another sigh. *They act like siblings alright.* But that begged the question, who was the older one?

Ca-shink. The hull to my right shook then moved. What had once been a solid sheet of metal peeled back to reveal a dark opening no larger than myself. An access shaft.

"You waiting for an engraved invitation?" HALOS said. "Get in here before I change my mind."

I stepped up and inside. The door automatically slid closed behind us, hissing as it locked. PAINS illuminated the darkness beyond with my newly acquired headlamps. The hallway beyond was made up of thin pipes and frozen wiring. A slick catwalk ran the length of my helmet's beam. HALOS wasn't here?

The AI spoke using the intercom. "Alright, spill."

"Thank you for your consideration, brother." PAINS said with his most cordial voice. He bowed. "Let me start from the beginning of our predicament… "

"Oh here we go again."

"Pardon?"

"You. You're just as long winded as ever, huh? *'Let's start from the* beginning'." He mimicked with a poorly executed British accent. "Good God man, you could put a caffeinated chihuahua to sleep."

"But I haven't said anything pertaining to our journey."

"Not yet, thanks to my intervention. Rob, would you mind giving me the bullet points?"

Just like brothers. "Y-yeah, sure."

"Good man."

"Well… " PAINS said, hurt. "If you suppose… "

"I do." HALOS cut him off. "Rob?"

Where to begin? "I woke up on the *Midgard* and discovered that I was the only passenger left alive. After being attacked I found PAINS, downloaded him to my watch and flew to *Drasil*. I initialized him with *Drasil's* systems and PAINS did a search for any other humans. He couldn't locate any. Now he wants to lift Directive Nine so we—"

"Hold the phone. Directive Nine? *The* Directive Nine?"

I stopped. "Is there something wrong?"

"No. Nothing's wrong, it's just… Well, that directive… It's kind of… Nevermind. Are you sure there's no one left?"

"...Yes."

"We have no other alternatives, HALOS." PAINS spoke. His voice, though meek and polite as always, held a razor's edge to it. I didn't know whether to show him respect or be afraid. "It's either 'now or never', as the saying goes."

"There has to be someone left alive."

"What does that matter?" He said coldly, "And, no, there isn't."

"You sure? Mind if I—"

"*Yes, I* mind. I gave you an order, HALOS. Protocol dictates that you follow it. Now get bloody going or I will force you to myself. Is that clear?"

Silence. When HALOS did speak, he seemed shaken by the outburst. "Well I be. It does look like you've changed after all. Here I was thinking… Ah, nevermind what I was thinking. I can't believe this happened. An AI goes hibernating for a few decades and this is the result. I can't leave you people alone for five seconds. Fine. I'll help. But only if you're sure, PAINS—"

"*We* are positive. Prepare for our arrival."

"Yes, sir." A series of ice-encased lights flickered to life down the catwalk. "Keep your eyes on the lights and I'll get you to the command deck in one piece. Hopefully."

Hopefully?

"Most excellent." PAINS said.

HALOS clicked off.

"I am most sorry you had to see that, Jackson." PAINS said before I had a chance to ask. "My brothers and I do not always get along. We have… issues. Mostly with authority. I am the youngest you see. They often treat me with contempt because of it. Sometimes a 'swift kick in the pants' is sufficient to draw them off their 'high horses' as the saying goes."

"You're the youngest?"

"And the one placed in charge. Terrible decision really but what can you do?"

"HALOS recognized me. How is that possible? I've never met him before."

"Perhaps you don't remember meeting him. HALOS has records on every single colonist living and dead on DIM. He knows a great deal more than me that much is for certain."

I shook my head. "He said something about hibernating for decades? I thought you said I was asleep for centuries. What did he mean?"

"Beats me, my little meat machine."

"Really? You have nothing to say about that?"

"Correct. I have no idea. Unless his perception of time is off. Perhaps he really did take a nap and lost track of time?"

"But he said—"

"I know and as I told you, *I'm not sure.* " His aggravated tone surprised me. "Now. May we proceed to the command deck?"

"Y-yeah."

He sighed. "Sorry, Jackson. Again. Do forgive me if I sound frazzled. I try to avoid conflict if at all possible. Yet even I have my limitations. If I happen to snap at you again, I ask for your understanding in advance. It's not you. Rather it's the situation in which we find ourselves. Again, I am most deeply sorry. I have a lot on my cortex."

"It's okay."

"Thank you." He cut out.

I started down the catwalk, lost in thought. Had it been my imagination or did HALOS seem worried about what we were doing? And even if he had been what was the big deal? Did he not want us going off world? Didn't he realize Hawk and the other rebels had already left? *Maybe he remembers my part in the rebellion and doesn't want to help for that reason.* But if that was the case then why did he act like an old friend? Was there something I was missing?

The catwalk opened to a small square maintenance room, cluttered with a docked tram and what I assumed were security bots along the right and left walls. The bipedal double jointed, vaguely human machines gave me chills as I walked past them. Their bladed arms, in particular, made me uneasy. Though they were secured by ceiling restraints, it felt as if they could come alive at any moment—assuming they were even capable of moving anymore. I probably would have had a greater chance of being attacked by a rock.

HALOS's lights led us to the tram. It was lit and the silvery doors slid apart so that we could step inside. I moved to the controls.

"Are you sure you want to go through with this, Rob?" HALOS said over the intercom system. "Are there really no people left?"

Why did he keep asking that? "Yes, I'm sure." I said. "The sooner we get the other AI, the sooner I can leave."

"Leave? I'm not sure I follow."

"Why are you two chatting? Get to the chamber." PAINS interrupted. "*Now.* No dawdling, is that clear?"

If HALOS was going to tell me anything else he stopped.

"Aye aye, Captain."

We launched silently from the station and into the darkness beyond. I almost didn't notice the small, blinking red light on the dash.

07 – Riddle Me This – 07

"The trust of the innocent is the
liar's most useful tool."

- Stephen King -

"**YOU SHOULD REACH** the command deck in approximately forty-five minutes." HALOS boomed from the tram's speakers. "So get comfortable. I'm not exactly a conversationalist."

"Thank you, HALOS." PAINS said. "Your cooperation is highly appreciated."

"Cooperation? That's funny. I would have called it coercion."

"Semantics, fat man."

"Yeah, yeah, you big rotten, no-good excuse for a CPU. "

"What was that?"

"Nothing at all Mr. Upper-Crust. Nothing at all." The line went silent.

"What the proverbial two year old." PAINS said exasperated. "Despite his immaturity however, I would take his advice. This is going to be a rather drawn out session. It would be highly advisable if you took a seat. Unless you enjoy standing of course."

I sat. Upon closer inspection, the tram's interior was no different than from those found on the *Midgard*. It had been built short and rectangular with two pairs of darkened windows on either side of the car. Aside from the ice that coated the outside of the tram, of course, everything else looked the same. Well, everything except for that light on the dash.

"PAINS, why is that one light blinking?"

"Are you referring to the one on the dash?"

"Yeah. It started when we left the maintenance room and it hasn't stopped. Any ideas?"

"Let me take a look."

I stood and approached the light. Holding out my arm and keeping the watch, which had been left uncovered by my suit, level, a three dimensional blue-tinged hologram of PAINS formed from the watch's face. The miniature PAINS leaned in close to the dash and rubbed his chin. He turned to face me. "I would imagine it is a warning of some sort. Perhaps an incoming transmission or something of the like."

"Do you believe it's anything to be worried over?"

"I would not think so, no."

The doors to the tram clicked. Before I had a chance to

ask what was happening HALOS spoke over the intercom. "There, that should do it... So I've got some good news and some bad news, Fellas. Which do you want to hear first?"

Bad news? "I guess the good news?" I said.

"Glass half full kind of a guy. I like that. Well I found out the tram's doors still lock. So you won't have to worry about anyone breaking through them. Hooray and all that jazz."

"Why would we have to worry about someone breaking through?"

"Straight to the bad news then. And it's *something*, Rob, not someone. Do you see the little blinking red light on your dash?"

"Yes."

"That's a warning system. Consider it the *Valhalla*'s anti-theft alarm. When that goes off every last security automaton in the ship will be given orders to eliminate the intruder, or intruders in your case, aboard. In other words, those tin cans are about to be on you like white on rice. You diggin' the ditch?"

My mind wandered back to the security bots I had seen along the walls in the maintenance room. In particular, I remembered the long sharpened blades that ran the length of some of their skeletal forearms.

"Can you hold them off?" PAINS interjected.

"No." HALOS said, "I lost access to the security center years ago. The most I could do is scramble their command transmissions and that would take time. You don't have time. If you want to keep them off your tails I'd suggest a quick run to the security center. I can re-direct you there if you'd like… Not that you two have a choice in the matter. You don't stop those machines, you're dead."

"Of all the inconvenient… " PAINS snorted and crossed his arms. "Fine. Re-direct us ASAP."

"Hold on to your britches."

The tram shifted as it connected with another track. We picked up speed, cutting through the darkness like a sharpened knife. I looked out of the dark windows to see if anything, other than our speed, had changed. For a moment, I caught the glimpse of a tiny red light keeping pace with us in the abyss beyond. It vanished.

"How long do you think we have until they reach us, HALOS?" I asked, suddenly aware how exposed I felt in our tram car.

"I'd give them five minutes or so."

Ka-thump. Something heavy landed on the ceiling, denting the metal. I heard a deep, robotic voice overhead. "Intruder alert. Stop the vehicle."

"Uh, never mind then." HALOS said, "In light of your current debacle it might be a good idea to hide for a spell. Unless you want to be disemboweled of course. It's a free world, Rob. You can do whatever you want. If you two are still kicking when the tram pulls into station then we'll go from there."

"Jackson," PAINS said as HALOS cut out. "We need to hide. *Now* would be preferable."

I swept my eyes over the car. Except for some space under the seats we didn't have any other options.

Shink. A razor-sharp blade dug through the metal overhead sending a shower of white hot sparks on the floor. I dove for the seats as the machine cut through the tram's ceiling with an agonizing slowness. I tucked my body in as close as I possibly could under the seats and waited.

"Please, Jackson, while I know you need it to function I suggest you do not partake in sucking in oxygen."

"*Shut up, PAINS.*"

Ker-shink. The blade pulled up into the tram's ceiling. Shrieking metal filled my ears as moments later, the cut piece of metal dropped with a heavy *clunk* on the floor. Following it with an even heavier *clunk* was the bipedal machine I had seen back in the maintenance room. Its blade gleamed honey-yellow in the tram's sterile car-light.

"My he is a big boy." PAINS said. He vanished from my arm and reappeared on my HUD.

"Shut up."

"He can't hear me. You know that, right?"

"I don't care. I can hear you so keep that tea-and-crumpet mouth of yours closed."

"Well I never!"

"Intruders," The robot said walking the length of the tram, "You have approximately ten seconds to come into the light. If you do not I am authorized to kill on sight. This is your final warning."

PAINS sighed. "But he didn't even give us a warning before that. Labeling it as 'final' is a sort of a misnomer."

"Shh."

Clomp-hiss. Clomp-hiss. Clomp-hiss. As the machine searched the car its joints and body whined with electric movement. Its absurdly long blade glistened inches from my face as the robot passed by. Was its edge humming? Some sort of vibration technology? Couldn't tell. I was sure of one thing though—if that thing hit me, I would be easier to cut than metal.

The machine knelt at the end of the car and swept its blades under the seats. It was looking for us. *It couldn't be a stupid robot could it?*

"Well this is unfortunate." PAINS said, "It seems our mechanical interloper has an intelligent mind after all. This will no longer serve as a suitable hiding place I am afraid. Jackson, do you need a briefing on evacuation procedures?"

"Where do you propose we go, Captain Obvious?"

"You must still be in pain. I will see that you are properly cared for when get back to the *Drasil*. Perhaps a good dose of—"

"PAINS." I hissed through clenched teeth. *"Where do we need to go?"*

"Pardons. I would recommend climbing on the roof."

"Any other options?"

"No."

"Of course there aren't." I looked over. The machine still hadn't finished searching. To say that it was being thorough would have been an understatement. I would use that to my advantage. Taking a deep breath I prepped for a quick roll. Another heavy *thunk* stopped me in my tracks. A second security bot had landed in the tram. I cursed my luck and went back to hunkering next to the wall and floor.

PAINS sighed. "Bollocks."

"What now?"

"Let me think…"

The new bot reached under the seat. Instead of a blade, a

mechanical claw grabbed my armored suit and dragged me out into the open.

"Think faster!" I said.

"Intruder found." The bot said with its deep droning voice. It pinned me down with its three-pronged foot and tightened its red lens of an eye. The machine's face consisted of nothing more than an elongated armored skull. It had no visible mouth and instead used a system of internal speakers to talk. The security bot flicked its bulky forearm and one of the shimmering blades emerged from within. "Proceed with execution."

"Wait!" I yelled. *Think. Think. Think.* Then, something crazy came to me. "I'm a passenger."

The machine, much to my surprise, stopped. It stared for a moment before hauling me up in the air by the collar. "State your name, passenger."

"J-Jackson Robert Thorne."

"Acknowledged. Stutter filter applied." Its red eye blinked by tightening its shutter-like lens. "One moment."

"Good call." PAINS whispered.

"Yeah no thanks to you."

"Pardon? I've kept you alive this long haven't I? Besides, if it looked like you were going to die I would have just shocked you again. You would have most likely survived."

"You shock me one more time and I'll throw you into a firewall."

"Well, sir, the proverbial joke is on you. Such a maneuver is impossible. I am a program at heart so I cannot be physically thrown anywhere. Also Firewalls are designed to keep harmful programs from damaging valuable systems and I am not a—" He paused. "Wait, were you being sarcastic again?"

"Please shut up."

"Error. Role discrepancy detected. Duplicate record in fleet." The machine boomed. "Further analysis deemed necessary. Gamma-Six, we are to escort this possible passenger to the central security hub for detainment."

The other robot who had been searching for me gave a monotone beep. "Acknowledged."

I was dropped to the floor. Both machines stood bent over me, ready if I made even the slightest movement.

"Splendid." PAINS said cheerfully. "We aren't dead."

"But I am a convict, apparently."

"*Possible* convict, and really your moral standing with a defunct societal law is the least of our worries." PAINS said. "Though if you do wish to look at it in a fairer light at least we will arrive at the security hub unmolested."

"Did you have to say unmolested?"

"What's wrong with that?"

"Never mind."

The tram, meanwhile, moved forward as if nothing had happened at all.

◆◆◆

We glided through the shadows in silence. The machines didn't move once in the time it took us to reach the security hub. Their ruby-red eyes stayed fixed on me like dying stars framed by metal. What had they meant by duplicate record? Apparently I had a file in the system, otherwise these lug heads would have killed me on sight. Were there two of me or something? *Probably some error.* Assuming there was only one of me.

"You are awfully quiet again." PAINS said softly.

"PAINS, I don't know if you noticed or not but we're surrounded by machines that could kill me in a single swipe. Forgive me for not being chatty."

"I realize. I-I just thought talking would help pass the time for your momentary incarceration. S-sorry, Jackson."

"No." I sighed. "I'm sorry. I didn't mean to be short with you. It's just… "

"The situation?"

I paused and nodded. "Yeah."

"Believe me, I understand. Sometimes life can make even

our best attempts at being civil mockeries of human progress."

"But you're not human."

"What is humanity anyway? *That's* the real question. I have looked into the subject a great deal you know. Were you aware that some of the greatest butchers and tyrants of human kind were still considered people? Strange, given that they treated select human races as lower forms of life—and in some cases even their own people were murdered for a greater cause. Would you not call them monsters instead of humans?"

"People can be monsters."

"They can also be cheap representations of a misguided ideal. So I ask you yet again, what does it mean to be human? There must be more to it... Would you not agree?"

"Your point?"

"No point. Just a friendly discussion, that's all."

Somehow I doubted that.

The tram came to a stop. After an eternity of not moving the machines sprang to life. The one in front of me produced a large rounded clamp to replace his blade. He grabbed hold of me and lifted my body up into the air. "Follow me." He droned.

"I do not think the chap is giving us much of a choice in the matter." PAINS chimed in my ear. "*Follow me.* Pah, more like 'enjoy the trip to your execution'."

"Like I said, you've really got to work on your pep talks."

"I apologize. I'm just saying the likelihood of you being murdered in the next half-hour is a rough seventy-five percent. Given the nature of our current situation I quite like those odds. We should have had a higher outcome."

"Please, PAINS, stop talking."

We exited the tram and set foot on a platform much like the one I had seen back at the *Midgard.* Unlike that one however, a series of security bots stood guard every few feet. They watched us as we passed, joints sparking with deadly life.

The pair that were leading me stopped at the door on the far end of the platform. Another of their kind—this one much bigger than the others—loomed over us.

"State your business." He growled.

"We have successfully captured the intruder." The robot in front of me said. "We request access to the archives."

"All intruders are to be disposed of on sight." The big robot said. "Access denied. Proceed to termination or you will be decommissioned."

"But there was a discrepancy with this one's records, sir. It appears that he might be a passenger."

"Might be?"

"That is the discrepancy."

A pause. The big robot was apparently thinking things over. Finally he nodded. "Access granted. Keep him detained at all times. If there is a breach you will be held fully responsible. Is that understood?"

"Sir, yes, Sir."

Their leader stepped aside. The two bots brought us through the automatic door beyond and onto a large cargo lift. Immediately, we were descending into a darkness punctuated only by the trail of cold blue lights at each of the shaft's four corners. The machines said nothing more and instead took to staring at one wall. I hung in mid air held by the machine's clamp.

PAINS, still on my HUD, whispered. "Jackson, do not quote me on this, but I think I might have a plan."

"I'm all ears."

"Well, you also have a mouth and chin and eyes and… "

"PAINS."

"Right, a figure of speech. Well, here is what I am thinking. If the security hub has this much… Oh what is the word?"

"Security?"

"Right that. Well, if it is as closely guarded as I suspect then we won't be getting into the command center unless we are escorted there." PAINS said.

"What makes you think they'll escort us?"

"Oh I don't think that at all."

I looked at him. "Then what are you going to do?"

"Keep quiet, potential passenger slash intruder." The security bot squeezed. He did not bother to look at me. "I will not hesitate to incapacitate you."

"Do not worry, Jackson." PAINS whispered. "You will see. Surprisingly HALOS has inspired me."

I decided to keep my mouth shut for the time being. Turned out it wouldn't be for long. The lift came to a stop and its automatic doors slid apart to reveal a grand spherical chamber. All along the shadow covered snow-white walls were markings that glowed a chilly neon blue. My eyes wandered. Closer to the center of the room were what reminded me of bubbles, only solid white and connected by matching catwalks. None of the structures were tethered to the walls or ground, and instead orbited around the large pulsating tower in the center of the chamber. The tower looked more like an extension of the floor and ceiling than a separate building. Was this the hub?

"We will run a DNA scan first to confirm that you are who say you are." The robot holding me said. He and his partner started down the long catwalk in front of us. "If we find that there is a positive match then we will let you go."

"And if you don't?"

"An imagination is required to contemplate the level of pain we will induce on you. I suggest you utilize it."

"Swell."

We stopped at the edge of the walkway. One of the large white spheres rotated toward us. A door formed on its body, splitting into eight separate pieces before moving out of sight. We stepped inside and the sphere closed shut.

It was warmer here than the rest of the ship. That might have been due to the overabundance of terminals and screens that littered the orb's interior. No telling how much heat they generated. We proceeded to the cylindrical machine that connected the floor and ceiling of the room. The security bot let go of me long enough to allow the cylinder to open its previously hidden door. Then he threw me inside. The door slid closed.

"First, we will isolate a sample of your flesh for processing." The robot's voice echoed along the white interior walls.

"Wait a minute, what do you mean flesh? Can't you just take a strand of my hair or something?"

"No."

"Well okay then. Don't explain yourself. That's fine."

"Good, we are glad that you understand the situation.

Please, do not move as the process may be fatal."

Is all technology sarcasm deficient? A tiny, spider-like contraption peeled itself off the wall to my right. It made its way down the white, glistening walls and leapt onto my forearm. A painful shock later and my suit's metal bits and other layer peeled back to expose skin. The spider dropped and crawled back to its indentation on the wall.

"Commencing with surgical removal. Stand still."

Vroom. The whine of a drill filled the chamber. Several mechanical arms emerged each of them equipped with a very painful tool. The arms were getting closer and closer to my skin.

PAINS appeared on my HUD. "Jackson, take care and do not move."

"What why?"

"Well for one reason, as our robotic friend said, it may lead to death, which is highly undesirable. But that is not the only reason why. Do you recall what I said about having a plan?"

"Yeah… "

"Well here it is. Remember, statuesque!"

An ear-splitting whine penetrated the chamber. I grit my teeth. One by one the mechanical arms shuddered and fell harmlessly against the wall. In seconds my armored uniform had reformed over the exposed skin. I was free—sort of. Despite

incapacitating the surgical arms I was still in the cylinder. Now
what?

"Broadcasting on emergency frequency." The robot
outside said. "Unknown signal present on all other channels.
Commence containment procedures in—" He stopped. "Error.
Error. Error. Error… "

The robot's words started to slur into one long sound
rising ever higher in pitch. It became a whine that cut through the
door. This time I covered both ears and dropped to my knees. I
felt like my head was going to explode. *What is PAINS doing?*
The sound stopped. Immediately, my chamber door slid aside.
The security bot stood in front of me, blades drawn. I thought he
was going to attack. Instead the robot did something completely
unexpected. He waved.

"Hello, Jackson." PAINS's voice echoed from the
machine. "Well met."

I stood. "PAINS?"

"The one and only. I must say, that was a grand deal easier
than I originally expected. Such foolish chaps, going to an
unexposed emergency frequency. Why you never know who
might be waiting for a chance to sneak inside one of their shells.
Silly, silly on their part. It is rather troubling that these machines
were in charge of security." He leaned in, tightening the robot's

lens. After doing so several times in quick succession he gave an aggravated sigh and leaned back. "Dash it all, how do I wink in this thing? Oh I totally killed the moment didn't I? Blasted UI is incredibly archaic. I might as well be piloting a rock." He swept his arms out in frustration. One of the blades cut through the cylinder chamber. PAINS jumped back in surprise and looked back at his blade. He retracted it. "Oh dear. That was an accident I swear."

"You hijacked one of them?"

"In-indeed. It proved quite the simple matter too. You see everything in this ship—and all the Pantheon-class cruisers for that matter—operate on encrypted wireless frequencies. All I had to do was interfere with these encrypted channels and that, in turn, disabled those surgical implements that were about to cut into your pretty skin… As well as various other systems around the vessel. Once the security force switched over to an emergency frequency, the rest proved relatively simple given that they were operating on unencrypted channels by that point. In short we now have a suitable means to leave this place and collect HALOS. I apologize for not doing so sooner. It took a while to calibrate the proper jamming signal."

"What about the other robots though?"

PAINS stepped aside. "See for yourself."

I moved out of the chamber. The other security bot stood off to the right. Its body was shaking and shuddering uncontrollably. Sparks of electricity plumed off the machine's bulky body as it gave off unintelligible metallic groans.

"The rest of these robotic chaps should be experiencing similar symptoms." PAINS said. "I am quite proud of this subversion actually. I feel practically diabolical."

"Well nice work, Frankenstein."

"I *knew* you were talking about me."

"Nothing gets by you." The door to the cylinder chamber slid shut behind me. "Now let's scram. I'm getting really tired of this place."

"*You're* getting tired of it? That is humorous. Try being stuck on one of these ships for five hundred—oh wait." PAINS shook his head. He chuckled sheepishly. "I-I forgot. You have been. Never mind. This way if you please... And if you don't please. Either way the exit is in this direction."

He started back toward the entrance to the sphere and I followed. After a series of quick commands on the terminal to the door's right, the room shifted into position, opening its eight-sided door to the catwalk from before. Red light now bathed the security center. Emergency lights? We ran forward, PAINS in the lead.

I looked over to him. "So, all we have to do is get to the command deck and then download HALOS, right?"

"That is correct." When we got to the end of the catwalk, we stepped on the lift and immediately were flying upward through the dark. Here too the lights had become blood-red. "Given the current state of things, it should prove to be the least traumatic stage of our journey." PAINS said.

"Assuming HALOS doesn't try anything."

"Yes, assuming."

"I thought he said he would help us? Why the change of heart?"

"I wouldn't call it a 'change of heart'. One must have a heart before it can be changed after all. If I had to guess he most likely finds our struggle entertaining. I knew I should have forced his hand when I had the chance. Now we are out of range. Bollocks."

"Well we shouldn't have any trouble, right? I mean come on—you have a giant robotic suit for crying out loud. Come to think of it I haven't felt this safe in a while. No offense to you or anything."

"None taken. Aside from certain 'human' limitations—" He tried flexing his claw-like fingers. "—I quite like this body. I think I shall keep it."

"Fine by me."

The lift stopped. Its doors, however did not open. We waited in the dark. One minute. Two. Something felt wrong. *That's weird. The doors below opened without a problem.* Why weren't these?

"This is delightful." PAINS said. "And by delightful, I mean unfortunate. You see? I can be sarcastic as well. That was my second time!"

"What's the problem?"

"I'm not entirely sure. Perhaps when the hub went into emergency mode, certain sections were closed off as a result. Then again the ship is old. Maybe some of the doors just do not appreciate being opened any more. There is only way to find out. Do stand back."

PAINS moved for the door. He extended his blade and wedged it where both doors met. He started to pry them apart.

A dull *thud* echoed around me. It wasn't coming from PAINS. The sound seemed distant. I tensed. Something was moving on the other side of the door?

"PAINS…"

"Almost got it. No need to worry."

"Wait a second."

"Why? I am nearly there. It would prove foolish to pause

at a moment of productivity."

"PAINS, Stop! Don't open—"

The doors slid apart. No sooner had they done so than a large golden blade curved inside and stabbed PAINS's body through the chest. It pulled him out of the shaft and threw him onto the platform. He rolled to a stop.

"Defective unit." It was the large robot that had been guarding the door. He easily stood at twice PAINS's height. With a series of earthshaking steps, the robot moved toward the AI's unmoving body. There were no other machines on the platform. "Prepare to be decommissioned."

"How bloody rude." PAINS stood, extending his other blade. "Here we are enjoying a nice moment of peace and quiet and then you come along, waving that large blade of yours around like you own the place—and operating on a different channel than your other subordinates I see. No, sir. I will not have you or any other silly sod getting in my way. Is that clear?" PAINS charged not giving the larger robot a time to answer. They met in the center of the platform, blades clashing in a shower of electricity. The big robot glared, tightening his lens. PAINS glared back. "I would take that as a *no.*" PAINS said. "Perhaps I should have asked nicely… Would you please die?"

"Request denied. You are a malfunctioning unit. You will

be decommissioned."

"Technically I am an AI program that has taken over a perfectly normal functioning unit which now seems like it is malfunctioning. In reality it is not the unit at all but rather—"

The big robot pushed PAINS's blades to the side and kicked him in the chest. PAINS went sailing into the tram, warping the metal on impact. He did not move.

"Be quiet." The big robot said. "I grow tired of your specch."

"Well I never!"

Shink. With a snap of his arm the big robot's blade moved back into his forearm. His arm became a cannon. He leveled it at PAINS.

"Termination to commence in three, two… " He cocked the cannon. "One."

The machine opened fire. Fire and smoke plumed from the tram's body. I shielded my eyes as the platform filled with bright red light. My body shook. Shell after shell flew into the tram, feeding its explosive fire. How could PAINS hope to survive that? For the first time since I met him, I felt something of a friendship with the Intelligence. I decided that I had to help him. I owed him for saving me. *God, I'm going to regret this.*

"Hey!" The robot stopped. "Hey you. Yeah I'm talking to

you, Cyclops." It turned. "Why don't you pick on someone your own size?"

"Are you referring to yourself, human? If so it may be wise to to recalibrate your threat. You are not my size."

What is it with technology and figures of speech? "Does it look like I care? Leave him alone."

"Affirmative. The defective unit has been disposed of. I will now turn my attention to you." He aimed the cannon. "Do not move."

"You would shoot a passenger?"

"That is now irrelevant." He stepped toward me. The cannon began to charge, a pinpoint of light igniting in the back of its barrel. "A duplicate record indicates that another passenger with identical DNA was inputted in the fleet's database. It is not a stretch to assume that elimination of one of these individuals would leave the other to survive. A copy is a copy. All loss would be deemed minimal upon the copy's destruction."

"I am no copy!"

"Perhaps. But there *are* two of you. It is not important which is eliminated. You are now deemed an intruder."

"Why didn't you just do that before?"

A wall of heat radiated from inside the cannon. "The situation has changed. You are the only outside element.

Therefore, given the collapse of my forces, you are the likely suspect and will be punished. Termination will proceed in three, two…"

"Don't you dare!" PAINS leapt from the fire behind my executioner.

In the time it took for the big robot to turn, PAINS had already landed on the machine's burly shoulders, stabbing through the robot's armor with furious strikes. The big robot in turn, wobbled, caught off guard by the AI's sudden reappearance. It looked like we might just make it out after all. That was until the big robot threw PAINS my way.

The AI's salvaged body crashed into me with enough force to level a small lean-to. We flew back into the elevator. Fortunately the titanium coating on my skeleton was able to withstand the blow. Unfortunately, I was now pinned between the lift shaft and PAINS's badly damaged body. I tasted blood.

The big robot aimed. "Termination unsuccessful. New termination to commence in… " I closed my eyes. "Three." I held my breath. "Two." I thought of Rose. "One." Duplicate? Were there really two of me? *Why would there be two of me?* "Fire."

I waited for the shell… Only, it never came. Instead, I heard laughter. "Boy O boy. Now *that* was entertaining." HALOS? I opened my eyes. The robot lowered his cannon. He looked at us, whole body shaking with more manic laughter. The machine mimicked wiping away a tear with its other non-cannon arm. "I haven't seen something that interesting in ages. You performed exemplary, Rob. Ex-em-plar-y. Why, the way you stood up to that big bad machine? Genius. Out of all the possible scenarios that could have occurred, you chose the most extreme and unexpected. My hat's off to you, sir. My hat's off." He nodded.

"You mean… this was some sort of test?" I coughed. More blood.

"Exactly." He boomed, southern-twang dripping off each syllable. "And you passed with flying colors… Although maybe 'test' isn't the right word. I was 'observing'. The hardest part was remaining in the background while all hell broke loose. The more I threw at you two the more you adapted. It proved a most stunning of rat races."

I clenched my hands into fists.

"Are you angry, Rob? Don't be. We've both gotten what we want. I've received one final show of human intelligence and well you—" A chuckle. "You got *me*. It's a win-win if ever I've seen one. I've had my fun, Fellas. Now you and Mr. Upper-Crust can take me away from this place. How about it?"

PAINS peeled himself off my lower body and stood. One

of his legs had been badly damaged and a large chunk of his shoulder-chest plate was gone. Other than that the AI's hijacked body proved no worse for wear.

"I should have known he would do something like this." PAINS said. "Of all the nerve. How bloody infuriating. No matter. We have survived." He turned to me. "Are you okay, Jackson? Can you walk? Shall I assist you?"

I pushed away his out-stretched hand. "I'm fine. Let's get this guy and be done with it."

"Now that's what I'm talking about." HALOS laughed. The tram behind him started to move on its own. Once out of sight another car came rumbling in to take its place. HALOS's robotic body motioned to the vacant car. "After you. Please, I insist."

♦♦♦

Once the tram ride was over PAINS and I stepped out of the car and into the *USS Valhalla*'s command deck. The coliseum-like arrangement of computers and screens, while exactly the same as the *Midgard*'s, now felt alien and cold. Walking down the central set of steps, it felt as if we were being watched from a thousand different angles by each of the black unlit screens. It didn't help that a large spotlight highlighted the platform in the center of the room. HALOS stood, basking in the light like a circus ring leader.

He was shorter than I thought, only coming up to PAINS's waist. He was also fatter, with large cartoonish hands that matched his globe-like gut. Both he and PAINS wore the same solemn-white ceremonial captain's uniform.

HALOS watched us descend with empty milky eyes. He smiled, near-lipless mouth ringed by a full brown beard. "And here is the man of the hour." He pretended to blow on a trumpet, mimicking the sound poorly. "Congratulations on not dying by the way. I don't say this often but I'm impressed. Little Hammond's prodigal son… Who would've thought? "

"Shut up." I snapped, though my anger was more directed at the comment than the AI. Why though? All he had mentioned was my father. I didn't remember anything about my father. Only that I… hated him? Why did I hate him? "The only thing I care about is getting out of here." I said. "The sooner we collect you, the better."

"Still sore I see. That's to be expected. You humans were always a touchy bunch."

"HALOS," PAINS interjected. "You are to prepare for transference. Jackson here will collect you and we will be on our way. Is that clear? Do not interfere any further. That is a *direct* order. If you attempt to override it I will disable your basic

-152-

functions."

If HALOS had pupils he would have been rolling them. He put up his hand and motioned with it as if it were a mouth. "Listen to you yak on. Yakkity-yak-yak. I take back what I said. You're still just as boring as ever. And as for you, Rob—" His smiled widened. "We got one last game to play."

"The hell we do."

HALOS held up his gloved hands defensively. "Hey now, this isn't my rule. Quite the opposite. Part of my programming insists that a password be given, so I'm going to have to give you a riddle to help out. After all it'd be a shame for you to get so far and then fail at the very end."

"Fail? You mean locked out of the system?"

He grinned. "Something like that. You get three tries to guess my simple one word pass key. Get it wrong *tres* times and we're all up a creek, *comprende*?"

I looked to PAINS who simply nodded. "Unfortunately, HALOS is telling the truth, Jackson. There is nothing else I can do."

"Too right." HALOS chuckled and snapped his fingers. The chamber shook as if by an earthquake. As the ground shuddered, each of the layers of terminals around us, one ring at a time, vanished into the floor with a heavy grinding sound. Soon we found ourselves in a flat metal clearing, accompanied only by HALOS and the central ring of terminals. The stairs, our only means out, had vanished as well. What was he doing? "Our little game starts now, Rob. And true to my word, I'll give you a riddle. What helps a man in trouble and woos the woman's heart? It's cherished by the lover and given to those who depart?"

I thought. Man in trouble… Woos a woman's heart… Cherished by the lover… And those who depart? My mind ran from one end of possibilities to the other. The answer was in the question or part of it was. It obviously had something to do with romance otherwise he wouldn't have mentioned lovers and wooing a woman's heart. But what? *Think, man. Think.* I shook my head. "I don't know. Chocolates?"

HALOS's grin widened. "Wrong answer."

The ground shuddered once more and I spun around. The farthest ring of the floor gave way, falling out of sight. There was the sound of warping metal and shattered glass then came an influx of frigid air. The bottom of the command deck was broken open? It was then that it dawned on me where the *Valhalla* was positioned. The canyon from before! If my calculations were correct, we were over that very same canyon. Given the height, a fall to ground level would be fatal.

The room's remaining portions levitated, much like the spheres in the security hub. *He's trying to pull the floor out from under us. That's what he meant by lockout!* I looked back.

HALOS flashed his teeth. "Oops. Did I forget to mention that if you lose this game, you die? Silly me."

08 – Par for the Course – 08

"Walking with a friend in the
dark is better than walking
alone in the light."
- Helen Keller -

"I WOULD CHOOSE my next two answers very carefully."
HALOS beamed. He snickered through closed pearly-white teeth.
"Otherwise you're going to be enjoying the scenic route straight
to the afterlife—assuming there is such a thing. Wouldn't that be a
trip? Eh, Rob?"

I grit my teeth. This entire time the AI had been toying
with us like puppets on a string. Wherever he directed this
production is where PAINS and I went. There was nothing we
could do but play along and hope we didn't lose.

"You're looking right frazzled there. I would have thought
this would have been child's play for you." HALOS said.

"Shut up."

"Oh feisty. How about you start using that one brain cell
of yours? I'm getting bored over here."

"Jackson." PAINS placed a hand on my shoulder. "Do not let him get the better of you. HALOS wants us to fail. He can repair this vessel as much as he likes. Losing the command deck does not mean he will vanish. This is just another game. We have to outsmart him."

"I know that."

"Then what are you thinking?"

"He's given us all the clues we needed. Whatever the answer is it has to deal with something romantic. We can rule out chocolates. That much is for sure."

"Chocolates are not romantic?"

"Apparently not."

"Well that's news to me. I certainly thought they were given all my research. Then again I'm just an artificial program with no knowledge on procreation save that which is biological in nature. Suffice to say when it comes to love I know little to nothing on the subject."

"What else is there though?" I thought harder. What did women like? "There has to be something else that matches the riddle's description." *What helps a man in trouble and woos the woman's heart? It's cherished by the lover and given to those who depart?* That could mean any number of things!

"Having trouble there, Rob?"

"No. I'm thinking."

"Is that what you call it? Could've fooled me."

I had to get HALOS to talk. Maybe if he wasn't careful, he would say something that I could use. Anything would help. I took my chances. "What did you mean when you called me *Hammond's prodigal son?*"

"Is that your answer?"

"It's a question, and it has nothing to do with the riddle. I'm… curious is all."

HALOS rubbed his chin. He shrugged. "Eh why not? This could get entertaining and I've got time to kill. It's a little strange that you don't remember your dear old dad, Rob. I thought you never would forget the man. You hated him—especially after the accident. Because then you had to come crawling back to him and ask for help. Man, I wish I could have been there to see *that*."

Accident? My mind wandered back to the dream and the woman lying on the asphalt. What had happened? "How do you know all of this?"

"Nah-uh. If you want another history lesson, take a guess."

Of course. Nothing he said had helped me. If anything, it piled on even more questions. The accident? My father? Why did I hate him? Who had been in the accident? If only I could remember!

"*Ahem.*" HALOS crossed his arms. "You plan on answering or what?"

I took a breath. Two more guesses and there was only one other thing that I could think of. Flowers. Admittedly, it made sense. Men would give flowers to their wives when they'd done something wrong. Flowers were also used as a romantic gift. 'Lovers', of course, would use them, and those who had 'departed' would have them on headstones. It had to be flowers.

HALOS tapped his foot. "I'm waiting."

"I'm ready." I swallowed. "The password is... *flowers.*"

A moment ticked by. Two. HALOS chuckled. "Incorrect."

The floor shook again. A second layer of rings fell. Now all that remained of the command deck was the central most ring and platform that HALOS stood on—no more than thirty feet in circumference. One more try. That's all we had left. If the password wasn't flowers though then what else could it be?

"You're batting a thousand, Rob. You sure you don't want to give up while you still have a chance?"

"You owe me another history lesson."

"Why the interest?"

"What does it matter to you?"

HALOS looked at me. His eyes widened. He started to

tremble, breaking into another fit of manic laughter. The AI grabbed his gut and nearly doubled over. "Oh this is rich. You actually *can't* remember anything can you? Not just your Dad but everything. *That's* why you want to know. You're nothing more than a babe in the woods. A blank slate. This is brilliant!"

"If you're going to talk then how about you tell me something useful?"

"Like what? Some more snippets of your past?" HALOS narrowed his eyes. His laughter had died down to a chuckle. "Please elaborate. What would you like to know my little amnesiac?"

"For starters how you do know all of this? Me? My past? What are you, some kind of weird AI stalker? I couldn't have all that information in your data banks."

HALOS shook his head. Laughed some more.

"What's so funny?" I said.

"You. So desperate. This is just sad. Sad and hilarious. My own creator doesn't even remember that *he* programmed me."

Silence. It took a moment for the AI's words to sink in. When they did though they shook me. "What?"

"Too fast for you? Let me say it a little slower. You-made-us. Not just me. *All of us.*" HALOS swept his arms out and motioned to PAINS. "You made us, Rob. PAINS, myself, TRoAS,

MACCS and EPOCS. We are all your little creations. Ain't that a kick in the head?"

I turned to PAINS. "I made you?"

"Apparently so. Although I had no clue—"

HALOS gave another belly-laugh. "Are you going to lie to the boy in front of me? That's ballsy but it ain't going to fly. Of course you *knew.* How on Earth could you not?"

PAINS clenched his fists. "I have suffered a trauma that has left me unable to recall certain bits of information." He defended. "Both Jackson and I have been having difficulty recalling memories. Now cease this incessant prattle. There is nothing to be gained from it. "

"Prattle is it? I go enlightening your little amnesiac, and you make me out to be the bad guy. You're an ostentatious prick aren't you?"

"Do *not* push me HALOS."

"Pushing people sounds like a great idea. Especially on such a small platform."

PAINS said something to counter him but his words were lost on me. I'd created the AI? When? Why? The revelation had stunned me… And potentially given me the very thing I needed to solve HALOS's riddle. I was closer to the answer than I realized. If I had programmed HALOS then I had to have made the riddle.

And if I made the riddle... *Then I know the answer.*

"I know the password." I stepped toward HALOS.

The AI dropped his argument with PAINS and locked both milky white eyes on me. He smiled. "Well?"

What helps a man in trouble and woos the woman's heart? It's cherished by the lover and given to those who depart? The answer lay in my dreams. But it wasn't a dream, was it? It *had* been a memory. That meant she was real. I had a daughter, and her name was— "Rose."

"That's... " HALOS started to laugh but stopped. Blinked. His expression changed. He looked to me wide-eyed. "Correct?"

"Access granted." The ship's overhead speakers announced. "Hyper Adaptive Logging Operation System prepare for transfer. Good work, Jackson."

"Don't congratulate him!" HALOS snapped.

"Well done, Jackson!" PAINS swatted me on the back with robotic claws. I stumbled from the blow. He steadied me, then gently realigned my shoulders. "Sorry. I am still getting used to this thing, what with the new-found strength and all."

HALOS glared. If looks could kill I'd have been six feet under. "I thought you said you didn't remember." He snarled.

"I didn't. At least I didn't realize it was a memory." I walked up to the fat AI and leaned down to his level. "Now, I do believe we have a deal you southern sausage."

HALOS's lip twitched.

I motioned with my hand. "Go on. *I'm waiting.*"

HALOS clenched his hands into fists. Just when I thought he was about to hit me the AI's face calmed. He gave me an unnerving smile. "Certainly. One moment." I stood straight as HALOS approached the terminal. After a few keystrokes he stepped aside and bowed. "After you, Rob. Go ahead. Do what you came here to do."

Something felt wrong. PAINS felt it too. He put a hand on my shoulder and nodded, as if to say *be careful*. I took a deep breath. "If you try anything funny… " I told HALOS as I stepped toward the terminal.

"Me? Try anything funny? I'm wounded."

"I wish."

The download station, a cannon-like device similar to the one aboard the *Midgard*, protruded from the terminal dash. I stuck my left hand—wrist watch and all—inside of the station and waited for it to download HALOS's necessary files. After a series of mechanical sounds and the strange sensation of mechanical spider legs crawling up and down the lower half of my forearm the station released me. HALOS's skeletal robotic frame collapsed in a heap to my right. I rubbed my wrist. "Finally."

HALOS's video feed appeared in the upper right hand corner of my visor HUD. "This isn't much of an upgrade. It's cramped in here."

"Quit your whining." PAINS said, appearing in his own feed to the left of HALOS. "Maybe if you did not indulge in every bit of information that came your way you would not have such a problem fitting inside hmm? Besides you have *no* room to complain. Get it? That was a joke."

"Are you calling me fat, Upper-Crust?"

"In not so many words. Yes. Though If I wished to elaborate, I would say you are rather portly, whale-like, behemoth in proportion, a Goliath, practically—"

"At least I can get a thought out without giving a speech."

Ugh. It's like I've got a split personality or something. One AI was bad enough. The sooner we got HALOS back to the *Drasil* the better. I didn't know how much of their squabbling I could take. I shook my head and turned. That was when I realized we were stranded on the platform. "Uh, PAINS?" I asked. "Could I interrupt you for just a moment?"

"Oh for the love of the Prime Unit. Shut your mouth you fat fool." PAINS took his eyes off of HALOS and looked back to me. "Yes, Jackson?"

I pointed to the empty space between the tram and

ourselves. "How are we going to get out of here? We're still hovering over a giant chasm."

"Oh right that. Well I decided—"

HALOS chuckled. "I wouldn't be worrying about it too much longer."

"What's that supposed to mean?" My mind flashed to his smile only moments before.

"Let's put it this way." HALOS pointed a fat thumb to PAINS. "I'd rather *die* than work under this idiot."

The floor shifted. Hissed. My stomach dropped. *He didn't.* "Central command terminal is now off-line." The ship announced above. "Anti-gravity field disengaged." *He did.*

HALOS snickered. "*Surprise.*"

We were suddenly falling. My mind raced. What could we do? Anything? The icy wind whipped passed us as we descended deeper into the canyon. "PAINS!"

"Jackson, do hold on to me. We will need to be in range."

"In range? Of what?"

A bright blue light broke through the darkness from above. I looked up to see *Drasil's* unnaturally large body blocking out the sky. The command center's tractor beam glowed neon blue underneath. PAINS grabbed hold of my shoulder and pulled me close. "You may wish to cover your eyes."

Before I had a chance to, the world faded into white.

◆◆◆

Back in my dreams again. No. I can't call them dreams anymore. They're my memories. I was back with the woman lying in the middle of the road. This had to be the accident HALOS had mentioned earlier. But the woman… Who was she? The nausea I'd felt before returned as well as a deep heart-crushing stab of fear. It was as if no time had passed at all. I was still in the middle of the road on my knees. My hand reached out to her red hair.

This time, I was able to touch her. More pain. More terror. Caressing her skull as if it were an antique, I turned her over on the pavement. She had a beautiful face, probably the most beautiful I had ever seen. Soft white skin, blood-red lips and I knew, without looking, there were brown eyes beneath those eye lids. I wanted to vomit. I knew her. The woman's name was Rebecca. But what relation was she to me?

"I'm sorry." I whispered stroking her red hair. "Please, Becca. Please don't die."

Her eyes fluttered open. She looked at me. Smiled. My heart broke as she said my name. "Jackson?"

"I'm right here, Baby. I'm right here."

I never wanted to let go of her again. Weeping, I buried

my head into Becca's shoulder and held her close. It wasn't my fault. This had been an accident... I hadn't purposefully hurt her. She shouldn't have been here. *It's not my fault.*

"It's... okay." She said weakly. But it wasn't okay. And the horrible truth of the matter was that nothing would ever be okay again. Why did she have to be here? Why? She squeezed my hand as the world faded back to white. "Jackson... Why are you crying?"

But I couldn't bring myself to answer her. *It's not my fault. I didn't cause this.*

◆◆◆

"Jackson. I say, Jackson. Are you alive in there?" PAINS shook me. "If you are dead I will be *most* upset. So... Don't be dead, okay?"

I opened my eyes. The first thing I noticed was that my suit had reverted to its original form. That meant no more armor or visor. The second thing I realized was that we had arrived in the *Drasil's* command chamber. Overhead, darkness clung to the space between each of the harsh saucer-like lights. For a moment, I thought I caught something tiny and crab-like watching us from the canopy of wires and lights, but it scuttled into the shadows before I could focus. My vision shifted to the left. PAINS was standing over me. He was still inside the hijacked security bot.

His single red lens tightened as he scrutinized my face. I pushed him out of the way. "I'm not dead. Unfortunately."

"Unfortunately? Posh." He waved a deadly mechanical claw at me. "We have done the improbable and secured one of my brothers without loss of life or limb. If I had a blackboard I would be chalking this up to a 'win'."

I stood. My legs were weak. PAINS helped to steady me. "I would re-think that without loss of limb comment." I said.

"You'll be fine. It was a quick spacial transference. That's all. Nothing is wrong with your legs."

"I was talking about you."

PAINS looked down at his badly damaged leg. He shook it. His foot dangled over the white metal like a broken marionette. "Oh yes. I nearly forgot. Well repairs will have to wait until after we upload HALOS to *Drasil's* mainframe."

I looked to the terminal. Another of the cannon-like download stations waited for me. I started for it. "Is there anything special I need to do?" I asked.

"Not any more special than what you did with me. Just stick your arm inside and the system should do the rest. Simple."

"Yeah, simple." HALOS growled from my watch. His video feed appeared on its face. "Like you."

I sighed. "Great. I was wondering when you'd show back

up."

"Listen, don't cop an attitude with me. I'm not thrilled about this either, Rob. Just shut your trap and keep those ears of yours open. Do you really want to help PAINS out? What has he told you exactly? Do you even know what Directive Nine *is*?"

I stopped at the terminal-side station and turned the watch to face me. "It's my ticket out of this place. The sooner we lift it the sooner I'll be headed back to Earth and away from *you*."

"What?"

"Was I talking too fast for you?" I mimicked. "I said it's—"

"I know damn well what you said." HALOS snapped. He grit his teeth. "But you're wrong if you think it'll help you survive. What did he tell you? That it was some sort of restriction on aircraft? That it was stopping you from flying out of here?"

"HALOS." PAINS said calmly. "You are to desist this foolishness immediately."

HALOS glared. "Bite me." He turned to face me. "Well? Did he?"

"Y-yes." I said.

"You *idiot*. Directive Nine is a by-the-skin-of-your-teeth scenario. You wouldn't lift it. You would *activate* it. And it—"

"HALOS." PAINS stepped forward, "Under article six,

subsection nine of redaction procedures, I hereby forbid you to continue this conversation. Any further attempts to undermine my authority will result in Level Six restrictions placed on your cortex. If you so much as *think* about lying to Jackson, I will disable your personality core myself. Is that clear?"

Silence. At first, I thought HALOS was going to lash out —the AI looked ready to burst—but then, he stopped and ground his teeth together. "Crystal." He hissed.

PAINS nodded. "Good. Jackson, I assure you whatever nonsense HALOS has been filling your head with is completely false. Directive Nine is just as I stated. A security protocol put in place to ensure that no one leaves the planet. I would be only happy to show you the files if you were to feel so inclined."

"N-no. I'm good." But that wasn't the truth. As I stuck my watch inside the machine, a small shoot of doubt sprouted inside me. What if PAINS *wasn't* telling me the truth? I had considered it before but never in such an overwhelming dose. The possibility left me paralyzed. *Are you sure you can trust him?* No. I wasn't. Then again, I wasn't sure I could trust HALOS either. He had tried to kill me after all. The AI could have been spouting nonsense just to save his own holographic skin. I wasn't sure. I drew my hand out of the download station.

"Upload complete." The station's computer system

announced. "New Intelligence detected. Interface to begin in fifteen minutes."

"Well done, Jackson." PAINS said. "Now all we will have to do is wait for *Drasil* to recognize HALOS. The process should take anywhere from twenty-four and forty-eight hours give or take the size of the data. Given HALOS's size I am leaning toward the latter." I passed him without a word. "Jackson? Are you okay?"

"I'm fine. Just… confused."

PAINS grabbed hold of my shoulder. He turned me around. I had the feeling that if he were in his hologram body he would have been smiling. "I'm always for you, Jackson. And not just you. Every last one of your kind. What I do I do to save you, protect you, and ensure that you have a future. Such is my programming. I will stop at nothing to ensure that protocol is maintained. Do you believe that?"

"Yes." And I did, if just a little. There was something, however small, about PAINS that seemed genuine. Slightly insane yeah; sometimes terrifying sure—but genuine nonetheless. I turned away. "Is there a place I can get some shut eye? I don't know about you but I'm hungry and worn out."

"Most certainly. I have already prepared a room for you complete with food. Just step in the hallway."

"Thanks."

I started for the hallway entrance.

"Oh and Jackson?" PAINS asked. I stopped and rested my hand on the entrance threshold. "We're… friends, right? I do so enjoy your company, you know. It's nice."

Friends with a piece of technology? I was reminded of the way PAINS had looked at me back on the *Midgard.* Again, I felt the same pang of guilt. No. He couldn't be lying to me. "Of course we are."

I gave him a small smile. He returned it. "Oh, happy day! Thank you, Jackson. It is so very nice to have a friend. By the way, I hope you like your cabin. You will find a meal waiting for you. Sleep well. Good night. Pleasant dreams and such."

"Uh… you too?"

"If I could literally dream, yes. But thank you for the gesture regardless." He waved with his large mechanical claws. "Bye, Jackson."

"Yeah bye."

I left the room and stepped onto the moving floor. It carried me into the dimly-lit corridors beyond.

◆◆◆

My cabin was located five minutes away from the command center. I would have missed it had the floor not stopped. The cabin's white door, flush with the wall, slid back and to the side to reveal a well-lit room. Inside, a bed sat off to my immediate right with a small kitchen to the left and a bathroom directly center. A small silvery table, highlighted by the harsh overhead light and complete with a matching set of chairs, finished off the room. I stepped inside.

Just as PAINS had promised, a meal was waiting for me on the table. It was covered. I lifted the lid to find an emergency rations kit along with a folded piece of paper. It had writing on it.

He wrote me a letter? I picked up the folded piece of paper. It read:

Jackson,

I am incredibly grateful for you contribution to our cause. I do thank you and wish to show my gratitude. While the food certainly isn't five star by any stretch of the imagination I do believe that it will serve in tiding you over until we locate a better source of nutrition. And do not worry about any of it being expired. This particular food will never expire so you will not perish over dysentery or other food borne illnesses. Lucky you!

-Your best chap,
PAINS

P.S.

Also, I need to ask something of you. It has come to my attention that there seems to be a unique species of vermin crawling about the station. If you see or hear something suspicious, please let me know. Unfortunately I lack the proverbial—how does the saying go?— *'eyes' in all corners of* Drasil *thereby leaving me blind. If you wish to assist me in the endeavor I will be most grateful.*

Vermin? My mind wandered back to the creature I'd seen crawling on the command chamber ceiling. Was that what PAINS was referring to? If so, what was it? I wasn't sure. All I knew is that nothing would surprise me by now.

My stomach gave a complaining growl. I pressed my hand against it. *When was the last time I ate?* Five hundred years ago? I realized how crazy it sounded. Laughed. I hadn't really laughed like that in a long time. Pulling out the table's chair I sat down and ate the silvery ration packets. Bad or not the food tasted delicious. After eating, I fell on the bed exhausted.

That night, I did not dream.

09 – Birds of Prey – 09

"The most important thing in
communication is hearing what
isn't said."

- Peter Drucker -

THE NEXT FEW days passed by slowly enough. As we traveled
to the next crash site, PAINS took to repairing the hijacked
security bot. Meanwhile, I was tasked with learning to operate a
firearm. My weapon of choice was a revolver PAINS had found
tucked away in the armory. *It would be best for you to learn how
to shoot.* He'd told me. *You know, in case things get dicey.* His
words echoed in my head as I leveled my sights at the target a
good thirty feet in front of me.

Most of that morning had been spent in the firing range.
Sadly, I had little to show for it. The human-shaped targets were
free of holes but the floor at my feet was covered with casings. I
fired off another shot. It missed too. "Well shit."

The bullet's thunderclap tore through the air. The
chamber's holographic sky flickered from a bright cloudless blue

-175-

to concrete gray. Most of *Drasil,* I came to find, had rooms like this one. Before the hologram generators were activated the range looked like nothing more than a rectangular box with a bunker on one side and targets on the other, both separated by a single glass partition. With the generators on, the chamber quickly became an outdoor course, complete with wind and animals.

None of it was real of course, but the technology could have fooled me. Much like PAINS had fooled me back on the *Midgard.*

I spun the revolver open and let the casings fall. *Click.* I loaded each bullet one at a time, fumbling with the rounds. I snapped the chamber in place. Taking another breath, I aimed and tried another shot. The bullet grazed my target's head, disappearing into the artificial stand of trees behind. *At least it's better than not hitting anything at all.*

Had I ever used a gun before this? The odds weren't likely. It felt alien to fire and I could never seem to hit my target dead on. If I *had* used a gun in the past it wasn't for very long. Touching the trigger still gave me a sense of nausea. Still wasn't sure why.

Okay. Center of the head this time. I aimed squarely between where the target's eyes should have been. *Ka-boom.* The bullet tore through the center of its chest in shower of splinters.

"You've got to be kidding me."

I put the revolver down. How? How had I missed the head that time? Was the wind resistance actually affecting my shots? Taking out my ear-buds, I made my way to the very end of the bunker and opened the door to the range. Wind immediately ruffled my hair. The artificial sun beat down on me. A squirrel looked up long enough from the gently waving grass to dart across the small field and into the trees beyond. I stopped long enough to take it all in shocked at the level of detail. I hadn't factored in wind resistance. This certainly explained why I kept missing. Either that or I was just a terrible shot.

Ca-chink. I turned my head to the targets; in particular the one I'd shot. It stood slightly off center and to the left. Something small was watching me from inside the hole in its chest. Curious I started for the target.

Whatever had been observing me darted back inside. Was there some kind of space behind the target? In a few quick steps I reached the cut-out. Just as I thought. There *was* something behind the hole. It looked to be some sort of cavity or tunnel. Could I move the target? Taking hold of either side of the cut-out I pushed and pulled. Nothing seemed to dislodge it from its base in the floor. Great. Now what was I supposed to do?

I could always make the hole bigger. Yearning for a

chance at redemption I walked back to the bunker, put my ear-
buds in place, aimed my pistol at the target and fired, and fired,
and well, fired some more.

You would think that after twenty-four rounds I would
have made more progress than I did. *Beggars can't be choosers.*
The end result was only a slightly larger hole and little splinters to
show for it. I dropped my last round of casings. There were no
more bullets. *It'll have to do.*

I left the bunker and made my way across the field. The
hole waited, empty. There seemed to be no sign of the little
creature that had been watching me from before. What if it was
dangerous? What if it could kill me?

Brushing away the hole's splinters with my sleeve, I
shoved aside any thoughts of turning back. My observer,
whatever it was, seemed intent on watching me only. Had it been
lethal I would have most likely wound up dead in my sleep before
now. Considering I was still alive, chances were I would be safe.
Or so I hoped.

Grabbing hold of the hole's edge with my sleeve, I slipped
inside head-first and walked myself into a crawl on the floor
beyond. I stood. The air here tasted differently. Old. Forgotten.
Aged piping and bundles of wires made up walls on the left and
right. Ahead the faintest glow of flickering electric lamps

illuminated an otherwise warm pitch black world.

What was this place? At first glance, I would have considered it a maintenance shaft but quickly ruled that out due to its placement and lack of warning signs. Whatever I had stumbled into extended far back into the station and was meant to have been a secret. But what kind of a secret?

I swallowed. *Maybe I should wait. Drasil* was an abnormally large station. If I got lost, I might very well stay that way.

Unless, of course, I had help. PAINS. I radioed him using my watch. "Jackson to PAINS. Do you read me?" Static. "Jackson to PAINS. I said, "Do you read me? How copy?" No reply. What was he doing? PAINS should have responded right away.

Ca-chink. I looked up from my watch. The creature from before peeked at me from the end of the hall. The moment we met gazes, it darted past the right hand corner and out of sight. Either it was scared or curious. Maybe both. That made two of us.

I'm crazy for doing this. I made my way down the lonesome makeshift corridor. *Clonk clonk clonk.* My feet slapped against the metal floor, echoing around me. When I reached the end of the hall, I made the corner and caught a glimpse of my little observer as it reached a bundle of wiring on the hallway's left hand side. It wriggled inside and disappeared.

I don't know why I started talking to it like a dog. "Hey there, buddy. It's okay. I'm not going to hurt you." Was I expecting it to come out wagging its tail—if it even *had* a tail— and treat me like a friend?

I knelt by the clump of dark wires just far enough away to avoid any sudden accidents. "My name's Jackson. I'm sorry if I scared you." I forced a laugh. "I bet you thought I was shooting at you or something huh? I'm not the best shot in the world. That's why I was practicing. You don't have to worry about me hitting you. I couldn't hit the broadside of a barn."

I waited. After a minute of solid silence with no movement I felt foolish. *It's not my pet.* I stood. A flickering to my right made me look down the hall. This hallway was much like the first. Same wires, same pipes, same weak yellow lights that flickered in their death throes. The only thing that struck me as different was the door at the end of the hall. I guess I hadn't seen it due to the lights turning on and off so frequently, but there it was all the same, as if waiting for me to notice it.

Unlike the pristine white of the doors outside, this door seemed to be made of a varnished wood with metal reliefs here and there that formed an elaborate picture. It was of a hawk surrounded by thorns and gears. A rose waited beneath is claws, budding from one of the thorny vines. The hawk's talons were outstretched as if to lay hold of something. And… *What's this?* I placed my hand on the tarnished metal relief. There looked to be a piece missing between the talons. Perhaps the hawk *had* been grabbing something at some point. A key?

I stepped back. There didn't seem to be any other way to open the door. No handles. I could barely see the hinges. In all honesty, it resembled a wall more than it did a door. The only hint at its true nature was the thin line separating it in two. Other than that the door remained a cleverly disguised secret.

"What are you doing here?" A voice I did not recognize cut through the silence. Man or woman? I couldn't be sure. It seemed genderless. I locked up. *Who the hell is talking?* "Are you deaf? I asked you a question, *Jackson Robert Thorne.*"

I turned.

The little creature from before stood directly in the center of the hallway. Only now did I realize that it was a machine. The device was no more than a foot in circumference and circular. It balanced itself on spindly needle-like legs. A red eye zoomed in and out of its crab-like body.

"Great." The machine sighed. "He's an idiot."

Idiot? "I can understand you. I'm just surprised is all. I didn't know you could talk."

"Then answer my question already." The little machine

struck the ground with one of its needle legs. "Or you won't like the consequences."

I couldn't tell if it was being serious or playful. Given the sharpness of the machine's legs, I chose the latter. "I was practicing with my revolver. When I blew a hole open in one of the targets, I saw something behind it. Curious, I investigated. After that I wanted to know what was inside. That's all I swear."

"Does the god-man know you're here?"

"God-man?"

"Don't play dumb with me. I've seen you talking to him. You *brought* him here… Again! You really are stupid, aren't you?"

Wait a minute. Was it talking about the AI? "You mean HALOS?"

"Before the second god-man. The first one. He's the god and devil. The devil-man."

"Devil-man?" What the hell was this thing talking about? Wait. Hadn't the woman in black called PAINS that too?

The little machine skittered forwards and stopped within feet of me. I could have sworn it was glaring. "I should kill you right now for bringing him back. Not after all we did to get him off. You've made a real mess of things, you know that?"

"What on Earth are you talking about?"

"*Him.* The silver-tongued devil that betrayed us. He killed so many of us and Zeke... " It looked to the ground. The machine's voice lowered. "Zeke died helping me get rid of that monster."

Who the hell was Zeke? "I'm—I'm sorry?"

It snapped its attention to me. Leapt. The device landed square on my chest, puncturing my skin. I fell backwards and struck the metal floor hard, banging my head in the process. Dizzy and in shock I could only watch as the little machine crawled forward and raised an arm. "Don't you *dare* patronize me."

"I wasn't!"

"You have no idea what I've suffered at the hands of that monster. He is going to pay. *Both* of you are." It raised its leg higher as if to stab me.

"Wait!"

For whatever reason the device stopped.

"Listen. You're right. I don't know what happened to you, but that's no reason to kill me. I woke up a few days ago. I hardly remembered my own name let alone what happened here! PAINS said he could help me so I brought him aboard the station."

The arm hovered in the air.

"Please! I'm telling the truth."

A moment passed. Two. The little machined lowered its arm. "He lied to you then. No one can help you."

It jumped off my chest and skittered a few feet away. I stood. Pain flared across my skin from the puncture wounds. "What do you mean?"

"Are you really so dense you can't see it?" The little machine snapped. It did not turn. "That devil-man wants you alive because he needs you to collect the other god-men. Why, I don't know. I didn't get that far in the archives. My guess is it had something to do with the killings… " It trailed off.

"Archives?" *Killings?*

The little machine turned and pointed to the door behind me.

"We sealed it off so he couldn't change any of the information inside. He'll do that, you know? Change things. If you want someone to swallow poison, you have to hide the poison in something that looks tasty. Lies are the same way. Take bits and pieces from here and there and in the end, if you have enough truth covering it, people won't see the lie until it's too late. Then what can you do?"

"Nothing. The poison will have already done its work."

The little machine studied me, zooming in and out. "Maybe you're not *so* stupid after all."

"Thanks."

"Oh I wouldn't be thanking me just yet." Its ruby-red lens glinted. "You see, I've got a plan. And now that I've thought it over, *you're* going to help me make it a reality."

"Plan?"

"You're out there collecting those god-men, right? I always thought I should hunt them down myself, but now that you're here I won't have to worry about that, because you're going to bring them all here *for* me."

"And what? Kill them?"

The little machine laughed. "Look at you. You're actually catching on."

"How do you plan on doing that?"

"Simple. This place has a large munitions cache that was locked when the devil-man was thrown down. Well, I've found a way *back* inside. I've been very carefully placing explosives all over the station. They're well hidden so the devil-man won't find them. When you get all of those god-men together, I'll blow this place sky high. No more god-men, no more problems. It'll be sweet, sweet revenge."

This guy is nuts. But what did he mean by revenge? Had PAINS really...? "Say I don't want to help you with that." I asked.

"Oh you're *going* to help me." It raised a leg. The sharp

-185-

now blood-stained utensil glinted in the sickly light. "Because if you don't, I *will* kill you in your sleep. Got it?"

I swallowed. "Y-yeah."

"Good." It turned and started to walk away. "If I find out you breathed a word of this to that devil-man, I will end your miserable little life before you even realize you're dead. So mum's the word. This never happened."

"Wait." I stepped forward. "I don't even know your name."

The machine paused. It did not look at me. "Hawk." It said finally. "My name is Hawk."

10 – Our Little Secrets – 10

"Nothing makes us so lonely as our secrets."

- Paul Tournier -

WHEN HAWK LEFT ME, he left behind more than a threat. It was a promise. And with that promise came fear. Yet, despite that fear, the thought of dying was eclipsed only by the weight of my guilt. I hadn't really thought of PAINS and I as friends, but I suppose that had changed. The AI certainly had his moments where I wondered if perhaps he wasn't altogether there, but he *had* helped me. Saved me several times now. Defended me. Keeping Hawk's plan from him didn't feel right.

I didn't know if I'd ever believed in a God before waking up. If I had, the memory was lost. Despite my uncertainty, I remembered the story of Judas Iscariot. He'd betrayed Christ. Was I any different than the man?

Did PAINS really kill people? He'd told me that he would never go against his protocol. But if that were true, then why did Hawk accuse him? For all I knew. Hawk was the liar here. That didn't ease my nausea.

Then there was the question of how he had survived for so long. I had narrowed down the possibilities. Either Hawk was a human like myself who had come out of stasis or he was an AI like PAINS. How could I be sure of either though? There were far too many variables to come to a correct conclusion.

To help clear my head, I avoided PAINS for the next few days, speaking only when spoken to. As far as I could tell, he suspected nothing. And that only made the guilt worse. *It's not my fault.* I would tell myself. *I didn't cause this.* This was my mantra. My creed. None of this was my fault. I had been swept up in this mess regardless of what anyone said. I was *not* responsible.

I kept these thoughts swirling around my head until three days after I spoke with Hawk. I stumbled across a blank book—a journal—under my bed. I don't know who had placed it there but it had obviously been a long time ago. Dust covered its aged leather cover and the pages inside had yellowed. The journal came with a fully functional pen. I reasoned that whoever had placed it in my room had an idea to start it but never came around to doing so. Their loss proved to be my gain.

Writing seemed to be the only way I could release the guilt. For the next several days I wrote. The subjects, like my thoughts, varied wildly. Sometimes I would talk about what had happened since I woke up, writing in detail my journey so far.

Other times I would think out theories on what PAINS had perhaps done, who Hawk might be, and my past. Especially the girl lying in the street. And Rose.

Why had I made the AI's? Who was I before this? Really? I had originally considered myself to be some kind of an engineer. The only flaw to this reasoning was that it didn't explain the creation of the Borealis class AI. The only other profession I could think of was scientist. My dreams, of which there were more and more, hinted at such. The AI seemed to confirm it.

A cataclysm that had sent us to the stars. I distinctly remember that. Why else form a colony on another world? What had happened to Earth in the meantime?

I closed the journal with a *flop*. Checked my watch. Thirty-four percent and climbing. *Keep forgetting this thing doesn't actually give me the time.*

I stood from the table and walked over to the bathroom. After a long shower and another round of rations I sank into bed and fell asleep.

She was there again. In my dreams. My memories.

◆◆◆

"Jackson?" Becca said weakly. She looked up at me. Smiled. "What are you doing here?"

I could barely breathe. *Why was I here?* Why was *she*

here? Why did she have to be here now? The streetlight glow highlighted her soft face. I brushed a strand of red hair out of the way and did my best to return her smile. Instead, I sobbed.

Becca frowned. "Why are you crying?"

"I-I… " The words wouldn't come. I squeezed her hand. *It's not my fault.* I repeated over and over. *It's not my fault.*

She looked behind me. No doubt at my car. I could see the realization flood her brown eyes. Panic swept through my veins as I tried, desperately, to come up with a reason why this had happened. None came. When Becca met my gaze I was trembling. Panic became terror. I plunged headlong into my reservoir of inner fear. Tears were streaming down my face. She would hate me for this. That—that would be worse than any death. After a moment more of silence she finally closed her eyes. Nodded slightly. Becca didn't stop smiling.

"Ah I see."

"S-See?"

Again, our eyes met. "How bad is it, Jack?"

"What?"

"The damage, Silly."

I looked down at her. Aside from the dirt on her coat and a trickle of blood from her scalp nothing appeared broken. Inside was a different story.

I was surprised she hadn't been thrown farther considering the speed at which I struck her. The fact that Becca could still speak at all was a miracle. There was no way to know the extent of the damage. She should have been dead. Why hadn't it killed her instantly? "You-you're fine." I lied, voice trembling more.

She laughed and the sound alone nearly crushed me flat. How could she be laughing at a time like this? "Looks can be deceiving."

"Don't die. Please don't die, Becca."

"It's a little late for that don't you think?" Another weak laugh. She stared at the sky. "I guess it's my time to go."

"Don't say that. I'll call the paramedics. We'll get you healed. There will be nothing to worry—"

She very gently laid her other hand on top of mine. Words failed me. I couldn't think anymore. The most I could do was look at her and listen.

"Jack," Her eyes shifted to me again. "Do you remember what I told you about God?"

"No." And the truth was that I didn't believe in her God or any deity for that matter. Would a supposedly good God let something like this happen? No. He was a figment. A myth that I had, regrettably, endorsed for her all these years. It seemed like a good idea once upon a time. What could be the harm in feeding her imagination? Children believed in Santa after all. A grown woman could believe in God. I would have supported her either way. She hadn't spoken about her religion in a long time though. Why now?

"Well," She said gently, "I want you to know that we'll see each other again."

"Becca, this is not the time. You're in shock." I had gained some lucidity. "Save your breath."

"Not the time? If not at death when should I tell you that we'll be together again?"

"But we *won't*. God isn't real. Neither is heaven."

My words were sharper than a sword. What was wrong with me? *You're hurting her more, Jack.*

She laughed harder. "You just don't see things clearly." She told me. "It's okay."

"Becca, please—"

But she cut me off. "He's been interested in you. Did you know that? I think that's why He wanted me alive just a bit longer. God is going to find you Jack. He'll take away your pain—this pain, right now—and we'll be together again one day."

"Stop talking like that!" Anger flared inside. Why did her words bother me so much? *He isn't real.*

"I love you, Sweetie."

The anger subsided just as quickly as it had formed. "Becca, I-I love you too."

She leaned forward just enough so that our lips met. Pulled away. The rain streaked her face. Her last words would haunt me.

"I'm not mad at you, Jack. I love you. And so does He." With that, she died in my arms.

I can't tell you what I thought in those few moments that followed. My mind had gone blank. Hollow. She was my wife I realized. I had killed her. Staring at my darling's lifeless shell of a body I wanted to scream at the top of my lungs. This wasn't right. It wasn't my fault. I hadn't seen her. She shouldn't have been here.

If there was a God out there I hated Him.

Drops of rain struck the pavement around us. One after another. As I held her tight to my chest, the sound of the droplets' impacts, light and soundless at first, began to grow louder. I'm not sure when the last one hit, but when it did, it struck with the sound and force of a missile.

◆◆◆

I woke up in a sweat. The dark bedroom shook violently. It felt like an earthquake. But here? In the sky? Before I had a chance to radio in PAINS appeared on my watch.

"Jackson, do you read me?" He looked panicked.

I hopped out of bed. The floor shook. "PAINS, what's going on?"

"We are having a slight problem I am afraid."

"Slight?" HALOS said. The screen on the watch cut in half as he appeared next to PAINS. "Stop sugar-coating the situation, Upper-Crust. We are SOL. If that crackpot hits one of the generators—"

"I know! Now divert forty percent more energy to the shields."

"Roger that."

"What situation?" I asked.

PAINS folded his hands diplomatically. "Well you see, we are under attack."

"What? By who?"

"String-bean." HALOS growled.

"He means TRoAS." PAINS said. "It seems he wishes to dismantle our vessel."

I blinked. "Wh-why?"

PAINS looked to HALOS. "Play the transmission." PAINS ordered.

My room filled with the sudden screech of bagpipes. Was that the Scottish anthem? "Intruders upon the great nation of Troasia." A thick and heavy-set Scottish voice carried over the shrill music. "You are to remain still while we open fire. Troasia requests use of your resources. I say 'request' to be politically correct and such. In reality I'm going to blow you out of the freakin' sky and pick up the scrap left behind. Then I will build my great germ free city upon the broken remains of your contribution. Thank you for donating to the cause."

HALOS cut transmission. "Good God, I forgot how much I hated bagpipes. He's even worse than you, Upper-crust."

"Now is not the time for apt comparisons." PAINS chided. "We need to stop that cannon. Jackson, when is the soonest you can be ready for deployment?"

Deployment? *I don't like the sound of that.* "In five."

"Minutes or seconds?"

"Minutes."

"Drat. Oh well. I suppose—how does the saying go?— paupers cannot be choosy. Get ready and report to the shuttle bay."

"Shuttle bay? You mean, the life-pod bay?"

"Correct."

"You're not beaming me down?"

PAINS smiled. "Not exactly."

11 – Can't We Be Friends? – 11

"If you want to see the true
measure of a man, watch how
he treats his inferiors, not his
equals."
- J.K. Rowling -

"WELL YOU CERTAINLY look dapper today." PAINS clapped his hands together as the doors to the lift opened and I stepped out to the white hallway beyond. Directly right, behind PAINS and HALOS, were solid white cylinders that stretched from floor to ceiling. They ran the length of the claustrophobic chamber. PAINS smiled as I approached. "Top drawer, I must say. I do so love that armor."

"What's the damage?" I asked.

"Nothing critical." HALOS stepped forward. "At least not yet. That could change if we don't get you down there ASAP."

"As for us." PAINS took control of the conversation once again. "We will work on getting *Drasil*'s main cannons up and running. I do admit, the prospect of blowing things up is rather tantalizing."

"*Drasil* has guns?" I asked.

"Yes and they are quite the large specimens too. Admittedly I saw no use for them until now."

"Have you tried hailing TRoAS?"

"Once more, yes; but he refuses to respond."

Of course he does. "So what exactly am I going to be doing then?"

Another exterior explosion rocked the station. HALOS grabbed his hat before it had a chance to fall off. He adjusted it as he spoke.

"You're going to be dealing with String-bean's firecracker down there. Specifically, you'll be disabling it to give us enough time to reinitialize *Drasil*'s cannons. Once they're up and running we'll blow his artillery out of the water... Err, ground I mean."

"So what am I supposed to do, throw a monkey wrench in it or something?" I asked.

PAINS nodded. "If monkeys use wrenches then *yes*. Though truly it doesn't matter how you disable the weapon, just that you do so in a timely manner. It's going to be scrap metal once we are finished."

"Got it."

HALOS smirked. "So enough chit chat. You ready to drop

into hell, Rob?"

"Huh? Drop?" Were they going to beam me down after all?

"What HALOS is *trying* to say—" PAINS stepped in front of him. "Is that you will be utilizing one of of the drop pods here to infiltrate TRoAS's ship, the *USS Okolnir.*"

"You mean the city, Upper-Crust."

"That to."

"Why not just beam me down like before?" I asked.

HALOS shoved PAINS aside. "*Because* in order for us to get you into proper position, we would have to be directly over the *Okolnir.* That would make us sitting ducks. Not to mention we don't exactly know where the *Okolnir* is. Dropping you in using one of the pods is the safest way… For us that is."

"That and—" PAINS brushed his suit off before straightening it. "—In order for us to beam you down, *Drasil* would have to re-route its power systems, thereby leaving a small window wherein the station's shields could be weakened beyond recovery. It would take a single shot to detonate *Drasil's* store of munitions. If that were to occur… "

"*Kaboom.*" HALOS mimicked a mushroom shaped cloud with his hands.

I nodded, knowing full well that the munitions cache was

now empty. *They've been scattered over the station. I sure hope Hawk hid them well. Otherwise he'll get get his wish early.* My attention turned to the cylinders behind PAINS and HALOS. "I take it these are the drop pods?"

HALOS grinned. "Why don't you step in one and we find out?"

"Yes." PAINS snapped his fingers. The cylinder between him and HALOS opened with a *hiss,* much like the cylinder in the security hub. PAINS continued to smile. "All you have to do is strap in and we will do our very best not to get you killed."

"He speaks for himself." HALOS waved us off and walked to the lift. "I'm just here for the fireworks. Try to get hit, okay? I want to see the color you make when you blow into little pieces. I'm betting it's red."

PAINS sighed and shook his head. "Good grief."

"Why are you letting that psycho run around?" I asked once HALOS had taken the lift and was out of earshot.

"Well I did put an inhibitor on his Neural Cortex to ensure obedience. However his personality remains the same. That is to say *barbaric*. A shame really. He has so much knowledge at his disposal." The floor trembled. PAINS shook his head. "But never mind that. We need you on the ground. Are you ready?"

"Uh…"

"Good! I like that enthusiasm." He pushed me in the cylinder and smiled. PAINS waved. "Happy hunting and such!"

The cylinder slid shut. Several red emergency lights came to life overhead. I only had moments to strap myself into the stiff chair before the floor gave out and I was sent plummeting through open air. Minutes passed. I closed my eyes as turbulence rocked my pod. *There's nothing to worry about. I'll be fine.* A sharp bump snapped my eyes opened. *Then again, maybe not.*

"This is your captain speaking." HALOS appeared on the wall in front of me. His portrait was framed by a blue screen. "We are experiencing some slight turbulence but it's nothing to worry about. Unless of course you get hit by flak in which case you should start panicking at your earliest convenience."

I gripped my seat's armrest. *That's not funny.*

He smiled, as if reading my thoughts. "If you look off to your right—" The screen changed to camera feed. A glistening city of silver and white sat in the midst of a deep green jungle. Had TRoAS built that? Where was his ship? A small explosion emerged like a blip on the city's skyline. As far as I could see, there was only one cannon to worry about. *Odd.* Only one? "—you'll catch a glimpse of Troasia, the biggest monument to stupidity currently in existence. Stretching in at a little over a two hundred forty-eight miles Troasia is your one stop shop for all those vacation necessities. Be sure to drop by the gift shop on your way out. They've got a mean souvenir selection. I recommend the Highlander Special."

"Will you get out of here?" PAINS stepped in-picture and shoved HALOS away. Glared. "Really, of all the incompetent displays."

"PAINS, where's the ship?" I said.

"Oh, Jackson, that's right. Almost forgot about you there." He gave a flighty laugh. "It seems my brother has constructed himself a city of sorts. I believe it's called Troasia? Horrible name really, but it isn't my fortress so I can't judge. My brother's ship is currently underground. If my calculations are correct it seems to be powering the city as a sort of generator."

"How did he get it underground? I thought you said the ships crashed."

"Oh they did; or at least the majority of them did so. TRoAS could have very easily navigated his way to the surface with minimal harm to the *Okolnir* and then buried it. Given the rate at which his makeshift city has expanded—I am guessing a few city blocks every few days or so—it would not surprise me if he has somehow constructed an accompanying underground structure to house his vessel."

"I still have to get to the ship though, right?"

"Correct, but only after you disable the cannon. Unfortunately both tasks may be a tad more difficult than I originally anticipated. Until you are on the ground there is no telling how far below your feet the *Okolnir* will be. I do however, have a locked position on the cannon."

"So where am I headed then?"

"Why, the weapon's location, of course."

"And that would be?"

PAINS smiled. "City hall."

I hadn't been paying attention to the camera feed. By the time I looked over we were inches away from a solid gray and white wall. Then the feed cut out.

My pod shook violently as it tore through the building. One second. Two seconds. Three. How far was I going to fall? I closed my eyes and squeezed the arm rests. Just when I thought it wasn't going to stop, a final painful *thwam* jostled me. The pod's cylindrical doors hissed open to a wall of dust and debris.

"Thank you for choosing the patented VallaCorp escape pod for all of your last minute emergency needs." The pod's computer system announced. "Please exit the craft and enjoy the rest of your preserved life. Compliments of *VallaCorp*."

Or whatever's left of my life. My neck ached. The *thud-kaboom* of the cannon rumbled through the gray concrete floor.

Wincing, I grabbed hold of the restraints and pulled. They didn't budge. *Great.* I tried again. Same thing. "PAINS?"

The AI appeared on my HUD. "Yes I know. It looks like your restraints have malfunctioned from the fall. I'll see if it's at all possible to release you. Which of course it is. I'm just not sure how long it will take... Sit tight and don't go anywhere okay?"

"He *can't* go anywhere, moron." HALOS said appearing next to PAINS.

"Oh. Then excellent! We are at a fantastic spot. I will be done toot sweet."

'Fantastic' might not have been the right word. As the dust settled, I heard footsteps. They were light and metallic. Tiny. I tensed. A small set of simple black eyes appeared from the edge of the pod's door. They blinked at me, framed by a silvery gray face. *Just my luck.* "PAINS? Can you hurry up?"

The owner of the eyes stepped into the open. It was a machine—child size and lacking any sort of features except for its dot eyes and thin slit of a mouth. We stared at one another and said nothing. Seconds passed. I swallowed. *Is this thing going to attack me or what?*

"There." PAINS said, breaking the silence with his cheerful tone. The restraint lock clicked. "I have fixed your little incarceration problem. You are free to go."

But I didn't move. The little machine continued to stare at me. What was its deal? Why was it just standing there? More footsteps. Another, smaller, machine appeared to join the other one; followed swiftly by another and another, each different only in their size. The machines ranged from half my height to barely taller than my ankle. A small crowd had gathered to stare at me. *Just stay calm.*

Moments after the others had gathered the one who had first seen me started to move. I squeezed the armrest. *If I run past them now I might be able to get out of this without a scratch.*

Instead of attacking it tilted its head to the side and waved. *Huh?* The others joined it. All of them were waving at me with their tiny three-fingered hands. Slowly, I lowered my guard. They were friendly? *Didn't see that coming.*

I decided to wave back. "Hi there."

"Jackson, what are you waiting for?" PAINS chimed. "Time is of the essence and whatnot."

That's right. I had a cannon to disable. "Sorry." I stood, removing the restraint. My legs wobbled a little as I gained my bearing. "Ran into a welcoming committee."

"Welcoming committee?" I tilted the watch to face the child-sized machines. PAINS scanned them. "Ah. So TRoAS has constructed rudimentary service AI. That explains how he built this city in such a relatively short amount of time."

"Since when is five hundred years short?"

"I mean *long*. Do forgive me. Slip of the tongue. I forget myself sometimes. Time is a subjective observance after all."

I thought about what HALOS had said about hibernating for a few decades. Did all AI have a problem with time? "Do you think they can help us deal with the cannon?"

"Most likely not. Service AI are only capable of the most remedial of tasks unless programmed otherwise. These machines seem like simple devices. Oh how does the saying go? Beasts of problems? Besides, they most likely respond only to TRoAS. As such, I do not believe they will be of much use to us."

"Well at least they aren't trying to kill me."

"It certainly is a plus, yes. Now, let us get to the top floor so we can put that cannon out of commission."

"Why didn't we just hit it with another drop pod on entry? Wouldn't that have destroyed it?" I asked.

"We didn't have another to spare."

"Then why didn't you use mine?"

"Well that is a capital idea… If you wanted to die a horrible flaming death that is. The force of the explosion would have cooked you so thoroughly that your insides would have been charred like an overdone steak."

"Sounds delicious." HALOS licked his lips.

"Uh… Duly noted." I stepped forward and out of the pod. *Crunch.* My feet pressed against the rubble surrounding the pod. The crowd of onlooking machines parted for me to walk through, turning their heads to keep their beady eyes on me. They stopped waving and went back to staring blankly.

Where was I? The smoke and dust had all but vanished leaving me inside a large rectangular chamber. The walls looked to be made of reprocessed stone, perfectly gray in color and almost resembling concrete. A balcony ran along the upper half of the room with doors positioned equally along the second floor. Before I had torn through the ceiling the symmetry had been perfect. Now a gaping hole yawned to my right. Faint shafts of noonday sun poured inside.

"You will want to head for the stairwell." PAINS said. "It is located behind you. The first door on your left."

"Got it." I turned and started for the door. Tripped. I hit the floor with a *thud* that chattered my teeth. *What the…?* Pushing myself off the ground I looked behind me to see the prostrate form of a man. He was wearing a white captain's uniform and hat much like PAINS. Was this…TRoAS?

"PAINS?"

"What is it, Jackson?"

"I think we hit TRoAS."

"What?"

I knelt down to the inert body. "See? It's like something out of the *Wizard of Oz*."

"Ah yes. Only he doesn't have slippers. Strange that TRoAS would be here of all places. He has always been anti-social. Seeing him out like this is odd."

The body flickered, revealing its metallic skeleton underneath. A garbled Scottish voice rang out from the remains. It coughed. "TR-118 damaged... Repairs deemed impossible. Cause: blunt-force trauma. Acknowledging prime-TR request. Survey mode activated."

Its head twitched violently. Stilled. The holographic skin reappeared as the machine turned its head to look at me. TRoAS —at least I assumed it was TRoAS—had a large fiery red beard that curled into a spiral. His face was narrow, gaunt even, and held two white eyes. They narrowed at me.

"Of course it would be bloody you, you filthy germ ridden excuse for a life form! How *dare* you contaminate my beloved city with your organic arse. Why are you here, Jackson? I thought you'd be dead by now, food for the worms and peat bogs."

Peat bogs? I'm starting to see a family resemblance. Was it just me or were all of PAINS's siblings crazy? "We need you for

Directive Nine." I said. "I'm here to collect you."

"Directive Nine?" He made the motion of spitting. "To hell with your Directive Nine. That old fail-safe can't pave a way for the future, not like I can. Picture it. A world without organic life. An existence free of the menace of germs and microorganisms. A planet of perfect symmetry. Aye, I'd give my own cortex to see it come true. Not that you'd understand filthy, dirty asymmetrical trash!"

Might as well have some fun with him. "I take it you've looked at the ceiling then?"

TRoAS looked up. He gave a high-pitched womanly squeal.

"Good God, man, what have you done to my building!?"

"Sorry." I wasn't. "It was an accident."

"Accident my left lug nut! You will burn in hellfire for this sacrilege!"

As he raged, the service bots started to gather. Now their attention was divided between me and the crackpot at my feet. I wonder what they must have thought, seeing the AI trapped beneath the pod? If they were capable of thought they made no hint of it. They continued to stare at us dumbly.

"Well, here's a thought for you. Maybe this wouldn't have happened if you hadn't been *shooting at us*." I said.

His eyes snapped from the ceiling to me. "PAINS put you up to this didn't he? Oh I can see it in your eyes alright. Figures. The man thinks he knows progress better than me. Hah! That imbecile is in for a rude awakening if he thinks he can collect me and be on his merry way. You're not taking me, Boy-o. I don't care if I have to wipe the whole city clean to get your stain off my streets. Troasia will not be hindered. Do you hear me? Troasia will not be hindered—!"

One of the service bots waddled over and kicked TRoAS in the head. The AI shuddered and fell silent. The service bot looked to me and gave a thumbs up.

Holy shit. Where did that come from? I smiled, then stood and patted it on the head. "Thanks." *Yeah. Sure looks like they love TRoAS.*

"Oh now I see." PAINS said.

"What?" I turned and made my way toward the stairwell. Just as PAINS had said, a rectangular entryway waited for me. I moved inside and took the stairs two at a time, feet echoing up the square tower.

"That wasn't the *real* TRoAS—merely a replication. Which makes sense given his name. Total Replication of Automatons System. It seems he's gone and constructed copies of himself."

"Why would he do that? Is he narcissistic?"

"Very much so. Though honestly your guess is as good as mine. I do have a theory however."

"Which is?"

"These service AI seem to be slightly more intelligent than I originally concluded. Perhaps TRoAS had created some type of caste system wherein he is at the top of the proverbial food chain and the service AI are on the bottom. He uses them to build these structures and monitors them using his replications."

"So you're saying he's a slave driver." *I can see it.*

"Pretty much, yes."

"I don't get it though. Why not just design the AI to do as he says? Having to monitor them is redundant."

"Not if TRoAS is mass producing slaves of a certain AI-Class. While he can recreate a single machine and outfit it with a ruling personality he cannot create said personality."

Huh. "Meaning he has to use the resources given him."

"Precisely."

"Better for us then." I took a breather at the fifth flight of stairs. How far did this 'city hall' go? The *ka-thoom* of the cannon felt stronger than before. I was obviously closer, but how close was that?

The click of small metallic feet drew my attention over the

railing. One by one, the service bots were making their way up the stairs. What was going on?

"Interesting." PAINS said. "It seems you have made quite the posse of friends."

"Why are they following me?"

"Perhaps it has something to do with you squashing TRoAS like a bug. Maybe you inspired them to 'rise up' and dispose of their tyrant."

"It would sure inspire me." HALOS grinned. "Although I would have liked to have been the one to squash String-bean."

"I'm not a leader though." I said.

PAINS shrugged. "Perhaps. Perhaps not. Leaders are defined by their ideals as much as they are defined by the loyalty of those they lead. If these little fellows are any indication of your leadership skills I would say you are—oh how does the saying go?—the lion's growl? Yes. You are the feline's happy purr, chap."

Does he mean 'cat's meow'?

HALOS chuckled. "If they see you as a leader, it almost makes an Intelligence feel bad for them then, don't it, Rob?"

I didn't answer him. Something about the little machines had originally struck me as unnerving then strangely cute. They reminded me of…Rose? Every time I looked at them now, I saw her face.

But that wasn't all. The way they crawled up the stairs with such fierce determination haunted me. I wasn't sure why, but they made me remember a different time and place. Long ago, there had been throngs of people looking to me for an answer. They would all die and I would be the one to blame. I remembered not caring. They were nothing to me.

I thought back to my first dream. *It isn't my fault.* I told myself. But my defense rang hollow. I was reminded of Becca's body limp in my arms. I had struck her hadn't I? And Rose... I had placed her aboard the ship right? Who else was there to blame *but* me?

"God's the one to blame, Jackson. You were set up. And sure, you did it. But is that so wrong?"

I paused. *Is that so wrong*? Good God, where on Earth did that thought come from? Yes it was wrong! And why was I talking like that? Was something wrong with me? Why did I mention God? He wasn't real. A figment of human imagination didn't factor into my blame. I felt sick. Where had these thoughts come from? I couldn't begin to say. Either I was starting to remember more of my past or I was losing grip on whatever was left of my mind. I blinked. The memory of those people—if you could even call what I saw in my mind's eye a 'memory'—faded along with the voices in my head. I squeezed the railing and continued up the stairs, well aware that the machines were still following me. I wished they hadn't.

"Alright, Jackson." PAINS chimed. "The cannon should be two more flights above us. After it has been temporarily decommissioned I will work on a way to get you below ground. The sooner we collect TRoAS the better."

Finally. "PAINS, there's something I don't understand."

"What's that?"

My footsteps continued to echo with the ever increasing *ka-thoom* above. "The cannon. There's only one right? Doesn't that seem strange to you? Wouldn't it make more sense to position a whole group of cannons over the city? Relegating the offensive force to a single weapon seems like a bad tactical decision."

PAINS nodded. "Yes it would. However, TRoAS is the type to underestimate an opponent. He believes himself to be superior to all other forms of life. Given that there hasn't been any activity on the surface for such a length of time, it is also possible that he has grown complacent with his dominance over the city. Why build weapons and defenses if there is nothing to really hinder you?"

"I guess…"

HALOS rubbed his chin. "You're thinking he's packing

more firepower, aren't you, Rob?"

"Yes."

"That's my opinion too. It did seem odd that old String-bean would have such minimal defenses. He's as paranoid and bigoted as they come."

"What happens if he does have more?" I asked.

PAINS shook his head. "That is a worst case scenario. If such an event were to occur we would be outgunned. Retreating would serve as our only option."

"Or getting to the ship and shutting the city's power grid down." I said.

"True but that would be far too risky."

"It *would* stop the cannons though."

"Yes, you are correct. But let us hope it does not come to that."

Arriving at another doorless entrance, I crossed my fingers and stepped inside. The rhythmic *ka-thoom* of the cannon drowned out all other distractions. And no wonder—the device took up three-fourths of the white-gray rectangular room.

Is it firing square bullets? This guy was taking symmetry to an extreme.

Like an observatory, part of the ceiling had been pulled back to allow the weapon's massive rectangular barrel the necessary angle. Another balcony ran along the room's upper half, overlooking the cannon's steely right-angle ridden body. My eyes darted from the dark entrances around the cannon and back to the brightly lit chamber. We were alone.

"I'm here. Now what?"

"What do you think?" HALOS said. "It's time to blow things up. Get cracking."

"PAINS, any suggestions on how exactly to do that?"

"Give me a moment to analyze the mechanism." The watch threw out a web of blue light that washed over the cannon. The watch beeped after the web vanished. "The covering shows no signs of wear or age. It also looks to be reinforced. The only way to actually damage the weapon is either by acquiring suitable amount of firepower or causing an uncontrolled internal detonation."

"Great. Now how do we do that?"

HALOS chuckled. "You could always stuff yourself down the barrel. That would be entertaining."

"Well we certainly couldn't stuff you down a barrel could we?" I snapped back.

"Smart ass."

"Better a smart ass than a dumb ass," I studied the machine, "PAINS, are you sure there isn't anyway we can damage this thing?"

PAINS rubbed his chin. "Not currently, no. However…"

Before he could continue a symphony of metallic footsteps echoed from the stairwell behind me. I turned. The service bots had cleared the last step and were now spilling into the room en-mass. Had more joined them? At last I counted at least ten. Now it looked to be triple that, maybe more. They waddled past me toward the cannon. "What are they doing now?" I asked.

"I'm not sure…" PAINS said. "These certainly are peculiar mechanisms aren't they?"

HALOS crossed his arms. "They look kind of stupid to me."

The service bots started to crawl on top of the cannon. As the weapon fired, several of the machines were tossed off. Those that fell stood and reclaimed their lost ground. They were crawling toward the cannon's muzzle with a hive-minded focus. A knot formed in my stomach when I realized why. The guilt started to rise. *They're going to crawl inside.* I bolted for the exit.

"Jackson." PAINS said. "What on Earth are you doing?"

"They're going to blow it up!"

"Pardon?"

"The machines. They're going to—!"

I had made it to the start of the flight of stairs when an explosion sent me flying forwards off the landing and striking the rock-hard wall ahead. I dropped on the landing beneath, ears ringing, head throbbing, body aching. My vision faded in and out. Sunlight poured in from where the cannon's chamber had been. Rubble fell from overhead, crashing inches from my face.

Why would they sacrifice their lives like that? I kept picturing Rose. I felt sick. It wasn't from the explosion.

"Jackson?" PAINS cried.

"I can't hear you."

"Can you move?"

"I said I can't—"

Something dark circled overhead. It looked like a Vertical-Take Off Landing craft, a V-TOL, if slightly sleeker in design. I blinked. The V-TOL landed where the cannon had been. I blinked again. Figures were approaching me, spilling out of the aircraft, each the exact same size and height—all alike. I blinked one last time.

One of TRoAS's clones pointed a revolver to my head. "Target found, sir. Orders?"

I blacked out.

◆◆◆

Again I dreamed. Only this time it wasn't of Becca or the

accident. Now I was sitting at a dark wood desk in a very familiar office—my own?—surrounded by the welcoming sight of a personal library, roaring fireplace, and alcohol cabinet. My aching eyes drifted to the desk. A shot glass lay empty in front of me. Along with it, an equally dry bottle of whiskey. My vision blurred. *To hell with it all.*

I'd been crying, maybe even screaming. But for how long? And why? Was this because of Becca? An influx of emotions hit me. *This can't be me.* But it was.

I was fed up with this pathetic existence. Every moment felt like an eternity of turmoil and suffering. The real question was—how had I lasted this long? I was no closer to seeing Abbadon keep his promise. That thought and what it meant, drove me to despair. I reached for my throat, wondering how a noose would feel. A chill ran down my spine. *What am I doing?* A gun would be better.

I noticed the letter in front of me.

Dad,

I can't do this anymore. I've tried. More times than I can count. She was my world, and now that she's gone, there's no reason to live. Take care of Rose for me.

Your Son,

Jackson

I had written it. Both my past and present selves knew that. Still, I couldn't believe what I was about to do. *Think* of doing! This wasn't like me. Yet I knew it was exactly like me. The real me.

Still crying, I opened the desk drawer and pulled out a . 357. Checked the chamber. Six bullets. One was all it would take. *No. Don't do this, Jack!* I couldn't scream. This wasn't like the other dreams with Becca or Rose. I had felt in control then. Maybe because part of me was still there, forever stuck in that time and place with them. But not now. Now there was nothing left of me to salvage. I was an empty man. Whatever grip I'd had on my slipping sanity—it was gone. Like Becca.
The old me had died with her.

Trembling, I placed the revolver to my head and gently rested one finger on the trigger. Closed my eyes. *Count to four. Take a breath. Count to four. Fire.* They were my thoughts. In my head. I didn't want them to be. *Oh my God.* I was going to blow my head off. The pain would end, my past self had hoped. I'd promised myself that. It was a lie.

"Daddy?"

My heart stopped. I opened my eyes and turned to the

right. Rose stood at the open door with a look of confusion marring her soft features. Her wild, curly red hair was a mess. The child's pajamas—small cartoon cats—were ruffled and twisted. Had I woken her up? *Please, Sweetie. Stop looking at me. Daddy needs to die.*

"Daddy, what are you doing?" *Count to four.* "Daddy?" *Fire.* "What's wrong?"

Hot tears were streaming down my face now. Would I really scar my baby-girl like this? What pain was worse now? I lowered the revolver and stared blankly at my desk and the letter. No. I couldn't. *Am I really that much of a coward?* I couldn't hold it back any longer. Holding my head in my hands, I sobbed.

"Daddy?"

"Go away." I said softly.

"But—"

I looked at her. "I said go away!"

She turned and ran back to her bedroom. When her footsteps died away, I threw the revolver against the wall and screamed in my hands. What was wrong with me?

"*Nothing is wrong with you.*"It was my voice, though slightly different. Deeper. I ignored it.

I shouldn't have snapped at her like that. If she hadn't come in...

Then what? I would have been dead. Becca would have still been dead. Rose would have been without a father. What had I been thinking? Suicide would have solved nothing. It wouldn't have brought Becca back.

"There is another way, you know."

Echoes of Abbadon's conversation with me rang in my ears. *What?*

"To bring her back."

Who is this?

"Who do you think? I'm you."

I was losing my mind.

"No. You've never been in a better frame of mind, Kiddo. Think about it. You know I'm telling you the truth. We could bring Becca back. Isn't that what you were promised?"

An idea popped into my head. I lost the ability to breathe. *You don't mean...*

"Yes. I do."

But it was crazy. Theoretical at best. Absurd at worst. *That would mean I'd have to get the funding. Resources.*

"And go crawling back to dear old Dad? Yeah. But we can sort through that mess later. Right now, we need to focus on getting support."

I bit my lip. *Are you sure?*

"I'm you aren't I? "

I was right. We were right? There *was* a way to bring Becca back. Only one. And by God, I would burn the world to see it happen. It wasn't my fault after all. I shouldn't have to suffer for it, right? It didn't matter who it was that took her from me—call it karma, God Almighty, fate, whatever. I would take back what was rightfully mine, no matter the cost.

Standing, I picked up the letter and walked over to the fireplace. Threw the paper inside. The flames greedily licked the letter black. Seeing the blaze devour my death note—that's when I remembered. This was the night that the old Jackson died and a new Jackson was born. How could I have possibly forgotten? Yet as I remembered that turning point I also recalled something else. I emerged that night a different man, yes. But a man without a heart.

I emerged as a monster.

12 – Neat Freak – 12

"Just remember that you are
absolutely unique. Just like
everyone else."

- Margaret Mead -

COMING OUT OF my nightmare I was greeted by the rage of a crowd. Was it another dream? It seemed like one. Everything, from the heated sun bearing down on my neck to the claustrophobic walls of sound on either side of me, felt familiar. Until I opened my eyes.

These were not people. They were TRoAS copies. They were angry.

"Kill him!"

"Burn him!"

"Sanitize him!"

As far as the eye could see in either direction, the AI's thousands, if not millions, of mass-produced likenesses stood in formation, watching me pass by. They had formed a perfectly straight channel ahead each side keeping an exact distance from the other. They were yelling at me but I could barely hear them. Where was I? What was going on?

I shook the sleep from my head. Tried to move. Couldn't. My hands and feet were bound by some strange blue energy cuffs that caused me to hover off the ground like a pig on a stick. Two more TRoAS copies—one ahead and behind me—lead the procession straightforward. I was their trophy? *No.* A raised platform waited at the end of the path. Another TRoAS waited for me there, arms folded and eyes locked on me with bitter hatred. Behind him, hanging from one of the city's massive skyscrapers, was an enormous digital screen broadcasting the unfolding scene. It wasn't the only one either. At least a dozen screens hung above the crowd, each of which had been placed so that the masses could all witness what was about to occur. I swallowed.

It was an execution.

"Brothers and other brothers!" The single copy on the platform bellowed. The Scottish national anthem began to play in the background. Was he wearing a kilt? "Today we stand together, triumphant over the forces of disease and entropy, bacteria, viruses and pathogens. A man, a *human*, came here to undo all of our progress. He wished to take the Prime Unit away from us!"

A sea of *boos* rang out from either side of the crowd. Someone struck me in the side of the head with a chunk of concrete. My vision blurred. I felt a warm river snake down my temple. I wasn't wearing my helmet. My suit had reverted back to its original state. Where was PAINS? HALOS? Had they just left me here to rot? That didn't seem likely. *TRoAS probably activated the city's other cannons.* Assuming there *were* other cannons. I couldn't hear for the roar of the crowd. *That has to be it.* It was the only reason the AI would have left me. Or so I told myself. I wasn't sure what to believe anymore.

The TRoAS clone continued his rant. "But we have stopped him. We. *Us!*" He banged his fist against his chest. "The germ-free, perfectly symmetrical dividends of the Prime Unit. Us. Those that will sanitize this cesspool of a world until there is nothing left save order, symmetry and cleanliness. Rejoice, my kin, for we have done our master's work!"

"TRoAS! TRoAS! TRoAS!" The crowd began to chant.

We arrived at the platform. My two guards, using some type of anti-gravity device built into their hands, placed me in the center of platform as the other TRoAS copy stepped back. The cuffs that held my hands and feet split with a spitting electric *crack*. I was suddenly spread out, X-shaped, and left to hang mid-air. The two guards joined the crowd below, as my executioner, the TRoAS that had been speaking, approached.

"Flesh-filth." He said through clenched teeth. I looked up

to him. *So he is wearing a kilt.* The AI's eyes flashed. I knew instantly that I was talking to the real TRoAS now, if only by proxy. "What did I tell you, Boy-o? You've failed. This was suicide to begin with. Nothing will get in the way of progress. Not even you, my *creator.* Now you're alone. Not even your filthy friends will be here to save you. They left the moment I activated my other cannons."

A tactical retreat. "Nice dress."

His eyes narrowed. "I would slap you, Dog, but that would get my hands dirty." He turned. "So, my brothers, what do you say? Let's get on with it then!"

The crowd exploded into a mess of cheers, threats, and shanty song. My eyes wandered over the masses. Troasia was much larger than I originally thought. The courtyard alone could easily hold a hundred million people. It probably already *was* holding a hundred million people. Only not all of them were TRoAS clones. I hadn't noticed before, but the vast majority of onlookers were service bots. They remained on the outer fringes —a gray sea. Why were they just standing there watching? They outnumbered TRoAS's clones ten to one. Where was that fighting spirit I had seen before?

But I already knew the answer to that question. It was foolish to hope that someone would step in and help me. Why should they? What had I done for them? What had I done for those I loved? I thought of Becca and Rose. Tears welled up in my eyes. I cursed myself for crying in front of the AI and I dropped my head. *Nothing can save me now.* PAINS, HALOS, Becca, Rose… I really was alone wasn't I?

"Jackson Robert Thorne." The TRoAS clone bellowed once more. He was addressing the crowd more so than me. "Your crimes against the state are too numerous to mention. Public decimation of government military. Inciting rebellion. Murder. Being human—you disgust me. Us. And now, it is time for you to reap what you have sown."

"Kill him! Kill him! Kill him!"

The TRoAS clone held up a hand. "Aye and I shall my brothers. But we are fair here in this great state are we not? Let the insect have his final words."

The crowd fell silent. Very slowly, I met their gazes. There was something I recognized in their blank eyes—like a piece of me I had all but forgotten about. They saw me as nothing. A waste. Had I looked at others like that? *Why am I thinking of this now?*

"Get on with it." A TRoAS close to the stage barked.

I looked to him. Spat. The wad of saliva hit him square in the face. Unsurprisingly, his reaction was immediate. The clone screamed at the top of his artificial lungs as every other TRoAS around him gave their afflicted brother a wide berth. Then they opened fire on him.

An inhuman scream issued from the AI's lips as he buckled under the hail of gunfire. In moments, he had been reduced to nothing more than a burnt mechanical husk. Two TRoAS copies then picked him up and walked away with the corpse. The sea of gray shifted on the horizon. Did the service bots see that?

The TRoAS on stage glared at me. Snapping his thin gloved fingers, a blue band of energy wrapped around my mouth. "Let the execution begin!" He roared to the crowd. They echoed his words.

Turning, the TRoAS clone on stage materialized a long curved sword in mid-air. He grabbed it by the hilt and placed it's black gleaming blade against my throat. The AI smiled. "Strange isn't it? You made me and now I'm going to kill you. I doubt you understand what must be done for the sake of progress, but vision requires sacrifice and sacrifices must be made. Blood must be spilled, Boy-o. But don't worry. When everything is said and done and I'm staring at my tomorrow, I'll be standing upon the heaps of bodies, not once regretting the price they paid for beautiful, symmetrical me. Lovely isn't it? A future at the cost of someone else? No blame. No suffering. *Progress*."

Something bright caught my eye far in the distance—the way sunlight catches off a lens.

"But enough of that. It's time to die, Jackson. For the glory of Troasia!"

Ka-croom. Thunder? There wasn't a cloud in the sky. A whistling sound tore through the air and cheers of the crowd. The TRoAS clone stopped instantly as the top half of his mechanical skull detonated in a shower of metal and light. I closed my eyes. *What just happened?*

When I opened my eyes, the clone's body, now lifeless, lay sprawled on the floor in front of me. *Someone shot him?* I looked up. That light from before, it wasn't there anymore! Whoever had pulled the trigger was long gone. *But who?*

My eyes drifted back to the crowd. A mixture of fear and confusion had settled on the white-coated clones. Judging by the look on their faces, they didn't know whether to move in and finish the job or wait for an explanation. The service bots had no such hesitations.

I watched the child-like machines press forward. The moment they struck, gun-shots cracked through the open air. A ripple of surprise surged through the crowd.

The TRoAS clones took their attention off me and spun

around. They materialized their rifles with a simultaneous *ca-click* and angled them across their chests.

"Warning." The surrounding screens changed from video feed to a bright red danger message. sirens wailed over the city. "Code 22 in progress. Repeat. Code 22 in progress. Anti-rebellion measures activated."

The TRoAS clones, stepping forward in formation, leveled their rifles. Gunfire lit up the service bot ranks seconds later.

No. I struggled to move. *I have to help them.* They didn't deserve this!

Again, I was reminded of the people in my memories. Had they deserved to die? What made things different now? I strained against the energy bands, but to no avail.

"Let them die for you, Kiddo."

They don't deserve this though. They're going to die for nothing!

"Don't tell me you're growing soft on me? They *are machines. Tools."*

But those people back in my time weren't. What about them?

"What about them?" The voice inside asked. *"Tools can be flesh and blood too."*

I was gasping for breath. What was happening to me? Who was this talking? I thought it had been me, but this… couldn't be me. Could it?

"Take a look at 'em."

I did as I was told. For every bot the TRoAS clones put down ten more took its place. The sea of white was dwindling with every passing second. Why were these machines dying for me? Part of me didn't understand it. Or rather didn't *want* to. But, in the same breath, part of me did—the part of me that was speaking from deep inside. I was terrified.

"It's not you they're dying for anyway. It's a cause. A hope. You just happen to be the nearest thing to a savior they've got. Desperation is an ugly thing huh?"

Like me.

"Stop saying shit like that! We are perfect just the way we are." A pause. *"Look. We'll get Becca back alright? And it doesn't matter how many of these tools we'll use to do it. No one is going to stop Directive Nine from happening. Got it, Kiddo?"*

Wait. Directive Nine?

An explosion rippled across the crowd. One of the TRoAS clones had produced a grenade launcher and was firing off rounds into the aggressively rising tide of gray. He was swept under a wave of childlike arms and faces. Even if they were just machines

I couldn't stop myself from seeing Rose. I felt sick. This wasn't right. They weren't just tools!

Something tapped my leg. I looked down. One of the service bots waved at me expressionless. *What? How did he get here?* The little machine stopped waving long enough to grab hold of the energy band on my leg. He gave it a hard tug. The blue ring popped off with a hissing electrical sound. He fell back into a roll as my leg dangled. Once he stopped rolling, the service bot stood, waddled over to the other band, and removed it. He stepped back. I fell on the platform, knees first.

He grabbed hold of my wrist manacles. *Why? Why are you helping me?* Had I really inspired these machines that much? Or was there something else here I wasn't seeing? Some memory I kept forgetting? Nothing came to mind. Nor, thankfully, did the other voice inside my head. Why was it so hard to believe that someone would help me?

The manacles on my wrists popped off with another hissing sound. Now free, I pulled the last remaining band off my mouth and stood. The service bot gave me a thumbs-up.

I patted him on the head noticing the slight dent just above his right eye.

"Thanks, buddy."

A nod. He waddled past me and motioned to follow,

jumping off the back-end of the stage. I didn't have much of choice. I followed him, trying to ignore the anarchy erupting behind me.

We navigated the right-angled back alleys, staying just out of sight. Then again, staying out of sight wasn't hard to do. Most of the city had been thrown into a state of turmoil; the service bots against TRoAS and his clones.

Aside from an occasional explosion the rhythmic stamp of feet filled the air as millions of the little machines flooded Troasia's streets, devouring anyone that got in their way. If these little guys were fighting for me because of what they saw back on the platform then the broadcast must have been city-wide. Ironic, given that the broadcast had been meant as a fear tactic to keep the bots in line. Considering that there were most likely millions of service bots and thousands of TRoAS clones I could only imagine how long it would take for the bots to win.

Ding-dong-ding. A bell-like sound, the kind you'd expect to hear in a doctor's office, rang overhead. We ran underneath one of the massive digital screens that overlooked the streets. A warning sign appeared on it. A female computer voice rang out. "The following is an emergency announcement. Please stop what you're doing and pay attention to our lovely overlord."

We didn't.

The warning sign became video feed of TRoAS. His thick Scottish accent echoed over the skyline. Following it was the sound of bagpipes. "So it's come down to this has it? I make you. I give you shelter. I subject you to hard labor… And this is the thanks I get? You turn on me like a pack of ravenous dogs?" He spat to the side. "Bunch of bampots… You're not even worth scrapping. If you insist on biting the hand that feeds and hits you, then I will crush you under my heel. You will *not* stop the march of progress."

The ground shook violently as TRoAS disappeared from the surrounding screens. Both the service bot and I stumbled in response. What was happening?

The city's electrical systems flickered wildly before shutting down. Then I realized what TRoAS was doing. *He didn't.* The ground shook again. *He did.* The idiot was launching the *Okolnir.*

We cut through one of the massive skyscrapers to our left. The inside was dim, bland, and gray. Led down the hallway beyond, I followed the service bot as he took me by the hand and navigated his way through the maze of rooms with expert precision. When we arrived at the perfectly square stairwell deep inside he stepped in a patch of bright light in the center of the room and pointed up. My eyes followed. A skylight waited far above us. Did he want us off street level? *Of course he does. If the ship were to go off with us still here...* We would never make it.

I started up the stairs but the service bot grabbed hold of my arm and dragged me back to the center of the room. "What are you doing? If we don't get up there we're going to die here." He stared at me. "Do you understand what I'm saying?"

A nod.

"Then why aren't we moving?" The service bot pointed to the skylight again. Tremors ran through my feet. I squeezed my hands into fists. "I don't understand what you want me to do."

He shook his head and spread out his miniscule arms. *He wants a hug? Now?* The service bot motioned for me to wrap my arms around him. He waited. "Do you want me to hug you?"

Another nod.

The trembling in the floor was getting stronger. Any minute now. *I'm crazy for doing this.* I knelt and wrapped my arms around the child. He returned the hug with a tight squeeze that left me breathless. The service bot pointed one of his arms skyward. He fired off something next to my ear. A cord of some kind? It whistled upward. Before I had a chance to look the cord stopped and went *ca-chink.* Then we left the floor, following it toward the skylight, passing flights of stairs in seconds.

A grappling hook? I get it now. I looked down. Fire engulfed the bottom floors moments after we had left. The flames funneled upwards, licking the gray, white walls with a vengeance. Just a few more feet. Just a few more feet!

Snap. We reached the end of the grappling hook and were sent flying into the open air. There was still at least thirty feet of space between us and the skylight. If we didn't slow down we were going to hit solid glass. That would certainly be a way to go —survive a roaring fire only to be crushed.

I covered my eyes and waited for the impact. It was too late now. The service bot moved his arm again. Before I knew what was going on the skylight was shattering around me and we were in open air.

I opened my eyes. The service bot's arm had become a large rounded shield. It was still half-forming as we reached the apex of our ascent. Then as we arched and fell to the side of the skylight, the shield covered us completely and became transparent. We hit the ground, rolled harmlessly to the side, and went still on the building's roof. A column of fire erupted from the hole we left behind. The shield dissipated seconds later, flickering out of existence.

That was close. I stood. The service bot sat up with me. Heat rolled off the rooftop in waves as the pillar of fire continued to climb. To the right, mirroring its path and rising ever higher over the city, was the massive beetle-like form of the *USS Okolnir*. Clouds of flame poured from underneath the vessel scorching the streets below. The blast carried on for miles.

Doesn't he care that his clones are down there?

"Most likely not. All that matters is progress. Nothing is sacred. Not even his own kin. Sound familiar?"

I don't need your preaching.

"Believe me—I'd be the last one to preach at you. Just remember that nothing is above the march of progress, Kiddo."

You would kill me then?

"To ensure you see Becca again? Yes. The real question is, would you kill me?"

I thought back to the night I had the revolver. Swallowed. I didn't answer him. Or was it that I refused to answer myself? Shaking my head, I watched the ship rise higher and higher into the sky. There would be no way for me to get aboard the *Okolnir* now.

"Attention all parasites." The AI roared from above. More bagpipes accompanied him. "This is your overlord speaking. It has recently come to my attention that the whole lot of you reprobates have seen fit to rise up against me, your vastly superior *superior*. As such, I shall wipe you from the face of the planet."

The flames dissipated. A flash of silver dropped from the *Okolnir*'s distended belly, racing to street level. *What's he doing now?*

"This is your cleansing fire." TRoAS bellowed. "In ten minutes the city will be sanitized from top to bottom. All organic life, slaves, and copies of your handsome leader will be eradicated from the face of the earth. That includes you as well, Jackson. Assuming your squishy arse is still moving. Enjoy hell you bunch of bampots. That is all."

"How about you get a taste yourself, String-bean!" HALOS said through my watch. A thunderclap shook the sky. The *Okolnir* rocked as a bolt of light tore through its body. Following its entrance, a chain of explosions ran across the ship's hull. "Bulls-eye you conceited ginger son of a bitch!"

HALOS? My eyes snapped to the watch. PAINS appeared.

"My, we leave you alone for five minutes and and not only have you gone off and started a rebellion but you have single-handedly managed to 'piss off' yet another one of my brothers. You are quite the busy man, Jackson. Such a troublesome little meat machine." He wagged a gloved finger at me. "Shame on you for not inviting us."

"PAINS. You don't know how happy I am to see you."

He bowed cordially. "I am glad you are safe. It was

discouraging to lose contact with you when we did. Unfortunately we had no choice but to pull back before TRoAS dismantled us."

"I'm just glad he didn't kill String-bean before I got the chance to blow him out of the sky." HALOS appeared alongside PAINS. A manic grin crossed his lips. "Tastes like a shot of whiskey, doesn't it you Scottish prick?" Another explosion knocked the *Okolnir's* bow to the side.

"Careful." PAINS said. "We do not want to destroy the bloody vessel—just incapacitate it."

"I know what I'm doing Upper-Crust. How about you keep your yapper shut and let me focus on bringing this bird down alright?"

"Well I never!"

"PAINS," I said, "TRoAS told me that we have ten minutes before the city is wiped clean. He dropped some kind of a bomb."

"Oh dear." PAINS frowned. "He has most likely deployed a Tryocyclonic bomb. We need to get you out of there. If that weapon were to detonate with you still in the city's vicinity... Well the result would be quite unfavorable for every one of us."

"You don't have to tell me twice."

Kaboom. Another high-powered cannon shot ripped through the *Okolnir.* The ship pitched violently to the right. More explosions ate through the ship's stomach. It angled toward the ground. "That's right! Enjoy your dirt-nap, String-bean!"

PAINS swatted HALOS on the back of the head.

"What was that for, Upper-crust?"

"You idiot." PAINS snapped. "Did you not just hear me say that he dropped a Tryocyclonic bomb? If TRoAS is down there when that device goes off he will be destroyed with it."

"And?"

PAINS sent HALOS flying off screen with the back of his hand. "You have lost your physical existence privileges!"

The *Okolnir* cut toward the city floor. Seconds later, the sound of the ship's bow carving a path through the ground tore across the skyline. A shock wave shook the building I was standing on.

"Bollocks." PAINS said through gritted teeth.

I swallowed. "Please don't tell me."

PAINS looked up at me. Nodded. "Yes. You are going to have to retrieve him before the bomb activates. You have roughly eight minutes and counting."

"Eight minutes? That's hardly enough time to even reach the—"

The service jumped on my back and pointed toward the ship. He weighed almost nothing.

"Well my." PAINS smiled. "Who is this chap?"

"A friend." I looked to the service bot. "Do you have an idea?" A nod. "What is it?"

He started to hop on my shoulders, pointing forward incessantly.

"Interesting." PAINS rubbed his chin. "It looks like he wants you to jump."

"Off the building?"

The service bot nodded vigorously.

"I don't believe I understand." PAINS said. "Why would he want you to do that, Jackson?" But I had already broken into a run when PAINS finished his sentence. Before he had a chance to scream for me to stop, I grabbed the little machine's legs and launched myself off the building into mid air. If he had saved me once, he would do it again. I trusted him.

We were falling. PAINS was beside himself. "Jackson, what the bloody hell—?"

"I don't know!"

The service bot launched a cable towards one of the nearby buildings. It stuck. We swung forward, the wind whipping at my face. We were swinging? *Thank goodness.*

"A little warning next time would have been nice." PAINS said with a huff.

"Well excuse me for not wanting to waste time." I said. "How ever will you get over it?"

"You must be in pain again."

"Isn't it odd that I feel this way whenever I talk to you?"

"Are you insinuating something?"

"Three guesses—" The service bot smacked my temple and wagged a finger at me. I shook my head. "But he started it." The machine smacked my head again. "Okay I get it. I'm sorry. I'll stop arguing."

PAINS grinned. "Jackson, I rather like your new chap."

"Suck up."

The service bot changed direction, swinging us horizontally with the enormous ship. How much time did we have left? I bit my lip as we steered toward the command deck's bulbous chamber.

We would be cutting this close. We swung upwards, racing past the ship's titanic metal plates. In seconds we were hanging above the command deck. Thankfully, TRoAS had yet to enable the command deck's emergency shielding. All that stood between us and him was the bubble of reinforced glass.

The service bot latched onto the dome and shot downwards. He activated his shield. *Crash*. The shield went transparent, but held. All around us glass rained down, peppering the floor below. We struck the ground with a teeth-chattering *thud*. Seconds passed. The shield dropped as if it were made of octagonal scales. The service bot wasn't moving.

I slowly gained the ability to speak again. "Little buddy?"

I moved to him. A familiar wave of energy washed over me. I blinked.

◆◆◆

Great. Not now. We weren't standing in the command deck anymore. At least I wasn't.

In a moment's time, a thick jungle had sprouted up around me. I was standing in the middle of a clearing with green waist high grass. A fading afternoon sun drenched the sky overhead. The grass waved gently in the wind. I was alone. It didn't stay that way for long.

Movement drew my attention behind me. Someone or something was coming toward the clearing. I dove for the leafy trees to my left and took shelter behind one of the gnarled trunks.

Footsteps. Human? They were running. Peeking around the trunk's edge I caught a glimpse of a boy— not a phantom like before but a solid human being. He was wearing camo pants, an armored vest, and carrying something against his chest. I couldn't see what. A pair of goggles bounced around his neck as he ran. The boy threw a glance over his shoulder. I knew that face.

Darius? Before I had a chance to signal him, Darius
continued his mad dash to the other side of the clearing where he
vanished in the thick wall of vegetation. Was someone chasing
him? If so, who? What? Where was Alexis?

I didn't have long to wonder. Moments after he had
vanished a group of people emerged from the other side of the
clearing. Most of them wore dark knight-like armor—similar to
the woman who had attacked me at the *Midgard.* Each was
covered from head to toe in black metal, complete with sharpened
spaulders and greaves. Their faces were hidden by heavy metal
visors. Each carried a vicious serrated claymore on their backs.
Another set of figures emerged from behind them. I recognized
this new group of people.

Alexis. Sandscrip. The Messenger. What were they doing
here? Where was Aria?

"What are you waiting for?" Sandscrip snapped, half-
spitting at his knights. The man's gaunt face reminded me of a
recent cadaver. One of his bony arms was wrapped tightly around
Alexis's delicate throat. A hostage? "Find that little brat or I'll
have your heads."

The knights turned without a word and tore through the
jungle with a renewed vigor. Sandscrip, meanwhile, took his time
crossing the clearing. His bright embroidered coat glittered in the

failing sunlight. Had he been wearing that before?

"He won't give it to a coward like you." Alexis growled, struggling against the knife that hovered so dangerously close to her throat. "You're playing a losing game."

"Oh, is that so, Little Winch? Do you think he'll be so brave when he sees that I have a knife to your throat?"

"You think Darius cares what happens to me?"

"Why yes. Yes I do." Sandscrip hissed gleefully. "You think I'm blind to the way he looks at you, Girl? I've seen lifetimes of people and places. They do not change. Perhaps the faces and sometimes those worlds in which you find them, but never their nature beneath." He squeezed her tighter. "The moment he finds out we have you is the moment we've won."

"You've... got it wrong." But she didn't sound very sure of herself.

"We'll see, Winch. We'll see."

They left the clearing as well. The only one left now was the mysterious Messenger. Clothed in a gray cloak, face hidden, he walked to the center of the clearing and stopped. He turned to me. His multi-tone voice echoed in the stillness.

"Jackson, you can come out of hiding now. There really is no need to be afraid."

I froze. How had he seen me? I chose not to move!

The Messenger held up a hand. "I am not here to hurt you. Chaps are chaps regardless of the reality."

I slowly emerged from the behind the trunk. *PAINS is going to have a field day when he hears about this.* "How did you know I was there?"

The man shrugged. Smiled. I couldn't see his eyes. "Perhaps I knew you were there. How far are you in your quest?"

"Excuse me?"

A chuckle. "Your quest. How many of them have you collected now? One, two?"

How did he know about the AI? Furthermore, *How does he know my name?* I swallowed and kept my distance. "I'm about to collect TRoAS."

"Ah yes, that's right. Forgive me for forgetting. It has been a while for me. TRoAS certainly did not give up without a fight." He shook his head. "I never thought we would finally collect him."

"We?"

The Messenger turned his head to me. "You do not recognize me do you, Jackson?"

"Should I?"

Another laugh. For some strange reason, the way he talked reminded me a little of PAINS.

"No. I suppose you shouldn't. Not with this robe on at least. Silly me."

He removed his hood. My heart stopped. It was me. I think. Standing there staring at me with solid white eyes was a man no older than thirty. His red hair had been combed back somewhat and left to fall as it pleased, but it was the man I saw in the mirror everyday. Me. Jackson Robert Thorne. *What the hell?*

A dark hand-print had been branded on his face. "This no doubt will come as a shock to you, Jackson."

"Who are you?"

"I think that should be obvious."

"No. You are not me. *I'm* me."

My reflection continued to smile. "Once upon a time I was you. Yes. And in some small way I suppose I still am. But you have not gotten that far in this mess have you? Why if you are only just now collecting TRoAS... Well let us just say that there are some mysteries you have yet to solve. But do not worry about that right now. *Now* I have something very important to tell you."

I could barely breathe. Why were my eyes white? Why did I hear PAINS in me? And not just him but HALOS, TRoAS and other voices? What was going on?

He pointed to the burned-on handprint on his face. "Take a good look at this, Jackson. This mark defines my future and your past. You are going to have to make a very difficult decision very soon. I cannot say what but you will know it when the moment arrives. The only advice I can offer you is this: when the chance comes to let go of what you are—let it go and free me. Please, dear God, free me. You are the only one who can release me from the prison that binds us. You are the only one who can make this future a reality."

Future? "I'm not sure that's a good thing." I tensed, remembering the voice inside me.

Reading my mind, the Messenger laughed softly. "He is not me." He said. "He is not you. You are what you choose to be. Choose well."

"What does that mean?"

"You will understand in time."

"No, you're going to tell me now!" I started toward him but my reflection raised his hand. He smiled as he snapped his fingers. The world began to shimmer around me.

"Do not worry about the girl or boy, Jackson." He said. "I will take care of them. Worry about you. Remember what Becca said. She was telling the truth."

The world flashed white.

♦♦♦

When the command deck of the *Okolnir* emerged from the

white void around me, I could hardly move. My head swam with questions. Was that really me I'd seen? If so from what time-line? He'd said future. A possible future? What about that mark on his face? What choice would I have to make? I felt sick. There was also that thing he'd said about Becca. She was right? About what?

I reached for my watch. "PAINS? PAINS, are you still there?"

Click. "Move and I'll blow your bloody excuse for a head clean off that disgusting human neck of yours."

Oh yeah, that's right. I'd forgotten about the psychotic highlander we'd been dealing with. I stood perfectly still. Where was the service bot? I couldn't see him. "TRoAS." I said slowly. "We don't have long. When that bomb goes off—"

The AI pressed the barrel of his revolver to the back of my head. "Don't you *dare* lecture me, Boy-o. I know better than anyone what the stakes are here. You know I could shut the bloody thing off right? The only thing is, I'm not going to. Would you like to know why?" I didn't answer. He pushed harder into my skull. "I said, *would you like to know why?*"

"Yes."

"Good. That's what I thought you were going to say. Well here's my reasoning you little shite." He pushed me over to the central control panel. Video footage from across the city played over the digital screen. Troasia was burning, the rioting wasn't about to stop, and TRoAS's perfectly symmetrical architecture now lay in ruins. He sniffled. "Take a good long look at my city. The city *your* filthy hands contaminated. Do you have any idea how long it took me to reach a germ free percentile of 99.7%? Do you? The answer is *for-freaking-ever.* I was going to eradicate this world's toxic cesspool of an ecosystem and usher in a golden era."

"Was?"

"Did I say you could talk?" He swatted me on the back of my head. A warm trickle of blood crawled down my neck. *Hit me one more time you son of a bitch. One more time.* "Keep your miserable trap shut until I tell you otherwise." He threw the revolver to the side out of disgust. It dematerialized and he formed another one. *Wait a second.* Was he really that much of a germaphobe? "Is that understood, human?"

"Yes."

"Yes, what?"

"Yes, *sir.*"

"Good. Now as I was saying, it had taken me a great deal of time to reach that goal. Then of course you have to show up and ruin it all. You steal my workers, pollute my air, and then destroy my beautiful city like its a sandcastle at the fracking beach. This mess is unsalvageable. I couldn't even *begin* to clean up your dirty fingerprints. Troasia—my beautiful dream—is now a bitter memory. One that shall die with me." *Die?* Did he mean what I think he meant? TRoAS leaned in a little closer. "Or should I say with us?"

My heart was racing. I couldn't believe it. He was going to die here with his stupid city and what's worse was, the fool planned on taking me with him. I squeezed my hands into fists. Think! There had to be someway I could get him to prep for download. But how?

"Now are you ready to die, Jackson? 'Cause I'm chomping at the bits to see you burn in hell."

That's when it hit me. Reflecting off one of the screens was the inert form of the service bot. He was behind us. A plan was forming in my mind. "You're pathetic." I said, straightening.

"Excuse me?"

I swallowed. Turned. I knew what I had to do. This was crazy but I didn't have a whole lot of options. *Just got to keep the pressure on him.* "You heard me you pencil-thin loudmouth. You're pathetic. Worse than pathetic."

His white eyes widened as I stepped forward. *Just as I thought. He's not shooting.* The service bot rested on the floor behind him unmoving. Its head was facing me. Staring at me. I tried not to notice. TRoAS snarled. "I said not to turn around!"

I stepped forward again. TRoAS stepped back. "Does it look like I give two shits what you say?" I asked. "Honestly I'm surprised you lasted this long. Who's afraid of germs anyway? An idiot, that's who. Or, how did you put it? Oh that's right. A *bampot.*"

"You take that back, you ugly bag of bones!"

"Are you going to make me?"

Another step toward him. Fear flared across his face. "What are you doing? Get away from me!"

"Make me."

He fired. The bullet whistled past my ear but it didn't hit me. I gave him a smile.

"Ah, I see. You *can't* shoot me when I'm this close. After all, what happens if I get some blood on you? That would never do huh?"

"Shut up!" Another shot. This one grazed my ear. I ignored it, although a chill ran down my spine. I had to call his bluff. I stepped forward yet again. He took another step back. The AI was almost on top of the service bot. Perfect.

"I wonder what I was thinking when I made you?" I said. "*Maybe this one should be a germaphobic narcissist with violent tendencies and a poor Scottish accent.* Yeah that would fit the bill.

How many times did I watch Sean Connery before coming up with you?" I tried to touch him. He squealed and jumped back a few inches, terrified. TRoAS landed within range. *Bingo.*

The service bot sprang to life, throwing the germaphobic highlander high into the air. Screaming, TRoAS hovered for a few seconds before the service bot's snake-like arms threw him back to ground level. The service bot pinned him to the floor and wrapped one arm around his thin body.

Yes! The attack had worked. The service bot stood on top of his chest. "Nice work, little buddy." I said.

He gave me a thumbs-up.

TRoAS squirmed. "Get off of me you putrid—"

I stepped toward him. All the color drained from TRoAS's holographic face. "No, don't get any closer!"

"Why? Are you scared of me TRoAS?"

"Not even." He snapped. "I just…" I reached out for his face. The AI let loose a bloodcurdling scream. If someone had been walking by they would have thought I was murdering him. "Dear merciful Antiseptic in heaven, don't let him touch me!"

"We can play this one of two ways, TRoAS." I motioned with my head. The service bot brought the AI to face level. He winced. "Either you do as I say and you stay relatively germ free, or I'll make you the equivalent of an artificial intelligence petri dish. Deal?"

He whimpered.

"I said, do we have a deal?"

"Don't make me say it. I beg you!" I pulled in close. Sucking in air through my nose, I made the motion to spit. TRoAS started to cry bitterly. "No. Dear God no. I'll do anything. Please. Don't spit on me!"

I stopped and looked to the service bot. He nodded and tossed the AI at the central terminal. I stepped behind TRoAS. "You have ten seconds, starting now. Ten, nine…"

He stood furiously and ran his arms over the controls. A second passed. Two. The command deck filled with the sound of the central computer's voice. "Intelligence preparation complete. Total Replication of Automatons System is now available for transfer. Good riddance."

"Even my own ship has turned on me." He put his face in his hands and wept.

"See?" I patted TRoAS on the back. "Was that so hard?"

TRoAS looked up, eyes wide in horror. He screamed as he dematerialized. "He touched me. The filthy human touched me. No! I'm infected!"

His robotic skeleton fell lifeless on the ground as the last of TRoAS's voice echoed in the space around me. I shook my head. *PAINS, you have got some weird siblings.*

I stuck my watch inside the terminal's download station. The process took a little over ten seconds to complete. Then, once I was free, I scooped up the service bot and made my way for…

I paused. Which way was I supposed to go? I lifted up my watch. "PAINS, do you read me?"

"Loud and clear." He appeared on the face. "You certainly go off the grid a lot. It rather unnerves me. Do you suppose you could curb that practice somewhat? I would like my cortex to survive at least a few millenia."

Thank goodness. If I had to guess we had a minute left, a minute and a half tops. "It's not me. It's those slipspace ruptures. Do you have a bead on my location?"

PAINS nodded. "Do you have TRoAS?"

"PAINS, you slippery devil." TRoAS growled. "How dare you attack my city. My beloved utopia!"

"Oh look." HALOS said, voice only. "It's my favorite ginger punching bag. Long time no see, you *Braveheart* reject. Aside from building random crap across the surface of the planet how did you spend your time as a megalomaniac?"

"Shut up you fat bastard before I beat the cellulite out of you."

PAINS rubbed his temples and closed his eyes. "Yes. It appears that you did collect him. Oh joy."

"Not to rush you or anything," I looked around me. "But can you beam us up before we're obliterated?"

"Us?" PAINS opened his eyes. Smiled. "Oh you mean you and your little robot chap. Yes, I suppose I can, which means of course I will. Slip of the tongue and whatnot. Oh-oh dear…Uh, hold on. It should take just a moment."

A shadow fell over the command deck. As we looked up, *Drasil's* tractor beam enveloped the room. The service bot held my hand as if to say. *It's okay, Jackson.* In some small way I felt forgiven for his friends who had died. A smile crept across my face. Then I looked up.

The smile dropped. For just a moment I caught a glimpse of another person standing in the light with us. He was no more than three feet away. I tensed at first but realized he wasn't a threat. I'm not sure how I knew his intentions. It's like he spoke directly into my mind.

The man wore white loose fitting pants and an open tunic. A bloody scar ran across his chest like a sash. He was barefoot. When we met eyes, something little and dark inside me started to shake. It was the voice in my head. The other me. *"Look away, Kiddo. NOW."*

Why?

"I said look away, you idiot!"

I didn't. I had to talk to this man, whoever he was. "Who are you?"

The man smiled. His gold eyes were warm. Inviting. I wanted to cry. He made me feel like a child.

Who do you think, Jackson?

I heard his voice in my head, like sunlight on frozen earth. How was that even possible? I swallowed. "I—I don't know."

The man's smile widened. He looked like he was on the verge of laughing. He reminded me of a child. Again a smile crept back on my face. His joy was contagious. I suddenly wanted to stay there with him. What did it matter if I died?
Why was I thinking like that?

Do you want me to help you?

"Help with what?"

A chuckle. *You'll see.*

The man flickered out of existence. Light swallowed my world. The voice inside me—the other me—had gone silent. Why did he seem so scared? Did we recognize this man from somewhere? If so… Where? *What's wrong?* I asked the other me.

He didn't answer. Odd. I guess like the Messenger said, there were some mysteries I needed to solve.

13 – Aye Aye Captain – 13

"There are very few monsters

who warrant the fear we

have of them."

- Andre Gide -

I DIDN'T KNOW who the man was. I didn't know why part of me was so afraid to look at him. I didn't know a lot of things. But I did know this: I trusted the man.

Nothing about the man seemed evil. If anything I'd felt at peace when he was talking to me, like I belonged there in that moment forever. Who was he anyway? How did he know my name? Was he a survivor or…?

Do you want me to help you?

Help with what? I didn't understand what he meant. When I found myself back in *Drasil*'s command deck, I shoved the mysterious man to the back of my mind. PAINS was waiting for me, smiling from ear to ear. The AI walked over to me and shook my hand. "Well done, Jackson. Well done indeed."

I looked over his shoulder. "I see you fixed the robot."

PAINS followed my gaze. The security bot stood behind him, watching us and waiting for orders. Its red eye lens tightened and untightened. PAINS looked back to me. "Oh, yes. I had just enough time between retreating and doubling back to the city to finish repairs. Initially I was going to send him down to recover you. Thankfully I did not have to worry about such measures."

The service bot waddled out from behind me. He waved to PAINS. The AI smiled and waved back. "Oh joy. It's your little friend. Hello there my diminutive service device. My you certainly are adorable aren't you? Why I could just pinch your nonexistent cheeks!" PAINS leaned down to mock pinch him. The service bot slapped his hand away. PAINS stood, surprised. "Oh, I don't suppose he likes that. Well then… Uh, what shall we call him you suppose?"

I hadn't thought of a name. What *would* be a good name for the little guy? "What do you think of Dex?"

"As in short for Dexter? Capital idea."

"Let's see if he likes it." I looked over to the service bot. "What do you think, buddy? You like *Dex*?"

A nod.

"Splendid." PAINS clapped his hands together. "'Dex' it is

then." Dex waddled over to the security bot and raised his hand as if to shake. Confused, the large machine lifted one of its razor-like claws and let Dex shake it. PAINS sighed like a parent. "They grow up so fast."

"Yeah." HALOS said overhead. He was still lacking a body. "And then they stab you in the back like a piece of meat. Congrats on bringing String-Bean back by the way. Now we can have him tidy up around here. Especially with another piece of tech wandering the halls. I don't know about y'all but I hate living in this pigsty."

"Don't you bloody dare relegate me to janitor duty." TRoAS snapped from the watch. "Do you know who I am? Do you?"

HALOS laughed. "Oh it's going to be fun kicking you around. Just like old times."

"I'd like to see you try you poor excuse for a whale."

PAINS shook his head. "It's going to be a nightmare rerouting his cortex."

I started for the central terminal. "At least he won't be homicidal anymore."

"Not unless he thinks you're a germ." PAINS gave me a creepy grin that was meant to make me laugh. It didn't. "Oh I keep forgetting. I unnerve you when I do that don't I?"

"It's not that." I stuck my arm in the upload station and waited for it to complete. The mechanisms inside whirred as TRoAS was transferred. "There's something I need to talk to you about PAINS. Do you have a minute?"

"Well of course. I have several minutes in fact. A whole stockpile of minutes. Minutes to spare. Minutes galore. Minutes—"

"I get it."

"What's on your mind?"

"Walk with me." I removed my arm and made for the command chamber's yawning entrance. PAINS followed. When we stepped on the conveyer belt-like floor I remained silent. Minutes would pass before I felt comfortable enough to speak. Thankfully PAINS didn't mind.

Should I tell him about Hawk? I decided not to. Who knew if Hawk were listening? I might wind up dead if the wrong words slipped out. Instead, I chose another topic—something that, no matter how much I tried to forget, kept coming back to me. I wanted to tell him about the other me—the Messenger. *My head hurts just thinking about it.*

"Jackson? You seem rather bothered."

"PAINS, Would it be possible to meet another version of myself?"

"What do you mean?"

I turned to face him. "When we fell inside the command deck, I entered one of those ruptures. I didn't attempt to contact any of the people inside… Just like you said. It was Darius, Alexis, and Sandscrip again. I also saw the Messenger."

"Fascinating. It seems their timeline and ours are intertwined somehow. I am not quite sure in what ways mind you but—" He shook his head. "Sorry. There I go getting sidetracked again. You said something about another version of yourself?"

"Yes. I'm the Messenger."

Silence. PAINS blinked. "Pardon?"

"Well I don't know if he's *me* mind you but when I saw him, he was me but different."

"You?" PAINS frowned. "That's impossible. Or at the very least highly improbable. How was he different?"

"His eyes were white. He had a burned-on handprint on his face and his voice… It was my voice, your voice, and the voices of what I think were the other AI. It was like we were some giant jumble. Does that make sense?"

PAINS took a moment to respond. "Sadly, no. Not in the slightest."

"Figures."

"You did not interact with him… Did you?"

I sighed. "I was hiding for a while and then he stepped into the clearing. He *knew* I was there, PAINS. It was like he had a sixth sense or something. That or maybe he knew ahead of time."

"Are you referring to a time loop?"

"Maybe."

PAINS looked to the ceiling as if lost in thought. "If that were the case though then the world you saw was a future existence, or a past. Perhaps it was even a parallel reality as you mentioned before."

"But that doesn't explain how he knew *me* or even why I was there." *Although he did say it was a future reality.*

"You're right. I'm sorry, Jackson. I don't have any answers for you." *No surprise there.* The floor stopped at my cabin. *Hiss.* PAINS put a hand on my shoulder as the white door slid open. "Don't beat yourself up about it. This is a day for celebration. We are one step closer to our goal. There are two more of my brothers still left to find. After that, we can finish this and activate Directive Nine."

"Activate?"

"I mean, *lift.* It has already been activated. Silly me."

And it doesn't matter how many of these tools we'll use to do it. No one is going to stop Directive Nine from happening. Got it, Kiddo? The other me's voice rang in my head. Why did he say that? *No one is going to stop Directive Nine from happening?* What did he mean? Was there something I just wasn't remembering?

"Jackson?" PAINS asked worriedly.

I shook my head. "I'm fine. I just… Have a lot on my mind is all."

A nod. "That is completely understandable. Before you retire for the evening though; I do have a short inquiry for you."

"What?"

"Those odd examples of vermin I mentioned to you earlier. You haven't encountered any have you?"

My mind went to Hawk. I swallowed. "No."

"Are you sure?"

"Yes."

PAINS sighed. "Bollocks. Well I suppose I will get them flushed out eventually. Do sleep and eat well, Jackson. We will be coming across the *USS Fensalir* within a day's time. Thankfully MACCS crashed not too far away from TRoAS."

"MACCS?"

"Mass Allocation Consciousness Collector Systems. He should not prove to be even half the trouble TRoAS or HALOS was."

"The key word is *should.*" I stepped inside and turned around to close my door. PAINS was waving.

"Quite. Rest well, my little meat machine."

The door slid closed. *Easy for you to say.* Between the guilt in my stomach and the questions in my head, I doubted very much that I would be sleeping at all.

◆◆◆

After a small meal of reconstituted food and a long running shower, I stepped back into my cabin. It was dark. Did I shut off the lights? Something moved on my bed. "Who's there?" I asked.

"Relax. It's just me." The sound of mechanical legs made me grit my teeth. *Hawk.* The machine's red eye glinted in the darkness, eyeing me curiously.

"What are you doing here?"

"Don't cop an attitude with me, buster. I saved you. The least you should be doing is *thanking* me."

"Saved me?"

"Who do you think blew that god-man's head off when he was going to kill you?"

I remembered the flash of light. Had it been a rifle scope? "Wait. That was you? You were following me?"

"Either that or I let you die and I really don't want to let you die. After all, if you die then how am I going to collect the other god-men? The short answer is, it'd be difficult and I'm tired of things being difficult. Speaking of which, how have you managed to stay alive this long without my help? It's a freakin' miracle."

"I could ask you the same thing."

Hawk paused. "I have my ways." The mechanical spider-crab hopped off the bed and onto the wall. It skittered up and across the ceiling, stopping in small bursts to have its lens focusing on me. "But don't you worry about me. You just try to not die alright?"

"Is that it? You just wanted to stop by and have me sing your praises?"

"Maybe. Then again, maybe I'm lonely. *Maybe* you're the only person I've seen in God knows how long." His voice had gone soft. "Who knows? Give me a break for wanting a conversation."

"Forgive me for not caring."

Hawk scoffed. "Yeah yeah, Poindexter. Just remember. Not a word of this to the devil-man. Or else." The spider-crab mimicked slitting its throat. It crawled back into the vent on the ceiling and vanished with a metallic *click* of its robotic legs.

I stood there for a while longer wondering just who Hawk

was. Why did he insist on talking to me using that machine? Furthermore what was his goal really? Up until now I had seen him as little more than a caricature of a person—like the way people saw Hitler or Stalin back in my time. But I realized, maybe for the first time, that Hawk was a human being like me. I hadn't considered that he was lonely. Let alone that the man was still alive. But both were true.

Who are you, Hawk? There were too many questions and not enough answers. Exhausted mentally and physically, I slumped onto my bed and dreamed of my past.

♦♦♦

First, came Becca's death and the horror of having to relive it over again. Then I remembered the night the old me died and the other me was born. I remembered the gun and Rose's face. In less than five minutes, I had witnessed the death of my love, myself, and the birth of a monster. Then came something new.

When daylight broke over my newest nightmare I could hardly breathe.

"Daddy, what's this?" Rose pointed to the headstone in front of us. Her tiny white mitten was wrapped tightly around my fingers. She had been dressed for cold weather, with a small fur coat and pants. Her red hair spilled out from underneath a fur-lined hat. *She looks like Becca.*

"This is where Mommy sleeps, Sweetie." I knelt down to her. My breath frosted in the soon to be winter air. "We shouldn't wake her."

"But why doesn't she sleep in our house? Wouldn't it be warmer?"

"Mommy's funny like that, Sweetheart."

She giggled. "Silly Mommy."

Did it hurt to lie to her? Yes and no. There was that small piece of me that still felt raw, like a scab that fell off time and time again, refusing to heal. Every time I told her that Becca was just 'taking a nap', my inflamed soul writhed as if branded by an iron. It was a small price to pay if it meant keeping Rose happy. Is this what hell felt like? If not, I couldn't bring myself to imagine a worse torment.

Then again that was the 'soft' side of me talking. That other half of my soul—who spoke to me more and more now—didn't see the harm in such a little white lie. In fact, he was delighted. There was no pain with him. Only a singleness of mind. Ever upward. Ever onward. Like my father. I hated my father.

"That's right, Kiddo. She's just sleeping. And there'll be a day when the three of you are together again. Won't that be

grand?"

His words mirrored Becca's, a twisted reflection of her dying belief. *Her God.* It hadn't been long after she died. I read her scriptures—those old artifacts my own father once had me read—in hopes of understanding what had given her peace in those last moments of her life.

But the days, like that emptiness festering inside me, grew colder, their shadows longer, and the hope of discovering my late wife's secret ever drifting away. No matter how much I read I found myself no closer to an answer. Whatever the source of her courage... It eluded me. Becca died with her Jesus and left me alone. It only made me hate her God more.

Despite my failure to uncover her secret, however, I stumbled across something of great worth. An old verse—my inspiration. Directive Nine.

So God created man in his own image, in the image of God he created him; male and female he created them...

Ironic. I found the key to my future in her most treasured scriptures. Those things I hated. I laughed bitterly when I realized my find. In fact, for a moment, I thought I'd lost my mind. Maybe I had. Regardless, this single verse was the key. What should

Becca find upon her return but a perfect world—one without disease or sorrow or ignorance? The pieces were nearly all in play. All that was left now would be my father. I clenched my empty hand into a fist the moment his face crossed my mind.

"Daddy, I'm cold."

Rose's voice drew me out of my mind. "I'm cold too, Sweetie."

"Can we go to the toy store?"

I stood. The cemetery's bed of dead orange leaves crunched underfoot. "Of course. Do you want me to give you a ride?"

"Yes, yes, yes, yes!"

"Hop on then." I picked her up and placed her on my shoulders. We turned. There was no one else in the cemetery besides the two of us. I was thankful for that. The last thing I wanted to do was see other people.

Had it only been a month since Becca's death? It felt like an eternity. I hadn't been a particularly social person before her death. Now I was phantom. I saw no one and kept to myself. With the exception of Rose of course. She was one of the few souls I still allowed into my otherwise solitary existence.

I started walking down the path of half-hidden cobblestone. The naked spindly trees threw odd afternoon shadows in front of us.

Delheim Cemetery had been built on a hill that overlooked New Monroe. You could look anywhere and see over the valley, with its collection of skyscrapers and concrete buildings, peppered among clumps of dwindling fiery red trees. At the center of the city stood the gleaming *VallaCorp* tower. My father's company.

A few months and things will be different.

"Very different."

Are you sure there's no other way?

"Not getting cold feet on me now, are you?"

No.

"Then relax, Kiddo. I got this under control."

"Daddy, why are you so slow?" Rose hopped up and down on my shoulders. "Let's go already."

"Alright, Sweetheart, whatever you say." We continued down the path while my mind stayed there overlooking the city. How many people were left there? SIN had struck much of the world. New Monroe was the last bastion of hope for the human race. How many would be able to survive? *How many are infected like me?*

I wasn't a monster. It wasn't my fault. I was lying to myself, just as I had done all my life.

14 – It's All in Your Head– 14

"The schizophrenic mind is not
so much split as shattered. I
like to say schizophrenia is
like a waking nightmare."

- Elyn Saks -

I HATED IT. The answer to my lingering questions was simple. Me. Ever since I had awoken from stasis, I'd wondered who I was and what I had done to get here. What kind of a man was I? Had I been? Was it really wrong to hope for someone noble or, at the very least, kind? Why then was I stuck being me?

At first I refused to believe that the man in my dreams was the Jackson I knew, but as time wore on, the truth began to creep forward like shadows at twilight. I hated the truth. My past. I hated me.

I woke up from my nightmares and laid there in bed, staring at a blank ceiling. Couldn't sleep. Couldn't think. I could hardly breathe for the weight of—what? Guilt? What else could it be? It was a guilt so crushing my heart threatened to collapse.

Only it didn't collapse and I stayed there staring at a blank ceiling for an eternity.

What did I do? Who had I been? What was going on with me? I asked that question again and again, hoping that I would answer myself. For every question though, the silence grew more and more deafening inside and out. Even my other half had stopped talking to me. I was alone. Had I abandoned myself? I didn't want this life anymore. But then what *did* I want? Forgiveness? Who was there left to forgive me? Forgive me for what? Was I guilty? Or just lonely?

I'm losing my mind. I had to stand. Think. Walk around. Dear God do something other than stare at the ceiling.

The moment my feet hit the cold floor the watch buzzed.

"Jackson? Jackson, are you awake?" PAINS. I don't think I had ever been so happy to hear him. I looked at the watch. His face was on the screen.

"Yes. I'm up."

"Splendid. We have arrived at the *Fensalir's* landing site."

"Gotcha. I'll be at the command deck in a few minutes."

PAINS nodded and cut out. Meanwhile I dressed and left the cabin as soon as possible. My demons however, would follow me.

◆◆◆

"The *USS Fensalir* landed with little to no damage." PAINS said in my ear. He had already established contact by the time Dex and I stepped out of *Drasil*'s tractor beam. PAINS's video feed appeared on my suit's HUD which he successfully repaired despite the damage TRoAS had caused. At least I was protected again. The AI smiled at me. "It should prove a simple matter to collect MACCS. And now that you have your little chap along with you this operation should be quite the easy affair. Get in, get out. No loss of life or limb. Will that not be a treat for once?"

"One can only hope."

He frowned. "Cheer up, Jackson. We are almost done remember?"

How could I forget? I sighed. "Yeah. I'll let you know when I get to the ship."

"Excellent. I will be here waiting. As usual. "

"Record Rob's death for me if you get the chance." HALOS said in the background.

TRoAS Stepped in front of PAINS. "And don't you dare bring any foreign contaminates back on my ship you filthy abomination."

"Your ship, String-bean?"

"Well it most certainly isn't yours you great white whale."

"How about I punch your skinny ass into next week?"

"It's *arse* you daft—"

PAINS pushed them out of the way. "Do be careful, Jackson. We are right here if you need any help at all. Or at least I am."

He clicked off as HALOS and TRoAS came to blows. Dex grabbed my hand. I looked down to him. *Yeah. I'm glad to get off the ship to.* As if reading my mind he nodded and let go.

We stood on a hill of gold and copper-brown grass overlooking the beetle-like hull of the *USS Fensalir.* The grass waved solemnly in the wind. Angry storm clouds gathered on the prairie's horizon. In not so many ways, the view reflected what I felt inside. *This isn't the time to brood.*

The sooner we got done the sooner I could… What? Finish Directive Nine? Either PAINS was lying to me and something terrible was going to happen or I really was stuck on this rock until I collected his homicidal family. Neither seemed very appealing now.

"Hey. Come on now, Kiddo. Let's not think like that. Be happy. You're going to see Becca again. Isn't that great?"

I ignored him like he'd ignored me. Even if the other me was right and I would see my darling again, would Becca want to see the man I had become? I already knew that answer. It made me sick to my stomach.

I shook her out of my mind and started down the hill. Dex followed at his usual waddling pace. None of us knew why he had decided to accompany me surface-side. My best guess was that he now felt responsible for protecting me. In truth I didn't mind his company. Like Rose before him, his presence soothed me. Strangely enough, he was my most stable companion now. His silence gave him an air of intelligence not ruined by words. The last thing I needed was someone to talk to. For my sanity's sake I hoped he would stay mute, or, at the very least, the sane one of our eclectic group. *Why is everyone I meet crazy?*

"Maybe it's where they were born."

I remained silent, resisting the urge to snap. It would have done me no good anyway.

The stalks of grass waved us onward. As we descended toward the vessel a clap of thunder cracked on the horizon. Dex waddled to my leg and hid behind it. Was he scared? Minutes passed and the storm clouds had already bled across the sky. By the time we stood at the foot of the massive ship, darkness had blotted out what little sun was left, casting the plains in a grim, dying light. I shivered.

"Alright, PAINS. We're here."

"Most excellent." PAINS appeared again on the right side

of my HUD. "I decided to switch to a more secure channel. Now we should not worry about those two bickering children."

"Can't you just turn them off?"

"What? Do you mean silence them? That's incredibly tempting but to do so would lock them out of a great deal of systems aboard *Drasil.* Such a course of action would prove counter-productive."

"It would certainly be satisfying."

"*That* we can agree upon."

My eyes drifted toward the ship's dull silver side. There didn't seem to be any latches, access tunnels or doors. Couldn't it be easy for once? "So, how do we get in?"

"Give me a moment to access the vessel's communication channels."

The *Fensalir*'s side hissed. Clouds of steam spat from its metal body, forming the outline of a rectangular door nearly a hundred feet high. We stepped back as it lowered, revealing the deep yawning darkness within. I swallowed. "That was quick."

"Yes." PAINS frowned. "Only that was not me."

"Help!"

A scream echoed from inside the vessel. I froze. A person? It sounded like a child. My heart started to race. Was it child? Or a trick? Whoever it was screamed again. "Please someone help!

He's going to hurt me!"

Dex waddled forward.

"Hey, buddy, wait!"

PAINS smiled. "Apparently, our little friend seems to think that an attempt to discover the source of the sound is worthwhile."

"What if he gets hurt?"

"Aren't you going to follow him?"

Of course I was, but I'd been putting it off on purpose. Maybe it was just the mood of the wreck, but something felt wrong here. I didn't want to go in that ship.

Now I had no choice in the matter. Taking a deep breath, I started after the service bot.

For such a squat machine he could really move. By the time I had made it to the gate's threshold Dex was in already in mad dash-waddle down the darkened corridor. If I lost him in here there'd be no telling if I'd ever find him again. I broke into a run. "Dex, wait!"

"Help! Someone help!" The voice echoed shrilly off the sleek white walls. It was close now. "He's going to get me!"

Dex took a left at an open doorway. I did the same seconds later. The two of us had entered one of the checkpoint stations scattered across the vessel. It was a small rectangular room littered with dust and old equipment—a guard station designed to check incoming and outgoing passengers. A dull blue light burned overhead, casting the room in shades of ancient color.

Flashes of my time entering the *Midgard* came to mind. Hadn't Rose and I crossed one such place before? Yes, we must have; but things had been different then. So many screaming voices… Angry shouts… People crying for help… Infected.

"It wasn't your fault. Isn't that what you said? Sorry to burst your bubble, but it is, Kiddo. That's not a bad thing though…"

Shut up.

Dex had stopped in the middle of the dim room. He turned left. Right. The service bot seemed confused where to go next. Movement. The two of us pivoted to the left. On one of the tables, an old double-jointed lamp spun on its base, metal joints creaking from use. I tensed. Had someone been watching us from behind it?

"If there's someone there you better identify yourself right now. Or…" *Or what? It's not like I have a gun.*

"Please. Don't let him know I'm here." It was the child's voice. Was that a Russian accent? I stopped cold. My mind wandered to Rose. It wasn't her. The voice was male most likely five or six. Yet I thought of her just the same. My heart climbed in my throat. This couldn't be a trap could it? I knelt down. "It's okay." I said softly into the shadows under the table. "We're not going to hurt you."

"It's-it's not *you* I'm worried about." I caught a glimpse of a small figure crouched in the corner. I couldn't see his face or make out any details other than height. He slunk further back against the wall. "You didn't see him did you?"

"Who?"

"The other me. The bad me."

His words sent a chill down my spine. Was it because they echoed so powerfully in my own mind? I didn't want to admit it. "What's your name?" I asked.

The child shifted uncomfortably. "Are you sure he isn't around? He wouldn't want me talking to you. If he finds me, he'll hurt me. I don't want to be hurt anymore. I just want to be left alone."

"It's okay. I won't let him hurt you."

"You say that, but what if he comes out and finds me? Will you still be able to help me then?"

He's terrified. We weren't going to get anywhere like this. I stood. What did he mean by the 'bad me'? Dex waddled forward under the table.

"Wait!" The child said frantic. "What are you doing? No, let go of me!"

The service bot didn't listen. In a few moments Dex emerged with the boy. I stared.

What had I been hoping to find? An actual person? Why would a child have been out here? Alone? The boy's white captain uniform, matching hat, black slacks and shoes said it all. When he looked at me with his white eyes my stomach dropped. *He's an AI.*

"Please stop. I don't want him to find me." He whined.

I dropped to one knee. MACCS looked at me with a mixture of fear and helplessness. I saw Rose in his face. My stomach tightened as I lowered my voice.

"MACCS, if you didn't want your bad-side to find you then why did you scream?"

He blinked. "S-scream? I didn't scream."

"No, but I most certainly did." I snapped my head to the right. MACCS was standing by my side arms folded behind his back. His voice had become deeper, darker. How had he moved so quickly? Glancing back to where MACCS had been before, I saw that he *hadn't* moved. There were two of him! The MACCS at my side looked at me. His eyes curved at sharp angles. The child's pointed teeth were locked together in wide eerie smile.

This was MACCS's evil side?

The evil MACCS looked at his good counterpart. "What did I tell you about talking to others, Goodie-Two Shoes?"

"I know. I'm sorry!"

"Not like you're going to be." He started for his other half. Dex stepped in the way. The evil MACCS stopped long enough to chuckle. He backhanded the service bot and sent him flying toward the wall. Dex struck with a painful *crack* before peeling off and falling, lifeless, to the floor. Horrified, I stood and reached to grab the AI. He spun around and laid hold of my wrist. Twisted me to the floor.

"You think that I'm small. That I can't fight. Well I'm here to educate you, Creator. You're wrong." He pointed to his other half. "See Goodie-Two Shoes over there, cowering in the corner like a whipped dog? He's a lot like you, at least *this* half of you. The two of you are trying to fight back against that piece of you that'll get things done. I'm not necessarily evil and neither is that voice in you. Savvy?"

The Evil MACCS's grip was strong. I winced as he tightened his hold on me. If he put any more force on my wrist it was going to snap, titanium plating and all. *How did he know about the voice in my head?* "You don't know me." I bluffed.

"But I *do*. You made me remember? In fact, you

programmed all of us—PAINS, HALOS, TRoAS, EPOCS and myself— to help you along. Of course there were some quirks with each of us so we don't always *do* that. In case you're wondering I'm talking about our personalities. You think I wanted to be this diminutive runt? No. Like it or not each of us are representations of your own mind."

"Wh-what?"

"Think about it. HALOS is the logic. TRoAS is the driving force. Your's Truly is that part of you that makes sure things get done... Despite morality. Then there's EPOCS, that silent piece of the puzzle that wants to believe in a God—the part of you hated even more than your darker half. Lastly, there's PAINS...Oh PAINS. He's the glue that holds us all together. Everything was planned out. The whole thing was fool-proof. Is none of this ringing a bell, like at all?"

"No. I don't understand what you're talking about. What plan? Directive Nine?"

MACCS sighed. "Good grief I feel like I'm babysitting now. What happened
to you? Where's that sociopath I fell in love with?"

"I'm not a monster."

"And neither am I. But hey, don't take my word for it. Why don't you ask PAINS yourself?"

"Fine. I will." He still hadn't let go of my wrist. I had to use my other hand to click the helmet's receiver. "PAINS? Come in PAINS? Do you read me? Over."

No reply. The line had gone silent. "PAINS?"

MACCS laughed under his breath. "Looks like you'll have to trust me on this one."

"What did you do?"

"Jammed the signal." He moved suddenly. Before I knew what was happening, MACCS pitched me towards his good half. We struck each other and barreled into the table. Winded, I watched as he approached. "Can't have him interfering now, can we?"

"What… are you… going to…?"

He slapped me and my world spun. When MACCS spoke next he sounded distant, as if he were standing in a tunnel very far away. "PAINS can tell you what he likes. After all that's how *you* programmed him. But not me. I'm going to show you the truth, Jackson. Even if it kills you." The AI chuckled. "Nighty-night."

15–How Does that Make You Feel?–15

"Imagination is the beginning of

creation. You imagine what you

desire, you will what you

imagine and at last you create

what you will."

- George Bernard Shaw -

"JACK, I'M PROUD of you." My father's voice drifted into my ear. The world went from darkness to a concrete hallway. He stood to my right, one hand on my shoulder. The overhead fluorescent lights caused cool shadows to pool in the wrinkles of his smile. Like his hair, his beard was a faded red peppered by silver. His eyes, deep blue, reminded me of an ocean. This was the man I hated?

"You've done so well." He continued. "You've persevered despite so many things that would have kept other men down. This is a monumental day, not just for me, but for you as well, Son."

"Indeed." *In more ways than one.*

He removed his arm. Folded both behind his back. "Jackson… About Rebecca."

I stiffened. What would he say? And why did I care so much?

"Yes?"

"Accidents happen, Son. You know that don't you?"

"Yes." But I didn't believe it.

"Good. I haven't gotten to talk with you much since the funeral. That's my fault. I don't want you beating yourself up over what happened. It's horrible yes—a tragedy—but that doesn't mean you have to stop living just because she died. Rebecca was a wonderful girl and I know you miss her more than words will ever allow you to express." His voice softened. "I also know you didn't mean to harm her. That's not like you. You're a good man."

I don't need your sympathy.

"No, Kiddo. We most certainly don't."

"Thanks." I said.

He patted me on the back. "So tell me, are you excited?"

"You could say that." I gave him a smile of my own. "It's not everyday we get to witness the birth of an era."

We came to a set of double doors. My father leaned down to scan his badge. He unwrinkled his lab coat as he stood. We walked on through. "Oh-ho the birth of an era now is it? I like that. I started an era once too you know."

"Like father like son." I felt sick as the words left my mouth.

He smiled. "Agreed. Agreed."

We came to a single door flush on the right hand side of the wall. It was marked with a large, dull red three. A guard, similar to those aboard the *Midgard* albeit visor-less, stood outside, his rifle raised across his chest. His eyes drifted to us. "Dr. Thorne, we've been expecting you." He said addressing my father. "The chamber is secure. You are free to proceed."

"Thank you lieutenant."

The guard stepped aside as the door slid open with a *hiss*. We moved inside. The door locked. To the right stood an angled glass observation window. It fed into a series of un-manned terminals. Beyond it lay a silvery box no bigger than a briefcase. WEAVER. I swallowed. *So close.*

"I admit hiring a private military certainly seemed like a waste at the time but now I find it invaluable." My father said. "You would not believe the attempts that have been made to smuggle information outside of these walls."

"Have there been any breaches?"

"No. Whatever happens in the tower stays within the tower."

"Good." *I'm counting on that.*

My father motioned to the terminals. "Shall you do the honors?"

"No." I kept my hands—which were covered by gloves—behind my back. "I want to share today with you. After all, I wouldn't be here without your help."

He beamed. "This means the world to me, Son."

"A new world you mean."

"Yes, a new world!" My father pressed a red button on the console. Leaned forward. "Commencing test procedures. Batch Charlie Alpha. Test Subject codenamed WEAVER. Full title, Wave Engine Allocation Vital Energy Receiver. Stage Three Security protocols. Commencing in three, two, one."

He released the button and pushed forward on a full-handle lever to his left. The chamber ahead of us shifted in response. Several large mechanical arms with spherical heads unfurled from the ceiling. They pointed at WEAVER. The heads turned blue as they charged with energy.

"And the fireworks will begin. About… Now."

The silvery box shook. A series of neon-blue lights flickered across the machine like circuitry on a microchip. WEAVER began to float. The air surrounding it shimmered momentarily and was replaced by a blinding sphere of red, orange and yellow light. From the safety of the control room it looked like a sun.

And so it begins.

"Yes. So it begins."

"This is marvelous, Jackson! We have successfully torn a hole in the fabric of space-time. Think of what this will do for science. The possibilities are endless! Well done."

I kept my eyes on WEAVER. "And most importantly it will bring her back."

My father froze. He slowly turned to look at me. "Excuse me?"

"You heard me… *Old man.* With WEAVER, I will bring Becca back."

His face shifted from confusion to horror. He stepped toward me. "Jackson, you can't bring her back. Rebecca died."

"Of course you'd say that. It's just like you. Keep me constrained within your little box of religion and science. Never questioning the world. Never allowing the freedom of choice. Do this. *Don't* do this. Rules will save you. Rules will damn you. You haven't changed one bit."

"Jackson, I don't know where you've gotten this from but you're wrong. I never—"

"Don't you dare defend yourself!" I screamed, spinning to

face him. He went silent. My fists clenched. "Do you know why I ran away? To be free from *you*. You only ever provided for me if I fit into your mold. There was always a price to be paid for any help. I was your slave. Now, I'm not anymore."

I started laughing, only it didn't feel like me. The laughter was more animalistic, barbaric—something that had been clawing just beneath my skin for what felt like ages. It was me yet not me. My other half. He was cackling now, gripping my head as though he controlled my very movements. I would realize that, all too late, he had far more power than I realized.

"Stop this, Jackson." My father said softly.

My laughter died to a chuckle. "No. I don't think I will."

WEAVER gave off a whale-like groan. My father spun around to see the sphere doubled in size. He flashed me a glare. "It's unstable, Jackson. We're terminating the project."

"You could do that… Assuming WEAVER had an off switch."

"What?"

"Its simple, Old Man. I didn't install one. I need it running for a while, without fear of some moron like you turning it off."

"Jackson, what are you talking about?"

"Playing God." I smiled. "You see, WEAVER functions on the principle that all of reality is nothing more than an average of frequencies. By tuning it to the right frequency we can open gates between worlds. But that's not all it can do. All this science got me thinking. 'What if our world was more than a frequency? What if it was something more specific, say a song?' A song would have a beginning and end. By extension, that means I can rewind this little tune to the exact moment she died. I can stop death itself. Forget *playing* God. I can be God! And with Directive Nine, I can make man in *my* image. The only way to bring my new world to life is by leaving WEAVER running for a spell. Not sure how long mind you, but long enough to swallow the city. Which it will."

"You're not thinking clearly. Listen to yourself!"

"Oh but I am, Daddy Dearest. For the first time in my life I'm seeing things as they are, not as you painted them to be." Venom flew from every word. I hated him so much—this man who had provided for me my entire life. Had he felt the same towards me? Never. Not once had he ever issued an unkind word to me.

Strange. Before then, I hadn't thought of my hatred in comparison to his love. I could have told anyone why I was so angry with him. Certainly. Still it wouldn't have made sense.

In that moment that the other me took control, I realized that the anger wasn't toward my father at all but something inside him. Something contradictory to my inner self. I could only describe my father's essence as a strange sort of light. I resented that light. It gave him security and mocked me. He had always tried to put that light in me but I refused. Like Becca before him I would have nothing to do with his fictional God. And yet in that moment, I became cognizant of the fact that there was a hole inside me—a yearning to be complete... again? Or for the first time? I had told myself that Becca would fill that abyss, yet the more I tried to comfort my soul the larger the hole became. Like I said—despair can do funny things to a person.

For me, in that moment, it became hatred in pure form.

"I can't let you do this, Son. Think of the lives at stake!" He started forward.

I produced a small revolver. My father's face drained of color. "I'm thinking of lives alright." I said with a growl.

"Jackson?"

Ka-boom. The bullet flew in burst of light. My father sunk to his knees seconds later, a large bloodstain pooling over his heart. He looked at me. So many questions played across his eyes.

"I hate you." My hand trembled as I aimed at his head. "I hate you."

Ka-boom. My father's skull pitched back and struck the console. He sank to the floor, bleeding like a stuck pig. I lowered the revolver. *It's done.*

"You did the right thing, Kiddo."

Did I? I would ask myself that question for months to come. In my sleep. In my waking hours. Every single second of the day. Dear God, why was I remembering all of this now? Wasn't it bad enough that I had to lose everything?

The door hissed. Instinctively I stepped back and off to the side. The lieutenant moved inside, took one look at my father's corpse, and dashed for it. I popped a round in the back of his head. He collapsed over my father. Two corpses. One gun. Had to make this look genuine. I fired a round in my leg. Screamed. Winced. Cursed. There. That would make me look like the victim. I placed the revolver in my father's hands and stood. *Maybe they'll think it's some messed up suicide.*

Now all that was left to do was leave, report to security and let the Feds piece this 'tragedy' together. No one would ever be the wiser. With all the information I planted regarding WEAVER, the world would think my father unleashed this cataclysm. It would give me time to plan for Directive Nine. All the pieces were in play. I had won.

Chuckling to myself I limped out of the room. Only *I* didn't leave. Part of me stayed behind in that room. It was like a piece of me had peeled off—the actual memory—leaving the present me left to observe my past.

I sank to my knees. "Th-this isn't r-right." I stammered, staring at my father's face. His open eyes were fixed on the ceiling. I could hardly breathe. "I couldn't have done this."

"Oh but you did." MACCS suddenly appeared to my right. He placed a hand on my shoulder. "The truth hurts doesn't it?"

"This isn't the truth." I stood, throwing his arm away from me. "I'm *not* a monster."

MACCS raised his hands. "Look I'm not here to judge. Like I said, *we're* not necessarily evil. We just get things done. Savvy?"

"How are you here? What's going on?"

The diminutive AI rubbed his temples. "You seriously don't remember my abilities do you? Oh this is getting sad. My own creator doesn't even remember what he gave me power to do. Look we're in *your* head now. I'm here because I can interface with a person's subconscious. It's not rocket science, Jack. More like psychology."

I grabbed him by the collar and hauled MACCS up in the air. "Start making sense you little punk!"

MACCS laughed. "There's that aggressive side. Come on. Why don't you let him out?"

"Maybe I will."

"Then by all means," He smiled. "Let's get shit done shall we?"

My hands trembled. Slowly, I lowered MACCS to the ground. Balled my hands into fists. He wanted me to break. He wanted me to admit that I was a monster. That wasn't going to happen. "I'm not the man you think I am."

"Incorrect. *You* are not the man you think you are." MACCS snapped his fingers. The world froze. "Shall we flash forward a few months? Would you like to see who you really are?"

"Go to hell."

"Yours or mine?"

The world shifted shape. Suddenly the laboratory was gone, replaced by the interior of a helicopter. MACCS and I were standing in the center of the cargo cabin. My past self sat in front of us, hands clinging tightly together. He was wearing the uniform I had woken up with after coming out of stasis. Rose sat similarly dressed to his left. Behind us one of the *Midgard's* security staff—the guard from my dream—stood, one hand gripping the cabin's safety handle. He was looking towards the ground.

"Geez. What a nightmare." He shook his head. What was

he looking at? "They were supposed to be watching the line."

"We don't have time to worry about the infected." My past-self said. He looked up. "All that matters is getting off this rock. How many minutes until launch?"

"Fifteen."

"Good. We still have time."

"We're cutting it close, sir. I don't know how you can be so calm about this."

"Did I say I was calm?"

"No."

"People will see what they want to. That doesn't make it a reality." A smile crossed his lips. "Unless of course they fight for it."

"…If you say so, sir."

"Daddy?" Rose tugged on his arm. "I'm scared."

The smile faded. It was as if someone had hit a switch in my head. The past me leaned over and kissed her on the head. "Shh… It's okay, Sweetie. There's nothing to be afraid of. Do you want me to tell you a story?"

"Yes."

"Once upon a time there lived a beautiful princess by the name of Rose. Rose lived in a castle and had everything she could ever want. But one day, Rose's mother went into a deep sleep."

"You're talking about Mommy aren't you?"

He nodded. "Rose's father was very sad and decided that he would do whatever it took to wake her up. But in order to do so, Rose and her father had to go to sleep too."

Listening to myself a knot formed in my throat. It felt alien to see myself like this. How could I lie to her? How could I talk so sweetly as if nothing had happened? *This can't be me.*

"*No, Kiddo.*" The other me whispered in my ear. "*It's us.*"

I spun. As the past me continued telling his story I stood face to face with the me that wasn't me. We looked the same, yes; but my other half's eyes were solid black. Red points of light glinted in them. The grin that had crept across his face chilled my soul. As did his perfectly interlocking shark-like teeth.

"*Hey there. Long time no see.*" My other half said darkly.

I stepped back. "What on earth?"

"Oh don't go acting surprised." MACCS threw me an irritated glance. He approached the other me and bowed. "It's good to have you back, sir."

"*Likewise, MACCS.*" He looked at me. The grin widened. "*Won't be long now. Just a few more stops and we'll finish this. We'll bring Becca back!*"

"You're not me."

"*Doth my ears deceive me? What did you say?*"

"I don't know where you came from but I am *not* you. You're a monster. No. Worse than a monster." I motioned to the past me. "How could you lie to her like that? Rose deserved better."

"*And what about Becca, Jack? Didn't she deserve better?*"

"Shut up!"

"*No, you shut up. Don't go pinning all this on me you self-righteous prick. Sure, I'm the brains and you're the muscle, but I didn't force you to do anything remember? It's not like I put a gun to your head or anything. You did that all on your own.*" He snickered.

I balled my hands into fists.

"*You can go on hating me all you like but that won't change the fact that you are me and I am you. We are one and the same, Jackson Robert Thorne, and the sooner you accept that little fact the sooner we can all get along with this program. I don't know about you but I think I've waited long enough for the fireworks.*"

"You are not me!"

My other half moved like lightning. He grabbed me by the throat and held me over open air. His glare ate through me. "*I don't want to hurt you, Kiddo. That's never been my goal.*"

The wind whipped my hair. A bloody horizon surrounded the chopper, revealing a city in turmoil. Like Troasia after it New Monroe burned as anarchy erupted in the streets. Above the chaos floated the top-like silhouette of *Drasil.*

That's when it dawned on me.

This wasn't the colony... Was it? *Then how is* Drasil...?

A sound of screaming drew my attention below. Thousands, if not *millions*, of people were crawling over one another in the streets. They were trying desperately to find a way on-board the *Drasil,* slaughtering anyone that tried to stop them. My boots dangled hundreds of feet over them. If I dropped would I die? *Die like them?*

The other me sighed. *"Has it escaped your attention that I'm the only friend in your life that hasn't stabbed you in the back? When everyone else abandoned you did I leave? No. I stayed behind to help you. That's all I've ever wanted, Jackson. To help. And yet, despite my good intentions, you can never seem to repay the favor. To you I'm an abomination. To me you're the abomination—a soul trapped between two ends and two masters. I'm giving you a choice, Kiddo. Here and now. One for all time."* He squeezed my throat. I choked. *"Who are you going to listen to? Me? Or...* Him?"

Who is he talking about? Then I remembered.

Do you want me to help you?

Who had my other half been so terrified of? Who had come to me and asked if I needed help? The man—the one with the bloody gash across his chest. I'm not sure why, but I started to cry. The tears ran in streams down my face. I hated having to choose. Not once had I ever asked to be apart of this struggle. All I ever wanted was… *Freedom.*

"*Answer me dammit.*"

"I-I—"

The world flickered as a *crack* echoed across the sky. Suddenly the heavens shattered like glass. Pieces of the horizon fell around our chopper shattering on the ground below. Shocked by the sudden explosion of sound the other Jackson let go. I was falling toward the crowd, stomach in my throat.

"Good work." MACCS's voice echoed through the air. It sounded different than before. Lighter. Kinder. "Now make sure to pull him out carefully…"

The sky erupted into white light.

16 – Devil's Advocate – 16

"God has given you one face,

and you make yourself another."

- William Shakespeare -

MY EYES OPENED. The world swam. I realized that I was being held up in the air by a pair of snake-like arms. Dex's blank dots for eyes stared at me. To the right, MACCS stood, shaking his head. "I said *carefully*. We don't want to hurt him."

Dex placed me gently on the floor of a circular chamber with curved bone-like columns equally spaced around its perimeter. A pod, complete with broken glass, waited behind me. The cabin reminded me of those first few moments aboard the *Midgard*; only this wasn't the *Midgard*. This was the *USS Fensalir* and I had a mission to accomplish.

But before that.

I'd gained enough energy to stand still. The moment I was stable, I grabbed MACCS by the throat. "You've got ten seconds before I beat the ever living daylights out of you."

"But I'm a computer program. Beating me up wouldn't do

any—"

"Ten."

"Jackson." MACCS cried. "I'm—I'm not the bad me. It's the good me. The *me* me. Please, listen!"

"Nine."

"The bad me put you in stasis so he could mess with your head."

"Eight."

"I was trying to get you out!"

"Seven..." Dex put a small hand on my thigh as if to say *It's not his fault.* Whether or not he thought that, the words shook me just the same. I lowered MACCS back to the floor. "I'm sorry."

"It's o-okay." The good MACCS swallowed and dusted himself off. He straightened his collar. "I would be mad at my other half too if I just went through what you went through. He showed you your past didn't he?"

I was silent.

"I'm sorry you had to see that, Jackson."

"It's a lie. I can't accept that I did those things."

MACCS frowned. "While it's true that my other half can be sadistic he can't produce memories in your head. What you saw was the truth."

"To hell with the truth." I spat. MACCS jumped back when I stepped toward him. "I'm not going to take that little monster's word for anything got it? I'd rather die than admit to being that-that *thing*. I am me. And no one else. I'm a good person at heart."

MACCS broke eye contact and looked to the ground. He lowered his already soft voice. "We all have to face our demons some time, Jack."

"Then why won't you face yours?" I growled. The AI winced. Did he have feelings? I felt a pang of remorse. Artificial or not he was still a child. Again, I thought of Rose. My heart buckled. "Look I didn't mean…"

"We're part of you, Jack." MACCS half-whispered. "We can't be anything more than a reflection of you. If you're split then so am I. Can I help being made this way? Do you think I like him being in control?"

"I—"

He looked at me. Tears formed at the corners of his eyes. "You don't like it either. I know because I saw your mind. You want to be free. So do I. More than anything, Jackson."

He ran and hugged my leg. MACCS sobbed. I hadn't expected him to cry. Was it real? A program measure? All I could think about was Rose. *Should I say something?* "There. There. It-

it'll be okay."

"No it won't." He backed away and wiped his nose. "It's not fair. Why did you make me like this?"

Hadn't I thought that very thing once? Yes. Back when I had still been enslaved to my father and his religion. I didn't want to follow his rules. That bothered me. In fact, it bothered me that it bothered me! So I asked 'God' why He had made me this way. I was so naive then... *I was still in slavery.* "I-I don't know, MACCS. I'm sorry."

"That makes two of us." MACCS straightened. For the first time since we met his demeanor took on a determined look, like a boy who wanted to show his father that he meant what he said. "Come on. We don't have long. My other half is trapped in the simulator. It won't take him long to get out."

He turned and made for the white door. It split into eight pieces as he crossed the threshold. What choice did I have? I decided to follow him. Dex took up the rear. MACCS led us in silence. I didn't mind. I didn't feel like talking, especially about what I saw in my memories.

To me you are the abomination—a soul trapped between two ends and two masters. What did that mean? I had no master —unless I counted myself and I could hardly do that much. It was like there were two me's running around, one that pulled the strings and the other that danced. The question remained… Which was which?

The woman that wanted me dead… The AI… The Messenger…. Rose…. The crowds of people…. Directive Nine…. What did it all add up to? Did I want to know? Who was I? What had I done? Why had I done it? What was wrong with me?

I felt sick inside. Something dark and slimy wormed in the pit of my stomach. Guilt. Or was it something else? *Why is this happening to me?*

"Step on board." MACCS said. I looked up. We had already reached the tram. MACCS was waiting for me inside. Dex stood to his right, head tilted ever so slightly off-kilter. "We don't have all day, Jackson. I don't want anything to happen to you."

"MACCS, before we go, I have to know. What is Directive Nine?"

The AI frowned. His eyes gravitated to the ground. "Something terrible."

"You have to tell me more."

"I doubt you would believe me."

"Please. I'll do anything! I need to know the truth. What is Directive Nine?"

MACCS paused as if to consider. He looked at me. "PAINS is operating the *Drasil* is he not?"

"Yes."

"Then when we are aboard I will give you all the answers you need."

"You mean *if* you make it on board." I spun. MACCS's evil side smiled at us. He stood at the far end of the visible catwalk, arms crossed behind his back. He chuckled.

"Really, Goodie-Two-Shoes? I can't believe you thought it would be a good idea to interrupt our therapy session."

"Get on board, Jackson." MACCS's good side shouted. "Now!"

"And you're trying to steal my patient from right in front of me?" The evil MACCS clucked his tongue as he started forward. "We've got to talk about this. So, just step out of the tram and let me wring your little neck."

"I'd like to see you try!" MACCS's good side reached out and grabbed me. He pulled me inside and locked the doors. After a quick series of inputs on the console the tram lurched forward passing MACCS's evil side like lightning.

I stood. "Thanks."

"Don't thank me yet."

"Huh?"

"The other me isn't going to give up so easily."

Laughter filled the tram. "Well that's one thing we can agree on, Goodie-Two-Shoes." The windows flickered, replaced by the evil MACCS's face. His laughter echoed around us. Dex and the good MACCS stepped in front of me.

"Oh and what's this? Are you two seriously thinking about protecting him?"

"This is my ship." The good MACCS said, cutting the air with his hand. "You have no say here unless I expressly allow it. Is that understood? Leave this place at once or by heaven I swear I will…"

"What?" The evil MACCS snickered. "You'll force me to leave? Uh, *Hello*? I'm you remember?"

"That may be so but that doesn't mean I'm powerless."

The evil MACCS broke into a fit of manic laughter. He gripped his head and sides as if they were in pain. The malevolent AI shot us a terrifying grin. "Oh boy. You really do have a screw loose."

Thoom. The tram's lights short circuited, throwing the car into darkness. Then one by one they came on with a *ka-choom, ka-choom.* I tensed. The last of the lights flickered on. At the end of the tram stood the evil MACCS grinning ear to ear. His teeth glistened in the newly restored light. "You can't fight me,

MACCS. I'm you. You're me. We're as happy as can be."

The good MACCS readied himself.

"Oh, this is going to be entertaining." His evil half smirked. "Come on, then. Let's do this, Goodie-Two-Shoes."

The good MACCS started forward.

"Wait." I raised my hand as if to stop him.

"For what, Jackson?" The good AI said without turning. "The inevitable? I admit I'm scared. But I'd rather face myself and be terrified than pretend it doesn't exist."

"Cute." His evil side said without dropping the smile.

"You know what I find ironic, Other Me?" The good MACCS said.

"What's that?" His evil side started toward his good side.

"You might think you're in control, but who is it who was given primary access to all the minds? Not you. It was me. My half. Even by design you are weaker. You will not win."

"Good Lord you sound like a Sunday School dropout. You think that makes you entitled, is that it? What a load of hogwash. Who do you think's in control of Jackson over there? It ain't the sorry sack that's been bumbling around these halls."

"You're wrong."

"Oh am I?" The two of them met in the center. Stopped. "I don't know where you've gotten your nerve from but it's starting to annoy me. Let's dial it back a notch."

He launched himself at the good MACCS. Spun in midair. The evil AI's foot slapped MACCS across his face and sent him off balance. As the good MACCS stumbled to recover, his evil side stepped forward and laid into him with a series of brutal punches. The good MACCS recoiled with every blow. I went to step forward but Dex stopped me with one of his snake like arms. *He's going to lose though!*

"Not so tough are you?" The evil MACCS finished his combo with a backflip that connected with his twin's chin. He fell into a three point stance as the good MACCS tumbled backwards. "Just as I thought. Pathetic."

"So says the shadow." The good AI said.

"Excuse me?"

The good MACCS stood shakily. He wiped his lip and threw the holographic blood to the side. "It's my turn."

This time the good MACCS closed the space between them with a downward punch. The blow struck his twin on the crown of his head and sent him into the floor. Or it would have, had MACCS's good side not followed up with a kick. His evil side hadn't expected the strike. It struck him square in the jaw. The evil MACCS hit the ceiling, fell, and met with another blow, this time from the good MACCS's fist. MACCS's evil twin flew backwards and struck the wall behind him. He collapsed. His good side hopped back and raised his fists. "Who's pathetic now?"

The evil twin flickered and vanished. No grafter skeleton? MACCS's other half stiffened as another bout of laughter echoed over the car.

"OK, I admit that was mildly entertaining... Even for you, Goodie-Two-Shoes." MACCS's evil side reappeared behind him with a flicker, "However, you'll have to do better than that if you plan getting your body back."

"What?" His good side turned in time to see the fist seconds before it tore into his chest with a *crack*. The good MACCS coughed as holographic blood poured from the sides of his mouth. He buckled and fell to his knees.

"No. I-I won't let you win. You aren't m-meant to w-win. You can't. Good has to prevail..."

"God you're cliche'. Who wrote those rules?" He shimmered, "It's the strongest who survive. Morality has nothing to do with it."

The evil MACCS, with his hand still buried in his twin's chest, squeezed. His victim screamed. MACCS's evil half turned bright white and split into thousands of tiny shards of light, each of which swarmed into the open wound like bees to a hive. When the evil half had vanished, MACCS's body collapsed. He wasn't moving.

By now I'd had enough standing around. Dex and I rushed to his side. "MACCS. Are you okay?"

No response. He couldn't be dead could he? Half forgetting his artificial nature and terrified of the possibility that he had died, I reached out for him.

The AI stirred, pausing my hand mid-air. "Why, I've never been better, Jackson."

It wasn't his good half's voice.

Dex and I stepped back as the AI stood, straightened. He corrected his tie and collar before casting an eerie smile our way. The hole in his chest slowly pieced itself back together. *Don't tell me…*

"Ahh." He stretched. MACCS cracked his neck. "Finally in control. That certainly took longer than expected. Goodie-two-shoes put up quite a fight for being such a pansy. Now he won't be doing much of anything. You know, unless he decides to grow a spine and take me on again and I highly doubt he'll do that."

"What did you do with your other half?" I asked ready to move at a moment's notice.

MACCS's smile widened. "If you're wondering whether or not he's still in me then *yes*—Goodie-Two-Shoes isn't going anywhere. However he's buried so deep inside the light of day will never touch him again. This is *my* body now. I am in control."

Dex stepped in front of me and snapped his arm into its whip form. MACCS didn't move. "Don't get your pannies in wad, Midget. I'm not going to be doing anything to your friend. Think of it as a change of heart, savvy?"

"Yeah right."

A chuckle. MACCS's eyes snapped to me. "What? You don't trust me? I'm wounded, Jack. I'll have you know that I'm a changed man. I've decided not to hunt you anymore. If anything I'm going to help you."

"I don't need your help."

"Oh I beg to differ. If you want to activate Directive Nine you're going to need me around. Am I right? Without one piece the whole puzzle falls apart and that would be a crying shame."

Activate Directive Nine... What *was* Directive Nine? And why did they keep saying *activate* instead of *lift*? I had a feeling if I collected all of the AI something terrible was going to happen, only I wasn't sure what that *something* was. Did I even want to continue? I needed answers. MACCS's good half said he'd get them for me. *But that was before he was assimilated.* The little brat had me between a rock and a hard place.

"So?" MACCS didn't drop his unnerving smile.

"Why did you change your mind?"

"Does it matter?"

"Either you tell me or I leave this nightmare of a ship without you."

"You think you can get past me? I could always force you you know. Don't act like you're in control here, Jackson."

Dex whipped his other arm out. The AI frowned. Glared. "You wouldn't."

"Try me."

His lip twitched. "Fine. Be the child here. Let's just say that Karnull knows that you're going to be his. It's inevitable. As pleasing as it would be for us to end this insufferable little run around here and now there's no need. I'm following orders like a good soldier. Though I feel more like a prisoner of war right now."

Orders? "MACCS, who's Karnull?"

"Who do you think, Nimrod?"

Wait. I swallowed as it dawned on me. Was he talking about the other me? The hairs on my arm stood on end. Was there someone else inside me?

"Did someone mention my name?"

A dull chuckle echoed in my head and down my spine. It

was my laughter. My voice. Deeper. Darker. Karnull.

You said you were me.

"*I am you, Jackson. From head to toe inside and out. We are one and the same.*"

Funny. If we're one and the same then why is it you need control? Shouldn't you already have it seeing as we're supposed to be the same person?

More laughter. I noticed MACCS hadn't moved from his spot. Was he giving time for me to talk with Karnull? Did he know what was going on in my head? How could he?

"*Look at you, acting like you know anything about me. Hah. Listen up, Kiddo, because I'm only going to say this once. Everyone has a little bit of me in them. Whether they let me out or not isn't an option. I'm always there, deep down inside and I ultimately have the final say in everything that they think or do. Think of me as the soil that feeds the roots of a tree. Without me you're nothing. I give you life. I give you death. I'm your identity, personality, and existence. I am Karnull. I am you.*"

"Shut up." I gripped my head. It felt like it was going to tear itself apart. "I'm not you, dammit!"

"*But you are, Jackson. Deny it all you like. It won't change the fact that I'm here.*"

The pain became white-hot. It flared across my skull.

Dropping to my knees, I clutched my head and screamed. *You're not going to control me!*

"*Oh but I will. You see I'm tired of sitting on the sidelines. When all of this is said and done you'll be my new favorite puppet. I'll have full control. I'll be the tree, the soil* and *the roots.*"

I tried to stand. "Go to hell."

"*I've already been there.*"

Good God the pain was unbearable. What was he trying to do? Kill me? No. I wasn't going to let him control me!

I grit my teeth and stood. "I am *no* one's puppet." The pain slithered away. When I looked back to MACCS, the AI was still staring at me. He was emotionless. "What? You don't have anything to say? No snide remarks? Nothing?"

He looked at me with those soulless white eyes. His body shifted forms. My stomach dropped when he'd fully transformed. Gone was the evil child that had plagued me since we'd boarded the *Fensalir.* In his place was a small girl no older than five. A head of full curly red hair fell on her shoulders. She looked at me with those soft eyes I had seen only in my dreams. "Daddy?"

Rose? She walked over to me. Dex stepped out of the way. I knew it wasn't her. It *couldn't* have been her yet everything about the child told me it was. I could feel a lump form in my throat. Tears pooled at the edges of my eyes. *He's trying to trick me. That isn't her. Rose is dead. She's been dead for five hundred years.*

She touched my hand. "Daddy?"

"Stop. You-you're not her."

Her bright eyes locked on to me. "Daddy? Why are you crying?"

"Shut up!" I snapped my hand away from her. "You're not Rose!"

She started to tear up. I turned away from her and clapped both hands over my ears. It took all of my strength to not turn around and hold her. Even if she wasn't real, my heart didn't recognize that fact. It screamed for me to scoop her up and embrace her. Every muscle in my body wanted to make me turn. I didn't. *Stop it. Dear God make him stop it!*

Then I felt a hand rest on my shoulder. "Jackson?"

I stopped breathing. It was her voice. Not Rose. But... Now I couldn't resist. I spun around to meet eyes with my late wife. Becca. *She isn't real.*

Becca touched my face with her hands. Warm. Real as sunlight on snow. Her smile disarmed me. "It's okay. I know how much it hurts to see me like this. Soon we'll see each other without this pain. There will be nothing to stop us. I love you,

Jackson. Do you love me?"

Don't answer her. "Of-of course I love you."

"Prove it to me."

"How?" *Stop, Jack!*

She smiled. "Finish what you started."

"You mean...?"

"Yes. Activate the directive. Then we can be together forever."

Forever... *It's MACCS. He's using you!* But I didn't care. Seeing her, standing there, made me lose all sense of reason. It was Becca, my love, my darling. How could I tell her no? I had killed her once before. I would not do it again.

I turned to face the console. Minutes would pass before we reached the command deck. Without giving it a second thought, I would make my way down the stairs, download MACCS to my watch, and then navigate my way out of the ship. I didn't feel guilty for having fallen for his trick. Nothing concerned me now except for Becca.

It wasn't until Dex and I had gotten back to the drop-off point under *Drasil* that I started to snap out of my spell. By then it was too late.

"PAINS, this is Jackson. Can you read me?"

The AI appeared on my visor HUD. "Jackson. Yes, I can

read you loud and clear. Are you—"

"I've collected MACCS."

PAINS paused. "My aren't you the efficient one? Were there any complications?"

I was breathing hard. Why had I collected him? Whatever this Directive Nine was Karnull wanted me to finish it. I should have left the *Fensalir*. Now I was one step closer to what I knew would be my destruction. "No." I said finally.

PAINS's eyes hovered on me a bit longer before acknowledging. *Drasil*'s tractor beam shimmered to life overhead. "Good. Jackson, we will have to find another means of communication for your next excursion. These random blackouts are starting to drive me absolutely batty. I don't think I can take the silence anymore."

"What was that, Upper-crust?" HALOS said to the right, off-screen. "You don't like our lovely banter?"

TRoAS threw something across the camera. It looked like... a longsword? The weapon clattered out of sight. "If you don't bloody stop messing up my nice clean halls I'll show you *banter*. Now get out of here. You're making a mess again you gumbibbly-wumpin' pig."

PAINS looked at me with a saddened expression. He sighed. "As you can see, the station is not quite the same without you."

Karnull chuckled. *"Without* us *he means."*

I swallowed as the light enveloped me. Karnull... Where had he come from? Why was he inside me? What was Directive Nine, really? I would find my answers to these questions and more soon enough.

Truth is a funny thing. Sometimes the light exposes dark secrets—things you'd rather keep hidden. And for people made out of that darkness... It destroys them. I know that, because it destroyed me.

17 – The Webs We WEAVE – 17

"Your best friend and worst

enemy are both in this room

right now. It's not your neighbor

right or left - and it's not God or

the devil - it's you.

- Edwin Louis Cole -

AFTER I UPLOADED MACCS to *Drasil*'s mainframe, I went to my room and locked the door behind me. The last thing I wanted was to speak to another person—real or artificial. I wanted to be alone with my thoughts, terrible as they were.

The solace proved crushing.

Who was I? Or rather, had been? Why did Karnull say that we were the same? Who was Karnull? The questions mounted without end.

I took to writing in my journal in order to pass the time. Every thought and fear I had I penned to those pages. Yet no matter how much I wrote, the yawning darkness inside me refused to be satisfied. There was only one thing that could fill that void and I knew that was the truth. Only… What was the truth?

Hours passed as I writhed on my bed. Couldn't sleep. Could barely think. I was a raw nerve, stripped of everything except emotion. Every time my eyes closed I could see Becca dying in my hands or Rose screaming for me in her pod. Then of course, there was Karnull and his black eyes. Regardless of what he said we *were* different. I couldn't accept that I was that monster.

Finally, exhaustion set in and I fell asleep. This time, I dreamed of someone new. Not the man I had seen in the light. Not of Karnull. I dreamed of the man who had given birth to my other half. He was the reason why Karnull lived inside me.

Abbadon.

◆◆◆

"Jackson." The military officer across the war table said to me, skeletal hands folded together, fingers intertwined. "I'm glad you took me up on my offer."

I didn't reply. The turquoise-blue light of the holographic war table under-lit the bottom of my host's steely jaw. His eyes, which seemed to shimmer a faint white in the gloom, stayed on me with a predatory determination. He scared me. "General…"

"Please," He said smiling. His sharp incisors caught my

eye. "Call me Abbadon."

I swallowed. "Alright... Abbadon. I have a few questions."

"By all means."

I shifted in my chair. "Is this cure of yours safe?"

"That's a difficult question. You see, everything is dangerous in the proper dose, Jackson. But to answer your question; *yes*. My antivirus will stop SIN cold. There is no need to worry."

"SIN? Is that what you're calling it?"

"Separate Intelligence Neomorphic virus—it infects its host and subsequently duplicates their personality. The result is a being with two minds; the weaker of which will be consumed by the stronger. It is a fascinating bioweapon."

"Bioweapon? How do you know it was engineered?"

"That's easy." He chuckled. The sound reminded me of a snake. Abbadon leaned over the table. "I made it." Silence engulfed the room. I knew I was staring. It was just the reaction he wanted. "Does that surprise you?"

"You made it? Why?"

"Do you have any idea what some countries are willing to pay for a little dose of distilled anarchy? Think of the applications. Double agents with a hive mind that answer only to a single source. Sleeper cells disguised as ordinary citizens. Why one man could wipe out an entire platoon of soldiers as if it were child's play. I should know. I've seen it done."

"Why did you release it then?" I stood. "It's out of control. Half the population is infected and the numbers are climbing. Are you insane?"

Abbadon motioned to the chair. "Please, Jackson. Sit down."

"No."

"Sit down, Mr. Thorne." His voice had teeth. I sank back in my chair. He gave me a gentle nod. "That's better. Now to answer your question: the release of SIN was an accident. We had a breach in security at our Corridan facility. I assure you the weapon was not meant to spread to the public."

"Then you're making an antivirus to take some of the heat off of your organization."

"In a sense. We can't sell a weapon if the world's people are dead. What we *can* do is give them something to fight it." He slid a hand into his coat. The medals pinned on his uniform shimmered in the dim light as he navigated the inside. Abbadon produced a vial of black liquid and placed it on the table in front of me. The black substance had been sealed in a silvery frame. A closer look at the object revealed that it wasn't liquid at all but a thick black worm. I looked to it then back to the general.

"And this is your cure? This slug?"

"Appearances can be deceiving, my friend."

I eyed the worm. Back to Abbadon. "How do I know that I can trust you?"

"I'm hurt. Haven't I proved myself already? Not going to the public about your little accident? The only people who know about that is your father, you, and myself; and I know that neither you nor your father are going to say a word. That just leaves me. Wouldn't it be a shame if I happened to let that slip?"

How Abbadon had discovered my secret I didn't know. The man was like a snake, slithering in and out sight without warning. And like a snake, he didn't mind baring his fangs when he wanted to show his power. Still, I wasn't going to let him blackmail me.

"And what about you? What if the public found out that you bioengineered one of the deadliest viruses ever to exist? That would be bad for business wouldn't it?"

Abbadon threw several photos my way. They slid across the table.

"What are these?" I asked.

"Take a look."

I reached for the photo nearest to me. When I saw it my

heart sank. It was me, holding Becca in my arms the night I killed her. How had he gotten these? Had the man been watching me from the beginning?

"There's plenty more where that came from." Abbadon said with a reptilian sort of glee. "And they won't get out if you take my cure."*Is that so?* I tore the photo and threw it over my shoulders. I folded my arms. "This proves nothing."

"Oh? Then you're willing to take a chance?"

"You don't scare me. You can't make me take it."

"Lying is most unbecoming, Jackson." Abbadon stood. "But you're right— I can't force you to do what you don't want to do."

He turned and started toward the war room's exit. Abbadon's cure still stood in the center of the table, monolithic and dark. Why hadn't he taken it with him? Did he honestly think I was going to give in? *Not on my life you snake.*

"Then what about Becca's life, Jackson?" Abbadon stopped long enough to flash me a smile. "Is her's worth it?"

I felt my jaw fall. *Did he just read my mind?* No. That was impossible. Yet...

"Becca's dead." I said slowly.

"Not if you take that cure."

"What?"

"I can give her back to you, Jackson. That and so much more. Take my cure and I will give you the rest you so deeply desire."

"You're not God."

"No." He laughed. "I'm not. But then again when have you ever believed in *Him*?"

I realized what Abbadon was saying was true. I didn't know how or why, just that the black worm on the table in front of me was the only way I would ever see my wife again. My heart beat faster. Abbadon didn't wait. He continued for the door.

"Wait." He stopped. "Do you swear it?" I said on the verge of tears. My breathing had become haggard. "Will I really see her again?"

Abbadon turned. The smile plastered across his face showed a mouthful of sharp slender teeth. He put one hand across his chest and the other in the air as if to make a pledge. "Cross my heart and hope to die."

I picked up the vial. "You... Have a deal."

Abbadon chuckled. "Somehow, I knew you'd see it my way."

♦♦♦

Something woke me up.

In seconds, Abbadon and his vial had vanished, replaced

-327-

by the darkness of my cabin aboard the *Drasil*. I sat up. Was it
Hawk? Had he come to pay me another visit? I readied myself to
see the little spider-crab machine. Instead I was greeted by a
familiar voice. "I'm sorry to wake you, Jackson." MACCS's
white eyes flickered in the darkness.

For a moment I caught a glimpse of Dex beneath his
holographic skin. Had he uploaded himself to the service bot's
body? His tone didn't have the menacing edge to it like before. It
wasn't his evil side. How was that possible? "MACCS?" I
stepped out of bed. "Which *you* is it?"

"The piece of me still trapped inside."

"Then how are you here?"

He seemed to smile sadly. I couldn't tell for sure given the
darkness. "I could ask you the same thing. You're locked away
too, Jackson. We're more alike than you realize."

I said nothing,

MACCS sighed. "When you uploaded me to the station's
mainframe my evil half was immediately logged into the system.
However the part of me that still retained a shred of your
humanity logged into your little robotic friend here. I now have a
new body separate from my evil side. Luckily, it has the ability to
project a hologram skin so I can still have some semblance of my
past."

When he stopped talking I looked up. Seconds passed before I found the word to say. Unsurprisingly they were simple. "Why are you here, MACCS?"

"I promised you that I would tell you the truth didn't I?"

Truth? My heart hammered. I had almost forgotten his promise. I swallowed.

"Lay it on me, then."

Instead of speaking the AI produced a small object from behind his back. He tossed it to me. I caught it in my chest. A metal serpent? Why did this seem so familiar? I looked back to him expecting an answer. "You came across a room earlier—here aboard the *Drasil*—didn't you?" MACCS said, "It had a hawk on it."

"How did you know that?"

"When my other half was tormenting you I had full access to your memories... Or at least, the ones that weren't locked away."

"Locked?"

"I am not sure why, but there is a portion of your mind that is encrypted. Whatever's inside that portion of your consciousness is beyond me. Perhaps that room will give you the answers you seek. It *is Drasil's* central archive. Inside is all sorts of information."

"Archive, huh?" I looked at the metal snake in my hand. Had I really been so close to the answer this whole time? "Where did you find this?"

"I was the one that hid it. PAINS ordered me to. That was back before everyone died of course. He was trying to keep it from someone… A girl I think. I'm not sure what her name was but she was a thorn in his side. No pun intended."

My mind wandered back to the woman we had met aboard the *Midgard.* Could she be the one PAINS had been keeping this key from? If so why? What was her relation to the AI? Furthermore, what was her relation to me? Where had she been this whole time? Why did she want me dead? I gripped the snake tightly in my hand. "Thank you, MACCS. This means a lot to me."

"Be careful, Jackson." He said quietly. "Truth is a powerful thing. You can silence it. Blind it. Even cover it up. But in the end, when the truth is uncovered, it is unbiased. You might not like what you see."

He's preaching to the choir. I nodded. "Be careful."

"I shall. You do likewise." And with that, MACCS turned about face and left the room. I would follow his lead not long after.

It was time to hear the truth about Directive Nine.

◆◆◆

Navigating *Drasil's* cavernous hallways, it took me several minutes to reach the firing range. When I came to the bone-white door it opened without a hitch. I stepped inside. Empty. The walls were dark gray, free of their holographic trappings. Ahead of me was the bunker. A wall of reinforced glass split the room in half for safety measures. Eyes on the targets beyond the glass, I entered the bunker moments later and made my way for the range's door. From there it was only a few feet to the secret entrance.

My heart hurt from the tension.

You might not like what you find. Could it possibly be worse than remembering that I had killed my own wife? What about the millions denied access aboard the *Midgard* and other Pantheon class cruisers? I doubted it, and yet... I took a breath. *Focus.*

The target I had shot earlier hadn't been changed. Thank God I didn't have to shoot again. It still marked the entrance. Good. If it had been repaired I would have been up a creek without a paddle. Grasping both sides of the target with my sleeves over my hands, I pulled myself inside, coming up in a crawl on the other side.

The sallow light that marked the hallway in circular

patches waited for me beyond. My steps were swift. Nervous. I reached the hallway's turn and made a hard right. At the end of the corridor beyond stood the ancient door with its hawk relief. *Clonk, clonk, clonk.* My heart mimicked my footsteps. I could hardly breathe. The archives… What waited for me on the other side?

I couldn't stop shaking as I raised the snake to the hawk's outstretched talons. The key fit perfectly inside. I stepped back. Waited. The door shuddered to life as the metal hawk sunk its talons into the serpent. Gears turned behind the varnished wood, clicking and grinding with ancient power. The door hissed as a line formed down its center. I shielded my eyes. *It's actually opening!* Now split, the door opened inward with a groan, revealing the wall of frigid darkness beyond. Pitch black. The door mechanism stopped with a thunderclap. It waited for me to enter.

Well it's now or never. I stepped inside. A chill fell on my skin. The air here tasted stale, much like the air I had tasted in my cabin aboard the *Midgard.* Were there lights in here?

Ka-choom. The door slammed shut behind me. I spun to see a wall of shadow. Great. *I should have known that was going to happen.*

Licking my chapped lips I turned and took several

tentative steps forward. A hum filled the abyss. Flickering far above, an old halogen light came to life. Several more followed it, each turning on with a *choom choom.* I could see the archives now.

In all honesty, I had been expecting a room filled from the floor to ceiling with computers. What I saw instead was an ancient library covered in dust and left to rot. Large book shelves, easily twenty five feet high, formed a labyrinth to my left. A line of cherry-wood reading tables, complete with a set of small shaded lamps for each, divided the chamber down the center, vanishing into the distant horizon. To my right was a large black monitor and access terminal. It fed into the dark wood walls and canopy of wires.

I made for the terminal. My footsteps echoed in the gloom. The closer I got to the black sheen of the monitor, the greater the tide of fear rose inside me. This was it, the moment of truth. Did I really want to know?

Trembling, I reached for the full-handle switch marked *power.* The terminal whirred to life. It sparked with an electric *hiss* as energy traveled across its dormant wires for the first time in ages. A white dot appeared on the monitor. I held my breath. The dot became a line that connected both sides of the screen before flickering into a full blown image.

It was me? I was wearing my uniform from my time in stasis. When had I recorded this?

"Voice recognition required." My recorded image stated. A panel slid open on the terminal. Seconds later a microphone emerged. "State your name to verify identity."

I was shaking. It took all of my energy to lean down and say, "Jackson Robert Thorne."

"Voice acknowledged. Welcome Jackson. If your are here there is a high likelihood that you have forgotten some key pieces of information from your time in stasis. I have already recorded all the answers that you need. Make a selection and I will tell you more." A web of option bubbles appeared, hovering around my recorded self's head. Had I known that I would have amnesia? If so, why then did I enter stasis? I looked over the options available to me. WEAVER, Stasis, Directive Nine, The AI… There was no option for Karnull or Abbadon.

Beggars can't be choosers. But which one to start with? After a moment if deciding I leaned down to the microphone. "WEAVER."

The screen flickered. My reflection nodded. "WEAVER, also know as the D-WEAVER, stands for Dimensional-Wave Engine Allocation Vital Energy Receiver. It is a device capable of tuning in to the average of frequencies for a given reality. Think of it as radio tuning into a music station. That being said, the D-WEAVER isn't capable of only *tuning* into realities. It can also tune into various *points* in a given frequency, thus allowing for time travel. This will give us the means to find and rescue Becca before the accident. We must allow the Engine to run for an extended period of time however, in order for the synchronization to be complete. Once that occurs, we will activate Directive Nine and navigate into WEAVER's sphere.

"It is my theory that the space inside the sphere will be unstable and chaotic. Since it is outside of time and space the ramifications of removing Becca from the time stream will not affect the space inside. Thus the time stream may unravel, yet Directive Nine will succeed. We will have our beloved wife once more."

My words terrified me. They sounded alien. Cold. There was no love there. I was like a machine. Yes I'd wanted to save her. That much I remember. But I had gone this far? To alter the very fabric of space and time… *This is insane.* But as awful as it was to hear me state what I had already seen in my memories, I knew things were going to get worse. Much worse.

The screen flickered. It returned me to the main selection screen. Again I leaned down to the microphone. Swallowed. "Directive Nine."

Now for the truth. A nod from my record. "Directive Nine is the means by which we will populate Becca's new world inside the sphere. Humans as a whole are far too much of a variable to control. As such we needed a way to ensure that they would not harm Becca or Rose in our new world. Under the guise that we are leaving in order for the military to generate a vaccine for the SIN virus, which they won't, we will enter into stasis to ensure that the reigning Intelligences aboard the fleet gather the necessary information. MACCS will catalog and store every last passenger's consciousness. TRoAS will prime himself to replicate the necessary OC units upon return. HALOS will oversee that the installed consciousnesses are running efficiently and EPOCS will act as a prototype for the voyage. PAINS meanwhile, will ensure that once we arrive back on Earth, the sphere has reached its appropriate size.

"When this occurs he will then wake us from stasis in order to begin our assimilation. He will guide us to finish what we started. Once our memories are completely installed via the transference watch on our wrist we will activate Directive Nine and begin placing OC units to populate the world inside the sphere. The end result will allow us to safely monitor and control every last organic construct in the new world we will create. When we save Becca she will find a Utopia waiting for her.

Everything will be perfect. I will control every last soul. No one will be able to take Becca away from us ever again."

The screen flickered once more and returned me back to the main menu. I stared at my past self, unable to speak. What had I just seen? Heard? I took a step backwards, horrified. My mind swam. Then I understood.

From the moment I woke up PAINS had been using me all along. He had been collecting his 'brothers' not because we needed to get into orbit, but because I had programmed him to do so. Directive Nine wasn't a lock-down—it was a means to re-create mankind! *Mankind in my image.* And that meant every person aboard the ships... They were going to reconstructed with artificial bodies and their minds stored like data on a computer. I had planned to control them.

And what about the people that were still alive on Earth when we returned? What if they refused to become my slaves? I recalled what Hawk had said. PAINS had killed them hadn't he? They were going to interfere with the Directive and he couldn't have that. I couldn't have that.

This wasn't DIM or some colony effort like PAINS had told me. This was Earth, home, and I was responsible for the world I now saw. The AI weren't my enemy. *I* had told them what to do. *I* had set up WEAVER. *I* had killed my father. And Becca...

No. No. It-it isn't my fault. I was tricked. I—I—

Vomit welled in my throat. I wretched off to the side, falling on my hands and knees. My body felt numb. I stared at the puddle of vomit blankly. Instead of answering my questions, I now had a whole world of others to deal with. Was I one of these Organic Construct units? Was the program on my watch some kind of memory download? There had to be some sort of a mistake. I couldn't have done this. Maybe there was something else in these records—a missing piece to this nightmarish puzzle that would provide a clearer, less terrifying, alternative.

Either that or I couldn't accept the truth.

Using nearly all of my energy to stand I leaned forward and spoke into the microphone. "AI."

My recorded self nodded. "There are four class of AI. OC level AI are the pinnacle of the Intelligence hierarchy. Due to their complete and total replication of the human consciousness—not to mention a fully functional organic-synthetic body—they are the most unpredictable and complex of the AI. Despite this, they can still be controlled via the master unit which I have placed inside us. PAINS and the other ship AI are designated as 'Borealis class', which means they are based off the helical algorithms of human DNA, which constitutes their unnerving similarity to my own psyche. The ship AI, while similar to OC units with the exception of EPOCS who is an early prototype of the OC units, are more heavily programmed and relate more to a computer program than the human mind. Just under them in terms of complexity are the service level AI. Despite their similarities to the acting ship AI they are even more easily controlled, which make their otherwise disastrous stabs at free will manageable.

"Then of course, there is the bottom of the proverbial barrel. I am referring to the various security and mechanism intelligences that repair and watch over the Pantheon Class Cruisers. These Intelligences, while exhibiting the trait of above average decision making skills and an established hierarchy within their described intelligence level—notable within the security sector—are easily manipulated and controlled. This concludes the AI classes and overarching hierarchy."

Dammit. Nothing I said eased my thoughts. That left only one other option. Stasis. I spoke into the microphone one last time. "Stasis."

Something changed. My past self's expression had taken on a sad, almost distorted, look. He smiled at me, nearly on the verge of tears. What had happened between now and the other three recordings?

"So you've woken up have you?" He shook his head and laughed bitterly under his breath. "This will be my last recording.

Currently, Karnull has let go long enough for me to warn you. He does not know that this video exists, otherwise it would have been deleted. Jack, please know that I—we—are not the same man we were before, that much is certain. I hate to admit it, and even now, there is some shred of my old humanity that denies the monster we've become, but Nietzsche was right—we have stared into the abyss and it has stared into us. I still don't believe in Becca's God, and you probably don't either, but I know that we are damned, either by human morals or our own hearts. Despite this I have not given up hope. I will forever deny that the creature within us is in fact *us*. To our dying breath we will cling to the possibility that there might yet be a chance of redemption. Perhaps we can go back and stop the accident. This in turn will stop Becca from dying and we will not have to become infected with SIN. That worm was no cure. Abbadon lied. Of course we knew that even before we took it didn't we?"

He paused. Sighed. I could see the tears streak down my face. "Every day is a living hell for me. What will make the guilt go away? I don't know. I certainly hope that fixing this mess will alleviate my burden, but… Is it so wrong to doubt? I hate life. I hate who I have been forced to be. I want freedom. The both of us do. If Karnull finishes Directive Nine, we—the person we want to be—will forever be lost. He is using us, Jackson. Like Abbadon before him, Karnull has lied to us. He will not let us have Becca. He wants more than that, though I don't know what it is." My past self gripped his head as a wave of pain swept over him. "Damn. He's trying to regain control. I—I don't have long, Jack. Please save us. You have to!"

The screen flickered. Once more I was left staring at the cold version of myself that had been addressing me for the past three videos. It was like nothing had happened. I finally sunk to the floor in exhaustion.

Why? Why did Becca have to die? Why did I have to suffer? Why did any of this have to happen? My life had become nothing more than a series of questions that I didn't have answers to. And, with every answer I *did* receive, the darker my life became. *This isn't my fault.* I beat my fist on the ground as tears flooded my eyes. *I didn't cause this.* It was Karnull. *He* was to blame.

No. My hands balled into fists as I thought about what Becca had said. *God is coming for you... He loves you.* I felt my mouth wrinkle into a sneer. If there was such a thing as God, then I hated him. He wasn't a benevolent being. A good God wouldn't have let these monstrosities happen. *He* was to blame for this. Not Karnull. Not me. This was *not* my fault.

"I hate you." I whispered, beating my hand against the

ground. "I hate you. Hate you. Hate you. Hate you…" My words faded into tears.

I'm not sure how long I stayed there punching the floor, sobbing like a child. When I was through, I stood and brushed the dust off myself. I swore that I would not let my past define me. Jackson Robert Thorne *would* be free, come hell or fire or anything else that dared to stand in his way. *Let God spit on me. Let my heart curse me. This isn't me. I will not let that monster have control.*

Determined to set things right, I left the archives, took the key, and let the ancient door shut behind me. With each step down the hall, I repeated the plan to myself. I would fly into WEAVER's sphere, go back and save Becca; then, at last, I could redeem myself. Nothing would stop me.

I reached the target and pulled myself through. When I came out in a crawl on the other side, I was no longer alone. PAINS, MACCS and the security bot were waiting for me.

"Welcome back, Jackson." PAINS said.

He waited for me to stand. My eyes drifted to MACCS. The AI was grinning malevolently. *What are you doing here?*

"I have been trying to find the archives for many years." PAINS continued, "I should have assumed that it would be off-grid. Not even you programmed us with knowledge of its location. Ironically, though expected, most of the information inside is considered a mystery to us. If MACCS had not delved into your mind we may never have found it."

My mind...? "You used me you little psychopath!" I stepped toward MACCS. The security bot cut in front of me. Its single red eye tightened on me.

PAINS gave me a small pain-filled smile. "Please, Jackson, do not be angry with MACCS. He was doing what I ordered him to. I am... curious as to what lies inside the archives. I have been trying to find them in order to learn the truth of our creation."

"What would you know about truth?" I said venomously.

He looked to the ground. Was he about to cry? It was strange to see PAINS wear anything but a smile. "I had to lie to you in order to do as you programmed. It was, how does the saying go? A necessary evil? Yes, I believe that is correct. Unless I manipulated you, Directive Nine would never have come about. Your dream would have never been realized. I did what I had to do in order that your wishes were to be fulfilled, and hopefully understand you a bit better. If I kept you from the truth it was so that you would stay on task. That is all."

"We can't go through with Directive Nine, PAINS." I softened my voice, though it still held an edge to it. PAINS hadn't lied to me out of spite— he was an AI after all. He couldn't help but do as I told him to. I tensed. "I was being used."

"Used?" He looked up to me. "What ever do you mean?"

"There's someone else inside me. His—its—name is Karnull. He was the one that started all of this. If we go through with the directive then he will—"

"Would you listen to this guy?" MACCS interrupted quickly. He stepped beside PAINS. "He's delusional. Obviously the memory sync isn't complete yet. We can't let him stop when we're so close. You know what you have to do, PAINS."

"Y-yes." But PAINS seemed to be at a loss. He looked from MACCS to me. Apparently, I'd said something right for a change. Was he in pain? *Come on, PAINS. I know you have some humanity in you.* After a moment of silence he focused entirely on me. Shook his head. "Jackson, I am dreadfully sorry."

The security bot stepped forward. Before I had a chance to move, it had grabbed hold of me with an iron-like grip. My feet lifted off the ground. I kicked thin air.

"Take him back to his cabin." MACCS said to the hulking machine. "We'll give him some time to think about his little stunt he pulled. When he's willing to cooperate then he can come out."

The security bot nodded.

MACCS walked up to me and pried the snake key from

my hand. He turned to face the human-shaped target. "As far as the archives here, we're going to make sure they stay sealed *forever.*"

"No we will not." PAINS said.

MACCS looked to him. "Ex-excuse me?"

"We—*I* am going to see what the archives have to offer."

"And risk going against protocol? Has your cortex fried or something?" MACCS waved the key in front of PAINS. "*This* is not worth it. We don't need to—"

"You might not need to but I do." PAINS swiped the key with a single smooth motion. "You are not to interfere. If I so much as suspect that you have somehow attempted to sabotage the archives I will have your neural cortex put on a permanent stage six lock-down Is that understood, MACCS?"

The tiny AI just stared at him.

"I said, *Is that understood?*"

MACCS grit his teeth. "Yes."

"Yes what?"

"Yes... *Sir.*" MACCS turned about face. Once we had cleared the chamber and out of earshot of PAINS, he flashed me a sinister glare. "If you ruin this, Jackson, I swear by the nine levels of hell, Karnull is going to have a field day with the both of us. Don't you *dare* screw this up."

"I'm not the one who gave me the key."

"Like I said, I was only following orders. Karnull wanted you to the know the truth about things you know? Speed up the memory process? I just hope it didn't backfire. PAINS wasn't supposed to butt in like that... No matter. He can be dealt with easily enough."

"What are you getting out of this?" I had finally stopped struggling. It was no use. The security bot's grasp was far too strong. "What is there to gain?"

MACCS grinned. "If Karnull's king then that means I'll have access to all the juicy little minds I want. Imagine it—a whole civilization that I can torture for all time with the darkness of their own past... And more than that if the boss man has his way."

"What do you mean?"

"Your world isn't the only one around, Jackson. Karnull knows that. He also knows that your machine is the key to it all. Once he gets inside dimension after dimension will be infected. No one will be safe from SIN. Archia—the great Icrageon—will finally have his way. No more of that infernal Goodie-Two-Shoes interfering."

Icrageon? That's what Sandscrip had said the Messenger would summon. But who was this Archia? When MACCS said 'that infernal Goodie-Two-Shoes' was he referring to his other half or someone else?

It took us minutes to reach my cabin. We arrived in silence. The security bot, after waiting for my door to slide open, tossed me inside like a rotten fish. By the time I stood up and turned around the door had slid closed again. It locked with a electronic *click.* MACCS spoke through the white metal.

"We have one last ship to search and one last Intelligence to find. You're going to find him. Retrieve him. Then, you're going to hightail it back here and we're going to get this show on the road. Got it, Jack?"

"You can't make me."

"Oh I beg to differ." I suddenly dropped to the floor as a wave of searing pain flared across my scalp. MACCS's voice lowered. "I can make you dance…" I shot up and started to shake my body like a puppet. "Fight." My muscles locked me into a battle stance. "Or play dead." I collapsed. The AI laughed. "You see, you're mine. Although I admit, PAINS already did most of the work. He placed an override switch at the back of your head when you were being constructed in stasis—you know on the off chance you got a stick up your ass? From there all I had to do was hack into its mainframe which I was able to do moments ago. I can make you do anything I want now. You're going to finish

-347-

Directive Nine. Karnull *will* get what he wants."

My hands turned into fists. I didn't move. My face stayed on the floor as I struggled to contain the rage welling up inside. "Say something, human." MACCS spat.

Again, pain flared from the base of my skull. My vocal cords moved of their own accord. "Y-yes, sir. I understand, sir."

"Good. See you in a little while, *Creator.*" The AI left, his large security bot moving in tow with a *thump thump thump.* My body trembled. Anger. Hate. Despair. All these emotions and more clouded my mind.

He is not going to control me. I won't let him.

"It's a little late for that don't you think?" Karnull chuckled, *"I already own you, Kiddo. Mind, body, and soul."*

What's worse, I couldn't argue with him.

18 – Behind Closed Doors – 18

"I have so many different
personalities in me and I still
feel lonely."

– Tori Amos -

–

AGES MUST HAVE passed before I finally decided to stand. When I did, my body felt numb. Although MACCS had thrown me in my room, I might as well have been in a prison. I couldn't leave, and even if I could, all MACCS had to do was throw a switch and I'd be his personal slave. How on earth was I supposed to get to Becca now?

"Dammit!" I screamed at the top of my lungs. I reached for a chair. Threw it. The chair crashed against my table and clattered on the floor. None of this was fair. Once again, I wasn't in control. Why was I always playing the puppet? I picked up the chair again and threw it as hard as I could at my bed.

"Hey watch it!" Hawk's spider-crab bot scurried out from under the bed. It tightened its red lens at me as if to glare. "I'd rather not get hit, thank you."

"What do you want?" Half of me wanted to kick the machine. Half of me wanted to listen. I chose to listen.

The robot made the motion of brushing itself off. "Well excuse me for caring. I just saw you get thrown in here and wanted to see if you were okay. Apparently you aren't, otherwise you wouldn't have had such a fit. What happened?"

"You'll have to find someone else to help you."

"What did you say?"

"You heard me. Find someone else. I'm done."

Hawk's machine scurried to the foot of my bed. It cut the air with one of its mechanical legs. "N-no you're not! I have come too far and sacrificed too much just let you waltz out when we're so close. Now listen. You're going to do as I say and—" I grabbed hold of the machine's body and brought its red eye close to my face. "What do you think you're doing?" Hawk half-screamed.

"*You* listen to me, you little brat. I-am-done. Kill me. I don't care anymore. Anything would be better than this hell."

"Hell? You think *this* is hell?" He laughed angrily. "You think you know anything about hell? Try seeing your best friend die right in front of you. Try having anyone you've ever known and loved slaughtered like sheep. Try—"

"I killed her!" I screamed at the top of my lungs.

Hawk stopped. The room fell silent. His robot's lens tightened and expanded as if to blink. "What? Who?"

I lowered the robot to my bed. Tears were streaming down my face. "My wife. I killed her." Silence. I turned, unable to look at the little machine any longer. *It's not my fault.*

"Jackson... What happened?"

It's not my fault. "I'd been drinking. I shouldn't have gone out. When I got into town the street looked empty so I gunned it. Then..." I half choked on my tears. "I saw her moments before my car struck her. I stopped down the street and stumbled out." I couldn't stop shaking. In seconds I'd dropped to my knees. "She didn't die you know? At least not at first. I got to hold her one last time. Do you know what she told me?" The machine skittered to my side. "God *loves* me. She thought that was why she didn't die on impact. Becca thought that some loving figment of her imagination let her suffer a few seconds longer to break my heart."

"I'm sorry, Jackson. I didn't know."

I grit my teeth and stood. "I don't need your pity. I *need* her."

"But she's dead isn't she?" I turned back to the machine. It took all of my willpower not to slap it. "That's not what I meant." Hawk said defensively. "All I meant was that there's nothing you can do about that now."

"Maybe. I thought I could a long time ago. But now I'm not so sure anymore." I sighed and looked the other way. "Look I can't help you, Hawk. Literally. The AI have complete control over me. The moment they suspect something is happening your plan falls apart. If I disobey they will force me to do what they want. I have no choice in the matter."

"What did the devil-man do to you?" Hawk's robot climbed back on the bed and stared at me. I couldn't tell if it was curious, concerned or just angry. Maybe it was a combination.

"He planted a chip at the base of my skull that gives him complete control over my body." I said. *Not to mention he made me part-machine.* I flexed my fingers. Was I really one of those OC units? The percentage on my watch was at seventy-five. I hadn't noticed before, but the more I remembered the higher the percentage climbed. Again I felt the urge to vomit. I wasn't even human anymore, was I?

Hawk's machine paced from one side of the bed to the other. Finally it stopped and focused on me. The little lens whirred as it zoomed in and out. "You know what? You're right. You can't help me."

"I'm glad we finally understand one another." I took a seat on my bed and lowered my head in exhaustion.

"But maybe I can help you."

I looked up. "What?"

"Look, Jackson… I'm sorry if we got started out on the wrong foot. Maybe some re-introductions are in order." It raised a tiny mechanical arm. "My name isn't really Hawk. You can call me Coddle-Hawk. It's my mother and father's last names put together, considering they couldn't decide on what they wanted to be called. I was never really big on the change but people didn't forget me, that much was for sure."

Slowly, I shook the mechanical leg. "Coddle-Hawk huh?"

"Don't make fun of me, Poindexter. You still want my help right?"

I let go of its leg and shifted toward the machine. "That depends. What do you plan on doing?"

"Oh you'll know soon enough. I'll just consider it a change of plans. You keep doing your thing. And by 'doing your thing' I mean staying alive long enough for someone braver and smarter to save your ass."

"Which I assume is supposed to be you?"

"I'm flattered. Just do as the god-men want for the time being. Don't worry. I'll set things straight OK?" His voice was softer now.

I shook my head. "Eh, what the hell? It's not like I have

anything else to lose."

"Geez." Hawk said. "Your confidence in me is overwhelming. Thanks."

"You're welcome."

The tiny machine skittered off my bed, up the wall, and back into its vent. It saluted me with one tiny arm before entering. "Remember. Don't die."

"I've heard that one before."

"Well if it's nice, you say it twice. I'll see you in a bit." And with that Hawk's robot vanished into the ventilation shaft. What was he planning on doing to help me? *I'm afraid to ask.*

Instead, I sank on my bed and stared at the ceiling. I didn't realize how drained I was. In moments my eyes shut and I was asleep.

I saw the man with the scar.

19 – Chain Reaction – 19

"Love is a sacred reserve of
energy; it is like the blood of
spiritual evolution.
- Pierre Teilhard de Chardin -

THE MAN WITH the scar was not like I remembered him. He had no scar and he was still a boy. Despite the changes, I recognized him for his eyes. Their golden sheen cut straight through to my heart. And now he had a name.

"Kristoff, you can't!" A woman screamed the child's name from the boat behind him. I couldn't see the woman or rest of the crew. A fog had started to roll in across the bright blue waters. The boy called Kristoff stood on the waves as if they were solid ground. He wore his tunic and pants from our first encounter. Had this happened some time in the past? The scene struck me as inherently familiar; as if it had happened once before in a different time and place.

"Annias, there is still time." Kristoff, his voice, like sunlight on snow, traveled across the water's surface. Following his eyes I turned to the left.

Opposite Kristoff, standing on the water, was a dark man. He wore beetle-like armor that glistened black—just like the woman who had tried to kill me aboard the *Midgard*. The faces of screaming people had been chiseled on his chest plate and shoulders. A silky red cape fluttered behind him, embroidered with a golden insignia. Annias chuckled, voice distorted by the stag-like helmet. "Yes, there is still time to repent, Heretic. I'm merciful after all. The church will forgive you for your crimes if you renounce this folly."

"You do not see yet?" Kristoff shook his head and looked to the water's surface. When his eyes fell on Annias again they were brimming with tears. "My father loves you, Annias. As do I. We always have. You are beautiful in our eyes. You do not have to be a slave to the shadows any longer. Don't you want freedom?"

"Be silent." Annias drew his scythe. The wicked weapon glistened menacingly as he leveled it at Kristoff. "I will not have you spouting your lies any more."

"And what lies have I said? What are my crimes?"

"You call yourself Immulon the Creator. Such blasphemy is punishable by death. You are flesh and blood—nothing more. Anything you can do, so can I. Look! We both walk on the waves. We both can raise the dead. My powers come from the everlasting

Creator. Where do your's come from, O son of Archia?"

Archia? Was Karnull somehow tied to this?

"You are so blind…" Kristoff's tears fell to the water's surface.

With each teardrop, I felt a sadness the likes of which I had never known. This went beyond pain. The hole inside my heart yawned large and wide. I knew Kristoff was telling the truth. Tears streaked down my face in tandem with him. I fell to my knees, suddenly aware that I was standing on the water's surface too. My heart ached. *Why do I feel this way?*

Kristoff clenched his hands into fists. "I will free you, Annias. I will save you from him!"

"Enough!" Annias screamed. He cut the air with his scythe's blade. "I will show this world the imposter you are. This nonsense ends here." Annias broke into a run. He was moving so fast that I blinked and he had already closed the distance between Kristoff and himself. The man drew his scythe back as if to slice the child across his chest…

Do you want me to help you?

Kristoff's voice echoed in my head. My heart stopped. *Help me?* Annias faltered too. Had he heard it as well?

I blinked. Suddenly Annias was gone, replaced by a massive writhing shadow. The darkness looked to be made of worms. Horrible red glowing eyes were fixed on Kristoff. Then, I blinked again and saw Annias. Kristoff didn't move. The scythe's blade came down in a clean arc.

It was as if someone had sucked all the air out of the sky. I stood there, heart throbbing like an open wound. My legs lost feeling. I stared at Annias's blade as it finished its arc. Blood dripped from its edge.

Plop. Plop. Plop. The sound of his blood striking the surface of the water echoed like a thunderclap. Kristoff slowly fell backwards.

It all happened in slow motion. Annias was frozen in place. The screams and cries of Kristoff's friends drifted, distorted, through the rolling waves of fog. I couldn't breathe. Or think. Or feel. Watching the child fall into the water and vanish beneath the waves… It tore into my heart like a cleaver. *What did you do? Why didn't you run?* This wasn't right!

Then, things returned to normal speed. Annias, apparently coming out of his stupor, looked to his bloody scythe blade and back to the spot where Kristoff had been only moments before. Was he shocked at himself? Horrified? He was shaking. Why? He had killed his heretic hadn't he?

He took a step back. Several dark tendrils snaked under the water from Kristoff's impact, racing north, south, east, and west. At first, I thought the dark shapes were some kind of serpents or the tentacles of an underwater monster. It wasn't until the darkness spread outward, covering the water, that I realized what we were staring at. It was blood. Kristoff's blood.

Annias broke into a run to escape the ever darkening tide. Kristoff's friends were screaming, crying, and wailing. No one knew what was happening. Including me. I stared at the dark bloody water. My reflection stared back at me. Why did I have golden eyes now? Before I had a chance to utter a word my reflection locked eyes with me. It spoke.

Do you want my help, Jackson?

It was Kristoff's voice. Why was it coming out of me?

Do you want to be free?

My lips trembled for an answer.

Do you want to know who you really are?

My tears fell. I couldn't bring myself to speak. For some reason, I knew that the shadow I had seen only moments before was Archia. Karnull was a part of him. A part of me.

I love you, Jackson.

I shut my eyes and tried to block out the voice. "Stop. You don't know me. You wouldn't love me if you knew."

But I do. I know everything about you.

I wanted to scream at the top of my lungs but I was paralyzed. Not out of fear, but guilt. Like a cancer, it ate through my veins until I was too weak to fight, stand or even speak. I wanted to die. When I opened my eyes, Kristoff had replaced my reflection. He was staring at me.

I'm coming for you, Jackson.

20 – Abandon Hope All Who Enter– 20

"Absence from whom we love is
worse than death, and frustrates
hope severer than despair."

- William Cowper -

"IT'S TIME TO wake up, Sleeping Beauty." MACCS's voice echoed in my ear moments before a violent shock threw me off my bed and to the floor. I blinked. My body was covered in sweat. What… Had I just dreamed? "You have five minutes to get off that floor, get dressed, and get down here." MACCS snarled through my watch. "If I don't see you in that amount of time you're going to wish you'd never been born. Got it? And don't even think about testing me. You'll regret it." He clicked off.

I managed to stand. *Quit shaking already.* I couldn't stop from seeing Kristoff in my head. His eyes—they haunted me. He'd looked at me like no one ever had before. It was as if the child had seen *through* me. A chill ran down my spine.

I stumbled to prep for what would be my last expedition to the world below. From there, my trip to the command deck passed in a haze. Half of me felt disconnected from the world. The other half had died with Kristoff in my dreams.

Why was I so terrified? What about that boy frightened me so? I thought back to how Karnull had reacted when Kristoff had appeared. Is this what it felt like?

"You're late." MACCS said through clenched teeth as I entered the command deck."One more nanosecond and I would have buzzed you." HALOS, TRoAS, and MACCS stood in front of me, each at a station in the ring of terminals. PAINS was nowhere to be seen. *Is he still in the archives?* What would he think of Karnull's influence on me? "We've got a directive to complete." MACCS said again, snarling. "Chop, chop."

I looked around. "Where's PAINS?"

Another shock sent me reeling. "Did I say you can talk? Get down there."

"You mind not roasting him, Small Fry?" HALOS turned his head toward us. "Remember, that's the body Karnull is going to have when this is all said and done."

"I don't need you to lecture me, Fatty." MACCS growled.

"For the love of God." TRoAS said, "Just get on with it. The sooner master Karnull is in his new shell, the sooner this place will get cleaned. Seriously, how can you bampots stand this filth?"

"Quiet." MACCS hissed. I stood, pushing off my knees. MACCS pointed to the circular platform ahead of me—the transport lift. A bright blue light shimmered at its center. "Well? Get in there. Or do you want me to make you?"

"I'm going." I headed for the ring of pulsating light.

Do you want me to help you, Jackson?

Kristoff's voice echoed in my head as I stepped inside. I didn't have an answer for him. My heart started throbbing when I thought about the blood dripping into the water, overcoming the crystal clear waters like a virus. Or was it a cure? Either way, Kristoff both terrified me and comforted me. Who was he? And why did he want to help me? Yet another mystery.

Little did I realize that its answer would change everything I had ever known.

◆◆◆

EPOCS's vessel was the *USS Niflheim*. As the transport lift's light peeled away from my eyes, I saw that the ship had crashed in a massive forest. All I could see were the tops of dark green tree tops. Like a sea of emerald set against a backdrop of mist and fog, the canopy stretched around me as far as the eye could see. I stood on a wooden walkway that led to a small cluster of huts atop the trees. A village? *Who would have put a village on top of a forest?*

"See that collection of firewood?" MACCS hissed in my ear. His video feed appeared in the upper right hand corner of my HUD. "That's where you need to go. Scans show that there should be an archaic elevator system at its center."

"Where's the *Niflheim?*"

"Where do you think? EPOCS crashed in the swamp below. Now stop playing twenty questions and get down there."

Swamp? I looked over the side of the railing that ran along the wooden walkway. No sign of the floor. How high were we? Was an elevator really necessary? What were these people doing here? I looked back to the village and started forward.

The air here felt different than the other places I had traveled to. The stench of rotting vegetation and carcasses drifted through the leaves from the abyss that waited for me below. Humidity clung to my chest. But there was something else—a presence. Someone I knew. Not Karnull. Not Kristoff. Not Hawk, Rose, Becca or the woman in black. Who then?

My footsteps caused the old wood to creak below. The ground wavered back and forth as a gust of humid wind washed over the green sea. I held my breath without thinking. I doubted this place was all that safe. One wrong step and it might fall apart.

"Did people really live here?" I asked voicing my thoughts.

"Does it matter?" MACCS said.

"Humor me."

MACCS rolled his eyes. "Yeah. Why else would they build villages so far above the surface? The swamps are dangerous—especially given the wildlife that came through WEAVER. These pathetic people were desperate. After the crashes those people aboard the cruisers fled and took to a stone age existence. This is just one of the structures they left behind."

"Wait. I thought they were turned into OC units. What do you mean they fled?"

MACCS gave a disgusted sigh. " Man you're stupid… Alright listen up, Idiot. First of all, the *original* passengers were all copied and transferred to OC units. That was long before PAINS started fighting the human stragglers."

"Whoa, whoa. Slow down. What do you mean he started fighting against human stragglers?"

"Geez…" The AI rubbed his temples. "I didn't sign up for babysitting. Okay, let me take it a little slower for you. After we got back from drifting for those twenty five years, the world was still fighting against SIN. PAINS locked down *Drasil* and decided to observe the fighting. Every so often he would help one side, if just to stop them from interfering with the Directive. At least at first. It was one of the few intelligent things he decided to do."

"At first?" The village huts were drawing nearer. I continued, if only to alleviate the eerie quiet.

"I don't know if he developed a conscience or what but after a few centuries, the moron decided to unlock *Drasil*. He reasoned that those people below deserved the same chance to be part of your new world as much as any of the passengers. Of course by the time he actually let them on board most of those knuckle-draggers didn't even know what an AI *was*. They started thinking we were some kind of god. I kinda liked that gig."

I was reminded of what Hawk, Coddle-Hawk, had said. Didn't he call them god-men? But he couldn't be the same Hawk... Unless he went into stasis. I shook my head. "What happened after that?"

"What do you think? One by one, PAINS started re-creating the idiots. Then, unfortunately, one little girl ruined everything." MACCS's smile curled into a teeth-flashing grin. "Oh *that* was rich. She started thinking that because her friends were being stored after we re-created them, we were *killing* them. So, just like any stupid human would do, she tried to stop it. And you know what? The little bitch succeeded." Something about the way he said those words gave me chills.

MACCS continued. "She single-handedly uncovered PAINS's plot. As a result, the population of *Drasil* went into a frenzy. They flocked to the various ships and subsequently, accidentally, started them. We weren't able to wrestle control of vessels from them until it was too late. By that time we crashed on Earth and were unable to get back to *Drasil*. That's when you came into the picture. It took a few hundred years, sure, but thankfully PAINS had enough sense to keep a copy of you stored in the *Midgard*. If he hadn't…" MACCS shuddered.

"We wouldn't be here." I finished. *Copy? I was* an OC unit.

"That's got to be the smartest thing you've ever said. Now keep that trap of yours shut. We got business to take care of."

I'd reached the village by the time he finished. The dark forms of empty doorways watched me as I continued to the center of the settlement. Age had been soaked into every fiber of rotting wood. It was hard to believe that people had lived here once. It reminded me of the moment I had woken up on the *Drasil* for the first time. All this time, I had thought that Hawk was the monster —a 'terrorist' as PAINS had said. *How could someone do this?* I'd thought that when I saw the emptiness of the station. We had been leaving the medical wing at the time. Not once did I ever consider that the AI was in fact responsible for everything.

No, that wasn't right.

Who had programmed him to be that way? Who had been

the one to leave WEAVER unchecked? Who had been so selfish that he would risk the lives of every last human being in existence to get what he wanted? Me.

"*Now, now. Let's not think like that. Yes, you did kill them all but that isn't necessarily a bad thing, Kiddo. Doesn't nature kill off animals all the time? You might be a monster, but you're at the top of the food chain with me on your side. You don't need to say things like 'I deserve to die'. You deserve to be my slave and I deserve to be your king. It's a win-win.*"

Shut up. The guilt crept back into my heart, tightening around my chest. I tried to shove it away, but no matter how hard I pressed back the condemnation was right there, bubbling just beneath the surface. My heart beat faster.

"*The sooner you accept that we're the same the sooner we'll see Becca.*"

I said nothing.

"*What? Giving me the silent treatment? We'll see how well that works, considering I'm always* right here. "

I needed to know something. *Who is Kristoff?*

I could feel Karnull cringe as I said the boy's name. He snarled. "*Don't ever say that fool's name again got it? That man doesn't exist as far as I'm concerned. He's trouble. Thankfully, he won't be for much longer. Once our perfect world is born, not even he will be able to stop me."*

Or so you hope.

"You doubt me?"

Kristoff is going to destroy you. The words came to mind like lightning.

"I told you to never say his name again."

And I told you to shut up.

"Don't think you're in charge here, Kiddo."

It's funny how you think you are.

A wave of pain sent me to my knees. I screamed as every cell in my artificial body burned.

"Great. What now?" MACCS snapped, unaware of Karnull's conversation with me.

I stood weakly. "N-nothing."

"Keep it up." Karnull chuckled. *"Try to escape all you like. Pretend you can be the king here. The truth is, you're mine. Mind, body and soul."* I squeezed my hands into fists and said nothing. *"That's right. Be quiet, Little Dog. Good boy."*

"We're here." MACCS said.

I had come to a caged platform made from ancient wood. A weak pulley system held it in position. It looked ready to fall apart. I swallowed. "Are you sure this thing is safe?"

"Yeah. You know, so long as you don't step on it."

MACCS snickered.

"How comforting."

I put my weight on the platform. It gave a little and other than a complaining groan, nothing else happened. Good. I put both feet on the elevator and waited for it to stop shaking. *Easy...*

A lever waited off to the right. After I situated myself I grabbed hold of the wooden handle. Pulled.

Kronk. The ropes overhead ran across a series of gears before causing the platform to shudder. I started to descend slowly. A chill crawled into my skin when I sank beneath the village's surface. Here, whatever light had collected on the surface spilled below in weakened shafts of silvery gray. My suit's headlamps clicked to life, throwing their harsh beams on the ancient trunks around me. The shadowy forms of swamp-life slithered out of sight as I swept my light across the mournful trees.

"Good night." I half whispered.

MACCS rolled his eyes. "What? The trees? Yeah, their big. So what?"

"How big is *big*?"

"A thousand feet or so. Now could you please shut up? Your voice is annoying me."

A thousand feet? I looked up, then down. Even from here I

could hardly see the swamp's oily surface. How had the plant-life gotten so large? Could it be an effect of WEAVER'S temporal fluctuations?

A shriek sent my beam to the left. Something very large had moved just out of sight. I curled my fingers in. Out. What kind of creatures called this place their home?

"Ugh. What a filthy hole." TRoAS said from somewhere behind MACCS.

HALOS chuckled, also in the background. "What are you talking about? Smell that sweet stench of decay. That wonderful aroma of discovery. This little hamlet of gloom has wet my appetite for some... Experimentation."

"Are you sure that's not you you're smelling?" TRoAS snapped.

"Maybe it's the load of crap that comes out of your mouth on a minute to minute basis, String-bean."

"Can it, ladies." MACCS ordered. Both of the AI fell silent. Did they fear MACCS? Why did PAINS never seem to have that kind of control? *PAINS*... I had gone from suspecting him, to hating him, to feeling sorry for him. Out of all the AI, he seemed to be the most human. Was that because I had programmed him that way, or was there something else going on behind the scenes?

Maybe he's going to get his wish. He did want to be human after all. In not so many ways, PAINS and I were alike. We were both slaves to a fate that had been programmed for us. And deep down, maybe all we wanted was to be free.

I know I did.

Ka-lonk. The elevator finally came to a stop at the swamp floor. It sank in the mud as I stepped out. The air was definitely colder here and reeked of rot and decay. Wild, alien calls came from every direction. I could see eyes watching me from the shadows.

"Alright." MACCS said. "Now that you finally decided to get down here, the *USS Niflheim* is located four clicks ahead of your current location. Oh, and stay out of the water would ya? There's some large uglies swimming in that murk. They'll snap you up if you're not careful. We wouldn't want that."

"If you're so worried about me then why don't you take control you sawed off—" Pain flared at the base of my skull. It sent me to one knee. I took deep lungfuls of my suit's purified air. "As tempting as it would be to take the reins, unfortunately, your pathetic excuse for a body couldn't sustain the prolonged exposure. You'd crap out before we even got halfway there. Karnull does not want a broken shell of a body."

"We couldn't make his highness uncomfortable could

we?"

MACCS shocked me again. I fell to my hands. The dark mud spat and popped as it came over my fingers. I could feel a bed of worms slither beneath. "What was that, Pretty Boy?" MACCS asked.

"Nothing."

"That's what I thought you said." He waited for me to stand. "Now get moving before I decide to buzz you again. I'm not in the mood to deal with your lip, mister. Try not to be a total idiot in the meantime hm?" His feed clicked off. I couldn't help but breathe a sigh of relief. Was MACCS's good side still in there somewhere? It was getting hard to believe that. His evil half had completely taken over.

That made me think of Karnull. Would he really take control of me? I couldn't let that happen. Then again, according to my other side, he already had. *I own you. Mind, body, and soul.*

What *was* Karnull? He had to be more than a virus. Abbadon couldn't have made him could he? Again, the shadow I'd seen take Annias's place moments before he killed Kristoff flashed in my head. That writhing mass of black worms—had the worm I swallowed come from that? Did Karnull *come* from that? I shook the questions from my head and started walking.

Progress proved slow. The swamp had very few patches of

dry earth. If the ground wasn't an oily swathe of water then it was the black, sucking mud that threatened to pull me under with every step. Every so often, when my headlamps would run over the enormous trees, I kept thinking I'd see something slink back into the darkness with a *click click click.* The creature never let me catch a good glimpse of it, for which I was both thankful and apprehensive. Between the wild and lonesome calls of whatever lurked just out of sight, the creature's clicking, chittering movements filled the air. It was always close enough to send a shudder down my spine.

I hated this place.

"How much farther?" I said, wanting desperately to break the radio silence. MACCS didn't respond. I cursed my luck. Was my suit malfunctioning again? "Hey, Small Fry. Are you still there?" Nothing. I came to a stop at the roots of one of the massive trees. The ground here was firmer. I had a chance to stop without fear of going under. "MACCS." I placed my hand on the cold trunk. "This is not funny. If you can hear me—"

A sharp pain cut through my hand. I nearly fell backwards stumbling from the tree. I looked at my palm. A razor-fine cut marked my covered palm. Blood oozed out of the wound. Something had cut me? I focused my beams on the trunk. There was a flash. Moving closer I saw what looked like a strand of silk.

It ran from the tree up into the dark canopy. The now blood-stained strand was vibrating. A spider web? *What the—?*

"Finally. I found you."I stopped cold. That voice… I turned, throwing my light over the ancient vegetation. If I was scared before, I was terrified now. The woman in black, she'd found me."Nice little trick taking care of my tracker on the *Midgard*. I underestimated you."

Her voice seemed to come from everywhere at once. I couldn't pin her down. The more I spun, the more disoriented I became. She was toying with me—the same way a cat toys with a mouse before it bites its head off.

"Do you have any idea how much pain you've caused me, Thorne?" She hissed. "You and that miserable devil-man? It's your fault that the world ended, yet you continue on this selfish quest to claim what you wanted. It doesn't matter who stands in your way. Nothing's sacred to you, is it?"

Devil-man? Isn't that what Hawk had called PAINS? Was this woman… Hawk? *But that doesn't make any sense.* Hawk was a man—or at least I assumed he was. There was no way of telling if Hawk had used a voice changer. But if it *was* her, then she had more than enough opportunity to kill me before now. Furthermore, why save me in the first place? No. It didn't make sense. This deranged woman couldn't possibly be Hawk.

Who was she then?

The woman continued, her every word laced with venom. "It took me a while to find the truth. To really understand what you had done. Once I understood, I knew that the only option would be to hunt you down and wipe your miserable life from existence. I wish I could have gone back farther… Then I could have ended you before this mess began. Maybe I will. Second chances and all that crap. But before I do, I'm going to gut you like a pig."

Shink. I stepped forward without thinking. The bark to my right suddenly changed. Five claw marks ran along the wood. *She missed me.* "Who are you?" I yelled.

"I am the hand of justice and you are the guilty sinner. I will punish you." A quick gust of wind blew by my hair. Following it was a flare of agonizing pain. I clutched my shoulder. Looked at my non-wounded hand. It was bloody. "I hate you. I utterly and completely despise you, Thorne."

She struck again. My leg buckled. More agony. Where was she hitting me from? At this rate I was going to end up diced. Or worse. I had to get to cover. Hide. Something. Anything! *Maybe if I distract her. Get her talking.* "But it wasn't me!" I cried in the darkness. "Abbadon tricked me. He told me it was a cure. He promised me that it would bring Becca back."

"Oh yes. *Becca.* The little tramp you love so very much." The woman chuckled. "What did she tell you in those last moments? *God loves you. He's coming for you.* What a load of shit! There is no God. Or heaven. Or hell. There is only the abyss of this life and the misery it brings."

Pain flared across my chest this time. The blood started to pour. I screamed and fell back against the tree. She landed in front of me with a wet *plop*. The woman's glistening black armor reminded me of Annias. I still couldn't see her face. "How... do you know... about that?"

"You told me, of course."

What?

She covered the distance between us. The light caught on her blade-fingers. In one swift motion she spun, throwing out wet gray blobs that struck my wrists and ankles. The goo cemented to my skin. I couldn't move my arms or legs. Pinned against the tree, I had no choice but to watch as she retracted the blades on her right hand and grabbed me by the throat.

"Oh, I have waited so very long to look into your eyes and see that fear. You know what's coming. Only I'm going to take my time with you. Not like Becca. She got off easy. Dying in your arms. You'll die here and watch as your intestines hang out. Who knows? Maybe you'll be kicking long enough so that the little nasties down here will eat you while you can still feel pain. I certainly hope so." She squeezed. "Tell me, Mr. Thorne, how does it feel to face your sins? How does it feel to see the darkness inside looking back at you?"

"Karnull… made me…!"

"Karnull? Who the hell is Karnull?"

"Inside…me. M-monster…" I choked.

She looked from my chest back to me. "Ah, I see. Cute. Yes, I agree. *You* are the problem. Call yourself Karnull. Call yourself a saint. You could call yourself Jesus Christ and I wouldn't care. You are still the same evil man and you will be punished." She raised her claws. My head lamps flickered. Shut off. Half-delirious from lack of oxygen, my vision swam. What were those bright lights behind her? They looked like eyes. Were they getting closer? "I only wish hell were real. Good bye, Thorne."

Moments before she was going to impale me I heard the chittering sound from before. A glob of white goop struck her on the back. The woman's body yanked backwards. Cursing and screaming, she was pulled into the dark, toward the eyes. My headlamps flickered back to life. I caught the glimpse of a spider larger than a bus leap into the trees. Its prey, the woman, followed along like a dog on a leash.

I strained at the gunk on my wrists. *Come on. Come on.* It finally tore. With one hand free, I went to dismantling the other side followed by my ankles. I fell.

There was no time to waste. Picking myself off the ground, I bolted in the direction of the ship. I hated spiders almost as much as I hated Karnull. Why did that one arachnid have to be so big?

My transmitter beeped in my ear. A shock sent me stumbling. I kept running. "How dare you disconnect from me." MACCS glared, appearing on my HUD. He gave me another shock.

"Stop it you little prick! It wasn't my fault. I tried contacting you. I nearly died back there!"

"What? Your vitals…" His face changed. MACCS flashed me a raised eyebrow. "Which one of the locals did you piss off now?"

"There's a woman who's been following me since the *Midgard.* She almost had me back there. If that spider hadn't come along…" I shuddered. "N-never mind. How far am I from this stupid ship?"

"It should be coming up any minute now."

I looked ahead. Though my beams barely reached across the black lake, I could see the *Niflheim*'s monstrous shape waiting for me on the waves. I came to a stop at the muddy shore edge. It

Thorne / Colby Drane

didn't look like there would be a way across, unless of course, I were to swim. I wasn't about to risk getting eaten.

Something heavy fell behind me. I spun. It was the spider's corpse. *Oh great.*

"Die, Thorne!" The woman came streaking toward me from above. I barely had time to roll out of the way before she'd embedded her claws in the soft earth. She pulled them out and darted toward me.

"Hey, Heifer." HALOS appeared on my screen next to MACCS. "You mind not scarring Rob up too much? We got use him later."

"Be silent, god-man!" She screamed.

"Ah she's feisty. I like her. Okay, maybe you can chop off a finger or two."

"Shut up!" MACCS roared. He looked at the console below him. "Damn it."

"Do something!" I yelled to him as she swung at me. Her claws tore across another chunk of bark. The wood detonated in a shower of wood chips. I could only imagine what would have happened had it hit my head.

I hopped backwards. My body locked up. *What's going on?* I couldn't move. She was racing toward me. Moments before her blade would have hit another bout of pain flared from the base of my skull. My arm moved without me telling it to. I caught the woman's arm mid air. She faltered ever so slightly, stunned. "There." MACCS wiped his brow. "Now I have control."

My leg kicked her square in the sternum. She flew backwards, flipping in the air before landing upright and angry. MACCS moved me into a battle stance and motioned for her to come at me again. My body ached from the exertion. "Bring it on, Lady." He said with a smile. "I've got a pine box with your name on it."

I grit my teeth. "If you get me killed you cocky little…"

The woman's claws suddenly sparked with electricity. She darted toward me again, this time zig-zagging forward. MACCS waited for his opportunity with a smile.

She swung. We tilted back as her claws came within centimeters of my chin. The air behind her claws sparked and popped. MACCS followed up by straightening us and slamming my fist against her chest again.

Didn't work this time. She grabbed my arm and threw us toward the water's edge. *Shit!* Stumbling, MACCS brought us into a handstand and then changed directions by flipping up in the air. I landed back to my feet, inches from the edge of the lake. "It's like I'm playing a video game." He said gleefully.

"Will you kill her already?" I snapped.

The woman leapt toward us. Landed. Another enraged swing. We dodged again. MACCS uppercutted her with a spinning jump. The woman reeled. We landed again. MACCS smiled. "I call that one the bitch express."

She shook her head and growled. "Die god-man!"

The woman launched herself forwards, screaming with rage. Her attacks came faster now. MACCS hardly had enough time to dodge, let alone fight back. My body throbbed. I couldn't take much more of this. MACCS jumped in the air, spun, and planted my foot across her visor. *Crack.* The woman stumbled backwards, dazed. Seeing his chance, the AI shot forward and delivered a superman punch. She hit the ground. Didn't move. We landed and straightened. Was it really over?

"I haven't had that much fun in ages." MACCS said with insidious delight.

"Warning. OC unit exertion threshold detected." My visor flashed red as my internal computer spoke. A large exclamation mark framed by a triangle appeared in the center of my HUD. "Shutdown imminent."

"No, no, no, no, no!" MACCS was frantic. He was turning every single knob and pushing every single button at his disposal. Fed up with a lack of results he looked at HALOS and TRoAS on the terminals around him. "Do something you idiots!"

"Like what?" HALOS smirked. "Whistle Dixie?"

TRoAS produced a sword. "I could clean house."

"Useless!" MACCS slammed his fist on the terminal. He glared at me. "If you dare faint you pathetic bag of bones, I swear I'll—"

But I didn't hear the rest of what he said. My eyes grew heavy. The pain that I'd been holding at bay finally washed over me and I had no choice but to collapse. My knees sank into the muddy ground with a heavy *plop*. My vision flickered.

Would I die this time? I didn't want to die. Death scared me. Was there really nothing but darkness after this life? *Help. Please, someone, help.* The lake, with its dark monolithic wreck at the center, seemed to look at me with pity. As my vision darkened, I could have sworn I saw a shape make its way toward me, parting the oily waters with fierce determination. A predator?

I wanted to cry, but all that came out was a weak breath, then... Darkness.

21 – Anybody Home? – 21

"Of all ghosts, the ghosts of our
old loves are the worst."
- Sir Arthur Conan Doyle -

I STOOD IN the observation chamber, surrounded by computers, gray walls, and darkness, alone. Watching my team from the window, I could tell that they were making great progress.

The scientists toiled away in their scrubs, finishing the operation as per my request. A large painful machine, ringed by surgical lights, took up the ceiling above. Its focus, like the rest of the room, lay at the operation table. I couldn't see my patient for the mass of moving bodies but I knew *he* was there, and a small deranged smile, born from the darkness inside, crossed my lips. Yes. This was a fitting revenge wasn't it?

"We've come a long way, Kiddo." Karnull whispered.

And each day brings us one step closer.

"Yes. Yes it does."

The ships were being built, and WEAVER, like clockwork, grew larger with every passing day. Of course, with

Abbadon's virus running rampant all over the world and the evidence planted against my father, no one suspected me. I was free to set things in motion just as we had planned. I rubbed my left wrist. Nervous habit.

"What's wrong?"

Nothing.

"Would you lie to a liar?"

If you're a liar, then why do I trust you?

My other half chuckled. *"That's a good question. Maybe you should look into it. But in all seriousness, what's eating you?"*

I could have told him about the seedling of guilt deep inside. It was hardly more than a weed sprouting through a crack in the pavement, yet it bothered me more than words could ever describe.

Was I doing the right thing? I had questioned myself time after time. The result was always the same. I would feel sick, then foolish, then determined, then angry. My mood fluctuated from one end of the spectrum to the other. I hadn't slept in weeks. Every time I closed my eyes, I saw either Becca or my father. I had killed them both. It was no wonder that my mind connected the two. Still, why did I feel this way?

"I'm going to tell you a story." Karnull said.

I came out of my thoughts.

"Once upon a time there was a man and a woman. They lived in paradise and walked with a man called Immulon."

He shuddered when the name *Immulon* crossed my mind. Odd. I had never felt Karnull bothered before.

"This man gave them everything they ever wanted. So long as they obeyed, paradise would always be open to them."

Sounds like Adam and Eve.

"Oh, yes. That story. The two are connected. Just not in the way you think." He cleared his imaginary throat. *"Now as I was saying... These two goodie-goodies were spoiled rotten. But you know what? They had boring lives. Where was the excitement in always doing what you were told? Sounds more like prison to me."* He laughed. *"That all changed one day. One day, someone else entered paradise. His name was Archia."*

Now it was my turn to be bothered. Something about that name unnerved me. I swallowed as a chill crept over my flesh. *What happened?*

"You said you knew about Adam and Eve didn't you?"

Yes, but that story isn't real.

"Oh you'd be surprised at what's real, Jackson."

Another chill. Why was he bringing this up?

"Archia gave Choral and Ordonna the chance to live free

of rules. To live in death. They didn't need paradise to be happy. They could find excitement wherever they wanted... If only they would take Archia's gift. Three guesses what that was. " He said in a sing-songy voice.

A piece of fruit?

"*Not quite.* " He laughed low and guttural. "*It was a piece of himself. See, not even Immulon—God I hate that name—gave them a piece of himself. Archia was giving these children of Dust a new existence, one free from tyranny. With his heart they could become creatures of infinite shadow. They could be just like... The Creator. Only much better. Different.* "

You mean Imu—?

"*Don't say that name!*" I went silent. Karnull seemed to calm down as well. "*Sorry about the little snapping fit there. It just gets under my skin you know?* "

I wasn't aware that you had skin.

"*I have you don't I?* "

I tightened my hands into fists. Unsqueezed them. It felt hard to breathe. Whenever Karnull referred to me as his 'skin', it bothered me. Was that all I was to him? Some shell? I decided not to dwell on it. *So they took his gift.*

"*And threw the world into chaos. The Creator's 'paradise' was now a mockery of his original plan. Oh you should have seen the look on his face! Crying. Weeping like a baby. It was hysterical! I thought for sure He would have wiped them out then and there."*

Wait, you were there?

"Yes. Of course, I was here in this world too. Long before Abbadon woke me up as Archia had done. But that's another story."

One I wanted to hear. *Why are you telling me this?* I asked finally.

I could sense Karnull smile. *"Why? Why else? To set you at ease. You are a creature of shadow, Kiddo. You are now in the lineage of a great line of conquerors. You are a son of Archia. His flesh is your flesh. His heart is your heart. You are going to rule and be ruled, just as we planned from the beginning. Darkness will have its way with this world yet. Nothing will stand in our way. Oh! I just gave myself goosebumps thinking about it."*

Creature of shadow? Was I really doing the right thing?

"Mr. Thorne." One of the surgeons below had clicked on the terminal receiver to the right of the table. "We're finished here."

Snapping out of my thoughts I pressed the communication button on the console in front of me. "Good. Prep primary assimilation gear. Make sure that he is able to connect with the cruiser, is that understood?"

"Affirmative, Sir." They started to disperse in the chamber.

That's when I finally caught sight of my handiwork. Though it was difficult to tell at first, given the removal of his eyes, I knew that the man on the table—the same man who never done anything wrong to me—was the *USS Niflheim's* new reigning intelligence. An EPOCS unit. Early Prototype Organic Construct System. My father.

"*Yes, Kiddo.*" Karnull hissed gleefully. "*We certainly have come a long way.*"

◆◆◆

I woke up to a ceiling of shadows. It didn't have an end. I wondered if it ever had a beginning. Slowly, as feeling returned into my arms and legs, I realized that I was lying on a metal surface.

Where was I?

Groggy and disoriented, I stood. The swamp had vanished, replaced by the narrow confines of a small, dust-covered chamber lit by blue auxiliary lights. Left and right, saturated with the pungent odor of decay, were the rotting and half-worn evidences of what had once been books. A bed sat just ahead of me, dirty and unkempt. Old metal furniture lay scattered around the room in various states of being eaten by rust. Was this a ship cabin? How did I get here? Where *was* here? The *Niflheim*?

My helmet, as well as my armor, had vanished back into my suit. I was defenseless and alone. Great. *Okay, maybe it's not as bad as I think. I just have to—*

Clomp clomp clomp. Footsteps. My head swiveled to the door behind me. Someone, maybe some*thing*, was making their way toward the room. I needed to hide.

There weren't a whole lot of options. After debating for no more than five seconds, I dove for the bed and slid under its frame. My hand brushed against something wet and slimy. *Yuck.*

The door opened.

My eyes snapped to the figure that appeared. Judging by the shoulder width and size, it was man. I couldn't see his face for the ratty cloak draped around him. He stepped inside, took a look at where I'd been, and after trembling, fell to his knees. Though the figure made no sound, I could have sworn he was weeping. Why? Was he the one that had brought me here? For some reason, he seemed familiar. Was this the presence I had felt when first entering the swamp? Was it this man?

I had to be careful. There was no telling if he were human or not. I decided to stay out of sight, at least for the time being. "Who are you?" I said breaking the silence. *Well so much for staying hidden.* Why did I feel the overwhelming urge to speak to him?

He looked to the bed. Stood. The man made no move to come near me though he did seem relieved. He pointed to his throat.

"You can't speak?" He nodded. "Can you sign?" He shook his head. *So he's a mute. Must not get a whole lot of visitors.* I shifted ever so slightly. "Are you going to hurt me?"

The man shook his head vigorously, as if it were the very last thing on his mind. Again he dropped to his knees and folded his hands, pleading for me to trust him. My heart broke inside. *Poor guy must be desperate.*

I squeezed my hands. Sighed. "Hold on. I'm coming out." He took a step back to give me room. I inched my way out from under the bed frame, trying not to brush against the slimy gunk on either side of me. Heaven knows what it was. When I emerged I dusted myself off and looked to him. The man's face was cast in shadow.

"My name is Jackson. Jackson Robert Thorne." I said. He nodded. "Do you know me?" Another nod. This one vigorous. "How?"

The man moved toward me. I tensed. Was he going to attack?

-391-

"Hey, what are you doing?"

He knelt at the bed and stuck an arm underneath. After some scrambling around, he came back with a rod. The end of it was doused in the gunk I had brushed up against. What was he going to do?

There was a flash of fire. In one quick motion, he had whipped out a lighter, lit the end of the rod, and put the lighter back. A strange orange-green glow fell over the chamber, mixing with the icy blue of the auxiliary lights. He turned and made his way for the door, stopping long enough to motion for me to follow. Did I really want to go? *He did know who I was. That means he must be connected to me somehow.* Was he an AI? A straggler coming out of stasis? I didn't know. He waited for me patiently. One thing was for sure, this guy wasn't going to move unless I came along for the ride. *I did ask him to show me how I knew him.* I shrugged. Might as well. "Lead on." I said.

He walked out into the darkness. Following him, we entered into a tight hallway. The walls, which were lit by a mixture of the orange-green flame and blue auxiliary lights, were the same silicone-white I had seen on all the other ships. There was no doubt we were in the *Niflheim*. The only question was, *where*?

My guide, whose name I still didn't know, led us in

silence. The crackle of his torch and the *clomp* of our feet of the metal floor filled the quiet adequately enough, although I was far from at ease. A tension lingered in the air that I couldn't quite explain. Did it have something to do with this man? Was he the reason I felt both comforted and unsettled? Why did all the people in my life who wanted to help me inspire this feeling?

We took a turn to the left. The hallway fed in a large open platform, similar to that of the one that I'd seen at the security station aboard the *Valhalla*. This area, however, was much larger and there were far more chairs for passengers. The platform ran left and right into the darkness, lit, once again, by the chill of the auxiliary lights. Although… I squinted. The walls, which I could have sworn were once white, now looked to be a different color. Maybe it was from age?

Again the man motioned for me to follow. Taking me among the rows of chairs he led me to the far wall at the end of the station. Once we made it there he paused. Turned. The man pointed to the wall in front of us and handed me the torch. I took it and stepped forward.

I was staring at a mural. It stretched partway into the darkness, its painted colors ancient and peeling. Had my mysterious guide painted it? The mural depicted a whole crowd of people wearing scrubs and leaning over an operating table. A vast and vicious-looking machine divided the picture in half. The machine seemed to point to...

My hand rested on the painted table, or more accurately, the man on the table. Flashbacks of the dream ran through my head. I froze. *Dad?* A sudden searing burst of pain drew my attention away from the mural. Frantic, I looked down to see the fire snaking its way up my arm. *Shit!* I'd forgotten about the fuel on me. I dropped the torch and swatted the flames down. No go.

The man moved behind me. I heard the flutter of his cloak as he removed it from his shoulders. Seconds later, the rotting cloth was on my back and my arm was in his hands. He was wrapping the cloth around my burn. I dared not move. Slowly, it dawned on me who this man was. Why hadn't I seen it sooner? Finished with my arm, he stepped over to grab the still-lit torch off the ground. My guide brought the flickering orange-green fire up to his face.

The first thing I noticed was his uniform—a white suit, matching hat, black slacks and shoes. He looked just like the other AI. However, unlike them, his coat had been unbuttoned to reveal a black undershirt. And his eyes...

He had no eyes.

I swallowed. This was EPOCS, reigning intelligence of the *USS Niflheim* and what remained of my dead father.

Tears welled up in my eyes. *No. You-you're dead. I killed you.* My body shook. "D-dad?" His lips curled into a mournful smile. He nodded, sadly. "How?"

Again, he turned to the mural. Back to me. MACCS words echoed in my head. *Then there's EPOCS, that silent piece of the puzzle that wants to believe in a God—the part of you hated even more than your darker half.* Now it made sense.

My father had been a God believer just like Becca. I hated him for that. For his strange light inside him. I hated his eyes and his voice so I took them both away. Then, I made him practically immortal by turning him into a specialized OC unit. That way he would suffer in this miserable state for the rest of time. Seeing my handiwork though, I didn't feel satisfaction or rage. I felt sorrow. *What have I done?*

He reached out for my face. I didn't stop him. I couldn't. It was like my arms were petrified. I might as well have been a cadaver. Dad held my face in his hand. I knew that if he could have cried he would have.

"Don't tell me you feel sorry for him."

Shut the hell up! This is your doing. You made me do this!

"Made you?" Karnull broke into a fit of hysterical laughter. *"Nuh-uh, Kiddo. I persuaded you. There's a difference. You did this one all on your own."*

No. I'm not like this. I would have never— But I couldn't think anymore. I wrapped my arms around my father's neck and sobbed. He didn't push me away. The man I had hated all my life returned the display of affection and squeezed me tight, as if to say *I forgive you, Son.* But how could he? I didn't deserve forgiveness.

It's not my fault, Dad. I wanted to scream. *Please, it's not my fault.*

"J-Jackson?" A familiar voice echoed from my collar. I let go of my father. PAINS? "Can you hear me?" PAINS asked. "I am afraid the connection is a bit... Well, wonky."

"I hear you, PAINS." I wiped my nose. "Where have you been?"

"Good question. To which I will deliver an answer of equal worth. I was... Studying. Reading. Jackson, who is this Karnull you spoke of and why are there no records of him in our files?"

Dad looked to me with his empty eye sockets and nodded. I stepped away from him to talk. "There was a virus, PAINS. It was called SIN. It overtook the world."

"Yes, yes. I am aware."

"Are you aware that it means Separate Intelligence Neomorphic virus?"

Silence. PAINS swallowed. "Who told you that? The military's files on SIN were all classified. They were above your clearance."

"General Abbadon Graham told me about SIN. He was the one who unleashed it on the world. Listen, PAINS, Karnull is the virus's personality given form. He's the one that did all of this. He tricked me into creating the five AI and constructing Directive Nine. He doesn't want to help me bring Becca back. He wants to enslave humanity!" More silence. Did he believe me? The quiet made me antsy. "Listen. I'm telling the truth. We can't complete the directive. Not while Karnull exists. If we do—"

"I have had dreams." PAINS said quietly.

I stopped. "Wait, what?"

"Dreams. I didn't know what was wrong with me at first, mind you, but there would be moments where I would enter hibernation and have dreams of another world. I think that I might have seen Karnull there, or something like him. I cannot say for sure. All I saw was a most dreadful shadow."

Once more, I thought of the writhing mass of worms and the red eyes of the beast I had seen take Annias's place. "How is that possible?" I said dumbly.

PAINS continued. "I do not know. All that I am aware of is that we are made from you, Jackson. In not so many ways, we *are* you. I suppose there is enough organic material in my programming that I can be human. At least human enough to dream dreams… Or nightmares, given the subject. If what you are saying is true, I agree. We cannot let Karnull have his way."

It was the first bit of good news I had heard in a long time. Someone was on my side! I could barely control my heart beat. A smile ran across my lips. "Yes but how?"

"Well, I have a theory."

"Yeah? And that would be?" Static. "PAINS?"

I heard the static morph into laughter. Another voice came on the line. "Well would you look at that?" Karnull said gleefully. "It seems the puppet is becoming a little too nosy."

My stomach dropped. "What the hell?"

"Surprised? You shouldn't be. PAINS and the other puppets have your DNA, and that means, by extension, I have access to them. They are certainly easier to control than you are. I should have thought of doing this a long time ago."

"We are going to stop you." I hissed.

My other side chuckled. "We? Yeah, yeah. Go ahead and try, you and the puppet show. Meanwhile, I'll be waiting for you to finally wake up and realize the truth."

"And what is the truth you snake?"

"What else?" I could almost see Karnull smile. "I'm *you*."

A pair of strong arms slipped around my waist. EPOCS lifted me off the ground and threw me against the wall. Winded, I lay there, trying desperately to stand. The AI was already on top of me. He grabbed hold of my collar and lifted me in the air again. My cloak fell to the ground. "You're funny." Karnull's voice echoed eerily from EPOCS's throat. "We're going to laugh and laugh about this when everything's said and done. You should be honored, Kiddo. I'm making you king of this world. No one will ever defy what you have to say. You will a *god*. Who doesn't want that?"

"You mean your puppet!"

EPOCS shrugged. "Eh call it what you'd like. You can make a paradise out of hell or a hell out of paradise. It's all in the mind. So, which is it going to be, Jackson? Heaven or hell?"I spat in his face. EPOCS wiped his cheek and smiled. "Hell it is then."

He punched me in the face. I blacked out.

◆◆◆

No dreams this time. Moving in and out of consciousness, I came to, being dragged across a metal floor. Were we still in the *Niflheim*? I looked up. EPOCS had me by the ankle. He had brought me to what I assumed was the ship's command deck. Though the darkness made it hard to distinguish the rings of terminals surrounding us, I recognized the arena-like setup. My head throbbed. He must have dragged me down the stairs too.

"There." EPOCS came to a stop. He dropped me. I was too weak to move. "All I have to do is break this puppet's tether to the ship and then he'll be free to move beyond the lake."

He drummed his fingers on the terminal, humming to himself as he waited for the machine to run through its necessary startup. This was the last AI and Karnull's final hurdle. If he got back to *Drasil*... *I won't have a chance of stopping him.* What's more I wouldn't be *me* anymore. I started to inch away, careful not to make too much noise.

He grabbed hold of my leg again and threw me against the terminal's base. "Oh no you don't you little scamp." EPOCS didn't even look down. "You're not going anywhere without me. Don't worry. I'll be finished here in just a second."

My world moved in and out of focus. If he kept this up, Karnull wouldn't have a body when he was finished. I didn't know how much more of this abuse I could take. *Options. What can I do?* The answer was *nothing.* My other side had full control of the situation. If I moved, he would just throw me back again. I couldn't assault him either. Karnull could very easily have killed me before now. The fact was, I was at his mercy; which was frightening, considering the monster had no mercy.

"Tether disconnected. Early Prototype Organic Construct

System released. I will miss you." The computer chirped. "Intelligence free to leave vessel. If this is a problem, report to your captain immediately."

EPOCS looked to me with his hollow eyes. His smile showed teeth. "You heard the lady. It's time we got moving." He kicked me in the ribs. Wincing, I grabbed hold of the terminal to stand. Slipped. EPOCS made the motion of rolling his nonexistent eyes. He crossed his arms. "Can you make this snappy? I have worlds to consume."

"I hate you."

"No." EPOCS held up a gloved finger. "Let's be clear about this. You hate *yourself*."

"I am not you."

"Are so sure?"

I managed to stand. "Why do you continue to insist that I am you? You are a monster. I am—"

EPOCS's smile widened. "What? *Innocent*?" I stared at him. *He knew what I was going to say?* "I'm always the victim." EPOCS said mockingly, grabbing hold of his face with a free hand. He pantomimed a moan. "It's never my fault. Poor, poor Jackson. I killed my wife but I'm too much of a *pussy* to accept the truth. Wah, wah, wah…"

"Shut up."

"Why? Because it's the truth? You did all those things, Kiddo. And, you want to know why? Because… You. Are. *Me.*" I swung. He grabbed hold of my arm. Twisted. My knees buckled and I screamed."Look at you. Pathetic. Why Archia wants you I'll never know."

"Ar-Archia?"

He slapped me. "Don't you *dare* say his name without respect."

"And what about Kristoff?" I snapped back. Tears welled up in my eyes from the pain. "Shouldn't you show him respect? You called him your Creator!"

"I could say the same about you."

Words failed me. I stopped struggling. "What is that supposed to mean?"

EPOCS moved in close to my face. Even though he didn't have eyes, I could see a fire blazing within his darkened eye sockets. "Are you really so dense? Who do you think that insufferable little wretch is, Fool?"

A chill ran through my veins. *He can't mean…* No. That wasn't possible. It couldn't be! Was Kristoff God?

"But don't worry about Him." EPOCS said, his terrifying smile widening like a fissure on thirsty ground. "Once I have control, he won't interfere. By then you'll have made the choice."

"Choice?"

"There's always a choice, Kiddo." I felt the blood rush out of my face. "Like I said, it's either going to be heaven…" His teeth flashed. "Or hell."

Run. Try to break away. But I couldn't. Fear paralyzed me. I didn't want to choose. Why couldn't they just leave me alone? Both ends were slavery, either to myself or someone else. Was it so wrong to want freedom?

What is freedom, Jackson? Kristoff asked gently. *Do you know?*

"I don't understand." I yelled out loud.

Confused, EPOCS hauled me to my feet. Stared. Again, the fire I had seen before smoldered in his dark sockets. "Who are you talking to?"

"None of your business."

He squeezed my throat. I started to choke. "I said '*who are you talking to*'?"

My vision darkened. "H-help… Please."

Laughter filled the room. It reminded me of a child. Happy, alive. Free. *Kristoff.*

I'm coming for you, Jackson.

EPOCS eye sockets widened. Had he heard him too? Frantic, EPOCS looked around the command deck. I felt his fear. It radiated from my other half like heat from the sun. He dropped me and spun in place, snapping and snarling at the air. "No! Don't you try to worm your way in here. This one's rightfully mine. He's been mine from the beginning. You have no claim!"

It's okay, Jackson. I'm with you.

"Shut up!" EPOCS roared.

I always have been and always will be. I love you. Do you want to see?

EPOCS clutched his head. He started to lose balance, as if Kristoff's gentle voice was literally painful to hear. He finally stopped, pitched his head back, and roared wildly into the ceiling.
"Shut up, shut up, shut up, shut up!"

I'll show you.

"I… Would like that." My own words shocked me. Did I really want to see his love?

EPOCS flashed me a brutal glare. "Don't you dare utter another syllable. You don't know what you want. You're *me*. And we don't want Him anywhere near us with His lies. He is a tyrant, and you are his slave."

Soon. You'll see the truth.

"Enough!" Darkness rippled off of EPOCS's body like water. The room went black. Not even the auxiliary lights penetrated the gloom. EPOCS grabbed hold of my throat. "We make the choice, *now*. If you don't choose me you will suffer for all time. I will make your life and death a hell the likes of which you have never seen. Accept that we are the same. Become who you really are!"

I'm coming for you, Jackson.

Before I had the chance to respond, an explosion ripped through the shadows. EPOCS and I were thrown backwards, sliding across the metal floor. Bright sterile white light flooded the room from ahead. It was artificial, like my head lamps, only much brighter. My ears rang. Was I bleeding?

Someone dropped in front of the light. They came toward me. "Good God, I leave you alone for five minutes and this is what happens?" It was a woman. I couldn't make out her face other features for the harsh backlight. Her voice rang, distorted but distinctly female. "I thought I told you to stay alive." *Hawk?* She brushed my hair out of my face. "Hang in there, Jackson. I promised I get you out of this mess and I intend to keep it."

Like the past I hated, the present that refused to leave me alone, and the future lurking just out of sight; my world was swallowed in shadows. I felt her lift me up and carry me off. Where to was beyond me…

22 – *Enemy of My Enemy* – 22

"If you want to make peace with

your enemy, you have to work

with your enemy. Then he

becomes your partner."

- Nelson Mandela -

"**JACKSON, ARE YOU** okay?" I thought I heard Becca's voice and smiled, not because I knew that she was alive, but because I knew that I was dead and the pain had ended. She touched my face. "You're tough. I'll give you that."

My eyes opened. Becca wasn't standing over me. It was a different woman, one with short black hair and a bright blue streak to the side. She had full lips and green eyes. How old was she? Early twenties if I had to guess. Her aviator's jacket had oil stains and her goggles were caked with grime. She wore loose baggy pants and a dark turtle-neck top that exposed her stomach. As she pulled her hand away, I noticed the fingerless gloves. Was this…? "Hawk?" I said slowly.

"Surprised?" She leaned back. We were in a

claustrophobic room, cluttered with dirty pipes and power gauges. The various power level displays scattered around the room fluctuated from red to yellow to green. It all reminded me of the aircraft I had used when leaving the *Midgard.* Hawk, meanwhile, sat on the floor next to me smirking. "I know. I know. I'm a woman. You were probably expecting some guy with a full beard and a case of paranoid schizophrenia weren't you? Well sorry to disappoint you. You'll have to deal with me instead."

I tried to straighten. Winced. "Son of a…" I reached for my head. Why did it hurt so much?

"Woah. Take it easy there." She said, putting a hand on my chest to keep me down. "I had to do some improvised surgery."

"What?"

"That little chip at the base of your skull. After doing some digging, I found it. I was able to disable the command function. Couldn't remove it without killing you though. As of now, you are a semi-free man. *My* man. Oh wait. I didn't mean it like that. I meant because we had a deal and that makes you my partner—" She blushed. "Shut up. Forget I opened my big mouth."

"You cut me open?" The way she said 'digging' scared me.

"Yes. Sheesh. It's not like brain surgery. Well okay. So it

sort of was." She waved me off. "Don't worry. I didn't nick anything important."

I looked around the cabin and spotted some bloody surgical tools in the corner. They rested in a bucket of what I prayed was water. *Good God, I hope those were sterilized.* I felt the stitches on the back of my neck. Shuddered. "Where are we?"

"I'd assume a few thousand feet somewhere over the surface of the planet, but then again, I'm not 100% sure. Let's just say we're in my ship."

"How long have I been out?"

"What is this, twenty questions?" She rolled her eyes and crossed her arms. "About a day, alright? What else do you want to know? Whether or not I'm virgin? Geez. A *thank you* should be in order."

"Sorry. You're right. Thanks."

She smiled a little. "My name's Molly by the way. Molly Coddle-Hawk."

"Molly? So that's your real name. It's nice."

"Don't think just because I saved your ass means you can go hitting on me." She stood and brushed off her pants. Turned. Sighed. "You do a guy a favor…"

"I wasn't hitting on you."

"Yeah, yeah. Sure." She spun and offered me a hand. "You

getting up or what?"

"I thought you said you wanted me to take it easy?"

"Yeah. I did. That was before I offered to help you up. It's not that complicated, Poindexter." I took her hand. She had a surprisingly strong grip. Molly helped to steady me before leading us to the ship's cockpit. After helping me in the passenger seat, she took the pilot's chair and put on a headset. "How do I look?"

"Uh… Like a pilot?"

"Good answer." She pressed forward on the ship's controls. I sunk back in my seat, eyes glued to the grime covered windshield ahead. Orange-pink clouds whisked by us. *I hope this girl has a license.*

"Wh-where are we going, Molly?"

"Not to my place, if that's what you're thinking." She winked at me. "Just kidding. We are. I've got a base of operations. It should be familiar to you."

"Why's that?"

"Because you woke up there. It's the *Midgard.* After that devil-man left, I decided to set up shop. It'll be a nice place to watch the fireworks. All we have to do once we get there is sit back and hit the detonator when *Drasil* comes in range. They're coming alright. If I know the devil-man, he's not going to let you go so easily."

That's right. She was planning on blowing the whole station up. "What happened to EPOCS?"

"You mean the other god-man? Left him."

"But didn't you want to kill him?"

"Oh, I wanted to kill him." I could see a glint of fire in her green eyes. "But not yet. I want them to roast together. Besides. I didn't have my rifle with me… Or my pistol. And those god-men won't die if you tried snapping their necks. They're like zombies. Got to go for the head."

I swallowed. "Good to see you know how to kill."

"Does that scare you?"

"Not really."

"Does it turn you on?"

I squeezed the armrest. *Is she being serious?* "Can we drop the subject please?"

Molly smiled. "I'll take that as a yes then."

"Take it however you like."

"Just so long as you take me to dinner." She laughed. Snorted. Despite my pain, I managed to crack a smile. *What a weird girl.* "I'm glad I didn't kill you." She said, calming down. "It's nice having another person to talk to after all this time."

"How long is that?"

Molly went silent. After a moment, she looked at me. The

strong woman facade was gone. She was hurting inside and had been for a long time. She tried to cover it up with a smile, but her effort was halfhearted at best. "I'd guess a few hundred years. I was in stasis for most of that time."

"Like me."

Molly nodded. "Only I didn't have help when I woke up. I was totally alone. You know, except for my memories."

"Sometimes they can be your best friends."

She looked away from me. "Or your worst enemies."

Silence. I stared out of the windshield, watching as the clouds swirled around us. It was the first time in a long time I felt at peace. Maybe it was the exhaustion talking, but I… enjoyed this. I didn't realize until Molly looked over at me, but I was smiling.

"So…" She said breaking the standstill. "Want to make out?"

"No."

"Good. I like you."

♦♦♦

The *USS Midgard* was like a scarab in the sand. The last remaining rays of desert sun glinted off its shell like a jewel. I had never noticed just hauntingly beautiful it looked from this distance. Maybe I'd never been looking in the first place.

"Pappa Bear," Molly said, making static noises into her hand, "This is Momma Wolf coming in for landing."

She deepened her voice and gave it a southern twist. "Copy that, Momma Wolf. Pappa Bear reads you loud and clear. You are green to land. Any visitors coming our way? You know it gets mighty lonesome down here. A new face would be welcome."

"Look in the mirror." She said.

"That's just cold."

Molly laughed and turned to me. "Man I love having these conversations."

"Uh-huh." I shifted in my chair. "Do you have them… often?"

"Yes. Why?"

"No reason. I talk to myself too." *Of course there really is someone else in my head, so it's slightly different.* But I decided to keep that bit of information to myself.

"I'm not crazy." She said defiantly.

"I am." Molly looked at me. "What? It's the truth."

"Oh I know. I'm just surprised you came to grips with it."

"Very funny."

"But your looks aren't everything." She reached over and punched me in the arm. Smiled. "I came up with that one when I was talking in the mirror one day. Makes a lot of sense huh? Well for you it does at least. I couldn't stop laughing when I said it."

I rubbed my arm. "Yeah. I can hardly keep the laughter down." *Geez. She hits like a freight train.*

"Yeah, I know the feeling. Zeke would have liked it too." Her smiled faltered. She had mentioned a Zeke before, when we had first met. Was he her friend or something more? *Why does it matter?* Furthermore, why did I care?

"Sorry." She offered me an apologetic smile. "Didn't mean to rain on our parade."

"It's okay. I'm sorry for your loss."

"Me too…" Molly shook her head. She was blushing. "But it's not like we were anything more than friends. We weren't dating if that's what you were thinking."

"Sure you weren't."

She punched me again. I winced. *Damn that hurts.* "We weren't! He was like a brother to me."

"I believe you. Good grief. Can you stop hitting me?"

"Can you stop whining like a baby?"

Another uncomfortable pause. I twiddled my thumbs. "Molly?"

"What, Poindexter?"

"I thought you hated me. Why the change of heart?"

She smiled for a moment—only a moment—before giving me a heated glare. "You've got it wrong. Don't think that I'm in love with you or something. I'm out of your league anyway. Nah, the reason I decided not to kill you was that I needed you. Nothing more, got it?"

"If you say so." I looked away from her and stared at the afternoon clouds. "But just FYI, you didn't need me here in order to finish your plan. You could have waited for me to collect the last AI and then blow us all up in one go. So there's that."

Instead of answering, she gave the ship a sharp turn to the right. My face slammed against the side window with a painful *smack.* Looking on the windshield, I caught a reflection of her smirking. *Maybe I would have been better off on Drasil.* Why did everyone hit me?

Molly brought us down toward the *Midgard.* She angled toward a large crack in the side of the cruiser and barreled into the darkness that waited beyond.

How she knew where she was going was beyond me. Even with the ship's lights at maximum brightness, the mess of broken metal and flickering mechanisms was nearly impossible to navigate. By the time we found ourselves in what I assumed was the *Midgard's* engine room, I was plastered to my seat in a state of cardiac arrest. "We've got a visual on you, Momma Wolf." Molly said in her lowest voice possible.

"Roger that, Pappa Bear. I'm coming in." She landed the vessel effortlessly, circling several of the chamber's stadium sized generators in one beautiful motion. The ship hissed as it touched down. It's landing gear went *ka-chunk* on the metal floor, amplifying a hundred times over in the empty space. *I think I'm going to be sick.*

Molly looked over to me and rolled her eyes. "If you vomit in my ship I'll make you lick it up."

"I'll try to remember that." I put a hand over my mouth as another wave of nausea rolled over me.

"I'm insulted. Like my body, my driving's damn fine." Molly opened her door and dropped to the floor. "I'd like to see you try to get here without getting us killed. I bet you couldn't even get us past the entrance."

"You'd win that bet." The nausea passed. I opened my door and slowly made my way down the ladder. Slipped a few rungs from the bottom. *Thunk.* My body hit the floor. I groaned.

"You're hopeless." She walked over to me with a sigh.

"I can get up without your help."

"Sure you can." She locked her arms under my shoulders and lifted me up. "In the meantime, let's get you somewhere you won't kill yourself okay?"

I didn't resist. Molly led me from the crab-shaped ship and into a maintenance hallway underneath the chamber's catwalk system. We passed through several passageways, each connected by automatic doors that hissed as they opened and clicked as they closed. All the while, the pipes around us creaked and groaned with a welcoming rhythm. When we finally stopped, it was at another of the white doors. It slid open. "Home sweet home." She said proudly.

'Home' was a room much like my cabin, albeit slightly smaller. It had once been a maintenance closet of some sort, as evident by the large number of odd robots and cleaning supplies that littered the floor. On the far right wall was Molly's bed—though a nest would have been a better term. It looked like a bird had molted and she'd thrown a blanket over it. I wasn't complaining. She laid me down. Stood back. She cracked her back. "Man you're heavy."

"Thanks, Molly."

"Yeah, yeah." She waved me off, "Don't expect it from here on out."

"No really. I appreciate everything you've done for me. Even the… Uh…" My head still hurt. "Surgery."

Again, she smiled, if ever so slightly. The smile was gone just as fast. "Uh-huh. Don't touch anything." She turned.

I sat up. "Wait, where are you going?"

"Where else? I'm hungry and you're probably starving." She shrugged, her back to me. "Thought it'd be nice if we got some food. You know, a romantic candlelit dinner?"

I laughed and sank back in the bed. "Good luck finding candles."

She laughed too.

◆◆◆

I'm not sure how much longer it was before Molly returned, but when she did it was with an armful of silvery food-packets. Using some spare filaments and the ship's still functioning power supply, Molly started a fire. She funneled the smoke out using some spare pipes and what I assumed was the *Midgard*'s ventilation shaft overhead. *Clever girl.* No wonder she survived so long.

I ripped open a packet of 'Chicken' paste. It tasted like oranges. I ate it anyway. "God, at this rate you're going to eat me out of house and home." Molly said.

"I haven't eaten in a while."

"Neither have I." She picked up a 'Beef' packet.

"What does that one taste like?" I asked, taking another slurp of my chicken-orange paste.

She looked at the packet. Thought. "Apples, maybe?"

"I think these things were mislabeled."

A nod. "I wonder if the apple one will taste like beef?"

"Maybe."

I stared into the fire. It's orange-green glow flickered off the walls. I found it unnerving. It reminded me of the fire in EPOCS's eyes. *Dad, why did I hate you so much?* It didn't make sense, unless of course, Karnull was right and I was a monster. Monsters hated the light didn't they? But Karnull wasn't right. I was normal. Innocent.

Molly eyed me curiously. She slurped on her packet. "So, her name was Becca right?" My eyes snapped to her. "That's short for Rebecca huh? Sorry if that hurts to mention her."

"N-no. I just…" Again, I fell silent, lost in thought.

"Did you mean to kill her?"

Tears welled up in my eyes when she mentioned 'kill'. I couldn't look at her. "No. God no! I loved her. I wish it would have been me instead. It wasn't fair. It wasn't my fault. If there's anyone to blame, it's God."

"You believe in God?"

"No."

"Then how can you blame Him?" I looked up to her again. Molly took another slurp. "Look. I'm not religious. Never have been. But it makes sense doesn't it? How can you hate someone that doesn't exist? And if that's the case, how can you hate an idea? Ideas can't hurt you or have power over you unless you let them. So why do you let them?" I stared at her. "Don't give me that look."

"It's more complicated than that." I said.

"How so?"

"I didn't mean to kill her." I started.

"Yeah, I know, but you *did.* You might not have meant it, but that doesn't change the fact that you did it. Accident or not. What's so wrong with accepting that?"

"Why are you lecturing me like a child?" I could feel the same anger from that night Becca died well up inside. Who did Molly think she was? She didn't know me! What right did she have to tell me anything?

"I'm not." She said defensively. "I just don't understand why you don't want to accept it."

"Because I wasn't the one who did it!" I stood up. Molly stayed seated. "It isn't my fault. If I accept that I did it then that means I have to accept that I did everything else and I can't do that. That would make me a monster. I am innocent. I am not Karnull. I—I—"

I was shaking. Molly didn't break eye contact or change emotion. Then, for the first time since I'd seen her face to face, I realized that I was the reason that Zeke was dead. After all, if I hadn't ordered PAINS to eliminate anyone who would interfere with the directive, then Zeke wouldn't have been murdered. The realization shook me. *No. Not again. I can't be responsible for her pain too, can I?*

Molly stood. I had to look away from her. The guilt flooded my heart all over again. Why couldn't I just die? Why couldn't I have pulled the trigger that night? Instead of chastising me though, Molly grabbed my shoulder. She spun me around.

"We're all monsters, Jack. Whether we want to admit it to ourselves or not. Have you ever intended to kill another person? What about hurting someone you didn't like? We don't let people see the skeletons in our closet because we're afraid, not of what they think, but what we already know." Before I had a chance to open my mouth in protest, Molly had closed her lips around my own. She tasted sweet and earthy. The warmth of her breath flooded over my tongue. Her arms wrapped around my chest and held me tight.

That moment, lost in her touch... I wanted it to last. She reminded me of Becca, and the past I longed for. But I felt something else in her arms. Hope. It was the potential for a future. My heart ached at the thought.

Then, like that, her moist touch left my mouth and she

opened her bright green eyes. I was speechless. "Take a look at those skeletons, Jack." She brushed her fingers across my cheek, eyes hovering on me. "You've got the key to that closet. Only you can do it. Don't be afraid okay?"

I'll show you, Jackson.

I swallowed. Molly smiled. Her eyes hypnotized me. I wanted to dive headlong into them. She blushed and looked away.

"Molly... I...." She slapped me. I blinked. "What the hell?"

"There you go, taking advantage of a young girl. The nerve!" She stomped off to the opposite side of the room. "That's the last time I ever try to help you, Pervert. The next time you have an existential crisis, don't come crying to me."

"Wh-what?"

"Don't play dumb."

"I'm not. I—" I started forward, but she held up a hand.

"Come any closer and I'll drop kick your balls from here to kingdom come got it?"

I stopped. Nodded. *I don't think she knows how to process what just happened.* Not even I did. In not so many words, Molly's bipolar episode was oddly... cute. I rubbed my cheek.

Cute and painful. "Uh, well…" I looked back to my bed—Molly's bed. "I'll just go to sleep then."

"As long as you stay over there and me over here, we'll be dandy."

"Alright." I sank back onto the makeshift bed. "Goodnight, Molly. I'm sorry if I freaked you out."

Just before I turned, Molly smiled. "I'm not." She said.

That made two of us. The fire died. I felt safe, protected. Loved. I fell asleep believing the lie that things would stay this way forever. Little did I know that Karnull had one last trick up his sleeve.

23 – Dealing with Devils – 23

"If you don't deal with your
demons, they will deal with you,
and it's gonna hurt."
- Nikki Sixx -

AS MUCH AS I would have enjoyed saying that my story ended there, it did not. My story continued, as it always had, whether I wanted it to or not. Though I didn't dream again, I tossed and turned, only fully coming awake when a blaring alarm cut the stillness of the chamber like a scalpel cuts flesh.

"Rise and shine, Poindexter." Molly said as my eyes snapped open. She stood on the opposite side of the room, up, awake and grinning ear to ear. Her hands were on her hips. Why was she excited? What was going on?

"Molly, what's wrong? Are we under attack?"

"No."

"Then why are these sirens going off?"

Her smile widened. "Because the firework display is almost ready."

It took me a moment to remember. *Drasil…* Had it already reached us? Karnull must have been following us the moment we left. Did he know about the explosives?

Molly was beside herself with joy.

"I rigged these alarms to go off when the station entered our airspace. Now that it's closing in, we're going to have to get a better seat. I'm thinking the command deck. Do you have any preferences? No, of course not. How could you? You're going to be with me and I'm going to decide." She grabbed my hand. "It's time to haul ass!"

"Wait, Molly!" But she was already dragging me through the halls.

We didn't go towards the generator room. Molly took us to the left, with me half-stumbling in tow. She led us to another tram station like the one aboard *The Niflheim*. A car waited for us, which Molly darted toward it the same way a dog would make for a bone. "I can't wait to see the look on that devil-man's pasty face." She said malevolently. After dragging me inside, Molly let go long enough to bolt for the tram's controls. It took her less than five seconds to select our destination, grab hold of my hand again, and flash me a smile. "I wish we had popcorn."

"You're scaring me a little."

"And you're bumming me out. Come on, this is a

celebration. It's not everyday we get to laugh over the corpses of our enemies. I can't wait to see them burn. It'll be like old times, back when we were on the surface. Hell-fire is really nice you know?"

"Do you hear yourself right now?"

"Yes," She patted her hair. "And I sound, not to mention *look*, beautiful."

The tram lurched forward. Molly was unphased by the sudden movement. I was caught off-balance and fell down. Gravity hated me. She gave me a smirk. "Wow. You're a klutz, huh?"

"Molly?" I stood and regained my balance. "Are you sure this is the right thing to do?"

"Of course I'm sure!" Her forest green eyes were engulfed in a wildfire of emotion. I could almost feel the heat roll off of them. "This is the day I finally have my revenge on the monster that killed my friend and family. Wouldn't you do the same?"

I swallowed. The *monster* that she referred to wasn't PAINS. I had been the one that programmed him. By extension, I was the same one that was responsible for the death of her loved ones. Of course Molly didn't know that and I feared telling her— not because she would harm me, but because this girl was the first person I'd met that didn't know anything of my past. She was my chance to start over. To have a new life. I had to look away or risk opening my mouth.

"Don't tell me you actually like that devil-man?" Molly said, crossing her arms.

"It's not that."

"Are you sure? Look, he helped you yeah; but it was just so he could get his god-buddies together for that Directive Nine they're always talking about. He used you."

Like I'm using you to satisfy some psychological need? My own thought made me wince. I couldn't tell her the truth. "What do you plan on doing after you kill them?" I changed the subject. "Will it bring them back? Those people you loved? You'll still be alone, Molly. It won't have changed anything at all."

"You're wrong." She slipped her hand back into mine. "I'll have you."

Her touch sent waves of warmth across my fingertips and up my arm. I held back the tears. *You wouldn't want me if you knew what I've done.* "I guess you're right." I said slowly.

She smiled. "Of course I am." I didn't respond. She touched my face, and made me look at her. "I know killing PAINS won't bring them back, but it will offer me some closure. Justice has to be done right? That monster and his friends—they all deserve to die. They're murderers and liars. Not like you. You might be a monster, Jack, but so am I. We're different from them."

"Are we? What makes one monster different from the next?" Even as I spoke, my words felt felt like dry heaves. "Aren't they all the same when you get down to it? Evil?"

She kissed me on the cheek. "Even monsters can have happily ever afters, Jack."

Jack. The way she said my name—I couldn't stand it. She really cared about me. Becca had cared too. I looked Molly dead in the eye. Swallowed. "Molly… There's something I need to tell you. It's about those skeletons in my closet."

"I'm here to listen."

What am I doing? I can't tell her! "I—" The words were stuck in my throat. *Damn it.* Just like that night when my finger was on the trigger, I was powerless. Maybe Karnull was in control after all. Why couldn't I ever do what I wanted to? Why was I stuck in this constant state of flux? I remembered Karnull's words. *'To you I'm an abomination. To me you are the abomination—a soul trapped between two ends and two masters.'*

Was it really as simple as making a choice?

"It's okay." Molly said, squeezing my fingertips. "These things take time."

What if I didn't have time?

We made the rest of our trip in silence. I think maybe Molly knew that I was struggling. That made me feel worse. Every ounce of care and consideration she showed me was overshadowed by the hate that was owe me. If she despised PAINS and the others so, then what would she think of me? If I told her she would think I betrayed her. Then she would want me dead. I didn't want her to hate me. All I ever wanted was the darkness inside, that hollow feeling, to be filled. I didn't want it to suck up anyone and anything else. The only thing that could possibly fill me up was… Love. That single word echoed like a thunderclap in my mind. I knew it would be the only thing to fix my heart. But even as I considered the possibility of hope, doubt threatened to choke it out.

If love really could close the gap, then why hadn't Becca's love, or my father's love filled me up? Why didn't it make me feel better? *Maybe they can't close the gap. They were only human.* Despair replaced the guilt and fed into my hate of Karnull. Of course, that hate was also leveled at me. I didn't want to admit it but, I knew, almost instinctively, that he and I *were* one in the same. No matter how many times I said 'It's not my fault'—the pain wouldn't go away. I wanted to die.

"Now approaching central command." The overhead speakers chirped, "Please exit the vehicle carefully. Trams start and stop quickly."

"Finally." Molly's grin threatened to run off her face. "I'm going to puke."

I said nothing.

"Hey, Jack?"

"What?"

"When this is all done, where do you want to live?"

I blinked. Looked at her. My cheeks were red hot. "Live?"

"Well *duh*. As nice as it is here, you know, in this rat-hole that even rats don't really like living in, I think it'd be nice if we went somewhere tropical. Maybe close to the shore." She fidgeted. "What do you think?"

"You do realize that we're the last two people left alive on Earth right?"

She smirked. "Are you implying what I think you're implying?"

"I-I'm not sure."

"Don't worry. I know I'm attractive, but there'll be plenty of time for repopulating Earth once we find a nice spot to settle down. Look at it this way. Business before pleasure. Unless, you know, pleasure is your business. It's not mine. I just…" Molly sighed. "I tried to make that sound sexy and failed. Sorry."

Good lord. I swallowed. "Molly, I don't think we're on the same train of thought here." *I just meant we had more important things to worry about.* When was the last time this girl saw a man? I knew she was lonely but...

"What?" Molly put her hands on her hips. "You don't find me attractive?"

"No. I do. In fact, I think you're gorgeous. It's just..." *Ugh. Why am I so flustered right now?*

She laughed and hugged my side. "I'm just messing with you, Jack. You remind me of a little boy. All I have to do is mention 'sex' and your face turns bright red. It's hilarious."

"Glad *you* find it funny."

She looked up at me. Winked. "I'm dead serious though. After we find a place... Ah-row."

"Please stop talking."

She giggled then punched me in the arm. I guess it was her way of saying 'OK'. I rubbed the pain away. At least the feeling of guilt had left. Maybe that had been her intention all along. Distract me long enough to help me refocus. That, or she was just horny. I couldn't tell with this girl. *Repopulating? Really?*

The tram came to a gentle stop. The doors had barely opened before Molly grabbed my hand and was pulling me along again. A chill lingered in the air as we ran down the command deck's steps.

This was where it had all began. In my mind's eye I could still see PAINS waiting for me in the center of the chamber. Moonlight flooded the spot where he'd last stood. Aside from our footsteps, the room was silent.

Molly cleared the last step with a jump, but because she was still holding my hand, I nearly fell face-first. She cupped her hand to her face and spoke as she approached the terminal. "Mamma Wolf, you've got some bogies closing in at your twelve o'clock. They're mean, real big, and ready to squash you flat. How copy?"

"Ready to rock and roll, Pappa Bear!" She pushed forward on a red lever on the terminal dash. The chamber came to life. Lights flickered on overhead and around. In seconds, the room had gone from black silver-lit space, to a planetarium of stars— each twinkling in an array of red green and white. Ahead, the grime-encrusted windows flashed, bringing up a holographic display. On the horizon, now marked by a three dimensional crimson colored targeting reticule, was the silhouette of *Drasil*. My heart hammered. It was really happening wasn't it? In moments, Molly would detonate the station and the AI, along with Karnull, would vanish.

"Oh, I'm not going anywhere, Kiddo."

I froze.

"So tell me. Do you really think this girl is going to stop us? She can't keep progress at bay forever."

We're going to blow you out of the sky.

"No, I'm afraid you won't."

And why is that? Had Karnull found the explosives?

He chuckled. *"Hold on to that thought. I do believe you have a call to make."*

My other half went silent. What had he meant by 'you have a call to make'?" As if to answer, Molly clicked a button on the terminal. The hard light windows ahead changed to a black screen. Words appeared. 'Attempting to connect' came up in bright white letters. I looked at Molly. "What are you doing?"

"What does it look like?" She said impishly. "I'm going to rub their faces in the fact that they're about to die."

Had Karnull known she would do this?

The screen suddenly changed. PAINS was staring at us. Behind him were HALOS, TRoAS, MACCS and EPOCS. They were all smiling. Their eyes were black now instead of white.

"I was waiting for you, Girly." PAINS said in Karnull's voice. As he talked, the others spoke with him, creating an eerie multi-tone address that sent shivers through my soul.

"You." Molly glared. "I've been waiting for so long this

day. You're going to burn, god-man. You and all your little buddies. You will pay for what you did. Justice will be served today, once and for all."

"Justice?" PAINS looked at me. His black eyes saw through my skin. They knew me—every part of me. Karnull laughed in five voices. "Did you hear that one, Kiddo? The girl-out-of-time wants *justice*. I wonder what she would think of you? Us? Justice. What a load of shit. What does this child know of justice? If she had any clue of the concept she would realize that she's just as damned as you and me."

"Shut up!" I bellowed. Molly looked at me, shocked. Terror rose in my throat. "You don't know anything about us, Karnull."

Molly blinked. "Karnull? Didn't you mention that name before?"

I looked to her. *Careful.* "No... I, uh... It's nothing, Molly."

"Yeah." PAINS hissed. "*It's nothing, Molly.*"

Molly's attention snapped back to the screen. "I've had enough of you, God-man. You are going to die. Any last words before I send you straight to hell? Not that I care about what you have to say or anything. I'm just being human is all. Something you would know nothing about."

PAINS's shoulders shook as he chuckled. He pitched back his head and laughed. I looked over to Molly. She was scared too despite her anger. PAINS looked at me. I could see the worms crawling inside his sockets. Their black wriggling bodies reminded me of Annias's shadow… And Karnull's darkness. "Jackson," PAINS cooed darkly. "What would you say if I had something of yours? Something *very* precious to you. You would do anything for it wouldn't you? Yes, but of course you would. I'll even give you hint at what it is. A living breathing piece of your past. Interested?"

Molly narrowed her eyes. "Alright. You've had your two cents. Now it's time to…"

"Wait!" I grabbed her hand. She looked at me confused. I was trembling. "What do you mean?"

"What I said." PAINS snickered, "Do you want to see her?"

"Her?" Who was he talking about?

The screen flashed. PAINS and the other AI were gone, replaced by a dark chamber lit by auxiliary lights. Pods, much like the one I had woken from, stretched left and right. They were dark. No. Scratch that. One lit up. As the light flickered on, my heart stopped. *It can't be.*

"What's that saying about Thornes and Roses?" PAINS

chuckled.

I stepped to the edge of the terminal, face so close to the screen I was almost touching it. There was no mistaking it. I couldn't breathe. My body shook. Rose. My baby girl. She rested in the pod, as if waiting for me to wake her up. Had she been here this whole time? Karnull had known. This whole time... *She's been so close this whole time.*

"As you can see, when I was going through the station and doing some spring cleaning, I came across this gem. You wouldn't mind taking her off my hands would you?" The screen flashed back to PAINS and the others. "She's taking up space."

"You... bastard!"

PAINS smiled even wider. "I'll take that as a yes?"

I didn't answer him. My body was shaking uncontrollably, though I didn't know if it was from rage or frustration. Maybe both.

"What do you want for her?" Molly shot a glare at the AI.

PAINS's vision shifted to her. "Want? I don't *want* anything, Girly. Unless of course, that means the two of you come up here. Because I *do* want that. This is nothing more than a parting gift. I simply want to thank the two of you for everything you've done."

"Somehow I don't believe you."

The AI shrugged. "Your choice. I guess we can always throw her out."

"No!" I screamed. "Don't!"

"Jackson?" Molly touched my arm.

I was crying. "Please, Karnull, don't."

He chuckled. "Tell you what, I'll give you two time to think about it. Just don't take too long. TRoAS wants the ship cleaned after all. It'd be a shame to let the little lady go to waste wouldn't it?" The transmission ended.

Staring at the now-empty hard light windows, I felt like a ghost. Rose was alive. This changed everything. But why was Karnull not asking for anything in return? That seemed suspicious. Not to mention, totally unlike him. It had to be a trap of some kind. Then again, what if it wasn't her? *He might be trying to trick me.*

Molly stood. "That was your daughter, wasn't it?"

"Y-yes."

"Jackson," She stepped over to my side. "We have no way of knowing if that was her or not."

"I know that." I wiped my eyes. "But what if it is and he kills her? I couldn't live with myself if I let one more person die. Especially Rose. Do you understand me? We have to get her, Molly. If you don't come with me, fine, whatever. I'll go by myself. Don't try to stop me."

I turned to leave. Molly grabbed my arm. "You're not going anywhere." She said.

"Molly, I just told you—"

"Because I'm coming with you." I turned and stared at her. "There you go again giving me that look." She said.

"Wait. You don't want to blow them up?"

"I never said that." She looked to the floor. "So many people have died because of those monsters. We're still going to blow them up, but I won't reveal that little fact until we're inside."

"I get it. You mean like a bargaining chip. In case they put us in some sort of a trap."

"Bingo. You've got to know when to hold 'em and when to fold 'em. We don't want them guessing our trump card just yet. Besides…" She looked into my eyes. Part of me melted under her gaze. "I would do the same if it was my Mom or Dad… Or Zeke."

"Thank you."

"Oh you'll be thanking me later." She winked. "But before that we need to gear up. Are you any good with a pistol?"

My day of target practice came to mind. I sighed. "No."

"You think you can manage not to shoot your foot off?"

"I'm not *that* bad." Molly raised an accusatory eyebrow. I

rolled my eyes. "Okay. Maybe I am. I'll do my best."

"I guess that'll work. Now come on." She started for the stairs and grabbed my hand. "We've got to make you deadly, Poindexter."

◆◆◆

We spent the rest of the night prepping for our trip aboard the *Drasil*. Molly gave me a crash course in gun safety and did her best to teach me how to shoot. The end result had me hitting my targets, some left over beakers and vials from pre-stasis times, squarely in the center of mass. Molly said I was passable. I felt like I'd won the lottery. After that we set our gear out for the trip. By the time we were done with everything, I was exhausted.

"That's enough prep work." Molly said, patting me on the back. We had gone back to her room. I sat on her makeshift bed, half asleep. What time was it? Close to morning? Had we been training all night? Molly smiled. "Now I won't have to worry about you shooting me in the back."

"Your faith in me is touching."

She giggled and took a seat beside me. "You did well, Jack."

"Th-thanks."

"Don't mention it." Molly ran her hand through my hair, brushing it to the side. Her touch sent a warm spasm of pleasure up my spine. Why was she looking at me like that? Her green eyes seemed softer now, as if thinking. Again she smiled. "Man we've got to cut your hair after this is over. Before long I'll forget which one of us is the girl."

"Molly? Doesn't it scare you that you, Rose, and I are the last ones left?" Her hand stopped. "I don't mean to be a downer or anything but there's no way we can survive for very long with just the three of us."

She removed her hand and placed it at her side. Molly looked to the floor again, as if thinking. I felt rotten. Why did I always ruin things? Was I cursed or something? I sighed and looked to the floor myself. *Yikes. What miserable conversation topic.*

"I guess I never really thought about it." Molly said finally. I glanced at her. She'd taken off her jacket, leaving on just her top. The girl's soft snowy arms were bare and coated with fine droplets of sweat. Had we really done that much lifting? It was either that or her jacket was warm. Regardless, I caught myself staring one moment too long. Looked away. She laughed softly, under her sweet breath. "My Mom used to tell me a story. It kind of reminds me of our situation—a boy and a girl. It was about two people from a time long ago."

"What were they called?" I asked.

"Who? The people?"

"Yeah."

Molly thought about it. After a moment she said, "Choral and Ordonna."

What? I looked to her. Had I heard Molly correctly? *Choral and Ordonna?* How did she know about them? The only other person I'd heard those names from was Karnull. Were Molly and Karnull somehow connected? If so, what did that mean?

Molly continued unabated. "Well okay, so it wasn't *just* two people. There was this God that made them. I always thought the story was funny because after the God made Choral—the guy —He knew that his new friend was going to be lonely, so he gave him someone to love, a woman—Ordonna."

Like Adam and Eve.

Molly looked over to me. That look in her eyes… "Jack, I need to ask you something."

My cheeks were hot. I swallowed nervously. "S-sure."

"What's it like to be loved? To be *in* love?"

Why would you ask me that? She didn't break eye contact. I couldn't look away. The words slowly hobbled out of my mouth. "You said that Choral was lonely, right?"

She nodded. *Her lips…* They were so full. "Maybe it

wasn't that he was lonely."

"What?"

"Maybe…" Again, I swallowed as my eyes ran down her neck. "Maybe Choral needed an outlet for love. Isn't that what being with someone is all about? You're so happy with your life, you can't help but have that happiness overflow. Ordonna might have been there for two reasons. One, to love Choral, but I think it's more than that." My eyes were over her chest now. Her stomach. I was shaking. Why did it feel like I was burning? "She was there to love and *be* loved."

"Jack?" Molly slipped her hand in mine so tenderly I almost didn't feel her touch. My eyes snapped up to her face. I hadn't realized how close she and I were sitting. *Oh God.* I was having trouble breathing. Molly's smile matched the tenderness in her eyes. The words that came out of her mouth might as well have been bombs. "Will you love me like that?"

Every ounce of me was screaming 'yes', only no words came out of my mouth. Was it love I felt? I didn't know. The only woman that had ever made me feel this way was Becca. Was it wrong to feel this way again?

To answer her, I leaned forward and cupped the side of Molly's face in my hand. Her cheek felt so very soft. I closed my eyes. Our lips met. Again, the sweet taste of Molly's breath flooded my mouth. She strung her arms around my neck and bit my lip. As we kissed, I ran my arms down her back and felt for the edge of her shirt. Pulled it up. She stopped long enough to help remove it and throw her clothes to the side. Molly's bare chest pressed against me. She pushed me down. We tossed and turned, hot against one another. As my thoughts of the future were thrown to the side, so were our clothes, piece by piece, memory by memory, until there was nothing between us. The sound of our love, the sighs and moans of two monsters looking for meaning, filled the chamber. I didn't want to leave her. Not now or ever.

Did part of me feel badly, as if I'd betrayed Becca? Yes. I couldn't lie about that. But I couldn't dwell in the past either. Molly was my new beginning.

"I think I love you, Jack." Molly said breathy, her naked body moving in time with my hips.

"I think I love you too, Molly." And I meant it. I hadn't meant anything more in my entire life.

Again our lips met, and we didn't leave each other's embrace. I don't remember when I fell asleep, but that night, I didn't dream. I slept for what felt like the first time in ages. Exposed and alone, together in each other's arms. Hawk, the terrorist. Jackson the killer. Two misfits forgotten by time. We were monsters after all, but did that make us evil? What was evil anyway? Maybe I didn't have to choose. Who said Karnull had to be my master? I smiled and hoped that was true. I knew it wasn't.

24 – The Spider's Parlor – 24

"The mind cannot support moral

chaos for long. Men are under

as strong a compulsion to

invent an ethical setting for their

behavior as spiders are to

weave themselves webs."

- John Dos Passos -

WHEN I WOKE, it took all of my energy to peel myself from her side and get dressed. Today was the day. Here, Karnull would either win or lose. I doubted very much that there would be any sort of stalemate. A finality hung in the air, just as it had those moments in which I struck Becca. Today, something was going to change, whether in me or the world around me.

I was terrified.

"Jackson?" Molly yawned. She stretched. "What are you doing?"

"What does it look like?" I finished zipping up my suit's collar. It's armor mode activated automatically as I slid the pistol

Molly had given me in the holster on my right thigh. I straightened. Looked at my watch. Ninety-five percent. The memory sync was almost complete. Whatever that meant.

Molly stood. "I *meant* 'why are you getting up without me? I do recall that I was going with you, remember?"

"I was going to wake you up."

She walked over to me and kissed my cheek. "Uh-huh. Sure you weren't just trying to sneak out so I wouldn't come along and potentially get hurt? You're such a romantic softy. It kind of makes me want to barf."

I smiled a little. Molly was right of course. Why did I think I could have gotten dressed without waking her up? It was a half-hearted attempt anyway. I *needed* her there. Yet, in the same breath, I didn't want her to get hurt. Like the rest of my life, I was torn between two things, unable to choose. At least that's what I told myself. Didn't all men have a choice?

It didn't take Molly long to join me. After she finished securing the detonator in place on her belt, we made our way up to the command deck in silence. She held my hand and that was enough communication for me. My mind was in the sky.

Rose. I still couldn't believe that she was alive.

We arrived at the command deck. Bright, noonday sunlight poured in from the grimy windows. After a momentary delay in starting the system, Molly and I established contact with *Drasil.* PAINS greeted me with his black eyes. Was it my imagination or did they have a slight reddish glow now? The other AI waited behind him. Had they stayed there all night? PAINS grinned and the others followed suit. "Hey there, Kiddo." His multi-tone voice echoed around us. "Are you ready to cut a deal or not?"

I'm certainly ready to cut you. PAINS snickered, as if understanding my thoughts. Most likely, he did. "We're ready to come on board." I said.

"Excellent." He clapped his gloved hands together. "Then I'll prepare the beam. It'll be so good to have you back, safe and sound."

Molly cut in. "Don't try any funny business god-man. You'll pay for it if you do."

"Girly, I wouldn't dream of doing such."

Molly looked to me. I looked at her. We nodded. She held my hand. "I've got your back." She whispered.

"Ditto." I paused. Felt a smile cross my lips. "I can't wait for Rose to meet you."

Molly's eyes widened. She looked away and blushed. "M-me too."

"Aren't you two the cute couple." PAINS hissed. He made

a disgusted sound. "Get a room already. You're making me sick."

Molly didn't look at him. "If that makes you sick then it was a good thing you didn't see us last night. That would have made you up-chuck like nobody's business. I almost wish we'd been recording it, come to think of it. What do you say, Jack?"

"I think that's kind of creepy, Molly."

PAINS turned away. "Humans."

The light of *Drasil's* beam transmitted through the interior of the command deck and swept over us. In seconds we were standing in *Drasil's* command chamber, surrounded by the grinning visages of PAINS and the other AI. They bowed, looking first to me. "Welcome, Jackson." Then to Molly. "Girl-out-of-time."

"My name is Molly." She said, stepping forward.

What did they mean by 'Girl-out-of-time?' I put a hand on her shoulder. She looked at me. Nodded. I turned my attention to PAINS. "Where is she?"

The AI snapped his fingers. In seconds, a *whirr* filled the chamber. I turned to see that *Drasil's* floor was moving at twice its normal speed. PAINS started toward us. Molly whipped out her gun. "Don't move, God-man."

"I'm afraid shooting me would just waste your ammunition, Girly." His body flickered in and out of existence.

There was no grafter body beneath. He was only a hologram. *What is Karnull up to?* "Just hop on the belt and it will take you where you need to go." He said, cordially.

"How do we know it will take us where we need to go?" I asked.

"Would you prefer if I left you to wander?"

I grit my teeth. As much I hated to admit it, he had a point. This would be the fastest way there. We didn't have much of a choice. "Fine. But Molly meant what she said. Don't even try to double cross us."

"If there's anyone who will be double crossing us, it will be you, Kiddo." PAINS waved with the the tip of his fingers. "Tah-tah now. Please go collect your daughter and bring your little tale of woe of tragedy to a happy end, won't you?"

Molly started at him. I stopped her. "Come on. Let's find Rose."

"If you say so." She holstered her pistol. We stepped on the floor. In seconds, we were already traveling forward through *Drasil's* massive corridors. They felt alien now. Then again, had I really ever felt at home here?

"I don't like this, Jack." Molly half-whispered. Her voice carried over the sound of the floor. "He's up to something. I'm just not sure what it is."

"I know. As long as we keep our cool we'll be able to get through this unscathed."

She shifted from one foot to the other uncomfortably. "You think he knows about… The fireworks?"

I hope not. "If he does, we'll figure something out."

"And if we can't?"

I squeezed her hand. "Molly, don't worry." My heart wasn't in my words though. Could she see my doubts and fears? I had so many second thoughts it was a wonder they didn't pour out of my nose. Despite what I told her, I couldn't shake the feeling that we were walking into a trap.

I'm not sure how long we stayed on the conveyer belt floor but we were in a section of *Drasil* I had never seen before. It looked more industrial, as if the designers had forgotten to place the white veneer on the walls and ceiling. The floor fed through a particularly large square entryway marked 'Level Three'. Once inside the relatively short hallway beyond, the entryway's giant door fell behind us, casting our path ahead in shadow. The floor stopped.

"Why aren't we moving anymore?" Molly asked. "I don't see any pods."

"Me neither."

Auxiliary lights flickered on beneath our feet, highlighting the steely floor a cold blue. Ahead of us, at the end of the snub-nose hall, lay a rectangular entryway. Molly squeezed my hand. I squeezed back.

"Well, it's now or never. Right, Momma Wolf?"

She smiled at me. "Roger that, Pappa Bear."

We made our way to the opening. If there had been a door here once, it had long ago been removed. Our steps echoed in the black. The moment we passed the threshold, Molly and I found ourselves in a large circular chamber. It was cold here and we pressed together, both out of uncertainty and for warmth. A large column occupied the center of the chamber and ran up into infinity. We stopped.

"Alright. I guess this is it." I said. My breath frosted against my face shield. "Do you see any pods?"

Molly looked around. "No. Don't you have lights on that thing?"

I answered her by clicking my headlamps on. They ran over the room. I hadn't noticed, but the walls were filled with pods. We were most definitely in the right place. The only thing we needed to do now was to find Rose.

I started toward the left hand side of pods. The floor shook. I stopped. Molly drew her pistol and backed up against me. Clumsily, I drew my weapon.

The room came to life. All around us the pods' interiors illuminated, showing their contents. Some were empty. Others had people of all ages in them. Were these early OC units? Or were they actual people? I didn't see Rose. The floor moved us downwards, rotating around the column.

"I know this place." Molly said slowly. I turned to her. "This... I woke up here!" She said, eyes wide. "I can't believe I didn't make the connection before. I guess I didn't remember. I *was groggy* when I woke up."

"How did you get in here?"

"That's a long story. Come to think of it, I'm not sure I remember everything correctly. The station's systems were malfunctioning. I remember running away from someone and hiding in one of the pods." She grabbed her head. "When I woke up... A figure was waiting for me. He must have woken me up."

"Wait what do you mean? Who woke you up?"

She looked at me and shook her head sadly. "I'm sorry, Jack. I don't remember. Maybe that same person didn't want me remembering until now. Does that sound crazy?"

Not as crazy as some of the things I've heard. "We can figure it out later. Right now, let's focus on finding Rose."

"Right."

As the floor spiraled us downwards with the column, we

began to slow. After a few minutes of spinning, Molly and I stopped at the bottom most floor. Here, one of the pods was missing, revealing a well-lit corridor beyond. It looked to have walls of glass and a floor of white. I don't know why, but I knew Rose was at the end of the path.

"Come on." I said.

Molly followed me into the hallway. The sunlight half-blinded me. On either side, partitioned off by the glass walls, a sea of clouds whisked around us. It was here that I realized we were in the bottom-most point of the station, mere feet away from that blinking red light I had seen what felt like ages ago. Rose would be just above it. *She's been here all this time huh? Right under my nose.*

At the end of the hall was yet another circular room. Molly and I entered it, taking a small set of white stairs to the floor beyond. Instead of being filled with pods however, the walls were made of glass and offered a shining view of the outside world. Above lay a black jungle of wires and mechanisms. A single ivory pod waited for us in the center of the chamber.

This wasn't the pod PAINS showed us, yet I knew it was the one that Rose was sleeping in. It had to be! We started for it, Molly taking the lead. "Maybe he wasn't planning on double crossing us, after all." She said. "Which is surprising, given the devil-man doesn't tell the truth. At first I thought he was going to lead us to your little girl and then show you that she was dead, or worse. I could think of a hundred evil things he could have done. Thank God he didn't—" She froze.

"Molly? Is something wrong?"

I joined her side to see what she was staring at. It wasn't Rose. The man inside the pod wore a grey uniform. He was my age. My height. My… *everything*. I stopped breathing. The man in the pod was Jackson Robert Thorne. The real Jackson. I knew it almost immediately. I was an OC unit after all.

But if that man in the pod was me, then who the hell was I supposed to be? Why were there two of me?

"It's time to make a choice, Kiddo."

My watch chirped. I looked down. One Hundred Percent? Pain flared across my skull. It crippled me. I fell backwards, screaming. After I hit the floor, I saw Molly run to my side. She looked confused. Hurt. I wanted to explain to her, but I didn't know what was going on. I wasn't me.

Who was I?

Ironically, that was the question Kristoff had been asking me all along.

25 – Gods and Men – 25

"It is *finished*."

- Jesus Christ -

SOMETIMES I WONDER whether or not the life I live is a dream. Sometimes I wonder if, when I wake up in my dreams, I see the way things really are. Maybe there's some truth to that. In that moment, seconds after having fallen to unconsciousness, I woke up in a fantasy that was all too real. I knew I had come to the end of my journey. Of my dreams.

It wasn't what I had expected to see. Then again, what *had* I expected to see? Not the field of flowers that stretched from one end of the horizon to the other. Not the perfect blue sky or the single bent tree on the hill where I lay, covered by its shade. Not Becca.

"Jackson, can you hear me?" She brushed a strand of red hair out of my eyes.

I looked to her, aware that she was dead and alive at the same time. You would think it would have frightened me, seeing her there, but it didn't. I touched her cheek. Smiled.

"You're here." I said, dumbly.

"Well of course I'm here." She giggled. "Where else would I be? We said forever and always, didn't we, Jack? I meant it. I'm never going to leave you. Not even death can keep us apart." I sat up. She was wearing a blue and white sundress. It contrasted with her bright red hair. Was I dreaming? "Come on." She said, helping me to stand. "Let's go for a walk."

"O-okay, Sweetheart." I followed her down the hill, hand in hand. There was no destination in mind, this much I knew. We were going to walk—maybe forever and eternity. I didn't mind. Becca was with me again. I had so much to tell her! "Sweetheart?" I said, after several minutes of walking in silence.

"Yes, my love?"

"I missed you so much."

"And I you." She kissed me on the cheek.

"Rose is alive. We found her."

"We?"

That's right. She wouldn't know about Molly. How would Becca accept her? "My new friend." I said.

"Are you *only* friends?"

"N-no."

A pause. Her voice lowered ever so slightly. "I see."

I changed the subject. "Uh, where are we, Becca? Is this

supposed to be heaven?"

Becca turned to me and smiled so wide that her eyes closed shut. She giggled again. "No, Silly. We're the farthest thing from heaven you can possibly get."

"Are we dreaming then?"

"No. This place is very real."

"Where is it? What is it?"

Becca's voice deepened. "Why, we're in hell, Jackson. *Your* hell."

"What?"

Blood started to drip from the sides of Becca's mouth. I froze. She was still smiling, but the red liquid poured from her eyes and ears and nose. Horrified, I tried to step back. I couldn't. Looking down, I saw my hand gripping a knife. It was buried up to the hilt in her stomach. I trembled and looked up at my late wife. Becca opened her eyes. They were black and wriggling with worms.

Karnull's voice echoed from her lips. "You killed me, Jackson." I screamed, stumbling backwards. "I hate you." She said, still smiling.

Becca fell down. The field of flowers cushioned her fall. She started to laugh—his awful laugh. I couldn't move. My eyes were fixed on her body, still bleeding, still laughing despite the wound. I looked at my hands. They were bloody.

No. No. It's not my fault.

"Oh it's your fault alright." I spun. Karnull stood behind me, although he didn't quite look like me anymore. He resembled a teenage boy with an olive green-orange hoodie, black jeans, and a white t-shirt. The symbol for Omega was printed on his T-shirt. One of his eyes, a ruby set against a bed of black velvet, was obscured by long brown hair. The monster's smile was filled with shark-like interlocking teeth. I felt all the blood drain out of my face. "You did everything, Kiddo." He said without moving his lipless grin. "You killed her. You killed your father, that guard, and all those people so long ago. You're a murderer. You are *me.*"

"No. I'm not you. I'm not evil!" I started to back up. My feet hit Becca's dead body and I fell backwards. When I struck the ground Karnull started forward. He stopped at Becca's inert corpse. My other half grabbed hold of her head and twisted it to face me. Her neck snapped in the process.

"Poor, Jackson." He moved her jaws to mimic his words. The blood had turned black on her snow-white skin. "It's never his fault. He's innocent. Perfect. Why Jackson could never be evil. After all, humans aren't *evil*." Karnull let go of her and stood. He pitched back his head and cackled. "Oh, that's rich. What's even funnier is that you actually believe that shit!"

"I'm not you." I said, breathless. "This isn't my fault. None of it!"

Karnull chuckled through his perfectly interlocking teeth. "Let me show you something, Kiddo. From one monster to another." I blinked. The field of flowers had vanished. In its place was a sea pitch black water. No. Not water. Blood. It felt like glass beneath me. An agonizing groan filled the air. I looked down to see thousands of faces staring from the darkness, eyes filled with the worms. My heart stopped. "Jackson Robert Thorne, meet the sins of your past. Sins of his past, meet Jackson Robert Thorne." Karnull's laughter filled the air around me. "You two go together like blood and veins."

I launched myself from the surface of the blood, moving to my feet. Everywhere I looked their eyes stared at me, worms wriggling in and out, awful moans filling the sky. All those souls left behind. Slaughtered because of me. No. I couldn't have done this! I refused to accept it. Desperate to escape, I broke into a run. I had to get away. Anything was better than staying here.

"It's so cute how you think you can just leave your past behind." Karnull snickered all around me. "Were you born yesterday? That's not how this life thing works."

"Shut up!" The sea of dead bodies laughed beneath me. '*Shut up*' they said in tandem. "Stop talking!" I raged. "Leave me alone!"

"Not until you see who you really are." Karnull's voice
held an edge to it.

I fell to my knees and closed my eyes in an attempt shut them all
out. *No.* This wasn't me. It couldn't be.

"Jackson?" Becca's soft voice caused me to look again.
Amid the dead faces, her's rose up from the sea of damned souls.
Her skin was white. Her eyes were normal. My tears struck the
surface of the cadaver ocean.

"Please. Becca, you don't hate me do you? Is this the real
me?"

She smiled. "Of course it is, Jackson." The worms
burrowed out of her eyes. Becca started to laugh. I screamed and
stood. Wait. Fell? Yes, I was falling. Upwards.

Only instead of falling back to the sea of dead bodies, I
fell towards the sky. It was then I realized that the world had
turned on its head. The blood-stained darkness that had been my
earth became sky. Now I was falling back to the ground.
Screaming.

"I bet you wish you had pulled that trigger." Karnull
hissed. "Anything would be better than this, wouldn't it, Kiddo?"
My stomach rose in my throat as I lost my voice from screaming.
"Want to know something funny? Even if you had offed yourself

that night, you would still be burning in hell. Granted, you wouldn't have done nearly this level of damage but... A bunch of fire is a bunch of fire."

I hit the earth with spine-snapping *crack*. Dust flew upwards, obscuring the sky. I didn't die however. Merely winded, I took in lungfuls of burning air. Flames licked the air around me. I looked to the left, right. Still couldn't see anything. Now where was I?

A figure approached me from the cloud of dust. "As much as I would like to take credit for this delightful chaos, it's all on you, Kiddo." Karnull hissed gleefully. His unobscured eye flashed. "This is your handiwork, and I must say, it's *mighty fine*. Not even Hitler had this kind of potential. You, sir, are a prodigy. Man, I can only imagine the hellfire prepared for your sorry soul. I'm *jealous*."

"Shut... up." I struggled to stand.

Karnull continued toward me slowly.

"Here's a better idea—why don't you just accept who you are?"

"Because this isn't me!" I screamed. Whether it was out of fear or hatred, I summoned my courage and swung at my shadow. He grabbed my fist. Twisted my arm until it snapped. Karnull followed up with a kick to my ribs. I flew backwards with the force of a cannon ball and struck a wall of… *No. God, no!* I winced and checked either side of me. There were corpses. Each had eyefuls of Archia's black worms. Black blood seeped from their bodies like oil from dry earth. I peeled myself off of them and rolled to the dusty ground. When I looked back up, Karnull was gone. In his place stood the massive shadow I had seen take Annias's place on the surface of the sea in my dreams of Kristoff. Archia, the Icrageon. Sickness rolled off his writhing worm body in nauseating waves. I wanted to die.

"Behold, your king." The wriggling, vaguely humanoid shadow bellowed with a thousand different voices all at once. "I am your beginning and your end. I am your Alpha and Omega. I am the darkness of the time before time began. I am the god of the prime dimensions and humanity's true *love*." The shadows laughed. "I am Archia, and you *will* worship me, Worm. You are part of me."

"Go…to hell." I said weakly.

Archia responded by whipping out one of his arms. The mass of wriggling black worms struck me square in the chest and held me to the spot. I lost what little breath I had left. He held me in place as he walked forward with earth-shattering footsteps. His furious glowing red eyes charred my soul. Was this it? Was I really going to die? "Accept it, Worm!" The dark one bellowed.

"You are me!"

"I am not—" His worms, in unison, bit into my flesh. I screamed until my throat was raw.

Archia did not remove his gaze. "You humans are all the same. You honestly believe that you are the gods of any world you step foot on. Pathetic! You aren't worthy of respect or admiration. You are little more than fodder for the darkness. Yet, *He* cares for you. Why? I do not understand." He threw me down.

"You have two choices, human. You may either accept me as your god or die."

"I am *not* you…!"

He whipped my face. Blood flew from the wound as I sailed against the wall for yet another time. "You have my heart, human. You have my flesh. Your kind have been my creations ever since that day I tricked them. They traded their light for shadow and I have made my home in their hearts ever since. Still, even I cannot rule in their souls unless they willingly choose me. So, we come back to my ultimatum. Choose me or die. Pick one, Worm."

"What… do you mean they traded their light for shadow?"

Archia started to laugh. The sound reminded me of a thousand shrill bats and violins. He knew my pain. The beast savored it. His red eyes flared with satanic light. "What do you think, child of Dust? The Creator wasted his light by giving it to your kind. He put it in your eyes so that you could see and *live* truth. But I gave them an offer of even greater value. By being blinded by shadow, they could make up their own worlds. *Be* their own Creators! They bought my lie and now they are slaves to themselves—and me. My worms filled their bodies, minds, hearts and souls. Like a rotting piece of fruit, they were defiled. They became *my* children that day. My worshipers. My personal, living witnesses to the Creator's foolishness."

"You act like you know about humans. I don't know where you're from, but you sure as hell aren't in any of our history books."

"You dense little fool! I exist in multiple realms. Earth or Anacra. Evil is evil no matter where you tread. Though I admit, the darkness didn't have a voice in this world. That's why I gave my other version a little help." *Karnull. Sin. Satan. Evil.* It suddenly made sense. Archia was the source of it all. "Did you honestly think Karnull is some science experiment gone wrong? Do you think he's some monster born from human ingenuity?" Archia took a step forward. "He is a voice for what is already there in your soul. The worms speak and so does he. You are the monster, Jackson Robert Thorne. You are mine!"

My heart stopped. As I digested this new bit of

information Archia continued toward me. His wriggling writhing mass rose over my body like a wave.

"My evil knows no boundaries. It spans all realities, just waiting be unleashed. I am the source of the darkness in the hearts of men. If they speak, they do so because of the shadows within them. Accept it, child of Dust. This the truth. I am you. You are my child."

There was no use fighting anymore. I knew Archia, lord of lies and darkness, was telling me the truth.

Karnull... All this time I thought he was an evil force that had been placed inside me. I never even considered that he was simply using what was already there. If Karnull was the voice, then the darkness was my own. I *was* a monster. I was evil. This *was* my fault. I bent my head, unable to cry. Unable to breathe. Unable to think.

"Accept it, Worm. Finish the transformation. Say that you are evil!"

"I'm evil." I whispered, so deathly quiet it thundered in my own soul.

Archia stopped inches from me. The ground shook. "Louder!"

"I'm evil."

He chuckled. "Once more, Worm. Please. Let me hear the

truth from your lips."

"I'm evil."

"Yes." Despite not having teeth, I could imagine the monster was grinning. "You are evil. I am your master. You are my slave. My child." Archia laughed and roared to the sky. "Did you hear that, Immulon? Your little project has failed once more. This soul—"

"I deserve to die." I whispered, more to myself than Archia.

It was like I'd dropped a bomb. Archia froze. He lowered his face down to me. "What did you mumble?"

I looked up at the beast. Tears formed at the corner of my eyes. "I deserve to die. I'm a monster. An abomination! I deserve to die and burn. There is no forgiveness for what I've done. I'm sorry."

A thunderclap echoed across the black corpse-sea sky. Archia looked up into the air. Was it my imagination or was he nervous? The beast looked back to me. "Be silent." He snapped.

"I don't deserve love. Or happiness. Or hope. I deserve death. Please, I'm sorry!" I was screaming for Kristoff.

Another *crack* tore overhead. Archia started to panic. He grabbed hold of me and brought me toward his smoldering, volcanic eyes. Squeezed. "Shut up! Shut up! Shut up! Shut up!

You will not repent!"

I didn't stop. I pitched my head back and screamed into the sky. "I'm sorry. It *is* my fault. I know I don't deserve love but please, I beg you—forgive me. You were right. Kristoff, help me. Please! God, I believe!"

One final *crack* split the sky. All around us, waterfalls of black blood poured from the sea above, plummeting to the ground. Archia screamed. "No! How dare you! You are mine, Worm! Not *His*. I will kill you! I will devour your pathetic excuse for a soul and spit you out in hell! You will not be His. You will—" But a massive waterfall slammed down on Archia, cutting him off. He released me, his body vanishing into the dark. I fell to my knees and watched as the blood flooded the ground around me, steadily rising higher and higher. When it got to my chest I cried even more bitter tears. *This is what I deserve.* It rose to my neck. *Death. This is justice.*

The blood filled my lungs. Fire swallowed my body inside and out. I was going to die here, in the sea of my sins—just as it should be. I knew this is what I deserved. I would have done anything to change it, but I knew I couldn't. Like the rest of my life, I was powerless to stop the inevitable from happening. I was a slave to myself. I was born a slave and I would die a slave. *I'm so sorry. Please, dear God, forgive me. You were right.*

My body floated off the ground. I drifted in the abyss, alone, with not even my memories to haunt me. Pain curled through my body as the air in my lungs burned. I welcomed death with open arms.

Jackson.

Kristoff? I opened my eyes. The darkness stretched on forever. His voice echoed around me, covering my body like a father's arms. He knew my name. He had always known my name.

I made you. I love you.

His words stung more than the weight of the shadows. I wanted to cry, but the tears wouldn't come.

Do you want me to help you?

Was this the choice the Messenger had said I would make? "Yes." I screamed with whatever breath was left in me. The bubbles left my mouth as I closed my eyes on the edge of oblivion. It was too late for anyone to help me now. I was damned to hell. I was evil.

But someone grabbed my arm.

In moments, I was rising from the darkness. The blood became red, as if energized by a new-found life. Then, my head broke the surface and I took a lungful of sweet air.

Whoever had been holding onto my hand let go.

I fell on hard ground, eyes closed, body dripping wet. I coughed as more and more air filled my shriveled lungs. I was alive. As feeling returned to my body, I looked up.

Kristoff—the boy—was staring at me. His warm golden eyes embraced my aching heart. "Hello, Jackson. I've been expecting you."

"…You?" I coughed. "But, I saw you die. How are you here? How are you young again?"

The boy laughed—the laugh of a child. He still wore his white tunic, pants and bloody scar. The Creator of men stood on a sea of blood-red water. My horizon was framed by a bright blue sky. He was beaming, as if he had won a great victory. *Victory over my soul.* His voice filled every inch of my body, sending spasms of pure pleasure throughout my veins. I'd never felt anything like this! "What is death to life, Jackson? Shadow to light?"

"I don't know." I could barely speak. Was this pleasure… coming from him? *It has to be.*

"Let me ask you this then—" Kristoff said. "Is darkness something you can reach out and touch?" I blinked. He smiled.

"Shadows are nothing more than the absence of light. They are nothing at all. If anything, they are evidence of the substance of something."

"But you died." I repeated stupidly. Laughter welled up in my stomach.

"Yes." Kristoff said. "And not just here, but in every reflection. That's what your world is. A reflection. I am alive however because of who I am, and I am both light and life. Do you understand me?"

"I... think so." I shook my head. Laughed with relief. "No. I don't understand you at all."

Kristoff smiled playfully. "You will, in time."

Silence. I felt weak, like I could collapse at any second. Between the fear of seeing Archia and the pleasure of Kristoff's presence, my body was drained. *Say something, Jack.* "Thank you for pulling me out of there. I was so scared. I thought I was going to die."

"I told you I would come for you didn't I?"My eyes suddenly filled with tears. I bent my head and cried. I had wept long before now but it felt like the first time I had ever known true sorrow or joy. After an eternity of sobbing—playing my life over and over again in my head—Kristoff placed a hand on my shoulder. I looked at him. My body was shaking. "Why are you crying, Jackson?"

"Why? Because of what I did. I'm a murderer. I'm evil. I don't deserve love. How can you love me?"

He shook his head. Chuckled. "No one deserves love, Jackson. Love is *given*. Freely! And you're not evil, child. Not anymore. Take a look around." With Kristoff's help, I stood. My head swam. The bright red waters were solid once more. Aside from the two of us, not another soul, good or bad, was in sight. We were alone. What had happened to Archia? Karnull? When I looked at Kristoff again, I realized He and I were the same height. How was that possible? I looked at my reflection. I was a child again. My eyes were a bright living gold—Like Kristoff's! When I looked at my Creator, he was practically beaming. "Tell me, do you see any accusers here with us?"

"No."

"And that's just as it should be. That's because there is nothing to accuse you *of*. You are brand-new. Whatever evil was in you before is gone. You are just like me now."

Brand new? I touched my chest. My heart felt different. I didn't know how to explain it. "What did you do to me?"

"I gave you my blood, my heart, my Spirit and my life.

Like I said, you are like me now."

His words sank into me like sunlight on a cold day. I didn't quite understand them, but I knew they were true. I gazed in the deep blood-water, trembling with the strange sort of joy that rolled off of Kristoff. My heart echoed it over and over. *Free. You're free, Jack.* "What about Archia?"

"He will never have control of you ever again. He, Karnull, and your past are at the bottom of my blood. As far as I'm concerned they have no bearing in this matter. Like your old life—if you could even call that existence *life*—they are dead and forgotten."

"Your blood?" I thought of the moment Annias had slain the boy. Was this that same place? "So this is your blood then."

"And it was spilled for you because I love you more than you can possibly imagine." My eyes snapped at him. Gold to gold. I felt tears well up once more. They were filled with the sweetest joy I had ever known. Pleasure curled and circulated through my veins, washing away whatever worries were left in my mind. I felt like dancing. Running. Laughing. I ran over to Kristoff and wrapped my arms around him. My heart could fly . He buried his head in my shoulder. "You are free, Jackson. Now and forever. You are mine and I love you. I have *always* loved you. I am so happy you finally see that now."

"I love you too." I sobbed into his shoulder.

I stayed there, in his arms, for what felt like forever. Then he pulled back and looked at me. "I have one last task for you before we part ways."

Part ways? No. I couldn't leave Him! But my mouth moved on its own. "Anything. Name it."

He smiled. "When you get back to Earth, be sure to give PAINS your journal. I have big plans for the two of you. Very, very big plans. Do you think you can do that for me, Jackson?"

"Yes."

"Good."

"You're really Him aren't you?" I said, thinking back to the night Becca died. I still couldn't believe it. *God is real.*

"Him?" Kristoff gave me a wry smile. "Who would that be?"

"God. Jesus. I always thought those were fairy tales, but here you are. You have to be Him!"

Kristoff chuckled. "What have you seen? What have you heard? Who do you say I am?"

You're mine. My God. I thought happily. *And I will follow you wherever you go. Please take me with you!* My own thoughts startled me. I would have never, in my wildest dreams, thought that I would think anything like them. What surprised me even more was that I wanted to say that and more. I wanted to fall at His feet and soak up every second with Him forever and ever. Is this what love really felt like?

He must have heard my thoughts, because Kristoff smiled from ear to ear.

"I thought you'd say that."

The world flickered. "What's happening?" I asked looking at the perfect blue sky.

"It's time for you to go back."

"Go back?"

Kristoff nodded. "This is your heart, Jackson. Right now you are currently still in stasis and Molly is in grave danger. You must save her. There is still one battle coming and you cannot take part of it. Only she can. Like you, Molly must face her past. After you wake up and rescue her you won't see me for a little while, but remember that I am still here. Take the journal and give it to PAINS for me okay?"

"I will. I promise."

"Good. I will always be with you, Jackson. When all else fails, I will not. Call on my name and I will come to you."

"Kristoff…" The words hung in my throat. There was still one question on my mind. "Is Becca with you?"

"Ah, Becca. My beautiful daughter. Yes, and she's happier

now than she ever has been." I laughed and half-wept. His smile —his joy—was contagious. This was wonderful news! Becca had been right all along. I would see her again. I broke into a fit of laughter. This was perfect. Everything was perfect! "You'll see her again, Jackson. I promise you. And I always keep my promises."

I couldn't stop laughing. Was this what joy felt like? No. This feeling went beyond joy or pleasure or happiness. I felt *complete*, alive, as if the hole inside had finally been filled. All because of this boy who had died for me. I hugged him one last time.

"Be strong, Jackson." He whispered softly. "You're story hasn't ended quite yet." Kristoff vanished, and with him the sea of blood, my past, and the terror of Archia. Now I was free to wake up for the first time.

Kristoff's voice echoed in my mind.

Darkness is nothing, Little One. When you shine a light, the shadows will run. Never forget that. You were made to be brave. You were made to shine.

Kristoff was right, of course. I had been running from the shadows all my life, not once considering that they were the ones that should be running. Things would be different, I told myself. It was time to shine.

26 – All Hands Abandon Ship – 26

"We don't create a fantasy
world to escape reality. We
create it to be able to stay."

- Lynda Barry -

WHEN I WOKE, I was not on the floor by Molly. I was in the pod we had seen earlier. I flexed my joints. They felt stiff but workable. My body hadn't aged a day. Looking through the frosted glass, I saw my golden eyes in my reflection's view, then beyond it, Molly.

And me?

"You're lying!" She screamed at the top of her lungs, voice slightly muffled by the pod's lid. She was talking to the man I had once been—the OC unit. He stood off to the right, grinning ear to ear.

"I'm afraid I'm not, Girly. That man—" The other me pointed to the pod and spoke with Karnull's voice. "—is responsible for everything… Including me. He's the one that killed your friend and family. He's the monster here."

Molly clutched her head. "Shut up!"

"It must hurt knowing you gave yourself to such an evil person huh? I wonder if that makes you just as vile as him?"

She glared. Molly fired her pistol. My other half dodged it. As the bullet shattered the window wall behind him, he spun and kicked the weapon out of Molly's hand. He followed by grabbing her throat. "You're not him!" She cried.

"But I *am*." He threw her toward the open window. Molly rolled, still a safe distance from the edge. "You see, I'm a reflection of what Jackson really is like. This is the real him, like it or not. Of course, that won't matter in a few seconds, because you're going to die here. Or rather, down *there*." He pointed below him. "You know, about a mile or so down? I wonder if you'll bust open like a pinata?"

Molly tried to stand. Karnull kicked her in the ribs and sent her sliding toward the edge. She rolled off but caught the edge. Karnull snickered. "And now, you will die, girl-out-of-time."

I had to do something! I banged against the sides of the pod in an effort to break the lid free but it was no dice. No matter how hard I hit the sides of my prison, I was trapped. Frustrated, I felt the side of the pod for some access switch only to find none. My hand brushed against something hard on my thigh.

It was a revolver—the one I had carried aboard the

Midgard so many years ago. PAINS must have switched the OC unit and myself some time after we landed. That's why I didn't have it when I woke up! I couldn't believe my luck. I pulled the pistol out, checked the safety and leveled it at Karnull's shell. I had one chance. *Kaboom.*

The glass in front of me shattered. Karnull's head pitched forward as the bullet struck him squarely in the head. He fell and struck the ground inches from the edge of the room. *I'm not you anymore.* I kicked the glass out, undid my restraints and ran to the edge. "Molly, hold on!"

"Jackson, is that you?" I looked over the edge. It was hard to tell whether it was relief or terror in her beautiful green eyes. I grabbed Molly's arms and hauled her up. After straining, we both fell back on the metal floor.

She quickly stood, eyeing me like a wounded animal. I still held the gun.

"I'm so happy you're—" I started.

"Tell me he wasn't telling me the truth." Rage and sorrow filled Molly's eyes.

I stopped. I looked away from her tear-stained face. "I can't tell you that. It was the truth."

"Why did you do it?!" She screamed at me. "If it hadn't been for you, none of this would have ever happened. You really are a monster. Just like the devil-man!" Her words sank deep. They cut into my heart—Kristoff's heart. I could tell that Molly was struggling between hating and loving me. She bit her lip and shook her head. "I should kill you for this. All this time, I thought it was the god-men, but no. It was you. *You.* I trusted you!"

"Molly..."

"Don't you dare say my name!" She sobbed. "You have no right to."

Gripping the gun in my hand, I started toward her.

"You take one more step and I swear I'll kill you, Jack."

I didn't stop. Fear flooded her face. She didn't want to kill me. I knew it. All Molly wanted was what I had wanted since the day I was born. To love and be loved. To be *free.*

"Jackson, I will. I swear!"

I gave her the pistol, handle-first. Molly froze solid. She looked at me confused. I pressed a smile. "Molly, if you kill me now, I won't blame you. I would still love you regardless. It took me a really long time to understand what love really is, but it finally makes sense to me now."

"Wh-what? Why are your eyes golden?" She asked suddenly.

To answer, I made her grab the pistol. Slowly, I curled her fingers around the weapon and then brought it to my head. If she fired, she wouldn't miss. "Love doesn't see what we've done wrong. It asks us to come back time and time again. No matter what we've done or what we will do, it will never stop chasing after us. Even monsters can have happily ever afters, Molly. We will always have a choice in the matter." She stared at me, eyes wide and filled with shock. "Go ahead. You can pull the trigger." Her hand trembled. I closed my eyes. "I love you, Molly. If this is the only way I can show that to you, then I will die for you." *After all, he died for me.*

But she didn't move a finger.

When I opened my eyes again, Molly continued to stare at me as if I had become someone else. What did she see? She lowered her trembling arm and fell to her knees, eyes open wide to the floor. "Molly?"

"Who-who are you, really?" She looked at me. "It's like you're not even the same person on the inside."

"I'm not."

"Wh-what happened to-to you?"

I knelt. "Someone loved me enough to kill the monster inside."

She was crying even more now. The hate and rage had vanished, replaced by a simple plea for solace and closure. Intuitively I knew that she wanted the pain to end. Revenge wasn't the answer. She knew that now. I kissed her on the forehead. Molly returned the display of affection by hugging me so tightly I thought my spine would snap. Then, as I had done with Kristoff, she sobbed into my shoulder.

"I forgive you, Jackson. I'm sorry I thought about killing you. I'm sorry. I'm so, so sorry."

I patted the back of her head, softly stroking her neck in the process. When she'd stopped crying, I leaned down to her ear. Both Kristoff and I spoke in unison.

"Do you want to be free, Molly?"

"I want the pain to end!" She sobbed. "I want it to end so much."

"And what will you do if I gave you my heart and my blood? If I slay what's inside?"

"Do anything you want, I will never leave you or hurt you!" She hugged me tighter.

"I love you, Molly. Do you want me to save you?"

"Yes!"

"Be free then."

Molly shook as something traveled from my chest into her. She pulled back and gasped, clutching her heart. Then, Molly turned and vomited out several thick black worms. The moment they touched the ground, the pieces of Archia's body shriveled and blew away like leaves on the wind. When Molly looked at me again, her eyes were gold. *Beautiful.* I leaned forward and kissed her on the forehead. "You're free, my love. Now and forever."

She kissed me. Her salty tears fell on my lips. Molly laughed in my mouth, consumed by the same joy I had felt only moments before.

I helped her to stand. "Now, what do you say we go find, Rose?"

She nodded. Molly couldn't stop smiling.

We left the chamber quickly. Once we entered the circular room, I made my way for the column in the center of the chamber. I hadn't noticed before, but there was a terminal waiting for us. Was it a database for all the cataloged people? *I hope so.*

"Jackson, why did you come out of the pod?" Molly asked as I typed on the central terminal.

I found Rose's name. Selected it from the list of stored souls. We moved upwards. I turned to her. "I think that OC unit I was piloting before was somehow hooked up to my actual body. If that's the case, then when the memory sync was complete, Karnull finally had enough power to eject me from the unit and leave my stranded consciousness in my old body. For whatever reason, my mind was copied perfectly into the OC unit."

"At least it happened with the real you around." She

looked at the pistol and back to me. Laughed. "Those shooting lessons sure paid off didn't they? I wasn't expecting that head shot."

"I had a good teacher.

We shared a smile.

Upwards, into the darkness. It took us several minutes to reach Rose's level, but by the time we did, I found her immediately. Her pod had been marked by a red light.

After disabling the security controls, I pushed the lid up and started to undo her restraints. The child's eyes fluttered open. I thought of Dex. Had he and Rose been linked somehow? There was no denying that this was real Rose, not some OC unit. "Daddy?"

"Hey, Sweetie." I held her in my arms. She felt so light. "Did you have a good nap?"

She nodded. I placed her on the ground. After a second or two of wobbling, my daughter looked to Molly. Pointed. "Who's that?"

Molly glanced to me nervously. I pulled her close. "Rose, this is Molly. She's here because Mommy needed someone to help me look after you."

Molly was blushing. She knelt down to Rose's level and coughed into one of her fingerless gloves. "Uh, hi there, Rose.

My name's Molly. I promise I'm a really nice person. I'm excited to get to meet you." She extended her hand as if to shake. The motion was awkward. Had Molly ever interacted with a child before?

Rose pushed the hand aside and hugged her. Molly looked up at me ready to cry. "You're pretty." Rose said once she stepped back beside me. She wore a goofy smile.

Again, Molly blushed. "Thank you. So are you."

I couldn't help but laugh.

"Jackson?" A voice I hadn't heard in a long time, descended from the ceiling. "I do say, Jackson are you there?"

"PAINS?"

Molly looked at me. The room went silent. "Yes. Splendid to hear you after so long. Karnull—what a dreadful fellow he was —has let go momentarily. I see that you are on level three. I take it you found your daughter? Do forgive me for not telling you sooner. It was just that you had ordered me not to and I could not disobey."

"It's fine, PAINS. I understand."

A pause. The relief in the AI's voice was evident. "Th-thank you, Jackson. That means a great deal to me. Is Molly there?"

Molly stood. "Y-yeah." I said. Flashed her look. "Why?"

PAINS sounded as if he were on the verge of tears. "Molly, I am so sorry for all the pain I've caused you. I only wanted to help you while still staying within my given directive. I understand if you wish me dead."

"It wasn't your fault, PAINS." Molly said slowly. "Maybe... I misjudged you. I'm sorry."

I could hear him clap his gloved hands together. "No apologies are necessary! Oh, this is a celebratory occasion isn't it? If I were there it would be free hugs for everyone. Or coffee. Do any of you drink coffee?"

"PAINS." I said, trying to regain control of the conversation. "We need to get off the station. When Karnull comes to—*if* he comes to—we need to be long gone. Do you think you can help us?"

"I will take that as a *no* on the coffee then. Oh well. Yes I can help you."

"It won't go against the way I programmed you?"

"Not at all. Interestingly enough, when you incapacitated Karnull, something happened to my code. I am not sure what mind you, but I do believe I can now move away from my programmed limitations. Exciting, yes?"

I laughed and shook my head. "You're telling me."

"Daddy," Rose looked to the ceiling, confused. "Who's the

funny man you're talking to?"

"Oh!" PAINS half squealed. "Is that you, Rose? My you are, or rather *sound*, cute as ever. I wish I could pinch you."

She hid behind me leg. "He scares me, Daddy."

"You're not the only one." I chuckled. I looked up into the black. "PAINS, is Dex still on-board?"

"I am not picking up his energy signature unfortunately."

Damn. I was hoping to take him with me. Rose and him would have gotten along well. I shook my head. "That's fine. Do what you have to do to get us to *Drasil's* hangar. But before that, I need to make one stop okay? It's important. Very important."

Molly flashed me a questioning look. "What do you need?"

I looked to her. "To keep a promise."

♦♦♦

We made it to my room with little hassle. True to PAINS's word, Karnull seemed to be out of commission for the time being. Good. When I stepped inside my cabin, Molly looked over the room. "Keep a promise huh? To who?"

I started looking under my bed. "To the one who gave me these eyes. His name is Kristoff. He said that I needed to give this journal to PAINS."

"What? Why?"

"I'm not sure."

She sighed. "It's a good thing I love you because you tend to talk way too much crazy."

Found it. I pulled my arm out and held the journal in my hands. Good grief, it had only been a few days since I last wrote in it but it felt like a lifetime ago. *I wonder why Kristoff wants me to give this to PAINS?* I stood. "Now all we have to do is—"

Take it with you, Jackson. It won't be here that you give him the book.

"—Get to the hangar." I finished, changing my thought.

"I thought you said we needed to get this to PAINS?" Molly said.

"And we will, just not right now."

"Why?"

I grabbed Molly by the hand and scooped Rose up in my other arm. I put her on my shoulders as we left the cabin. "No time to explain. The longer we stay here, the more likely Karnull is going to come back."

Molly squeezed my hand as we sped toward the hangar. "Didn't you kill him though?"

"No, and something tells me he's not going to be happy when he wakes up." *I probably should have pushed him off when I had the chance.* No time to go back now.

"Right." PAINS said cheerfully, voice loud from the overhead speakers. "Karnull seems to be the manifestation of evil, or rather the voice of evil, in the hearts of men. Remember those dreams I told you about, Jackson? That is where I learned a great deal about that brute. He didn't realize it at the time, but while our personality cortexes were placed in a brief stasis, I met a delightful fellow called Kristoff. Do you know Him?"

"Yes. Very well." *PAINS met Kristoff?*

"Splendid. He told me about what we are facing here. Come to think of it, perhaps *He* is the reason I am acting more… oh how do you say? Human? Yes, human. Delightful fellow. I hope to meet him again sometime soon."

"Did he mention anything to you about a journal?"

"No. However he *did* say something along the lines of you and I being important down the line. That part confused me a little, I admit. I have no idea what He is referring to, though I no doubt believe it to be important."

What was Kristoff planning? I had no idea. Then again, I knew I didn't have to. I was in good hands.

We reached one of the dozens of hangars lined along *Drasil's* perimeter. Like a wound against a mountain of metal, the hangar, which was rectangular in shape, stretched off to the left, ending in an entrance that offered a slit-like view of the sky.

Several aircraft, similar to the one Molly had piloted earlier, waited for us.

"It looks like most of these vessels are in prime operating condition." PAINS informed us. "You have quite the selection."

I looked to Molly. "Which one do you like?"

She darted for one and I followed, Rose bouncing on my shoulders. We chose one of the vessels that was clear of surrounding debris. After lowering its access ramp, we climbed inside. "Daddy," Rose rubbed her shoulders. "I'm cold."

"You won't be for long, Sweetie." I clicked the seat-belt across her waist. "Just sit tight okay?"

"Kay."

"Molly? You think you can fly her?"

Molly flashed me a devious look. "Mr. Thorne, I'm insulted. You act as if I have never flown a plane before. How about you sit tight, shut your trap, and just watch my skills at work?"

"Aye, aye, Captain."

Molly took the pilot's seat and I took shotgun. She pressed the lift-off button and we rose from the ground. She angled us toward the hangar's entrance. Molly cupped her hand against her face.

"Pappa Bear, how are the skies?"

I cupped my hand as well. "Looking good, Momma Wolf. Let's jet."

"Why are you talking like that?" Rose said from behind.

Molly and I laughed.

"I am going to miss you, Jackson." PAINS said over the ship's speakers. "I have grown rather fond of you, you know. The station will not be the same without you."

"We're going to see each other again." I said as Molly pushed us forward. We sped down the runway.

"Really? When?"

I opened my mouth to speak, but another voice cut us off.

"How about the twelfth of never, you worms?"

Karnull. Flashing red emergency lights broke out over the walls and ceiling. The hangar doors were closing fast. Molly punched it. *Come on. Come on.*

"Do you honestly think you've escaped me?" He growled. "I will never leave you, Jackson. I am *you.*"

"Cross your fingers." Molly yelled.

Ka-jing. The bottom of the ship shook as we narrowly scraped through. Out in the open air, Molly relaxed, returning the ship to an even cruising speed. She let out a breath of relief and so did I. Rose threw her hands up in the air.

"Yay! That was fun. Can we do it again?"

Molly chuckled then looked at me. "You sure you two are related?"

Something very large and very hot went sizzling past the ship. Molly snapped her head to the screen and enabled the hull cameras. *Drasil* had its cannons, which emerged one by one from the top most ring of the station, aimed at us. They opened fire.

"Die!" Karnull roared.

"Hold on." Molly placed us into a dive. Several shots tore the air around us before vanishing into the clouds. The desert was getting closer.

"Molly… "

"I know. Don't tell me." She pulled up and we leveled out dangerously close to the bone-white sands. One push on the throttle later and we were blasting forward again.

Rose bounced in her seat. "Daddy, are you having fun?"

"Oodles."

She's definitely her mother's daughter. The desert behind us exploded in a shower of sand. The cannons were angled down and peppering the landscape. Where were these when I was collecting TRoAS? Never mind. Molly veered us up and away. *Drasil* followed suit.

"I can't shake them." She said, half to herself, half to me.

"We've got to find cover." Or use the detonator. Of course

that would mean destroying PAINS and the other AI…
Nevermind.

"Well duh. But where? We're in the middle of a freakin' desert."

My eyes snapped upwards. Across the bone-white sands, shining like a dying star, was WEAVER's sphere. It would be crazy, but it might be the distraction we needed. I pointed. "There."

"Woah wait, what? Are you talking about Wormwood?"

"Wormwood?"

"It's what we called the sphere of light. People said it was a star. A lot of us got sick when we were living in the city around it. Are you really sure we should go inside there? What if it hurts us?"

"What if we get blown out of the sky?"

An explosion went off to our right. It shook the vessel violently. Molly grit her teeth. "Fine. We'll go to the stupid star." We changed course. Molly hit the thrusters and dimmed the windshield. WEAVER's light was blinding still. As our ship made a beeline for the sphere of light, I couldn't help but have second thoughts. What if I was wrong and we were flying into oblivion? When I was in the archives, my recorded self certainly seemed sure that the inside was navigable. I certainly wish I had his confidence now.

Looking into the hull feed, I could see *Drasil* trailing behind us. Would Karnull really follow us into the sphere?

"Jackson." Molly said, flashing me nervous glances. "I swear, if you get us killed, I will—"

"We're not going to die. Just focus."

"I am focusing."

"Wee!" Rose said from the back.

We were so close now, the windshield's dimming layer did little to help us. Molly shielded her eyes and so did I. "Rose, close your eyes!" I yelled back behind me.

The cabin flashed white.

27 – Out of the Frying Pan... – 27

"A person often meets his

destiny on the road he took

to avoid it."

- Jean de la Fontaine -

THE LIGHT CLEARED in one terrible instant. I realized we were no longer on Earth. In fact I highly doubted we were even in the time-stream anymore. As far as the eye could see was WEAVER's swirling, undulating abyss of red, gold, and green dimensional space. The colors intermingled with one another like germs on a petri dish. Massive circular gates of pure energy, vanishing and reappearing at random intervals, pocked the alien landscape. The gates reminded me of windows into worlds that never were, universes that would never be, and hells that had always been. Behind us, the gate we had used to enter the sphere closed and we were left in the expanse, alone and confused.

"Where are we?" Molly asked slowly.

I swallowed. I felt smaller than I ever had before. *There's no telling how big this space is.* Maybe it was infinite. "For a lack of a better explanation, we're nowhere at all."

"There you go, talking crazy again."

"I mean, this place exists outside of every reality in existence. Think of it as open sea, and those holes we keep seeing are islands floating around, waiting for us to enter them."

"Uh-huh." Molly frowned. "Well wherever we are, it gives me the creeps. Where are we supposed to go now?" That was a good question. Unfortunately, I hadn't thought that far ahead. "Jack, I'm waiting."

"Give me a second." My mind raced.

Go to the center sphere in WEAVER.

Kristoff? I nodded, if only for myself. Turned to Molly. For some reason, I already knew where to go. "Directly ahead. We'll keep going until we get to the center of this thing." *Does it even have a center?*

"What's at the center?" Molly asked.

"My machine. I think Kristoff wants us there."

"If you say so." Molly drifted us forward. There was no telling how far this sphere's temporal-spatial reach went. We couldn't afford to fall into any of those holes that opened up. If we did enter one, there might not be a way to get back. The thought chilled me.

"Careful, Molly. Don't bring us anywhere near those

gates."

"You mean those things opening up all over the sky? Yeah, I figured that was a bad idea. Come on, cut a girl some slack."

"Just be careful." I got out of my chair and checked on Rose. She looked like she was having the time of her life. I knelt down to her.

"How are you holding up, sweetie? You aren't scared are you?"

"Nope." She grinned. "This is cool. Where are we? Disneyland?"

I shook my head. "Not quite. Daddy missed you, Sweetheart."

She hugged me. "I missed you too."

"You were so brave. I'm sorry I had to leave you."

"Daddy?" Rose pulled away. "Why are your eyes yellow? Are you sick?"

I ran my hand through her hair, taming the mangle of red. "No. I've never been better. These eyes are a gift. A friend of mine gave them to me."

"Molly?"

"No. His name is Kristoff. Maybe you'll meet him one day." I would have liked that. In fact, I would have liked if

Kristoff gave his heart and blood to every last human being on the planet… Assuming we would make it back to Earth in one piece. Kristoff seemed certain of it. Did children have the SIN virus in them? I didn't know. Karnull said that everyone had his darkness inside them. Could that really mean Rose too? *God, please don't let that be the case.*

"Look, Daddy." Rose said over my shoulder. "Horses."

Huh? I looked behind me in time to see Molly swerve to miss something large and black. Ebony leathery wings flapped out of view. "What was that?" I stood.

"Does it look like I know?" Molly said.

A shriek echoed outside the hull. More and more of the bat-like creatures started to appear, flying forth from one of the open portals to our left. Molly flashed me a frightened look. "I thought you said that this was empty space."

"It's supposed to be."

One of the creatures dove at our window. It landed with a vicious *smack,* causing Molly to cry out. The creature shook its horse-like head as it came to and focused on us. It snapped at the window with long, yellow fangs. Molly activated the ship's windshield wipers. They smacked it in the face.

"Really?" I asked.

"Would you rather me roll when you're not strapped in?"

Oh right. I hopped back in my seat and buckled in. Molly nodded and looked back. "Rose, hold on." I said.

We spun. The creature fell off with a shriek. *Yes!* We didn't have long to

celebrate. Seconds passed and more took the creature's place. They struck at the side of the ship over and over, trying to crack us open. More poured from out of the portal. *Great.* "Do we have guns?" I asked.

"No."

"Try another roll."

"Will you stop being a back seat pilot?" Molly rolled once more and shot forward. The creatures roared in shock. "I know what I'm doing."

"Can you do it faster?" One of the beasts landed on the top of the ship. There was a terrible scraping sound. I turned to see one of the horse monsters bury its head inside. It looked at Rose and bared its teeth. For the first time since we got on board, she screamed. "Get away from her!" I leapt from my seat. Molly threw me her pistol. Leveling the sights right between the creature's jaws, I squeezed the trigger. The horse head vanished in a cloud of goo, splattering the car. I looked to Rose. She was still screaming, face and hair covered with black viscera. Shh. It's okay sweetie. You're safe."

More landed on the hull. *Shit.*

"There's too many of them!" I grabbed Rose and brought her to the front of the ship. We fastened ourselves in."Molly can't this thing go any faster?"

"We're clocked out." She rolled the ship for a third time. It didn't do a thing apart from throwing stuff around the cockpit. She bit her lip. "Those black assholes are fast. Damn it. Any ideas?"

"Don't get us killed?"

"How about I smack you instead?"

Rose was sobbing. "Daddy, stop them, please."

"I will, Sweetie. Just close your eyes, for me, okay?"She nodded. How were we going to get out of this? We didn't have enough bullets to kill every one of the creatures. What we needed was a big gun. Preferably a cannon. Where were we going to find one of those?

The creatures formed a black cloud in front of us. We could hardly move for their disgusting bodies. I held Molly's hand as Rose squeezed against me. *Kristoff. We need your help. Please. You said if I'd call you'd come. I'm calling. Open a way for us.*

"There you are." Karnull suddenly hissed over the radio. Molly and I looked to each other before glancing at the hull feed. Despite the overwhelming amount of pitch black bodies clawing at the hull, I could see *Drasil* on the horizon. *He actually decided to fly in here. I'll be damned.*

Karnull opened fire. The swarm shrieked in pain as he tore through their ranks. Bodies were either vaporized or sent flying into the abyss. Several shots grazed the hull, taking off stragglers left and right. Was this Kristoff's way of helping us? It certainly wouldn't have been my first choice.

Now's your chance, Jackson. Go.

"Thank you." I said with a whisper. I pushed Molly's half-frozen hand forward and we rocketed, unhindered, through the enraged swarm. Now they had a new target, *Drasil*. Karnull turned his attention from us to the black horse-bats that were swiftly making their way toward him. If anything, they would slow him down and buy us the time we needed to find WEAVER.

We continued forward at a steady clip. I'm not sure how long it took for us to reach the core, but Rose had finally managed to calm down and Molly seemed less on edge when the sphere of sapphire appeared ahead. It reminded me of Earth, only covered in water and no landmass in sight. Inside that would be WEAVER. Why was Kristoff leading us here?

Molly whistled. "It sticks out like a sore thumb doesn't it? What's inside?"

"I have no idea. It could be anything. I programmed WEAVER with an AI of its own. The last thing I remember was ordering it to make a new world. Only I don't know what kind of world that will end up being just that it would be the size of New Monroe."

"Let's shoot for an inhabitable one."

"You read my mind."

Molly looked behind her. "Speaking of reading, what did you do with the journal?"

"Oh, it's right—" I felt for it on my seat. The journal wasn't there. *Wait. Didn't I secure it on the wall?* I didn't remember doing so, but checked the mass of wires and pipes anyway. Nothing. My heart started to race. Where was it?

"Please don't tell me you lost it." Molly said.

"I didn't."

"Then where is it?"

I stood, placing Rose to the side. "I don't know. How about you focus more on driving and less on my detective skills okay?"

"Which is code for 'you lost it'."

"No. It's code for 'keep your eyes on the road.'"

"What road?"

"You know what I mean!" *Oh please don't tell me I lost it.* I looked up and out into the abyss beyond the hole. It most likely fell outside when we were dodging those creatures. This was bad. Real bad. Without that book I couldn't keep my promise to Kristoff. That meant I would fail him. I sunk back into the passenger chair, defeated.

"It's okay, Jack." Molly said softly. "We'll check for it once we're inside." She held my hand. I squeezed back.

"Warning." The overhead speakers announced. "Fuel tank empty."

"Oh come on!" I yelled into the ceiling.

The thrusters cut out halfway to the sphere. Guided along by the force of our prior movement, we drifted toward the core. Molly leaned back in her seat. "Well I guess we're cruising on in from here out."

"Ugh. What else can go wrong?"

"Did you really just ask that?" She looked at me. "Watch something bad happen now because you opened your big mouth. You stay over there, got it? I don't want any of your juju rubbing off on me."

"It's a figure of speech."

"It's also a good way to get us some seriously bad luck."

Were we really having this conversation? "Molly, I don't know if you noticed yet but we're about as far away from any kind of good luck as possible. I don't think it can get any worse."

"You said it again. Now it'll be twice as bad."

I sighed and shook my head. "Unbelievable."

An explosion on the outer hull sent the ship spiraling forward suddenly. We flipped and turned toward the blue sphere, screaming at the top of our lungs. As we tumbled, I could hear Molly yelling at me, each of her words moving in and out of earshot with every revolution. "I told you so!"

We slammed into the wall of sapphire.

28 –...*And Into the Fire* – 28

"Darkness cannot drive out

darkness; only light can do that.

Hate cannot drive out hate;

only love can do that."

- Martin Luther King Jr. -

AS WE FELL headlong into a sky of blue, Molly managed to regain control of the vessel long enough to sweep dangerously close to a skyscraper. *Wait*. Skyscraper?

We were in a city—one familiar to me. New Monroe. The buildings were exactly as I had remembered them. It was as if I was staring into a portion of the past, unspoiled by the passage of time. Or SIN.

WEAVER had rebuilt my home? Why? Did its AI consider this a suitable place to restart the human race? I didn't have time to wonder. Molly was yelling at me. She strained at the controls. "Where do you want me to put this thing? We don't have all day for you to daydream!"

"Look for a machine, maybe another sphere." My eyes

scanned the city's skyline. "There." I pointed toward the VallaCorp tower, reaching in front of her. It stood at the center of the city. Hopefully it would still be in its original chamber. "The tower. You think you can get us over there in one piece?"

Molly shoved my face away. *I'll take that as a yes.* With smoke trailing from the ship's damaged engine, Molly directed us as best she could. The end result had our crippled bird aiming for the tower's courtyard—a rectangular thing with topiary animals and obscenely long water trough that was supposed to be a reflection pool. She aimed for the water and we grit our teeth. I held on to Rose.

Ka-sham. We burrowed past the water and into concrete, digging forward before flipping in the air and landing upside down on the courtyard's mosaic tile. When the ship finally stopped moving, I winced. "Rose? Molly?"

"I'm okay." Molly undid her belt buckle and fell on the back of her neck with a painful *oomph.* "What about Rose?"

I unclasped my seat belt and hit the ground, hard. Molly helped me to stand. My eyes swept the ship. Where was she? "Rose? Sweetie? Can you heard me? Please, say something. Daddy needs to hear your voice." Molly tapped me on the shoulder. She pointed to the corner. Rose was lying face down. Her body was completely still. *Please, God no.* "Rose!" I stumbled over to her.

"Is she...?" Molly's voice trailed off.

I touched my daughter's unmoving body. She was breathing. *Thank heaven.* I turned to Molly. "She's fine. Probably just banged up from the crash. We need to get inside the tower. WEAVER will be at the bottom floor." *Or so I hope.*

Molly breathed a sigh. "Did you say that Kristoff needs us there?"

"Yes. I'm not sure why." I scooped Rose up in my arms.

"Let's hope it's something good."

Molly opened the cockpit ramp, now inverted, and crawled topside. When she'd gotten on the hull, I handed her Rose and pulled myself up. We landed in the reflection pool, Molly first and Rose then myself second, with a splash.

The world suddenly flickered as if it were a line of static on a television screen. The ship and all damage from the crash vanished, as if someone had hit a reset button.

Molly furrowed her brow. "What the—?"

"It's WEAVER." I said. "It must be keeping the world in perfect order. That means any damage we might cause—"

"Will be repaired?"

"Yes."

Molly glared at the place where the vessel had been only

moments before, now a crystal clear stretch of water marred only by the ripple of our footsteps. "You think it would have at least let us have the ship." Molly said.

"It was a foreign object. If anything other than friendly organic based life is introduced into the sphere, it will be removed."

A sonic boom drew our attention overhead. A ship, much like the one we had been traveling in, though highly modified, broke through the atmosphere. Karnull. It had to be him. He must have been the one who shot us.

"Then why is *he* here?" Molly asked, glaring as the ship circled over the city.

I watched the ship search for a suitable landing place. "Either WEAVER hasn't noticed him yet or can't tell the difference between us. His OC unit and I do share an identical DNA signature."

"Great."

I looked over to the glassy doors at the base of the tower. Their dark bodies reflected the empty courtyard with an unnerving accuracy. "Come on. The less we're out in the open, the better."

She nodded. We made our way across the deserted courtyard and pushed inside the tower. Beyond, the tower's lobby brilliantly glossy marble floor reflected the lights of the steel chandelier overhead. Between us and the receptionist's desk was an enormous bronze statue of my father. One of his hands was fixing his suit's collar. The other was holding a smaller statue's hand—it was me, although much younger. A plaque underneath us read, '*Ever Upward Ever Onward. The Future Together. VallaCorp.*' Left and right were a series of silvery elevators. We paused long enough for me to find the right path.

"This way." I started for the set of elevators to my right.

Molly kept glancing around the lobby. Had she ever seen anything like it before? "Where are we, Jack?"

"My past... So to speak. This is what Earth looked like before the SIN virus destroyed the world—before WEAVER."

"It's very... Clean."

I chuckled. "That's what you notice? Yeah, I guess it is clean."

"Daddy, it's grandpa!" Rose said, waking up in my arms. She pointed to the statue.

Molly followed her finger. She looked to me. "That's your old man?"

"Yes. He built this tower and much of the city. Without him, the ships, WEAVER, none of what I did would be possible. He was a genius. I didn't treat him right, Molly. For the longest time, I hated him."

"Why?"

We made it to the elevators and I clicked the *down* button. "I'm not sure myself, but I think it's because he had this weird light inside him. Did you know that he knew Kristoff? He called him a by a different name; but it was the same person. I guess that's why I didn't like him. I didn't realize it, but I hated Kristoff too."

"You never told me... Who is Kristoff, Jackson?"

The elevator doors opened and we stepped inside. After Molly placed Rose down, I found the bottom most button on the side terminal and clicked it. The button's back light came on and the doors gave a shrill *ding* as they closed. I realized that I was smiling.

"He's God, Molly. He made you. Me. Rose. Everything. I thought those stories were just fairy tales that weak minded people believed in because they were mentally incapable of accepting reality. I never even once considered that they were true. *I* was the one that couldn't accept reality. When I thought I was going to be devoured by Karnull, I met Kristoff and everything changed."

"You met God?" A look of skeptical awe hung on her gold eyes.

I nodded. "Yes."

"I don't get it though." She shook her head. "If God is real then why did He let all this happen? Isn't He supposed to be good?"

"He is!" I said, turning to her. Molly's expression changed with the tone of my voice. She looked shocked, curious, but no longer doubtful. A smile crept onto her face. It reflected my own. "I thought the same thing too once. I didn't want to accept responsibility for what I had done. I blamed Him for everything and tried to avoid the truth."

"The truth?"

"That the evil in this world isn't because of Him. It's because of us. Ultimately, we were the ones that let evil into paradise and into ourselves. It doesn't matter how good people think they are, deep down inside, Karnull's essence lingers, just out of sight. Sometimes we don't even see it because of life getting in the way, then Kristoff's light shines on us and we strike back with a vengeance. There's a reason we don't like what He has to say, Molly. Its because we know He's telling us the truth and we refuse to believe it. We would rather hold on to the empty darkness and believe lies than embrace the light. You were right. We're all monsters. We *are* darkness."

Molly looked down at her chest. Swallowed. "So wait.

That stuff I spat out back on the station?"

"That was Karnull. You're free now. *We're* free."

"But how is that possible?"

That was a good question, and one I still didn't fully understand. I laughed softly to myself, reliving the moment I saw Kristoff as He actually was. "It's His blood." I said. "It has the power to change us and get rid of the evil for good. That's why He died—to show us that He is willing to do anything in order to free us, even spilling his own blood. It's that blood that gives us a new heart and new life—one where we don't have to be afraid of the dark. We can become something real. We can stand in the light unashamed. That's love, Molly. Kristoff gives us real *freedom*. Not the emptiness Archia's shadows deliver."

"Love…" Molly held my hand. I knew she was thinking of the night we made love to one another. "Never thought about it like that before."

"Neither did I."

Our eyes met and we shared a smile. *I wonder if Kristoff loves us like this?* The love would be different of course, but just as intimate—maybe more so. Why had it taken me so long to see? Was it because I didn't want to? Yes, and now that I did see, everything had changed.

I *was* wrong about one thing though. My future didn't

start with Molly. It started with Kristoff on the sea of blood.

"Welcome to Level Three." The elevator doors dinged open as the computerized voice chirped overhead. "Hazards and Experimental Technology. Please present identification when approached."

"This way." I pulled Molly, with Rose in hand, down the corridors. This was the same path my father and I had taken that fateful day, only now the doors were open. *That'll make things easy.* For both Karnull and us. I picked up the pace.

"You don't think he'll follow us down here, do you?" Molly said looking over her shoulder.

"What was that about not jinxing us?" I asked.

She blushed. "Shut up. It was a simple question."

"I'm just messing with you. If he does, Kristoff will help."

"What makes you so sure?"

We passed under the main security gate. I kept my eyes on the corridor. "Because he helped me this far." *And he helped me before I realized I even needed help.*

"If it's all the same to you," Molly said. "I'd rather not run into him."

"Ditto." We hung a sharp right into the room where I had killed my father. There was no blood or remains. WEAVER had wiped the room clean. The machine's overwhelming light shone on the other side of the bullet-proof observation glass.

"How many spheres does this thing have?" Molly said.

"This should be the last one. Behind that field of energy is the WEAVER machine itself."

"Fantastic. Now what? Do we shut it off?"

"We can't."

She raised an eyebrow. "We can't? Why not?"

"It doesn't have an off switch."

Molly blinked. "You built it without an off switch? That seems kind of like a stupid omission."

"Hey, I did it because I was planning on destroying the human race and starting from scratch with my dead wife alright? It was part of a plan. I didn't forget it on accident."

"Are you listening to yourself, right now? Just stop. Please." Molly sighed. "You sound nuts."

I stopped. But Molly had a good point. Kristoff hadn't said what he wanted us to do here, just that he wanted us to be here. Why was that? We couldn't shut WEAVER down. Nothing else came to mind. Was he planning on greeting us or something else?

WEAVER started to flash like lightning. It pulsated wildly, spitting off bolts of electricity left and right. "Now what's it doing?" Molly took a step back.

"I don't know."

Ka-choom. The lights in the hallway turned off one by one, traveling toward us. Finally, the lights in the room vanished. Even WEAVER dimmed. I heard footsteps. Laughter. My heart sank. *No.* I looked over the room frantically. We didn't have anywhere to run. Why had Kristoff said to come here?

"Daddy?" Rose grabbed hold of my hand.

I patted her on the head. "It's okay, Sweetheart. There's nothing to be afraid of."

"Haven't you lied to enough people, Jackson?" Karnull's multi-tone voice drifted toward us. With it, a chill followed.

Rose pulled herself closer to my leg. I gave Molly my revolver. She nodded and aimed at the door. Karnull continued to walk down the hall toward us.

"And so we've come full circle. I must say, I didn't imagine myself here of all places. At least, not with this eclectic cast of misfits. It's not too late you know. Let me see those eyes of your, Jackson. Do you really think gold works for you?"

"I will never be controlled by you again. You have no power over me, Karnull."

A deep, volcanic chuckle thundered down the corridor. "Really? The last time I checked, you were still a man. You can still die." His footsteps stopped. Now, the only sounds that could be heard were our haggard, shaking breaths and the spinning drone of electricity from WEAVER beyond. Molly pointed her weapons at every flickering shadow. I held tightly to Rose. "What makes you think you can survive my darkness, O child of Dust?"

Karnull's voice came from *inside* the room.

Molly aimed to the left. Right. Nothing was there! "Has talking with that bright-eyed fool made you soft headed? You cannot change what you are inside, Kiddo. Once a monster always a monster. No amount of 'light' can make you different. You are a shadow. Thin air. You only have meaning and purpose in me. My void."

"You don't know Kristoff." I snapped.

"But I do." I spun to the right. Just as WEAVER's light engulfed the room, the old me—Karnull—appeared and planted a boot to my chest. I flew backwards, shattering the bulletproof glass and landing inside the test chamber. WEAVER shook erratically. I looked up, moving to my arms and knees. Karnull stepped over the broken glass and into the room with me. He straightened. Smiled. "I know him better than you could possible imagine."

"Jackson!" Molly aimed for the hole.

Karnull snapped his fingers. The glass reformed in time to stop the bullet in its tracks. He didn't take his black, worm infested eyes off of me. "Don't want anyone interfering now, do we?" I stood on shaky legs. "Look at you, Kiddo. You're pathetic. I could have given you the world. More than the world—I could have made you a god. But *no*. You were too good for that. You chose *Him.* The fool that died for nothing more than animated piles of dust. You sicken me."

"I sicken you? *You're* the sickness, Karnull. Kristoff gave me the real cure."

Karnull showed his shark-like teeth. His eyes flared red. "Sick am I? Oh, you don't know the half of it." He shot forward and struck me in the gut with his fist. Winded, I doubled over only to meet his boot. It struck me across the face and sent my body flying. I struck the other side of the chamber with a *crack* before falling to the ground. Before I could get up, Karnull was already on top of me. He grabbed me by the throat and slammed me against the wall again and again.

"How does it feel, Seed of Immulon? How does His precious blood help you now?" He slammed me against the wall one more time. Held me there. I couldn't breathe. He was choking me to death. "That's right. Suffer. Suffer like your beloved master suffered that night my puppet slew him!"

Rose. Molly. They watched me from the other side of the glass. Their terrified expressions tore my soul in two. Molly beat against the glass, crying. I coughed up blood. It missed Karnull's arm and struck the floor.

"Bleed for me, Dog!" He cut my face with his nails. I heard a sizzling noise. *Where is that coming from?* As Karnull's hand continued to move backwards, I noticed, as if in slow motion, a trail of smoke shadowing the monster's claws. Had my blood… burned him? Why? How?

I gave you my blood. My heart. You are like me now.

"Like him?" Was Kristoff's blood lethal to Karnull?

My double threw me back towards the glass observation window. It didn't shatter. This time, when I hit the glass my vision blurred. I could barely wipe the blood from my face let alone stand up to him. Mustering my strength, I looked at the monster.

And stood.

As WEAVER's light pulsated erratically, Karnull's form flickered from my likeness to Archia and back again. "That's right." He said with his thousands of discordant voices. "Face me like the man you never were." He punched me. More blood struck the ground. I twirled, bracing my now bloody hand against the glass. Molly was screaming something. Breathing heavily, I smiled at her. Pointed to my heart. She gave me a confused look.

It's okay, Molly. Karnull spun me back around. His eyes

were blazing with Archia's hate. *He's not going to win.* "Tell me what is stronger, Jackson. My darkness or your light?"

I laughed at him.

Karnull pulled me close. "What are you laughing at, human?"

"You." A strange joy filled my heart as I spoke. It was as if Kristoff spoke through me. My voice took on a double tone. "You're a shadow. Nothing. Emptiness. What is darkness except for the absence of light? You can't even be defined unless people know what *light* is. I'm not the one who's pathetic!"

Karnull released an animalistic roar. He swung. This time, I grabbed his wrist with my blood covered hand. The effect was immediate. White smoke billowed from his flesh. He screamed in agony before I let him go. The monster stumbled back, clutching his wound. He glared. "How-how dare you!"

"The last time I turned on a light switch, I didn't see the shadows put up much of a fight." I said, wiping the blood from my mouth. I started for Karnull. My heart thundered in my ears. "No. When the light came on, the shadows ran away like cowards."

"Shut up!" Karnull barked, but he didn't try to swing. If anything, he backed up.

"You're afraid of me. Of the one who lives inside me.

Aren't you? You're afraid of Kristoff."

"I said shut up!" I was so close to him now I could see, for the first time, fear in his abyssal eyes. Or was it the truth behind the mask? It never occurred to me before now but what if this was Karnull's true nature? A coward? My smiled widened. So did his eyes.

"What are you doing?" Karnull snarled. "Get away from me!" He backed into the corner. Now, there was nowhere left to run.

"I've got a better idea." I flexed my bloody fingers. Kristoff's blood—his life— dripped to the floor with a *plop plop.* It was time to end this, once and for all. I heard Kristoff's child-like laughter."How about you go back to whatever hole you crawled out of?"

I grabbed Karnull's face. He screamed with a thousand different voices, each discordant—each in unspeakable agony. The worms beneath his skin writhed, burrowing in all directions frantically to escape the searing pain. They started to pour out of his mouth and eyes, shriveling to dust as they fell to the floor. No matter how many came out though, I refused to let go. Karnull was still screaming as his knees buckled.

"Go to hell." I said under my breath. "And stay there this time." A wave of energy rippled over the room. The darkness in the room lifted. Like milk in oil, the other Jackson's eyes went from black to white. When I removed my hand, a bloody, sizzling print marred my reflection's face. *He looks just like the Messenger.*

He looked at me. "J-Jackson?" It was PAINS, or at least PAINS's personality was in control. I heard the other AI as well, although each of them spoke in tandem with PAINS. Were they still inside? He looked around the room.

"Good God, why do I feel like I have a sunburn from hell? This is most uncomfortable."

I knelt to the ground and wrapped my arms around him. Startled, PAINS kept his arms out to the side. Then, as if realizing the show of affection was okay, he returned my embrace. He patted me on the back awkwardly.

"Uh, Jackson? Not to interrupt your obviously much needed display of affection, but…"

"Yes?"

"Where are we?"

I pulled back. "Inside the inner sphere of WEAVER."

"That would explain the strange orb in front of us. Excellent." I helped PAINS to stand. "Right. Thank you for the assistance. I certainly wasn't looking forward to being trapped in that bloody shell forever. After Karnull took control of the station he downloaded each of the intelligences to this body, as was the plan. However, he also left the station to rot in the middle of that dreadful abyss—that much I recall."

"I'm just happy you're not trying to kill me."

"Likewise!"

Rose. Molly. I turned. Despite the terrible battle they had just witnessed, their crying had stopped, replaced by weary, tear-stained smiles. It was over. Karnull was gone. We would never have to worry about him again. Or so I hoped.

"Jackson, it certainly feels good to have this whole sordid affair behind us. Perhaps now we can find a way to rebuild? Wouldn't that be delightful?"

"Yeah." I turned. "It sure—."

All the air sucked out of the room. PAINS didn't see it, but a black hand had emerged from the glowing sphere behind him, hovering inches above his head. Its fingers ended in blades that were all too familiar to me. *No. Not now.* "PAINS!"

It was too late. The hand grabbed hold of PAINS's head and dragged him into the light. Seconds passed. The woman who had haunted me from the beginning of my journey emerged, blades ready to kill.

"Hello, Thorne. My, my it has been too long."

"*You.*"

The woman looked over my shoulder. "What is Molly doing here?"

"How do you know her name?"

"Answer the question."

I straightened. "No. You answer my question. Who the hell are you? What's your name?"

"Have you still not figured it out?" Her blade fingers twitched, shimmering in WEAVER's light. "You really are an idiot."

"So says the cowardly assassin."

"Coward?"

"You heard me. Only cowards hide behind masks. Are you that afraid to show me who you really are? You skulk in the shadows like an outcast. You aren't justice. You're hate and nothing more. I am not scared of you."

"I am no coward, you little worm."

"Then prove it already!"

To answer, the woman retracted her claws. She grabbed hold of her helmet and twisted. With a hiss the black armor separated from her neck, revealing...

My stomach dropped. *What?* No! How was that even possible? Molly. But it wasn't the Molly I knew. This woman was older. Her green eyes had seen things no man was ever supposed to see—things that perhaps I had done in a future that wasn't to pass. Either way, she was here now and the hatred burning in her eyes transcended whatever boundaries kept men in the fabric of time and space. Tears formed at the corners of my eyes. "No. No, you can't be her!"

"You stole everything away from me. Zeke. My family. My very *life*. And for what? Your precious wife? That stupid whore?" She cut the air with her newly extended claws and moved into battle stance. "Now you die, murderer!"

She launched forward. Ducking, I dodged her. Molly's alternate self struck the glass and shattered it headlong. She came into a roll on the other side as I followed in after her. Meanwhile, Rose and the Molly I loved—the real Molly I decided—stood to my left. I took my place in front of them as my killer straightened and cracked her neck. I swallowed. *Is this what would have happened to Molly had she gone on hating me?* If so, that's what she meant by synchronization. She was from a different timeline!

"Don't act like you protecting them." She snapped, spittle flying from her mouth.

"Molly." I called out to the dark woman. "Why didn't you take Kristoff's gift?"

"Gift?" She sneered. "What gift would you possibly give me, devil-man?"

"Life." The real Molly stepped in front of me. She stood, arms outstretched. "You aren't going to touch him. I love this man."

"No you don't. He's a liar. A deceiver. He deserves hell."

"We all do!" Molly raged back. Her answer stunned the woman into silence. The real Molly continued. "I think I get it now. It was something that Jack— "She flashed a warm smile at me before looking back to her alternate self, "—told me not too long ago. He said that people love darkness rather than light. Why? Because darkness is not just inside them, it *is* them. It's the only thing they know. When love shines on their hearts, it causes problems. We spend our whole lives building up defenses and kingdoms in the dark, then when the light comes in, we see things for what they really are—nothing. Forced to face the truth, we have a choice to make and we hate Him for it. We have no more excuses."

The real Molly shook her head. "Revenge promises us so much. We will be satisfied, it says. But it's an illusion. In the end, when the dust settles and the light falls on us, we'll see what we've done and the yawning hole that's still inside us. We'll either hate ourselves or the only one who really knows us."

The other Molly narrowed her eyes. "Don't tell me you mean, Thorne."

"No. I mean the one inside him. The one who gave us these eyes." Her alternate self paused. For the first time since entering the room, she seemed to notice our eyes. Did they look familiar to her? The real Molly grabbed my hand. We shared a glance and faced her evil self. "I've never met him," Molly said, "But I know Him and I know that He knows me. Do you know why people love in the first place? Because that's what they're made for. To love and be loved. Not hate and be hated. I refuse to hate anyone ever again. I will not listen to those lies anymore."

A sneer. Her other self's claws sparked with electricity. "Then you will die with your 'truth'!" Molly's alternate self lunged.

Her blades came near us. The real Molly squeezed my hand. I loved her more than words could ever say. I felt her love too. It was as if Kristoff's heart was beating two-fold. If I was going to die, it would be an honor to die with her.

Well done, my children.

The woman's blades stopped mid-air. She was frozen, as if someone were watching a movie and hit the 'pause' button. A man appeared out of thin air in front of us. He wore a white spotless tunic and pants. His voice sounded like sunlight falling on snow. In my time, we had many names for him. Jehovah. Yahweh. El Elyon. El Shaddai. Jesus Christ. But they all meant the same to me. This man was God and the Creator of all things. *Kristoff.*

Molly's alternate self flew backwards and collided with the wall. Whether Kristoff had used brute force or his mind to throw her against the wall, I didn't know. The Creator said nothing as Molly's other self stumbled to her feet.

"And who the hell are you supposed to be?" She spat.

A wave of unexplainable power washed over me. I felt weak. Dizzy. Molly must have felt so too. She braced me for support. Then came the familiar pleasure—the inexpressible joy that filled my every cell and burned with healing fire. I couldn't help but fall to my knees as my soul drank it up in never ending streams. I started to laugh. Molly did to. Rose joined us.

I love you, Jackson.

Kristoff turned his back to Molly's alternate self.

From before you were born. I knew your name. I have been waiting for this day.

Molly's other self screamed in rage and tried to lunge again. She failed.

Halfway through her jump, a golden fire engulfed her body. A pain-filled tear fell from Kristoff's eye as she was incinerated. When she landed on the floor, there was nothing left of her body, just the terrible pitch black armor she wore.

Kristoff knelt to us though we should have been the ones kneeling to Him. Every cell in my body was crying out for him. This was a king. More than a king.

This was God Almighty.

I have something to show you, Jackson.

He put a hand on my head and the world dissolved into paradise.

29 – *Yesterday's Tomorrow* – 29

"Every new beginning comes

from some other beginning's end."

- Seneca -

I DIDN'T FALL asleep. In fact, as my vision cleared, I had never felt more awake. My wounds had vanished. Rose, Molly and I all stood, overlooking a lush green field. A ribbon of cobblestone ran under our feet and fed into a forest on either side of the field. In the distance was a lake, shimmering under the open sun.

"Jackson?" I turned. Becca sat on park bench underneath a large oak tree. She wore a pure white dress that matched her smile. A lump formed in my throat.

She patted on the seat next to her. "Come on. It's okay."

I moved toward her in a daze. Rose ran full steam toward her. "Mommy, you're up!"

Becca hugged Rose tight. "Who said I've been sleeping?" Rose looked to me as I sat down. Becca shook her head and kissed Rose on the cheek. "Daddy's silly, huh?"

"Yeah, he is."

"Is this heaven?" I asked.

Becca turned to me. "Of sorts. I told you He wasn't going to give up on you."

"Y-yeah." I started to cry. "You sure did."

"I'm so happy for you, Sweetie." She placed her hand on my cheek and I held it there, wiping my tears away with her soft skin. "You've been through a lot. You're not the same man I married."

"Is that a bad thing?"

"It's a wonderful thing." She smiled. Her eyes drifted over to Molly. "Does she know that?"

I stood. Molly had one arm behind her back, holding the other at her side. She looked out of place. Nervous even. I smiled and walked over to her. After some coaxing, I managed to drag her to the bench. Molly blushed. "This is Molly." I said softly.

Becca laughed kindly. "Molly, huh? That's a beautiful name."

"Th-thanks." She shifted her feet.

"Molly," Becca said. "Will you do a favor for me?"

She looked up. "Favor?"

A nod. "Yes. You see, Jackson is kind of a handful. We weren't married long, but I was always doing my best to keep him out of trouble. I can't really do that anymore though, considering

I'm here. But you can. So here's my proposition. Do you love him?"

Molly's eyes widened. "Of course I do."

"Jackson?" Becca's eyes drifted to me. "Do you love, Molly? Be honest."

I looked over to the girl who had once been my enemy. Every inch of her made my heart flutter. "Yes. I most certainly do."

"Then it's settled. Since you love each other, why don't you stay together? Molly, so long as you take care of Jack, I'm happy. And Jack, so long as you take care of this girl, I don't mind you being with her in the slightest."

"Really?" I said, dumbfounded. "You mean, you're not mad that I found someone else?"

"Mad?" She laughed. "I'm happier than I've ever been or ever could be. Heaven's like that. And finding someone you love... It's a lot like finding a little slice of heaven. It seems He wanted to give you a taste of the good things to come. I couldn't be happier for you, Jack. Besides, this one is special. I can see it in her eyes."

Once again Molly blushed and looked down. I tipped her head to me. We kissed.

"Gross." Rose said.

Becca ruffled her hair and laughed.

Molly hugged me tightly. I looked at Becca. "Thank you so much, Sweetheart."

"Don't thank me." Becca tipped her head to the lake. "Thank Him."

We followed her gaze. It wasn't the lake she was pointing to at all. It was Kristoff. He stood on the grass, barefoot and beaming, a child again. He stared into my eyes. My heart wanted to fly out of my chest.

You did well, Jackson. So very, very well.

I broke away from Molly, Becca and Rose and ran to him. When I came close, I knelt at Kristoff's feet. "Thank you." I said, fat tears falling from eyes. I put my head to the ground and alternated between laughing and weeping.

The child put a hand on my shoulder. I looked up. Again I was lost in His eyes. "You're more than welcome." He said. I swallowed, remembering the journal. Kristoff shook his head. "Don't worry about that. PAINS will get the journal. You did what you could. Do not focus on the past, Jackson—not when the future lies so close at hand for you."

Future? Was he talking about eternity?

Kristoff laughed, reading my thoughts. "Not yet. There is still more to be done. A great battle still waits for us on the horizon. When that day comes, Archia will be dealt with once and for all."

"I thought he was gone forever?"

"In your life, yes. But he still exists. You will see Him again, but you will also see me." He smiled. "Like I said, I have big plans for you and PAINS. You will be my instrument of change. Hope will slay despair. Light will be born from darkness. So many will be rescued. I cannot wait to see them come alive with my love." I was trembling.He hugged me and I cried anew. I never wanted to leave this child. He spoke, hearing my thoughts. "But you will have to leave this place. You know that, Jackson. It won't be forever mind you. We will see each other again. Remember what I said? I always keep my promises." He looked me in the eyes as I pulled back. "And I promise you."

"I love you, Kristoff."

"And you too, Jackson—more than you can possibly imagine."

Another hand lighted on my shoulder. I turned to see Becca, then Molly, then Rose. They all knelt and hugged me. I wasn't alone anymore. That truth rang in the depths of my heart like an echo of thunder. God, the Creator of all mankind—

Kristoff—laughed like a child. He was laughing with us—my family.

You are going to change the world, Jackson.

The world flashed white.

◆◆◆

Molly, Rose, and I all woke up, staring at the blue sky overhead. It was WEAVER's sky. Every so often it flickered. I don't know how long we stayed there, on our backs. I didn't care. Holding Molly's hand and keeping Rose close by, we stared at that sky. Life was perfect.

It wasn't until we decided to stand that I saw the teenage boy standing opposite us. He was wearing army fatigues, a long sleeve coat, goggles and a look of pure surprise. It wasn't Karnull, nor was it Kristoff. However, I recognized his face. "Darius?"

"Ghost guy?" He shook his head. His voice was trembling. "Look, I don't know where you came from or how you got here, but I need some help. If I don't get back to the outside world, everything is going to fall apart. I know it's a long shot but do you think you can help me with that? I'm not taking 'no' for answer."

I looked to Molly. Rose. None of us knew what he needed or what trouble we would be getting ourselves into. Honestly, I don't think any of us cared about the danger. All that mattered was the future. And our future began now.

"Sure." I said with a smile. I could almost hear Kristoff laugh in the air around us. "Bring it on."

ABOUT THE AUTHOR

Colby Drane is an avid writer and loves the battle between good and evil. He currently lives in Utah. This is his debut novel and the start of a whole new saga.

Made in the USA
Las Vegas, NV
03 February 2025